The
SONG
of
KING GESAR

Also by Alai

Red Poppies

The
SONG
of
KING GESAR

Alai

Translated by
Howard Goldblatt and Sylvia Li-chun Lin

CANONGATE
Edinburgh · London

First published in Great Britain in 2013 by Canongate Books Ltd,
14 High Street, Edinburgh EH1 1TE

www.canongate.tv

1

British Library Cataloguing-in-Publication Data
A catalogue record for this book is available on
request from the British Library

ISBN 978 1 84767 233 9
Export ISBN 978 1 84767 235 3

Typeset in Van Dijck by Palimpsest Book Production Ltd,
Falkirk, Stirlingshire

Printed and bound in Great Britain by CPI Group (UK) Ltd,
Croydon CR0 4YY

This book is printed on FSC certified paper

MIX
Paper from
responsible sources
FSC® C020471

Myths are universal and timeless stories that reflect and shape our lives – they explore our desires, our fears, our longings and provide narratives that remind us what it means to be human. *The Myths* series brings together some of the world's finest writers, each of whom has retold a myth in a contemporary and memorable way. Authors in the series include: Alai, Karen Armstrong, Margaret Atwood, A.S. Byatt, Michel Faber, David Grossman, Milton Hatoum, Natsuo Kirino, Alexander McCall Smith, Tomás Eloy Martínez, Klas Östergren, Victor Pelevin, Ali Smith, Su Tong, Dubravka Ugrešić, Salley Vickers and Jeanette Winterson.

Publisher's Note

With the permission of the author and translators, the book has been abridged from the much longer text translated from the Chinese. We hope we have succeeded in preserving the spirit of the original.

Part I

BIRTH

The Story
First Beginning

It was the time when domesticated horses separated from their wild counterparts, and when the deities went up to live in Heaven while the demons stayed in this world.

It saddened the deities to see the humans struggle with the demons, although their sympathy never went beyond sending down one of their number to help. In fact, they often made matters worse. Their visits became rare. Yet once the deities stopped meddling, the demons seemed also to disappear. Perhaps they had plagued humans simply to taunt the deities, and lost interest when only the feckless humans remained. But it has been said that the demons never left this world, that instead they transformed themselves, perhaps into a beautiful girl or into a tree trunk that gave off the sweet smell of rot.

Then the demons began to wonder why they had changed only into wicked figures. Why not assume human form? So they did, and then there was no telling them from the real thing. For centuries humans and deities pursued them relentlessly, until they found the perfect hiding-place: the human heart.

Let us go to the place where the story begins.

It was called Gling, which is present-day Khampapa. To be more precise, the Gling of the past is now part of the immense land named Khampapa. Its grasslands are in the shape of an enormous drum, the plateau encircling a slight rise in the middle. Sometimes you can almost hear surging drumbeats or a pounding heart inside. Snowcapped mountains circle the grasslands, like fierce beasts galloping at the edge of the sky.

In those days, people felt that the earth was big enough to contain many different worlds. Not different countries, different worlds. We speak now of the earth as a village, but back then people looked towards the sky's edge and wondered if there might be more worlds beyond the horizon – wickeder than theirs, perhaps, or more prosperous.

Gling was a small world, its people divided into clans. By the time the newly enlightened inhabitants of Gling began to separate domesticated horses from wild ones, other worlds had long since left behind the age of barbarism. Those peoples cultivated the seeds of many plants; they smelted gold, silver, copper, iron, featherweight mercury and heavy lead. They erected statues; they wove hemp and silk; they became civilised. They believed they had destroyed all of the demons – or, at least, if there were still demons, they were hidden in human hearts, scurrying around in human blood, laughing like hyenas.

But in Gling the curtain was about to rise on a battle between humans, deities and demons.

The people of Gling began to pursue wealth – pastures, palaces, treasure and, for the men, beautiful women. Tyrants fought one another for power, and life in Gling became a struggle between the noble and the lowly, the powerful and the powerless. An unlucky shadow shrouded their eyes as desire burned in their hearts, just as rivers, wishing to flow beyond their beds, are muddied as they rush against their banks. The people of Gling believed that an evil wind had blown the demons into their world to destroy Gling's peace and quiet.

Who could have blown the evil wind their way? They were not expected to ask – if they did, the sages might look foolish. They could ask: *Where did the demons come from?* And the answer would be: *They came with the evil wind.* Once the evil wind began to blow, dark clouds covered the bright sky. The grass of the pastures yellowed. Worst of all, the kindly were revealed as wicked, and it became impossible for the people of Gling to live in harmony. War horns echoed over the grasslands and among the snowcapped mountains.

It was to these grasslands, riven with the cries of battle, that King Gesar descended from Heaven.

The Story
Second Beginning

One morning, the deities went on an excursion. As they floated into the great void, they saw clouds of sorrow rising above Gling. Their mounts – lions, tigers, dragons and horses – flared their nostrils at the scent of misery in the air. One of the deities sighed. 'There are so many ways to rout demons yet these humans do nothing.'

The Supreme Deity joined in: 'I thought they would fight back, but they do not.' In Heaven the deities had physical forms, all but the Supreme Deity, who was, in a way, the final cause of every effect. He was formless but for his breath.

'Then let us help them.'

'We will wait,' the Supreme Deity said. 'They have no solution to rid themselves of the demons because they do not want one.'

'Why—'

'Let me finish. It is because they hope I will send someone to save them. If we wait, they may find their own way.'

He pushed aside a cloud to watch a celebrated monk preaching to an anxious audience. The monk had travelled thousands of miles, crossed mountain ranges and traversed roaring rivers to spread his faith in the demon-infested land. He spoke: 'If we purify our hearts, the demons will vanish.'

How could he expect the common folk to believe that such fierce demons had been released into the world from human hearts to bring such harm? A black cyclone followed the demons when they appeared: how could that wild energy have come from themselves? The crowd, which had arrived full of hope, left disappointed.

Another deity, watching from above, said, 'You are right. They wish us to destroy the demons.'

The Supreme Deity sighed. 'We must send someone familiar with demon containment to evaluate the situation.'

So there came another monk, this one with powerful magic. The first, who had preferred contemplation to magic, had walked all the way, and it had taken three long years. But Master Lotus was different. He could catch a ray of light as though he were scooping up water, wave it as though it were a willow branch and fly on the light's back. When he arrived on the majestic plateau, he fell in love with the view before him: the undulating ranges, like running lions, seemed to stretch for ever, the rivers roared with clear water and lakes dotted the plain, like a chessboard, their quiet waters glittering, like gemstones. It was strange that in such a beautiful place the people were so unhappy.

Master Lotus inspected Gling's four rivers and six hills. The wearying number and power of the demons far exceeded what he had imagined, and it was no longer possible to distinguish them from humans. In some parts a king had been lured into the demons' Tao; in others the demons had infiltrated the palaces to become powerful officials. Master Lotus could fight demons one at a time, but he could not battle a countryful of them. Luckily he had been sent only to inspect, not to eradicate, them.

The people said to each other that Heaven would come to their aid, but a resentful old woman sobbed: 'Damn them! They have forgotten us.'

'Whom do you curse?'

'Certainly not my husband, who has become a foot soldier for the demons. I curse the deities who have forgotten the suffering in our world.'

'You must not be disrespectful of deities!'

'Then why do they not come to save us?'

They all began to wail.

★

Meanwhile, the demons howled with laughter as they feasted at a banquet of human flesh. First to be eaten were those who had spread rumours. Their tongues were cut out, then their blood was poured into jars and placed on the altar as an offering to evil deities. The demons consumed some of these poor souls, but there were more than they could eat, so the rest were left without their tongues, weeping in remorse and pain. Their wailing streamed past people's hearts, like a dark river of grief.

Above, the sky was a vacant blue that imbued sorrow and despair with beauty. Some who had heard the wailing sang in praise of the colour, but they could not be sure if they sang of the blue or of the despair in their hearts. It seemed that as they sang their sorrow became bearable, and their despair lessened. But the demons would not allow them to sing for long: they feared the sound would reach the heavens. They released vaporous incantations of an invisible grey that suffused the air, entering the noses and throats of the singers. Those who inhaled them were cursed, their vocal cords paralysed, and they could make but one sound, that of a meek lamb.

Baa!

Baa, baa!

Oblivious, they continued to sing. Bleating, they roamed the land like sleepwalkers. When they grew exhausted, they chewed poisonous grasses that even sheep knew to avoid. Then, coughing up grey-green bubbles, they died by the river and the roadside. In that way the demons showed their power.

The people of Gling sank into indifference, their usually lively faces blank. They no longer looked into the sky – what could they expect to see? No deity had come. Rumour spread that one had arrived, but no one would admit to having seen it. True, they had not seen a demon either, but that was different: anyone who had seen a demon had been devoured by it.

In those sad days, wise men let their hair grow long and meditated in caves. They decided that there must be past and future lives, more and larger worlds than the one in which they lived. They wondered what those worlds looked like and whether soaring mountains or vast oceans separated them. And they gave a name to the terror, suffering and despair that the demons brought: they called it Fate.

It was under such circumstances that Master Lotus set off on his return journey to Heaven, intending to report the results of his inspection. Along the way he met farmers, carpenters and potters, all hurrying past him. From their stiff smiles and marionette gait, he knew they had been summoned by the demons. He took them by the shoulders and shook them, imploring them to return home, but no one heeded him. Although he might once have waged a battle against the demons, he knew he could not vanquish them all. Besides, his warnings had not brought the people to their senses, and he comforted himself with a phrase that we still hear now, a thousand years later: 'What I cannot see cannot trouble me.'

Actually, what he said to himself was: 'What I cannot see does not trouble me, so I must avoid the main roads.'

He pushed through bramble patches to reach hidden paths. In his weariness he forgot that a simple spell could protect him, and now his arms were torn by thorns, which angered him. The force of his rage made the bramble bushes bow down at his feet.

The paths were little better, for the shepherds, who had abandoned their flocks in the meadows, and the shamans, who had been collecting medicinal herbs in the hedgerows, were rushing to the beckoning demons, jostling him as they hastened past. He wondered what magic could be so powerful. His fatigue dropped away, and he followed them to a mountain pass where the rocky surface had been stripped of moss by the wind. He saw a clear blue lake in the hollow below, and remembered that he had passed this spot before and had vanquished three demons there, demons that could move in and out of the earth, like dragons that soar above water yet are at home in it. He'd used his magic powers to pick up lakeside boulders and drop them one by one at the base of the mountains: the impact had exposed the demons – one had died underground, the other two were buried beneath a colossal rock. Even now, the meandering banks of the lake are dotted with these boulders; once pitch black, they have been turned a dark, lustreless purple by the elements.

Master Lotus realised that he had spent a long time in Gling. A year? Two? Perhaps longer. At the place where he had once vanquished the three demons, a new demon had appeared, a giant snake that hid its body beneath the water, while its long tongue showed as a peninsula rich with enticing red flowers. Above it floated an alluring woman, a sorceress, cupping her breasts in her hands. She sang, and the humans were enchanted. If they retained a trace of free will, it was simply to walk towards her along the demon's tongue and into its mouth.

Master Lotus flew to the top of a boulder and commanded the people to be deaf to the demon's summons. But no one paused, not even for as long as it takes a grain of sand to drop through an hourglass, and the naked sorceress made her voice even more beguiling. Then she lifted her snake's tail from under the lake and waved it provocatively, sending a gust of putrid wind towards him. Enraged, he flew to alight in the snake's mouth, now transformed into the entrance to a dragon palace. He settled his mind, steadied his feet, and recited an incantation that filled his body with air. Bigger and bigger he grew in the serpent's mouth, until the writhing creature stirred vast waves in the lake. The flowers and the lush grass vanished. The snake's long tongue flipped the people into the water and its head split around Master Lotus's giant body. He flung the snake's body onto the lakeshore, where it was transformed into a range of rolling hills. But the lake had swallowed the people.

'Rise!' he cried. The drowned rose out of the water and were flung onto the shore.

Master Lotus's strong magic restored many to life. As they got slowly to their feet, they knew they must flee, but their legs failed them. They lay down and wept, their tears falling, like hail, into the lake, made foul by the snake demon. The salt in their tears cleansed the filth, and a blue mist of sadness spread, soaking up the cruelty that had inhabited the water.

Then Master Lotus summoned sweetly chirping birds to gather in the trees, which cheered the people, who stood, stretched and set off for home, to their pastures and villages where barley and cabbage grew. Potters returned to their kilns, stone masons to their quarries; tanners gathered mirabilite crystals from the roadside to soften their leather. Master Lotus knew they might encounter bandits or evil spirits, and never find their homes, but he bestowed on them his blessing with auspicious words.

Master Lotus was not a deity, but he was a future deity. He had earned his power through his devotions and asceticism, and carried magic objects that guaranteed victory over the demons. His head was filled with powerful incantations. Although he could not travel freely into Heaven, he could fly up to the gate, where the Guanyin Bodhisattva, saviour of all those who suffer, would be waiting for his report on what he had witnessed during his journeys through Gling. The Bodhisattva would tell his story to those above.

He flew from Gling to Heaven on the back of a roc, holding on to its feathers to steady himself. Dizzy, fearful of falling into the great void, he recalled that he could soar aloft on a ray of sunlight. Why, then, was he afraid? The people he had saved must have shaken his inner tranquillity.

He sat on the roc's back, his long hair flowing behind him, the wind howling past his ears. Reaching out, he squeezed the water from the drifting clouds, twisting them into auspicious knots, then tossing them to the ground. Later, when he had become a deity, sacred signs appeared where the knots had landed.

A voice full of laughter spoke: 'After that, people will think of you wherever they are.'

He reined in the roc and, eyes downcast, hands at his sides, sat up straight. 'It was the whim of a humble monk . . .'

Above him, all was quiet.

'I shall go down to retrieve the knots.'

'There is no need,' the voice said. 'I am happy that you have returned from the human world in such high spirits.'

Master Lotus breathed a sigh of relief.

The Bodhisattva said, 'Dismount and we shall talk.'

How could he dismount in the void?

'Just climb down from the roc's back.' The Bodhisattva smiled and waved, turning the void into rippling blue water, from which emerged enormous water lilies, one after another, until they formed a path at the monk's feet. Master Lotus stepped forward, overwhelmed by their powerful scent. He felt as though the flowers were carrying him up to the Bodhisattva.

'You have had a difficult time,' the Bodhisattva said gently. 'The evil spirits were a match for you.'

'Bodhisattva, I should not have tired so easily.'

The Bodhisattva laughed. 'That was because the ignorant mortals could not tell good from evil.'

So everything was visible from up here, he thought. *Why, then, did they send me there?*

The Bodhisattva waved a plump, soft hand and said, 'Do not try to guess at celestial intentions. You will understand when you live here.'

'I see. I must gather enough karmic merits.'

On that point, the Bodhisattva was clear: 'Indeed. A human must acquire sufficient experience to become a deity.' Then the Bodhisattva added, 'There is no need for you to describe what you heard and saw in Gling. We see everything clearly from here, not only that which has already happened but that which is to come.'

'Then why do you not alleviate the suffering down there?' Master Lotus asked.

A stern look appeared on the Bodhisattva's face. 'All we can do is give help and guidance.'

'Then please allow me to return and fight.'

'You have accomplished your mission, and your karmic merits now allow you to be freed from *samsara*, the wheel of reincarnation. You will become a deity and take your place in the heavenly court. From now on, you will use your magic to protect the black-haired common folk who live amid the snowcapped mountains. You will never again appear in person to fight demons.'

The Bodhisattva turned and passed through the celestial gate on a pink, auspicious cloud. Master Lotus waited for a long time, long enough to burn several sticks of incense, but the Bodhisattva did not reappear. He did not know whether he could now enter the heavenly court, so he grew anxious and restless. Had he been his impatient, pre-transformation self, he would have hopped back onto the roc and returned to the mountains where he had undergone his training as a monk.

The Storyteller
The Shepherd's Dream

Yes, restless and anxious.

Those drifting, floating clouds. Anxious and restless.

The shepherd had had the same dream many times. And it always ended at the moment when the most revered Bodhisattva entered the celestial gate. Even in the dream he felt restless, that it was not the man pacing outside the gate but he himself who was anxious because he wanted to know what would happen next.

In his dream he had looked deep into the celestial court and seen a sparkling jade staircase. The steps closest to him looked sturdy, those further away soft, but the end of the staircase did not disappear into the cloud. Instead, as though unable to bear its own weight, it tipped at the top . . . but he could see no further. Once, at the edge of a summer pasture, he had climbed a five-thousand-metre sacred mountain that wore a helmet of snow and ice. There, too, the mountain had seemed to tip into the clouds that roiled beneath its cliffs. Beyond lay another world, but what that world looked like he would never know, not in this lifetime.

He dreamed that the other world would crack open before him, like a cave – those words appeared in his head. Although he was an illiterate shepherd, in his dreams he had become wiser. Strange how such a literary phrase popped into his mind just when he was waiting anxiously to see what would happen next. He heard a roar, like torrents of water sluicing down the rocky surface of steep hills when frozen rivers melted on a summer day. The noise woke him. He opened his eyes to find that he had been sleeping on a hill sheltered from the wind by Siberian cypresses. The sheep were scattered across the grassy floodplain, cropping tender grass, flaring their nostrils to capture the scents on the breeze. When they saw him, they raised their sad faces and called out to him.

Baa.

Half dreaming, compassion rose inside him: he was reminded of the people who had been manipulated by the demons.

He gazed into the sky, and the roar he had heard in his dream burst forth again, like thousands of mounted riders galloping towards him. Above him a great crevasse had opened under the thick layer of snow on the slopes of the sacred mountain, between the ice and the steel-grey rock. With a muffled rumble, the snow slid slowly down until it reached the fractured ridge where it became an avalanche, ice powder rising into the air. Wind buffeted his face, the chill purity of the air driving out the last remnant of sleep. He had been expecting an avalanche, a clear sign that summer had arrived. Purple gentians bloomed around him on the grassland, and giant buds formed on the fuzzy stalks of snow lotuses.

But he paid little attention to the flowers: he was thinking only of how tomorrow he would take his sheep closer to the foothills now that the grass was lush and green and the danger of avalanche had passed. The noise had startled the sheep, and cleared the last vestiges of his dream from his mind, but his agitation remained, like a dark cloud on the horizon. But then his dream came back to him clearly, and he saw the story that had played out on this very land. For thousands of years, bards had told the tale, on the grassland and in farming villages. He himself had heard it many times, the story of a hero, King Gesar, but from poor storytellers who could remember only fragments. Now, as he revisited his dream, he realised that he had seen the beginning of the story.

Silence reigned, yet he could hear thunderclaps in the mountains. He shuddered, as if struck by lightning, and sweat poured from his body. What power had let him witness the opening scenes that had eluded so many? Without knowing the beginning, others could not tell the whole story – the beginning, the middle and the end.

The shepherd's uncle was one of those bards. He was a farmer in a village two hundred *li* from the shepherd's home, and in his spare time, he carved sutra printing blocks from pear wood. He would sit in the lotus position under the shade of a plum tree in the middle of the yard and send wood shavings curling down between his fingers. Lines were etched ever more deeply into his face. Sometimes he would sip strong drink and sing fragments of King Gesar's tale. His song had no beginning or end, for he knew only how to describe the hero's mount, the weapons he wielded, the warlike helmet he wore and the powerful magic that enabled him to kill people like flies.

'What happens next?' the shepherd had asked his uncle many times.

'That is all my master told me.'

'Who taught your master?'

'No one. He saw it in a dream. He was sick with a high fever, and babbling when he dreamed it.'

'Could he not have dreamed the rest?'

'Jigmed, my dear nephew, did you come all this way, nearly crippling the little donkey, only to ask me foolish questions?'

Jigmed just smiled.

In the courtyard of the farming village, with its several plum trees, he watched as his uncle placed a length of pear wood on his knees and began to carve words, reciting as he worked. Jigmed had not wanted to stay inside with his cousins. The younger one, who went to school, had told him that the gamy odour he'd brought with him from the fields was offensive. He was puzzled: he did not smell bad when he was on the pasture, but in this hot village he reeked of sheep and cows.

'Don't worry about the smell, Jigmed. It will be gone in a few days,' his uncle said.

'I want to go home.'

'You must be disappointed by my story. But that is my master's fault. He said he had dreamed it all but could not remember much when he awoke. He told me he could not even retell half of what he had dreamed.'

Jigmed wanted to tell his uncle that he had had a similar dream, more than once: he, too, had always forgotten it upon waking, but this time, startled by the avalanche, he could recall it all. The hero had yet to appear, so he knew he had seen the beginning of a long tale. His need to know what happened next had impelled him to travel the two hundred *li* with a gift-laden donkey to visit his uncle.

'Something is worrying you, Jigmed,' Uncle said.

Jigmed held his tongue: he felt that he must keep the dream a secret, that it had been a divine revelation.

Uncle moved aside to give him half of the shade cast by the plum tree. 'Come, sit here.'

He sat down and Uncle placed the wood on his knees. 'Hold the knife like this. No, too straight, tilt it a little. Now carve . . . with more force. Good . . . very good. Keep going . . . more. See? Like this, and a syllable appears.'

Jigmed knew the syllable: it was the first on the list of combinations, one that even the unlettered knew. People said it was the origin of human consciousness, the mother of all poetry, like the first wind that blew over the world, the first drop of water from the melting river ice, a fable for all prophecies and, of course, the prophecy of all fables.

'My dear nephew, with so many people in the world, the gods cannot take care of us all, and that is why you feel out of sorts. When that happens, think of this syllable.'

'I don't know how to carve.'

'Then treat your heart as if it were the best pear wood. Imagine yourself holding a knife, carving this syllable one letter at a time. As you think about it and say it, only this syllable will flicker in your consciousness. It will bring you tranquillity.'

On his way home, Jigmed said to the donkey, 'I'm thinking of the syllable.'

It was pronounced *Om*. When that sound is made, water wheels, windmills, spinning wheels and prayer wheels begin to whirl. And when everything is whirling, the world turns.

The donkey did not understand but it ambled along, with its head lowered and its eyes cast downward. There was a sharp bend in the road by a sparse grove of pine trees. Swaying its narrow hips, the donkey disappeared from Jigmed's view as it made the turn. He raised his voice and spoke to two parrots perched on a wild cherry tree: 'Think of the syllable.'

Startled, the birds fluttered up, clamouring, 'Syllable! Syllable! Syllable!' and flew away.

He quickened his steps and found his donkey waiting for him by the side of the road. It gave him a dispassionate look, then set off again, the bell on its neck jingling as it plodded ahead.

For a long time after that, Jigmed spoke to all manner of living things that appeared along the way, telling them, in a half-serious, half-mocking manner, of how he was focusing on the syllable – serious, because he hoped it would help him return to his dream world and not forget it upon waking, and mocking, to help him prepare for the inevitable disappointment. Deep down he hoped it would work magic.

He said it to a lizard sunning itself on a rock as they crossed a valley.

He said it to a marmot that held its front paws together and stood up on its hind legs in a mountain pasture, gazing into the distance.

He said it to a stag that seemed proud of its wide antlers.

But they all ignored him, or scurried off, as though fearful of his muttering.

He spent that night in a mountain cave, while his donkey grazed near the opening. Moonbeams flowed like water on the ground; in the distance they were like a mist. It felt like a night made for dreams. He recited the syllable before he fell asleep, but knew as soon as he awakened that the dream had not come.

As the road rose higher, the sky grew brighter. He had planned to spend the second night in a town, at a hotel, but there was no stable for his donkey. The manager led him out to the yard behind the building, where cars, large and small, were parked on the tarmac.

The manager appeared puzzled. 'You seem to have travelled a long distance, but people usually take the bus. We have a bus stop in the town. I can show you how to get there.'

He shook his head. 'There are no seats for my donkey.'

He searched for a spot on a hill outside the town where he could spend the night. It was barren land, so he slept beneath a steel tower whose base sheltered him from the wind. He built a fire against the chill night air, made tea and roasted a little meat, wishing he had bought some strong drink in the town. He did not plan to dream here, for it did not look like a place for dreaming. From the dreary hill he could see the flickering brightness of the town below, and when the wind blew, the steel tower hummed – *Om, om.*

Curled up under a woollen blanket, he gazed at the tower rising into the starry sky. With it, the people in the small town could listen to the radio and watch television. They could make phone calls at the post office, with its many small rooms in which they could sit with a handset, flailing their arms as if dancing, talking animatedly, though they could not see the person to whom they were speaking. As he listened to the incessant *Om* from the tower, the noise became like the congregation of voices, the words jumbled together into a hum that made him dizzy. He tried to recite the syllable, the first of all sounds, but it merged into the *Om* from the tower. He pulled the blanket over his head, blocking out the starlight and the sound.

To his astonishment, he found his dream again, but this time it was unfamiliar. He saw a mysterious, crystal-clear light at the tip of the tower. It grew stronger.

It was not the steel tower. It was a crystal tower in the celestial court.

He was still restless and anxious.

But this time he was anxious not to be startled awake.

The Story
The Wish of the Deities' Son

The Bodhisattva, who had been gone for what seemed like eternity, emerged from behind the crystal tower and arrived at the gate of Heaven. 'Where has he gone?'

But the Bodhisattva was, after all, the Bodhisattva, and understood everything, with no exceptions. Her surprised and puzzled look changed to a smile that spread from her mouth outwards. 'He was so impatient. Too impatient even to wait. He has missed an opportunity to meet the Supreme Deity. Well, perhaps it is not yet time.'

The Bodhisattva returned to the Supreme Deity, who simply smiled. 'I once thought to let him become a leader in the human world. He would help to destroy the demons and bring peace to the world. Perhaps the humans would then have been able to build their own Heaven on Earth. But it seems now that that was wishful thinking.'

The Bodhisattva suggested that it should not be the Supreme Deity who was disappointed, but the demon-infested place called Gling. With the myriad sins committed during previous lives, the inhabitants of Gling had lost their chance to build a Heaven on Earth. And, besides, the world below was boundless, so there must be another place where the Supreme Deity could carry out a similar experiment.

Om! The sound of all praise and condemnation emerged from the Supreme Deity's mouth and sent a profound shock through the Bodhisattva's mind.

It was a summons. Instantly the gods in the celestial court gathered around the Supreme Deity. Ripples in the air confirmed the Supreme Deity's existence, and the auspicious clouds beneath the deities' feet floated away. Below them more clouds roiled, turning a cheerless grey and a sorrowful black. The Supreme Deity shifted again to reveal the world below: landmasses large and small, the Earth's continents, appeared in all four directions. On one continent, tens of thousands of people in battle formation were killing each other; on another, people were being whipped as they dug a canal. On yet another, skilful artisans had gathered to build a colossal mausoleum for their still living emperor. Around the construction site, the graves of artisans who had died from hunger or illness took up great swathes of fertile land. In a deep forest on another continent, one group of humans was chasing another, and those who lagged behind were roasted and eaten. The leftover flesh was dried as food for those who continued the chase. And still others appeared to have attempted to escape from their continent, but their ships had capsized in storms. Fish even bigger than the ships leaped out of the water and gobbled up the humans as they struggled to stay afloat.

The Supreme Deity said, 'One nation after another has been created. See how they war against each other and how they treat their own.'

'Supreme Deity, will it be like this in the land of Gling?'

'Perhaps that is what the people there are striving for, but they have no real nation yet. I may give them a chance to try to establish a different kind of nation.' The Supreme Deity paused. 'It seems to me that humans have but one kind of history and cannot follow a different path. When demons reign, humans need our protection and assistance, but once they are rid of the demons and have established their nation, they go to war again.'

The Supreme Deity shifted once more, to show them what was happening in Gling; the misery and chaos there elicited heavy sighs. Reproach appeared on the Supreme Deity's face. 'I do not believe that you need me to show you what is happening.'

In response to his mild reprimand, expressions of extraordinary compassion appeared on their faces. But one young deity seemed indignant. The Supreme Deity called him forward and, turning to the other gods, said, 'Your compassion for the suffering masses below is not as genuine as his.'

The young deity's parents and older sister ran to the jade steps to shield their son and brother. 'This foolish youth lacks self-control and wears his feelings on his face.'

The Supreme Deity's face darkened. 'Move back!' he said. And then his expression changed. 'Come here, young man,' he said.

The young deity stepped around his parents and approached the Supreme Deity.

'I, Thosba Gawa, am the Supreme Deity's servant.'

'The suffering down below . . .'

'Your humble servant's heart goes out to the people.'

'Your heart goes out to them. Well said. Now, if I were to send you down to rid the people of their demons and save them from suffering, would you go?'

Thosba Gawa did not reply, but the determination on his face spoke for him.

'Good. But you must consider it carefully. If you go, you will no longer be a deity. You will be a mortal who suffers misery and hardship from the moment you are born. Are you afraid?'

'No, I am not.'

'You may lose your divine qualities and sink into evil ways, as mortals do. Then you will never be able to return to the celestial world.'

The young man's mother and older sister wept.

'And you will lose all memories of your life here.'

The young man dried the tears on his mother's face and put his arms around his sister. He whispered to her, 'Do not be afraid.'

His father embraced him. 'My son, I have never been so proud, but you have plunged a knife of sorrow into my heart.'

'Father, pray for the suffering mortals in the bitter sea of Gling.'

'I shall pray for your future subjects. I shall employ all my powers to help you accomplish your task. And if you find trouble and wish to leave Gling, I shall help you return to the celestial court.'

The steward of the celestial court spoke: 'After Thosba Gawa leaves for the human world, all the deities will, on his behalf, beseech the Supreme Deity to grant his father another son as brave as he.'

With his wife at his side, his father replied, 'No. We vow not to use more energy and vitality to create another life, so that our son may return to our heavenly court.'

The Storyteller
Light in the Blind Eye

In his dream Jigmed the shepherd was moved to tears.

He awoke to see frost sparkling, like glinting needles, on the dying grass around him. Near his cheek, gleaming beads of ice had formed on his woollen blanket. He put one into his mouth. His teeth did not feel the cold of the ice, but his tongue tasted the salt.

As he recalled his dream he realised that the beads were his tears. He placed another on his tongue, its taste like that of water held in rocks or in the soil. His sheep often nosed up against cracks in the rock to lick the salt crystals. Each year, people travelled to northern lakes in search of the shimmering crystals, whose taste, once it entered their bodies, filled them with strength.

The morning air on the plateau was always chilly, and as he shivered, he thought of the village shaman. Whenever someone had a problem, whether they had lost a cow or lost their own soul and did not know if it would ever return, they would invite the shaman to their home. Once he had eaten, he would dim the light and recite an incantation, after which he would tremble all over. That was the sign that an all-knowing deity had possessed him, and would give the mortal helpful guidance through the shaman's mouth. His rigid body swaying, he would speak in a muffled voice that seemed to come from another world: 'The cow will not return because it has been devoured by three wolves'; 'The person lost his soul because he offended an evil spirit when walking by a river, but he can regain his vitality if he sends offerings and speaks admiring words.' Once the deity had left his body, the shaman would fall to the floor, like a log.

But this was a different type of possession. On the grassland, those who learn of heroic deeds are called divine messengers, for it is the deities who tell them stories in their dreams. In Jigmed's youth, a blind storyteller had once visited his village. The storyteller had dreamed that Gesar, a deity dressed in gold, had opened his belly with a dagger and stuffed rolls of written scripts inside. The blind storyteller could not recall if the deity had sewn his belly back together, and when he awoke, at the sound of a turning waterwheel, there was no scar. He knew he could not read a single word on the written scripts, but his head buzzed, as if a herd of horses galloped inside him.

Jigmed wanted to return to the dream world, thinking that perhaps the god who had given him this story would appear. But the donkey was now nuzzling at his blanket, pulling it away from his face. It brayed, and Jigmed muttered, 'Let me sleep a little longer.'

The donkey brayed again.

'I don't want to get up yet. Do you understand, my friend?'

The donkey would not stop braying.

'What an awful noise! The deities will not like it.'

The donkey tugged at the blanket until it slid off entirely.

'All right, all right.'

Jigmed and his donkey walked back along the road to the village. He could not see out of his left eye, the one that always watered in the wind. The donkey, the road and the mountains disappeared when he covered his right eye, and he could see nothing but streams of light coming towards him from the direction of the sun. When he uncovered his right eye, everything was clear as day.

After his journey, he took his sheep to the mountain every day. The snow line on the mountain rose as the ice on the lower reaches melted to feed the expanding lake below. Yet the door to the dream world refused to open. He would close his right eye and recite the syllable his uncle had taught him, the sound of all sounds, and greet the light that burst forth from the east with his blind left eye. Staring into the dazzling colours, he would recite, *Om*. He directed his consciousness to trace the outline of the syllable in his heart: *Om*. But no divine images emerged from the swirling rays of light.

He had to content himself with tending his sheep. At night, when he came down from the mountain into his village, he walked along a little-used road that passed a shop where beer and spirits were sold. On early summer evenings men from the village would gather on the grass in front of the shop to drink until they broke into song, mostly popular tunes they'd learned from the radio. But some sang fragments of the hero's story.

> 'Lu-ah-la-la mu-ah-la,
> Lu-ta-la-la mu-ta-la!
> In the early summer of the Ding-you year,
> In the early morning of the eighth day of a crescent moon,
> An auspicious sign will appear in Gling;
> Those of the phoenix, the eldest, the noble class,
> Those of the dragon, the second, the famous class,
> Those of the hawk, eagle and lion, the younger class,
> From the noblest of the noble,
> To the commonest of the common,
> All will come together to await the good news,
> That an auspicious sign will appear in Gling!'

The Story
The Deities' Son Descending

Regret had begun to eat at Master Lotus. It was not that the demons of Gling had frightened him, but that the barbaric people had exhausted him. Returning to his home from the gate of the celestial court, he heard of Thosba Gawa's descent to the human world. It was clear to him that he had lost his chance to return to Gling and do something remarkable. On the other hand, people were still talking about his great deeds, which, he knew, was their way of showing remorse for not adequately following his instructions and for not trying hard enough to keep him there when he had told them he was leaving.

'I've formed an indissoluble bond with Gling,' he said aloud.

A voice asked, 'What do you mean, indissoluble?'

He smiled. He could see a hundred years into the future, see the towering temples erected on the shores of the indigo lakes at the base of Gling's snowcapped mountains. Gilded clay images of himself stood in the central halls, laden with sumptuous offerings. But he did not respond immediately. The person who had asked the question was Master Thangtong Gyalpo, who was engaged in his own spiritual quest beside him. At last Master Lotus replied, 'It seems that I must ask you to tell the people of Gling that the son of the deities will soon be born into their world.'

'Why will you not tell them yourself?'

'Because I regret having returned here.'

With a smile, Thangtong Gyalpo agreed to his friend's request.

Thangtong Gyalpo's body remained motionless but his thoughts travelled to Gling, and the people sensed his arrival.

The leader of one of the many tribes of Gling was an old steward, Rongtsa Khragan, who enjoyed high prestige and the confidence of his people. Though he was not considered the most outstanding leader, his tribe knew that he was tirelessly concerned about them. That day, he had gone to bed just after sunset and was unable to sleep although he was weary. Battles among the tribes and power struggles among his family spurred in him a new will to fight. His regret at the departure of the powerful Master Lotus prevented him losing himself in drink. Lately he had been asking himself, *Will Gling be condemned for ever to suffering, to karmic retribution, never to enjoy the rays of celestial light?*

As the sun sank behind the mists on the broad horizon, he allowed himself to fall asleep. Moments later he awoke to a blinding light. The sun, which had barely set, rose in the east in radiant magnificence, as if a golden wheel spun in the sky. A thunderbolt sprang from within the wheel and struck Mount Jijiedari, at the heart of Gling. The sun was high, yet the moon rose in the centre of the sky, like a silver platter. Surrounded by stars, it reflected the glow of the sun, and the bright light intensified in the sky. The steward's younger brother, Senglon, appeared in his dream, holding a vast umbrella whose shadow covered a territory much larger than Gling, east to Mount Zhanting on the border with China, west to Mount Banghe near Dashi, south to the north of India, and north to the southern banks of the salt lakes in the country of Hor. Then a cloud drifted over, upon which rested Supreme Master Thangtong Gyalpo. He spoke to the old steward, 'Awake! If you wish the sun to shine on Gling, listen to the tale I am about to tell you.' Before the old steward could speak, the Supreme Master had settled on the sacred Mount Machen Bomra at the edge of the grassland to the east.

Rongtsa Khragan woke from his dream refreshed, apprehension swept away. He gave orders to welcome the Supreme Master Thangtong Gyalpo at the sacred mountain.

'But, Steward, the Supreme Master practises Buddhism in the west.'

He had no choice but to relate what had happened: 'I had a dream, one that has been unthinkable for three generations of Gling ancestors, and impossible for three future generations. I am not sure if we black-haired Tibetans can appreciate it. The Supreme Master appeared in my dream. We must invite him here to make it come true.'

'Is the Supreme Master really coming?'

'He is already here! He settled on Mount Machen Bomra. Take the finest horses and the most comfortable palanquin to greet him. Hurry!'

Then the old steward dispatched a flock of messengers to the senior, middle and junior tribes, requiring their presence at his castle on the fifteenth day of the month, when the sun and the moon appear together in the sky and the snowcapped mountains wear a golden crown.

In the meantime, Thangtong Gyalpo arrived at the steward's castle holding a rattan cane. He began to sing. But as the fine horses and palanquins sped past him towards the mountain, he was covered with the dust they kicked up. By the time it had settled, the procession was far off in the distance, so he began to sing again, drawing the attention of the old steward.

The old steward noticed the man's unusual appearance and saw that his rattan cane had come from a magical mountain. He went up to ask if he was Thangtong Gyalpo, the wise Supreme Master.

The Supreme Master got to his feet and turned his back to the castle, as if preparing to leave.

Instead of following him, the old steward recited an ancient song of praise:

'The sun is an uninvited guest.
What is the point of turning if it cannot warm the lives below?

The sweet rain is an uninvited guest.
What is the point of travelling on clouds if it does not nurture
   the broad fields?'

The Supreme Master turned to face the old steward, who stood at
the stately entrance. He laughed. 'The time has come.' His voice, though
not loud, travelled up to the celestial court, and the Supreme Deity
knew that Thosba Gawa's destiny was upon him. He gathered the deities
to give him a final blessing, which travelled into the ears of Master
Lotus, who sat down to pray for Gling's future.

In those days, the celestial court had many ways of helping mortals.
The Supreme Deity said, 'Since the Lotus sect of Buddhism has formed
a karmic bond with the people of Gling, why not let Buddhism become
their permanent belief?' He called upon all the deities who held Buddhist
beliefs.

Meanwhile, in the human world below, the old steward invited
Thangtong Gyalpo into the castle where, in the meeting hall, he knelt
reverently. 'The Supreme Master passed through my dream world last
night,' he said, 'so today I would ask the Supreme Master to interpret
the dream for me and the suffering masses of Gling.'

Thangtong Gyalpo laughed. 'Very well. Who is to blame for my
carelessness in passing through your dream world but I? Yet, though I
have some magical powers, I cannot interpret your dream when I am
thirsty and my mouth is dry.'

The old steward slapped his head. 'Bring water,' he commanded.

Cold, pure spring water was carried to him.

'No, milk!' He waved his hand.

The Supreme Master sipped the sweet spring water, then gulped a
bowl of milk. 'I have journeyed far, and although I did not walk one
step, my belly is empty.'

'Another bowl of milk?'

'No. Let us talk about your dream.'

The old steward sat at the feet of the Supreme Master and bowed his head. 'Your humble and ignorant servant asks for enlightenment.'

The Supreme Master began:

> '*Om*! There is no life or death in the Dharma realm.
> Ah! But I pity the masses who suffer the consequences of life and
>   death!
> Hum! I have come to interpret your wondrous dream,
> So, old steward, please listen carefully!'

The sun rising above the eastern mountain in the old steward's dream was a sign that the light of compassion and wisdom would shine brightly in Gling; the thunderbolt represented a warrior who would descend from Heaven to be born in the area under the old steward's jurisdiction. The warrior would found a powerful country called Gling. Senglon had appeared in the dream with a vast umbrella: he would sire the warrior from Heaven. The ground shaded by the umbrella would be the territory his son would claim.

After he had listened to the Supreme Master's interpretation, brightness replaced the cloud before the old steward's eyes.

As they had been speaking, the leaders of all the Gling tribes and their retinues were gathering at the old steward's castle, which rose up in the crook of a mountain range shaped like a bow. The waters of the Yarlung river surged from the north-west, then turned and passed by the crook, straight as a taut bowstring. Between the bow and the bowstring, a grassy plain was covered with flowers, and it was on this plain that the tribespeople were gathered, their horses whinnying, surrounded by pennants fluttering from tents. The people were dressed in their best. Their tents faced the river in a wide semicircle with a meeting tent in the middle that soared like the glistening peak of a snowcapped mountain, its golden dome as bright as the morning sun. Gold and silver seats were arrayed inside, the warriors' seats draped with tiger or leopard skins.

One of the tribesmen climbed to the top of the castle and blew a conch to summon the leaders to a meeting. They took their seats in the tent. The elders, who enjoyed high prestige and commanded great respect, sat in the seats of honour, while the young and brave were below them. As the saying goes, humans have heads, necks and shoulders; oxen have horns, backs and tails; the earth has mountains, rivers and valleys.

Once they were seated, the steward began to recount for them the auspicious signs in his dream and the interpretation of the Supreme Master, Thangtong Gyalpo. The good news spread, like a bolt of lightning, from the tent to the people of Glingkar, as they sometimes referred to their homeland, and they cheered with joy.

As his bright eyes swept over the faces of those in the tent, the old steward grew sober. 'You have all heard that people beyond Glingkar, to the north, the south, the east and the west, have founded their own nations, with magnificent palaces and an orderly life, where sages spread the seeds of their meditation to scholars, where abundant fruit and vegetables grow in the fields and where milk flows across the pastures in eternal sweet springs. But here in Glingkar the people eat the raw flesh of animals and drink their blood. We struggle under the evil spells of demons, and we suffer because our deeds do not deserve the attention of the deities. Today the people of Glingkar, especially those of us seated here, must examine ourselves carefully.'

All present nodded before bowing their heads to begin their contemplation. But some, such as Khrothung of the Tagrong tribe, disagreed. 'Then the leader of the leaders must bear primary responsibility,' he muttered. 'If *I* were the steward of Glingkar . . .'

'Hush!' the others hissed.

'Do not speak to me thus. I am not a beast of burden.'

'No, you are human, so you should follow the old steward's advice and reflect upon yourself.'

The members of the tribes, unaware of the surging debate inside the tent, cheered at the news that the deities would help them at last to end the chaos and suffering in their lives. The chorus of wild cheers from tens of thousands of people was heard even in the celestial court, blowing open the cloud curtains at the entrance.

The Supreme Deity said, 'It is time for Thosba Gawa to go down.' He sent a messenger to fetch him so he could witness the celebration in Glingkar. 'Young son of the deities, the suffering below aroused your compassion. You shall soon be born into their midst and become their king.'

Thosba Gawa was moved to tears as he gazed down. 'I see it.'

The Supreme Deity's face became grave. 'Perhaps you see only the outside, not the inside.'

'Inside? Does the Supreme Deity mean the evil spirits and demons hiding in shadows and caves?'

'Not only those. There are more demons inside the meeting tent, in the leaders' hearts.'

Thosba Gawa had never felt the weight of his own body as he floated in the celestial world. His sorrow was born of seeing the suffering of another world, and now the Supreme Deity's words had planted the seeds of doubt in his heart.

'Perhaps I should not have told you. I should simply ask those with greater powers to bless you so that you will be ready to face the tests of the human world. My son, when there is a plague in the human world, the medicinal plants have no right to be idle. Sit still, close your eyes and do not look down. Imagine yourself as a container into which magical powers are poured.'

Before he closed his eyes, Thosba Gawa saw that all the Buddhas of the west were gathered round him.

A light from Vairocana's forehead shone down on all corners of the world, transforming the origin of all thoughts – *Om* – into an eight-spoke golden wheel that spun above Thosba Gawa, then entered his body through his forehead. With this blessing, no matter how filthy or ugly his surroundings, he would remain pure in mind and body. That was essential for any deity descending to the human world.

The Joyful Buddha stepped forward now, a bright light shining from his bare chest. For a moment the light remained suspended in mid-air, then turned into a thunderbolt that pierced the chest of the son of the deities. Sprites flew up to wash his body with celestial dew, to protect him from contamination by the evil in the world below.

Then the Buddha of Blessings and Dignified Treasures, light pouring from his navel, cast blessings into the navel of the son of the deities; they would lead him to hidden treasures in the human world and endow him with the power to use them to build a prosperous nation in which the people would live in peace. It was exactly what he would need as the future king.

Amitabha, the Buddha of Infinite Qualities, shone a light from his throat that could transform the energy of all languages into a red lily. Any who accepted the light gained the right to use the world's sixty musical tones. Then he placed a thunderbolt that held all the deities' promises for the future in the right hand of the son of the deities. 'Take this, my dear young man, for it represents your vow that you will not forget to save the suffering masses.'

'How could I forget?'

'Once you are below . . .'

Then Amoghasiddhi, the Buddha of Unerring Performances, came to him and said, 'If this young man remembers his vow and does great deeds, then some of the frivolous and ambitious members of the masses will envy you.' The deity, an odd-looking figure, sent a light from his loins that entered the same spot on the son of the deities. 'This, my son, is a power that will shield you from the fire of jealousy, and will inspire your work.'

Om! Now the body of the son of the deities had accumulated all kinds of blessings, virtues and magical powers. He stood up, expecting to feel heavy with all that had been poured into him, but instead he felt light and springy, and his feet nearly flew off the jade step. He could not help a tinge of regret that he had received blessings from the Buddhists only when the celestial court was filled with immortals of innumerable abilities and beliefs. But, glancing at the Supreme Deity, he swallowed what he was about to say. The Supreme Deity smiled. 'Even deities have their rightful domains. Glingkar is predestined to bathe in the light of Buddhism.'

'It is only that . . .'

'Tell me.'

The son of the deities spoke in a low voice. 'I thought the other deities might offer more fun.'

The Supreme Deity laughed as he turned to the Buddhas, who were resting on the jade steps. 'He said that you are too serious.'

The Buddhas brought their palms together and, without moving their lips, uttered in a deep voice, *Om* –

The Supreme Deity said, 'Now return to your parents and elder sister. This will be a long separation, and we still have work to do. We must find a good family in Glingkar for you.'

'Perhaps we should ask Master Lotus,' one of the Buddhas said.

The idea was immediately transmitted to the mountain cave where Master Lotus was meditating. He walked out of his cave, sat cross-legged on a rock and gazed into the distance. Closing his eyes, he focused his mind and joined two fingers to form a bond, bringing before his eyes the whole of Glingkar. He picked a birthplace for Thosba Gawa, where the sky was like an eight-panel canopy and the land like eight auspicious lilies. Waves from the river lapped at the rocky banks, sounding as if the precious six syllables were recited day and night.

Then the Master searched his mind for a family. He considered the six oldest clans, but quickly rejected them. Then he ran through the nine most famous clans in the land and discovered that one, the Mu family, lived in Glingkar. They had three daughters, the youngest of whom,

Rkayngmusar, was married and had a son named Senglon. Senglon was kind and generous, suitable to become the father of the son of the deities. Using his fingers to aid his deliberation, Master Lotus saw that if the father was from the Mu clan, then the mother must be from the noble Dragon clan.

Metog Lhartse, the youngest and favourite daughter of the Dragon King, lived in the Dragon Palace, and for the Dragon daughter to leave the palace was comparable to the son of the deities descending to the human world. For the sake of the people of Glingkar, the Dragon King gave his favourite daughter to Senglon, with an ample dowry.

Everything was now in readiness. Thosba Gawa ended his life in the celestial realm and prepared to descend to the human world, a land of misery and suffering.

The Story
The First Sign of Magic

In the sixth month, when all the flowers were in bloom, the Dragon daughter, Metog Lhartse, was married to Senglon.

On her way to Glingkar, Metog Lhartse saw a white cloud in the south-west, on which sat Master Lotus. 'Virtuous and blessed woman,' Master Lotus said. 'Heaven would like to borrow your noble body that you may give birth to a hero who will save Glingkar. No matter what hardship you encounter in the future, you must hold fast and believe that your son will be the king of Glingkar. He may be a stern deity to the demons, but to the black-haired Tibetans, he will be their brave and wise king.'

The Dragon daughter said fearfully, 'Master, if my son will descend from the celestial realm and is destined to be the king, why do you speak of hardship?'

Master Lotus lowered his eyes. After a pause he replied, 'Because some of those demons live in human hearts.'

The Dragon daughter, who had lived a sheltered life, wept bitterly at this, and when she looked up again, he had drifted away on his cloud.

After the wedding, she enjoyed Senglon's love and the respect of the people, and it seemed impossible that any hardship could befall them when her son was born. She often looked up at the clouds with a smile, sure that Master Lotus had joked with her. But still she was visited by a nameless dread.

Senglon had a first wife, a consort from the distant Han tribe, and they had a son called Gyatsa Zhakar, who was a few years older than Metog Lhartse. He was a bright, brave young man, an indispensable member of the old steward's retinue. He treated Metog Lhartse with the respect due to his own mother. Sometimes his uncle, Khrothung, would tease him, saying, 'My good nephew, a hero should be paired with a beautiful woman. If I were you, I would fall in love with my young mother.'

Gyatsa Zhakar would pretend he hadn't heard him. But when his uncle would not desist, the young warrior, mortified, would stuff a ball of new grass into the older man's mouth. Often his eyes reflected a sorrow so deep that even a hawk would lose its powerful wings if it fell into such a light.

At this, Metog Lhartse would feel a tender, motherly love for him. 'Gyatsa Zhakar, why do you always look so sad?'

'My young mother, it is because I am reminded of how my birth mother misses her homeland.'

'And you?'

'Glingkar is my homeland. But though I have vanquished many powerful enemies, I cannot help my mother's endless suffering.' His words brought tears to her eyes, and he added, 'But do not let me make you sad.'

'If I give you a younger brother, will you let him suffer an ill fate?'

Gyatsa Zhakar laughed. 'How could Mother worry about that? I swear on my life . . .'

And Metog Lhartse laughed, too.

In the middle of the fortress there was a spring with sweet water that froze in the winter. On the eighth day of the third month, an auspicious sign appeared. Flowers bloomed amid the melting snow, and the spring gushed forth again, pushing through the layers of ice, nourishing and refreshing the pungent air. Clouds heavy with summer rain gathered in the sky where thunder rolled. It sounded to Metog Lhartse like the dragon songs in her father's palace.

During the winter, Gyatsa Zhakar had led his soldiers in battle against the invading God tribe. Every fast steed that appeared at the fortress brought news of victories, and that day was no different. Glingkar's troops had occupied all of the God tribe's mountain castles. The shamans who had helped the enemy had been beheaded, and the God tribe's land, livestock, people and treasure were now under the control of the Gling tribe. The conquering troops would return in a few days.

That night the wild celebrations kept Senglon and Metog Lhartse awake. Turning to her husband, Metog Lhartse said, 'I hope our son will be as righteous and courageous as the elder son.'

When sleep finally came, she saw a deity in gold armour hovering at her side, while above her a crack in the clouds revealed a glimpse of the celestial court. A flaming thunderbolt sped downwards, bursting through her head and penetrating deep inside her. When she awoke in the morning, she felt calm and light, and a thought touched her heart. Shyly, she told her husband that their son had been conceived.

Husband and wife walked out onto the balcony. In the early-morning sun, round the bend in the river, the victorious soldiers appeared in a cloud of dust, with flags and pennants, the light glinting from their weapons and helmets.

Under the protection of Heaven, nine months and eight days passed quickly, and it was now the fifteenth day of the twelfth month. Metog Lhartse's body felt as soft as fine wool, and her mind as clear as the finest jade. Of course, she had heard talk about the pain of childbirth and had seen many women die in the process. She whispered to herself, 'I'm afraid.'

But she felt no pain when her son was born, and her heart filled with joy. More wondrous: the baby was the height and weight of a three-year-old. Although it was winter, thunder rolled in the sky, sending down a shower of blossoms. Clouds of many colours surrounded the birthing tent.

Supreme Master Thangtong Gyalpo came to congratulate the Mu clan and gave the child a name: Conquering Hero and Precious Pearl Gesar.

At the banquet, everyone begged Metog Lhartse to show them her extraordinary baby. Gyatsa Zhakar held up the child, who gazed at his elder brother with shining eyes. Deeply moved, Gyatsa Zhakar pressed his cheek against his younger brother's, and at this Supreme Master Thangtong Gyalpo cried, 'The joining of two fine steeds is the basis for vanquishing the enemy. Close ties between two brothers are a sign of prosperity.'

Gyatsa Zhakar wanted to call out his brother's name but could not. 'The name given by the Supreme Master is too complex.'

'Then let us call him Gesar.' The Supreme Master turned to the steward. 'You must nurture him with milk, cheese and honey.'

Metog Lhartse was filled with joy at the sight of her son's full mouth, bright eyes and well-set brows. But she said, 'He is ugly. We shall call him Joru.' So Joru became his childhood name.

Only Khrothung, head of the Tagrong tribe, kept apart from the festivities. In his view, the Glingkar Mu clan had come from one ancestor but had later divided into three branches, the senior, the middle and the junior, though for a long time there was no distinction among them. After Senglon had married his Han wife, who had given birth to Gyatsa Zhakar, a son praised by everyone in Glingkar, the junior branch was in the ascendancy. The old steward had been born into the junior branch, so the wealthy Tagrong tribe came under his rule. In theory, when the old steward stepped aside, Khrothung should take over from him. Who could have predicted that Senglon would marry a Dragon daughter who would give birth to such an unusual son?

At that thought, an evil plan grew in Khrothung's mind, and he knew he must act fast, so he set out for home. At the crest of the hill he looked back down at the crowd gathered at the river, and his heart felt as if it were crawling with poisonous insects. Loneliness overcame him, and he knew that his vile plan against the newborn baby was that of a coward. As a young man, he had always been ready to fight, and fight hard. Frightened by his fearlessness, his mother had sought the secret to making a man more timid: the shaman had told her that he must drink the blood of a fox, a shy, cowering animal. She had followed the instruction, but the shaman had not told her that whoever drank the blood would also inherit the fox's devious and cunning nature.

Sitting on his horse at the crest of the hill, Khrothung recalled the magnanimity he had seen in the eyes of the newborn baby and those of Gyatsa Zhakar, and was reminded of his own eyes. He knew they were now the sly eyes of a fox, and he was suddenly ashamed. He, too, had been great-hearted, until Fate had intervened.

Within three days Khrothung reappeared, smiling, bringing with him cheese and honey. 'My newborn nephew is already as big as a three-year-old. He will surely grow even faster when he eats the food I offer.' His words were sweet as honey, but the food was laced with a poison powerful enough to kill a yak. Taking the baby in his arms, Khrothung began to feed his nephew.

Joru looked up at him with clear eyes and smiled, then held up his hands to show wisps of dark smoke rising from between his fingers. The powers given to him by Heaven had expelled the poison from his body. In his confusion, Khrothung licked a fragment of fresh cheese stuck to his fingertip. In an instant, he felt as if lightning bolts were lashing him, that his intestines were being tied in knots, and knew he had been poisoned. His burning tongue would not allow him to utter a clear sound. All anyone heard as he tore out of the tent was a wolfish howl.

Khrothung stumbled to the river, where he pressed his tongue to the ice for a long time. When at last he could speak, he uttered an incantation to summon his friend Mgonpo Redag, a warlock, half human, half demon, who could snatch a living soul and take control of the body. Soon a great raven appeared, whose wings cast a wide shadow on the ground. It tossed the poison's antidote to Khrothung, who stumbled to his feet as the raven flew off.

In the time it had taken for his uncle to run to the river, Joru had begun to talk.

'What ails your uncle?' his mother asked.

'He went to the riverside to cool his tongue,' Joru said, not answering his mother's question.

'But he is not beside the river.'

Joru told his mother, 'Uncle has sent a black wind in our direction, so let this black-wind demon be the first I vanquish.'

Though his human body was sitting beside his mother, his celestial body was already flying towards the black wind. Mgonpo Redag flew past three mountain passes before he met Joru's celestial body, standing tall between Heaven and Earth, with nine hundred celestial soldiers in silvery armour waiting to carry out his commands. Joru remained motionless, waiting for the warlock to show his magic. The black-wind demon saw that this was not Joru's real body, so he flew around the soldiers towards the next mountain pass. Again he met Joru, blocking Heaven and Earth, this time surrounded by nine hundred celestial soldiers in gold.

Twice more he met Joru, the soldiers dressed in steel and then in leather. Then he saw Joru's human form sitting in front of a tent. Joru flicked his hand and tossed four colored pebbles into the air, summoning the celestial soldiers to surround him like an iron wall. The warlock Mgonpo Redag quickly sent up a column of black smoke and vanished, but Joru pursued the black-wind demon to his cave and sealed the entrance with a giant rock. Mgonpo Redag summoned all his magical powers to blast a tiny opening in the rock, but the crevice he opened let in a bolt of lightning sent by Joru, which blew him to pieces.

Now the good Joru transformed himself into the warlock's shape and went to see Khrothung, telling him he had defeated Joru's celestial soldiers and killed the infant, for which he wanted Khrothung's walking stick as payment. Now, this was no ordinary stick, but a treasure given to Khrothung by the black-wind warlock. With this stick, a person could walk through the air as if on wings. The disguised Joru threatened to tell the old steward and Gyatsa Zhakar how Khrothung had plotted to murder him unless Khrothung gave up his treasure, and with reluctance, he did so.

Joru flapped his cloak and flew off, but instead of a black wind the light of a rainbow trailed him. Suspicious, Khrothung flew to the warlock's cave, where he found the giant boulder blocking the entrance. Peering through a hole in it, he saw what was left of Mgonpo Redag: the disembodied head. The warlock's hand, also detached from his body, appeared to clutch the stick, and Khrothung, unmoved by his friend's death, transformed himself into a mouse small enough to squeeze through the hole. Squeaking, he wriggled into the cave, but when he scampered up to the demon, the stick was gone. When he realised he could not see clearly through his beady mouse eyes, he tried to return to human form, uttering the incantation. He remained a mouse. Terrified, he repeated the incantation, and this time something happened. His head regained its human shape and size, but his body remained that of a mouse. He struggled to the cave opening where, to his horror, he found that his head was too big to pass through the tiny hole.

Joru appeared at the entrance, and, feigning surprise, said, 'What is this monstrosity? I should kill it. It must be a demonic transformation.'

Khrothung shouted, 'Nephew, I am your uncle, and I have fallen under the spell of demons.'

Joru slapped his forehead, confused. 'It seems he has suffered from his own magic, so why does he say he was affected by another's evil spell?' While he was thus questioning himself, Joru's magic power diminished, giving Khrothung an opportunity to transform fully and squirm his way outside. Seeing bewilderment in the child's face, he dusted himself off and said, 'Little boys should not play so far from home.' Then he swaggered round the mountain pass, out of Joru's sight, and flew away.

After returning to his house, many miles away, Khrothung wondered if Joru really had come from the celestial realm, since the child had so easily foiled his evil plans. If so, then he, resourceful Khrothung, would remain merely the head of the Tagrong tribe, with no greater future. The thought made him so gloomy he could neither eat nor drink for a day, and rumbles of hunger joined his sighs.

The Storyteller
Teacher

That morning, the dew lay heavy on the grass. Too much wet grass made the sheep ill, so Jigmed set out late. The sun was high when he took his flock up the hill. Thrushes, tired from singing, were resting, and lizards, after warming their cold blood in the sun, were searching for insects.

From far down the road, behind a cascade of brilliant light created by the sun, came a storyteller. First Jigmed saw a banner held high, then a hunchbacked old man on the horizon, moving towards him.

After greeting Jigmed, the old man smiled. 'Why am I thirsty even before I begin to sing?'

Jigmed poured a cup of tea from his heated bottle. 'There is a passage that confuses me. Will you sing for me?'

'Does the young man want to learn how to sing?'

'I have dreams, but what I see in my dreams is never complete.'

'Which passage do you wish to hear?'

'About the family into which the son of the deities was born. It is a story as tangled as a skein of wool, or as the branches in a grove of old azaleas.'

The old man sat down and gazed at the sheep on the grassy plain. But instead of singing, he talked. He told Jigmed that this might help him with the difficult part.

'Then you are my teacher.'

'I will be your teacher.' And with that, the old man began.

The Story
What Came Before

Since Gling was part of Tibet, let us talk about the land of Tibet.

The oldest six clans in Tibet were: Jure of Drikung, Gasi of Taglung, Khon of Sakya, Chos gyalpo Lang, Gya of Khyungpo and Lha of Nedong. But these old clans were unable to maintain their vitality, so in time nine newly risen clans came to dominate Tibet. Though fearful at first, eventually the old clans let the names of the respected nine clans gush out like spring water: Ga, Dro, Tong from one line; Se, Mu, Dong from a second; and Ban, Tag, Dra from a third.

The many tribes of Tibet were scattered across the plateau, and looking down from Heaven, it appeared that snowcapped mountains, rocky cliffs and sparkling light surrounded the Pureng, Guge and Mangyul in the Ngaraus area of Taziks to the west. At the centre, there were the four Wetsang tribes: Yulru, Weru, Yasru and Yonru. Next to them were the six hill tribes of Dokham, which were governed by six magic mountains, named Marza, Pobor, Tsawa, Selmo, Markham and Minyag. The Yellow, Jinsha, Nu and Lancang rivers lingered at the foot of the mountains, bordered by pastures and farmland, and the many villages dotted among the hills and rivers fell under the authority of towering castles.

'Dispersed to all corners like pearls from a broken strand,
Blown by the wind throughout the land like grass seeds.'

The story isn't finished yet. *Om*!

The wise old man had an adage: How can you see a towering tree just by looking at the trunk? You must remove your boots and climb it, touching every twig. *Om . . .*

I'll put on my storyteller's hat. *Om!* Let me tell you about that hat.
It looks like a mountain with gold and silver threads . . . Oh, very well.
I'll talk about my hat tomorrow. What are you saying? That I've digressed
from heredity to geography? Ah, people today have no patience!

Now we will speak of the noble Mu clan, who commanded all the
tribes of Glingkar. The Mu family had enjoyed a prominent position
in Glingkar for more than a hundred years when Qupan Nabu became
its leader. The father of the old steward Rongtsa Khragan had three
consorts, one of whom was Rongtsa Khragan's mother, Consort Rong.
Consort Ge's son was called Yukye, a warrior who fell into the hands
of the Hor during a battle in the north. Consort Mu's son was Senglon,
chosen to be father of the son of the deities. Rongtsa Khragan had long
been married with children – three sons and a daughter by his wife,
Metog Lhartse. Before following the will of Heaven to marry the Dragon
daughter, Metog Lhartse, Senglon had married a Han woman from China
to the east. They had a son named Gyatsa Zhakar. Gyatsa Zhakar also
had an uncle, Khrothung, the head of the Tagrong tribe, who was adept
at magic and transformation. It was said that Gyatsa Zhakar was born
with the brave and righteous appearance of a heroic figure, taller at the
age of one month than a grassland one-year-old.

Ah! Young man, now that you understand, the story can begin.

The Storyteller
Chance

The old man said, 'Young man, look at the river bend. The water laps against the stony banks but does not produce a hollow sound. Our meeting here must be seen as extraordinary. So let me help you work through the important lineage of our hero, Gesar.'

'What shall I do next?'

'I don't know. Perhaps you should think back to every time you have encountered this great story.'

'Encountered? I saw it in my dreams.'

The old man smiled faintly. 'Dreams are encounters.' He plucked the strings of his lute, and the crisp sound of vibrating metal made the shepherd feel as if the land were spinning at his feet, the clouds were rushing past in the sky and the entrance to Heaven was about to open for the deities to descend. But when the old man's fingers left the strings, everything returned to normal, as if a heavy curtain had blocked out the bright light of understanding.

Dreamily, Jigmed murmured, 'The sound of the lute, where did it go?'

The old man slid the instrument into its bag. 'If this is your village, I'll spend one night here. I'll sing for the people by the entrance to the village, where the branches on the old cypress tree have formed the shape of dragon claws.'

Jigmed knew that the old man would not receive enough money for his singing in such a small village, so he decided to kill a sheep for him. The old man said, 'A good shepherd never kills his ewes in the spring. All you need do to sing of heroes is listen to this old man sing with his lute.'

Jigmed lay down at the bottom of a hill dotted with azalea blossoms and gazed up at the snowcapped mountain, waiting for revelation. He quickly fell asleep in the warm sunlight, but did not dream of anything, although the familiar sense of agitation assailed him. So he rose and made his way to the lake below. As he walked, he spotted a tent near the shore. The style and fabric belonged to a distant past; it was the kind of tent used when the world had just begun. Then the boy appeared before him.

'You are . . .'

'No, I'm not.'

He was going to say, 'You are the son of the deities,' and the boy's quick response had proved that he was. How else could he utter a denial before the question was out? Yet the boy's face was filthy, and the gem-like sparkle in his eyes of supernatural intelligence was dimmed, replaced by a fierce glare. The boy turned to chase a fox that had emerged from its den. The fox conjured up more foxes, which in turn prompted the boy to conjure the same number of himself, each chasing a fox. All Jigmed could see now was a hill overrun with foxes and Jorus. When all the foxes were under the feet of the Jorus, the hill streamed with blood as the Jorus tore apart their foxes, flinging away limbs, organs, flesh. But one Joru, with a fox beneath his foot, stood still on the hilltop. That was Joru's true self. He seemed stunned as he watched his other selves engaged in a bloody slaughter.

'Son of the deities!' Jigmed shouted. The boy seemed to have heard the cry, and Jigmed saw him look up into the sky, perplexed. Then, gazing once again at the bloody entrails scattered across the hill, compassion appeared on the boy's face, and in an instant the Jorus and the foxes disappeared, as did the boy, who was dragging the dead fox behind him.

The dream world has its own logic and freedom, so when the son of the deities disappeared, Jigmed turned towards the squat tent by the water, where a woman, worry written on her features, stood at the opening and gazed into the distance. She was Joru's mother, the Dragon daughter, Metog Lhartse. But her husband, Senglon, was not by her side.

Why was she not in her husband's palace? Why was she worried?

Jigmed spoke these questions aloud in his dream, but the woman, a thousand years distant, did not hear him. Dreams are full of trickery, and suddenly a tree appeared, from which a thrush chirped incessantly. Jigmed realised that it wasn't the bird but the woman lamenting: her son had forgotten his celestial origins and, in using his magic to kill animals, had angered the people.

Jigmed tried to defend the son: 'But weren't the animals really demons and evil spirits?'

'That is what he said, but nobody believed him.'

'That fox must have been a demon in disguise – but are you sure that all the creatures he killed were evil spirits?'

The thrush darted from the branch, saying, 'Are you asking me to speak evil about that poor boy?'

'I feel sad for his mother.'

'Oh . . .' The thrush fluttered its wings. 'You are not as stupid as people think.' It let out a shrill cry, and flew off.

Joru had come to the tent, carrying the bodies of the foxes. He flung the bloody flesh, the fouled entrails and shattered brains to the ground, then wove the green intestines into intricate knots and hung them on branches, even at the opening of the tent. The stench of blood was overwhelming. Birds in the sky, animals on the ground, even many mice in underground caves fled from it. Joru, who had lost nearly all of his celestial qualities, bared his teeth at Jigmed – Jigmed, who would one day sing of his great feats but now was so frightened he wanted to escape from his dream.

And so he ran, crossing one hill after another, but the hills came in waves. He tried to call for help, but struggled in vain to make a sound. Suddenly the old steward, Rongtsa Khragan, appeared before him. With his white beard quivering, the old man said, 'Stop running, and don't be afraid.' At these words, Jigmed felt the grey clouds of sorrow and the mist of misery that were following him break apart, revealing a clear sky with downy white clouds. Yet worry knitted the old steward's brow. 'Did he frighten you?'

Jigmed nodded, and then questions erupted: 'How did he become like that? Why don't he and his mother live in the palace?'

The old man gave him a long stare and shook his head. 'I had a dream that told me you could receive news from the celestial realm. It said you could tell me why.'

'My dream isn't finished yet. I reached the gate but did not see the faces of the deities.'

'That is what I thought. I saw no celestial light in your eyes.'

With those words, the old man vanished, and Jigmed awoke. To his surprise, there before him was precisely what he had seen in his dream: the hills, the lake and the river. At dusk, as he took his flock back to the village, he was still puzzling over the dream. Why was it different from what he'd heard in the old stories?

That evening by the fire, after a simple dinner, he was dozing when the crisp sounds of a lute woke him, reminding him of the storyteller he'd met that morning. The old man had no sooner donned a long satin robe of the kind worn by actors than the people sitting below urged him to begin. But he kept his head lowered, running his fingers over the strings. It was only when Jigmed appeared that he jumped to his feet and began to sing in a loud, clear voice.

> 'Lu-ah-la-la mu-ah-la, lu-ta-la-la mu-ta-la!
> The fated one has come.
> Ignorant shepherd, which part do you wish to hear?'

Jigmed answered anxiously, 'The son of the deities is not yet five years old, but he has lost his celestial nature.'

The people, who were familiar with the story, heard these words and raised a loud protest. Waving his hand, the old man quieted them.

In the silence, there was the sound of the lute, like moonlight brightening the ground.

The Story
Exile

Shortly after the son of the deities was born, he went to live on the Ashug grassland between the Yalong and Jinsha rivers, where a sparkling glacier ran down to the edge of a lake.

The people had witnessed Joru's magical powers; they had also seen how he had used the powers bestowed on him by Heaven in a frenzy of senseless killing. But they failed to understand that most of the lives he took were those of demons and apparitions. And they could not have seen him vanquish the many shapeless demons and evil spirits on the land between the water and the mountains. His uncle, Khrothung, was the only one who could have seen Joru's good deeds, but his heart had been occupied by demons so he kept quiet when the people voiced their disappointment in the boy who was rumoured to be the son of the deities. 'Is it possible that Heaven is merely toying with us?' they wondered.

Only the son of the deities knew what was going to happen: Master Lotus had told him in his dream that the long, narrow strip of land currently occupied by the Gling tribe was too small. For the nation to be strong, it must expand to the west and north from the Jinsha river to occupy the far broader grassland on the upper reaches of the Yellow river. They had to go all the way north until they reached a land that oozed salt, where, in the dry weather, sparks flew off camels' hoofs when they ran. The future flocks of Gling needed all the tender grass they could find, and the warriors of Gling needed vast stretches of land on which to gallop their warhorses.

Joru, who was only five years old at the time, was already as tall as a twenty-year-old and enjoyed stealing glances at the prettiest girl of the Gling tribe, Brugmo, who chose to play with warriors of her own age; she liked to etch a subtle pain into men's hearts.

When he uttered her name in his sleep, his mother was concerned. 'My son, the girl for you may just have arrived in this world.'

The moonlight flickered on the lake. The night was cold, like water, and the constellations revolved slowly in the sky. Joru's mother, she of noble birth, could not stop crying. She wanted to wake her son, to sob against his chest, but Master Lotus, who had entered Joru's dream, blew a puff of air on her, and she curled up under her blankets and sank into a dreamless sleep, her breath turning to frost at the edge of the coverlet.

Above the rocky levees along the river there was a soaring fortress, lights ablaze. Glingkar had been bathed in the light of peace since the birth of the son of the deities: the finest grain was turned into spirits; the finest milk made into cheese. Gone from the wind were the inauspicious sounds made by the dark cloaks of demons on their nocturnal journeys. Now, in the evening light, poets savoured rhymes, and artisans fine-tuned their skills. Hardly anyone thought of offering sacrifices for the fire that turned clay into pottery, or rocks into copper and iron. Even Senglon forgot his son, and his wife of noble Dragon lineage, who lived, cold and hungry, on the grassy plain. At that moment, his body was aflame with drink and women. With a wave of his arm, he ordered his servants to sing louder.

Only Gyatsa Zhakar missed his beloved younger brother. When his longing for the boy became unbearable, he leaped onto his horse and rode out of the fortress to see him, but when his cloak began to flap in the night wind, Master Lotus, who had entered Joru's dream, felt the vibration in the air. 'Tonight does not belong to you two brothers,' he said, and threw up an invisible black wall. It gave way when Gyatsa Zhakar attacked it with his sword, but quietly closed again. He was left with no choice but to turn his horse and go back. He met the old steward on the hilltop, looking to where the land dipped on the far side of the river bend until not even moonlight reached it.

'I miss my brother,' Gyatsa Zhakar said.

'I fear for Glingkar,' the old steward said, 'but your brother has made it impossible to see what Heaven has in store for us.'

Joru slept on. In his dream he asked Master Lotus, 'Shall I be king?'

The Master shook his head. 'Not yet – you must suffer more.'

'If I am not to be king, I wish to return to Heaven.'

The Master sighed. 'I may still be here when you return to Heaven.'

'You are not a deity?'

'I am a future deity.'

'Then leave my tent.'

The Master stood up and smiled. 'Son of the deities, I am leaving your dream.'

When Joru awoke, the rising sun had already melted the frost on the grass. He mounted the magic walking stick he had taken from his uncle, and told his mother, who was weaving, that he wished to go back to the fortress. She begged him to promise that he would stop his killing – and avoid making the people angry. Believing that he had eliminated the demons, and recalling, with a pang of loneliness, how his powerful brother, Gyatsa Zhakar, had effortlessly pulled him up onto the back of his horse and how the eyes of the old steward, filled with expectation, always lingered on him, he promised.

'Go back and apologise to your father and the old steward,' his mother said. 'Tell them what you have told me. They will forgive you.'

Meanwhile, the stick beneath him began to make a grating noise, which meant that demons were nearby. He abandoned it, and continued on his way towards the fortress. Two figures, gazing in his direction, were visible at the top – the old steward and his brother, Gyatsa Zhakar. They wanted him to return obedient and cleansed, which would allow the people to forgive him. He kept walking.

This time, though, there was something in the water. Two monsters, half dragon, half snake, crawled onto the bank. They were dripping wet, yet flames shot from their mouths. With a heavy sigh, he cast a quick glance at the fortress, went back to retrieve his stick, and rushed at the water monsters, which appeared to everyone else in Gling, including his mother, as two pretty girls out walking by the crystal gate of the Dragon Palace.

They fought with him on the shore, then dived into a pool where the Yalong river merged with a roiling tributary, and where every eddy seemed to carry enough power to suck the world dry. The bottom of the eddy was like the waist of an hourglass. He slipped through the tiny opening to see another world appear before his eyes. Moving freely, the monsters flew out of the water into the clouds when they saw that he was stuck in an eddy. The sound of their laughter cleared Joru's head. Holding the stick sideways, he stopped the flow of water in the eddy.

The monsters and Joru battled their way to the glacier, the rivers' source. Their final resort was an old trick: they conjured up many lovely living things, all running towards him, all of which died under his stick. To everyone in Glingkar he seemed cruel beyond words. When he struck down the water monsters' illusions, the corpses dammed the clear water upstream, and the smell of blood was so strong that even the flowers on the riverbanks closed and spun around to show the backs of their calyxes to the river. Yet when he struck down the monsters, their corpses floated, polluting only a small area of water. The instant the demons were killed, the piles of bodies disappeared and the river returned to its pristine state. The flowers bloomed again.

Though he had proved to the people that he had battled the demons' transforming magic, they refused to forgive him. Indeed, one clever person said that the magic had created an illusion, but that the malevolence and cruelty were no less real. Furthermore, he said, when the people had given him a chance to repent, the boy had shown no inclination to do so. That man's words brought cheers from the yet unschooled people of Glingkar. Even the brave and intelligent Gyatsa Zhakar could not find the right words to refute this view, although he knew it traduced his brother. Neither could the old steward. Who had spoken those words? It was Joru's uncle, Khrothung.

As the crowd watched, a section of ice sheared off the glacier with a thunderous crack and Joru's body was swallowed up in white sleet. The crowd cheered even louder.

But Joru's mother, Metog Lhartse, who had been sewing a fur robe in the opening of the tent, doubled over and clapped a hand over her heart as if it had been pierced.

When the clouds dispersed and the sun shone bright and clear, Joru rose up from the scattered shards of ice and landed in front of the crowd. The glacier had cracked into pieces when it met the magic that protected him. He told the people that the demons that had been trapped underground had opened a passageway in the water, but that he had sealed it beneath the glacier.

Khrothung spat at him. 'Liar.'

Other voices chorused, 'Liar! Liar! Liar! Liar! Liar!'

'My dear nephew,' Khrothung sneered, 'do not try to deceive us with your illusions.'

From the hills to the valleys, the people cried in perfect unison, 'Illusions! Illusions!'

The angry shouts were invincible, and the handsome face of the son of the deities turned ugly. Even his imposing stature diminished, until Joru was a wretched creature at the mercy of the crowd: they had won, they had forced an impostor to show his true colours. Now they shouted, 'Truth! Truth!'

This marked the sixth year after the son of the deities had descended to the human world.

Joru's mother, Metog Lhartse, looked into the hollow blue of the sky, beneath which emerald green hills extended to the horizon. She wanted to call out, but the sound rose up from her belly and stuck in her throat. It was not a sound she coughed out, but a blood clot. She dug into the ground, pushing the grass away, and buried it deep under the turf. She did not want anyone, not even Heaven, to see a mother's grief for her son.

The people were now shouting, 'Killer! Killer!'

'So what shall we do with him?' Khrothung wished to kill him, but he knew that no one could do so. In the awkward silence of the crowd, he spoke: 'He is just a child, so we must teach him to repent by banishing him to a barbaric and barren place.'

Banishment. Exile.

The boy would live or die alone in the wilderness. That way, no one would bear responsibility for his death. Greatly relieved, the people shouted again, and this time the word that brought the sky low in sadness was: 'Banish!'

'Banish?' Gyatsa Zhakar asked.

The wise old steward repeated his question: 'Banish?'

Echoes bounced off the rocky cliffs: 'Banish!'

All the old steward could do was summon the Glingkar noblemen to seek divination from Heaven. Gathered at his fortress, the noblemen listened eagerly to the prediction.

The precious pearl on the head of the poisonous snake is now in the hands of the poor, but how will they recognise its value if the right moment has not yet arrived?

Heaven had asked the people of Glingkar a question that most had not considered and were unwilling to do so.

'Does that mean Glingkar does not deserve the son of the deities?' The old steward was not sure what to do.

Khrothung had an answer: 'Send him north along the Yellow river, alone. Then we will see what magic the boy can manifest.'

The noblemen nodded their agreement, so the steward stayed silent.

'I should like to go into exile with my brother,' Gyatsa Zhakar said.

'What nonsense is that? You are the commander of Glingkar warriors. What would happen to Glingkar and its people if the demons rose up again or an enemy attacked?'

Gyatsa Zhakar sighed. 'Then I will inform him of the decision.'

But Danma, one of the Glingkar warriors, was sad that Gyatsa Zhakar must bid his younger brother a final farewell. 'Noble Gyatsa Zhakar, please stay in your golden seat. I will do that for you.' He spurred his horse and galloped towards Joru's camp.

Banned by his mother from returning to his father's fortress after his terrible battle with the demons, Joru in his anger had pitched a tent made of human skin. Intestines, set straight and rigid, served as the supporting poles, and human bones formed a gruesome fence. More bones were piled high beyond it. Disgusted as he was, Danma understood that Joru could never have collected so many bones, even if he had killed every human in Glingkar. The boy must have conjured them up in a childish rage, he thought, and in an instant the skin and bones vanished, leaving a simple tent.

Taking off his hat, Danma entered the tent, where the air was filled with a heavy fragrance, though not a flower was in sight. Joru did not speak; he just smiled. Enlightened by the will of Heaven, Danma fell to his knees, pledging eternal fealty to the boy. Thus Danma became King Gesar's first vassal, many years before Joru became king.

'The barbarians will come to their senses,' Joru said. 'In order that they will come to believe in their future enlightenment, we must make them regret what they did to me today.' He waved Danma forward and whispered to him what he must do.

Danma returned to the steward's fortress. Following Joru's instructions, he told everyone that the boy was a *yaksha* incarnate, a nature-spirit.

Khrothung directed the troops of his tribe to force the boy into exile.

'There is no need to use force,' the old steward said. 'Just send a hundred women, each with two handfuls of ashes, reciting incantations and spreading the ashes. The boy will have to go to the place of exile.'

Gyatsa Zhakar, knowing that this was a vile and very strong curse, pleaded for his brother: 'Joru is a descendant of my tribe, the grandson of the Dragon tribe. Please use a hundred handfuls of fried flour instead of the ashes.'

Joru and his mother had readied themselves. Wearing the hideous leather robe that his mother had made, Joru sat on his stick, like a simpleton, leering at the pretty Brugmo. She threw grey-white fried flour over his face. In contrast with her son's ugliness, Metog Lhartse was exceptionally beautiful that day. She put every other girl to shame. Jewels from the Dragon fortress seemed even more radiant beside her. Sitting upright on her snowy horse, she glowed like the early-morning sun.

The people marvelled at her beauty, as if they had discovered it for the first time, and the sight of her sweet face sent hot tears to their eyes. 'Glingkar is so vast and yet there is no place for this mother and son,' they lamented. 'How pitiful they look!' And they blamed others for the boy's fate.

Gyatsa Zhakar had returned home for provisions, which he loaded onto his horse. Taking his younger brother by the hand, he said, 'Let us go.' Mother and son mounted their horses.

The sighs over their fate faded before they had taken a hundred steps, and the women again spread the flour and spat such curses at the three travellers that deities flew out of Heaven to block them. Eventually, Joru told his brother to turn back. He wept as he watched him retreat.

Joru felt truly alone. Deities and the local mountain gods had been ordered to protect him, but he could not see them.

The Story
Tea Leaves

Joru and his mother rode until they reached the broad banks of the winding Yellow river, where nothing grew except a profusion of reeds on the flood plain, so tall that only the powerful shoulders and alert ears of their horses were visible. Joru told his mother that this should be where they built their new home. When she complained that the place had no name, the mountain god responded with a roar of thunder that it had once been called Yulung Kulha Sumdo, but the demons had released moles that burrowed underground, criss-crossing the land with tunnels. When the pasture grass reached down with its roots, it grasped nothing but black emptiness. That autumn, as the moles destroyed the link between the earth and the vegetation, the surviving clumps of grass decided not to grow the following year. They entrusted what few seeds they had to the wind, which would take them to a far-off place where they could put down roots.

So, the autumn wind took the seeds of fescue, wild green onion, sow-thistle and wild lilies, with the promise that one day it would bring back seeds.

The grass had left, followed by the people.

By the time Joru and his mother arrived, the moles had built a kingdom of their own, with two kings and nearly a hundred officials. When Joru decided to destroy the kingdom, his mother was worried. 'Since it is only the two of us, the people of Glingkar cannot condemn you for killing again but, my son, the gods in Heaven see everything.'

Gazing up at the sky, Joru mused that if Heaven could see everything, the people of Glingkar would not have mistreated him, and his mother would not have suffered because he was her son. So he said, 'Mother, I have long tasted the bitterness of wandering. Now I want to help those who were banished by the mole demons to return to their land.'

His words hung in the air as he transformed himself into a hawk and flew up into the blue sky. Below him lay a vast, open valley and a river with enough swirling water to make a beautiful bend. A dozen or so towering peaks gathered at the valley, which, as Master Lotus had predicted, was the place where the Gling tribe would rise to form a nation.

As the hawk rose, panic tore through the mole kingdom. The kings sent for their ministers and counsellors to form a strategic plan. One of the counsellors had already discovered that the hawk was Joru, banished from Glingkar. 'He has magical powers, but was exiled here because he killed in a frenzy,' the counsellor said.

'It matters not how he got here,' one of the kings said impatiently. 'All that matters is how we shall avoid calamity.'

'The king must order all the moles back from their tunnels. There are tens of thousands of us, occupying every hill around the underground palace, and I am sure he would not dare kill us all.'

But the hawk heard their words, and, pulling its wings back, it changed into a giant warrior, who picked up a hill and dropped it onto the palace, crushing the kings and officials to powder and burying the moles in their underground tunnels.

Then the wind blew back the grass seeds, the seeds of azaleas, giant cypress and birch. And there were seeds of rosemary, too, with its dusty blue flowers. It took only a single night and a fine drizzle for the seeds to sprout, and on the third day, before the palisade around the tent was finished, flowers were blooming across the grassland. People who had left but had not yet settled elsewhere returned with their cattle and sheep from all points of the compass.

To these people Joru was a king, but he wanted them to feel it in their hearts, not to call him king or make ceremonial bows. 'I am less a king than a favour from Heaven,' he told them. 'And I want to bestow upon you more favours on Heaven's behalf.'

He thought he sounded like a king.

The people looked up at him and said, 'Great King, what could be greater than that which you have already given us?'

'Yulung Kulha Sumdo will become the centre of a world, and the roads that are closed will link with all other places in the world.'

An elder raised a question that was on everyone's mind: 'Great King, why is it the centre of *a* world and not the centre of *all* the worlds?'

He wanted to tell them that the place where the black-haired Tibetans lived was indeed not the only world, that there were other worlds under Heaven. But he did not want to confuse them, so he turned away to explore the lands to the east, the west, the north and the south, quickly identifying the paths that would lead other worlds to his. The snow-capped peaks in the south were too close together, so he summoned the mountain gods and asked them to move their roots, to open a wide pass between them.

One by one, merchants following the trade winds took the road. Rain came with the warm winds from the south, bringing life to the wild fields. Lakes formed in low-lying areas, providing water for untended oxen and sheep. Tigers, leopards, jackals and wolves mingled among them, so the timid deer had to keep one eye open even when they slept. To the east, torrents roared down riverbeds, keeping men and horses from crossing. Only the monkeys and apes were able to travel freely on vines that reached from one bank to the other. Joru led a group of people to the riverbank, where monkeys swung across the river to the far bank. Instead of flinging back the vines, he tied them to a solid rock. That was how his people learned to make a vine bridge, which opened the way for caravans from the east, sent by the emperor of a distant land.

The foreigners used copper to make coins and exquisite urns, and came west to collect the source of lightning, the ore beneath the ground, and the dreamscape of snow lotus herbs. They believed that these ingredients could be mixed with others from the Eastern Sea to make an immortality potion for their emperor.

They wore delicately carved pendants of a fine stone they called jade, and when they landed they waved them at the western barbarians, asking, 'Have you this stone?' When they saw the magnificent steeds the barbarians rode, they said, 'We wish to buy many of your fine horses.'

They needed many things, so more bridges were built, each one wider than the last. Rafts and boats appeared on the broad river. Little by little, Yulung Kulha Sumdo became a centre, bringing lines of caravans from as far as Persia to the west and India to the south. The Indians were uncommunicative, but the Persians, at certain times of day, would dismount and spread out richly coloured rugs on which to pray in the direction whence they came.

Yet they all shared a fear of the north, where the Hor tribe lived. The Hor people were skilled horsemen and archers; the finest bowman among them could simply pluck his bowstring to make a whistling sound, and the terrified merchants would fall off their horses, dead. So, since the merchants were afraid to journey north, the Hor tribe came south. They set up tents at the mountain pass near Yulung Kulha Sumdo, where they robbed the caravans from Persia, India and the Eastern Empire.

Joru knew it was time to open a northern route.

He rode, alone, to the well-guarded Hor camp, where he passed through nine checkpoints and beheaded eighteen guards. The leader of the bandits looked down at him from the watchtower. He was the archer who could kill with only the whistling sound of his bow.

'I will kill you first,' Joru called to him.

The man roared with laughter, for Joru had no weapon but the stick on which he rode. More importantly, the archer was a handsome man with an impressive figure, while Joru, though not ugly, was comical, with his misshapen stick, shabby robe and a pair of crooked antlers on his hood.

But the laughing face of the archer froze when he saw Joru point to the sky to call down lightning, which he took in his hand and transformed into a bow. The crackle sent the man tumbling off his tower, dead when he hit the ground. His followers stampeded northward, fleeing for their lives.

The men of the caravans offered rare treasures to Joru, to thank him for saving them. But Joru refused them.

'We must do something for you,' they said. Though the merchants spoke different languages, Joru understood.

'If you wish to help, load rocks onto your pack animals and each of you carry a rock to pile at the bend in the Yellow river.'

'Dear warrior, you have such powerful magic, what could you need the rocks for?'

'I wish to build a magnificent fortress.'

'But you have the power to move an entire mountain – why do you need us?'

'Your work will be the tax you pay for the profits you have made here.'

The merchants were beside themselves with joy. They had been to many countries, but this was the first time they had been asked to pay taxes by moving a few rocks to the bend in a river. And so strange legends spread about the tiny nation with a very young king who had great powers but acted in unusual ways. Ambitious kings sent messengers and caravans to search for the nation of gold and jade and for potions that conferred immortality.

When Rongtsa Khragan, the old Glingkar steward, heard the tales, he realised that Joru might truly be a son of the deities, using extraordinary means to demonstrate his powers.

'I feel tremendous guilt when I listen to these stories,' he confessed to Gyatsa Zhakar.

Gyatsa Zhakar dreamed often of his brother, and in each dream he had spoken to Joru: 'Gling is your country and the people of Glingkar will one day be your subjects. Do not forsake them because they exiled you.'

★

Soon it was autumn, with its frequent winds and shorter days; snow fell. Gazing at the desolate landscape, Joru's mother said she missed Glingkar, and her words aroused a strange malady in Joru. He had been told that he came from a celestial kingdom, but could not remember what it looked like; when he longed for his homeland, the sights of Glingkar appeared before him.

In a dream that night his brother seemed troubled.

'Brother, why are you distressed?' Joru asked.

'My aged mother is ill.'

'Have the doctors given her medicines? Have the warlocks used their magic?'

Gyatsa Zhakar shook his head. 'Mother yearns for her homeland, but it is ten thousand snowcapped mountains and hundreds of rivers distant.'

'Is there nothing that can ease her suffering?'

'Yes, but it has not helped.'

'What is it?'

'Metog Lhartse, your mother, knows.'

When Joru awoke the following morning, he told his mother about his dream. Metog Lhartse recalled how, at Senglon's fortress, a bird no one had seen before flew over one day and landed at the window of Gyatsa Zhakar's mother's sickroom. She cried, because she heard the accent of her homeland in the bird's chirping. The bird left a branch on the windowsill before it flew away. It had many emerald green leaves. The Han doctor told her servant to pick a leaf and cook it in water. Within an hour, the woman had left her bed to stand on the highest point of the fortress to look east, the direction of her homeland. The medicine, the green branch with emerald leaves, which had come from her country, was called 'cha'.

'Cha?' Joru said.

'Yes.'

'What a strange sound!' He laughed.

'You would consider it pleasing to the ear if you know how to use it,' Metog Lhartse said.

'Oh?'

'Many sick people recover after steeping it in water, then drinking it. Your brother probably sent you the message in a dream because the Han consort has used all her cha leaves.'

'I'll find some cha for the Han consort,' Joru said, and summoned a peregrine falcon. All the bird brought back was a leafless branch. He showed it to a caravan from the east. 'Bring me as much of this as you can find.'

'Tea?' They used the foreign word.

'Cha!' He used the local word.

The leader of the caravan said, 'News will travel to my country even before I get there. When I am ready to return, the tea leaves will be on their way here. The first shipment will be a gift for you, but after that, when your people cannot live without it, you will have to pay for it with the good things from your land.'

'What do you need?'

'If you could tame them . . .' The leader pointed to wild horses galloping on the grassland.

'Of course.'

Then the leader turned to gaze at the torrential mountain streams, under which precious gold was buried in silt.

'Gold.'

The leader now looked towards the rare flowers and herbs on the grassland, all useful medicines for illness.

Joru was displeased. 'Enough! I asked for only one thing, but you are greedy.'

The merchant laughed. 'Everyone says that of us, but as time goes by, the people in the world find it harder to live without us. So you may refuse our demands, but if you do, we will not give you what we have.'

'I want what you have.'

'The road you opened did not attract only the greedy. Many destitute and homeless people have also come to be your subjects, Great King.'

'I am not a king.'

'One day you will be the king of a nation, unless you seal the passes between the snowcapped mountains, then burn the vine bridges and ferry boats on the river.' Joru knew he could not do that now, and felt regret. When he had opened the roads, he had brought peace and wealth to a deserted, barbaric land. He had been powerful. But now he felt that he was under the control of something even more powerful, not demons, nothing he could see or kill, yet it drew closer and closer.

'Have some tea.' The merchant handed him a jade cup filled with a clear brown liquid.

'Isn't it a leaf?' Joru asked.

'This liquid is brewed from the magical leaves.'

He took a sip and found it bitter, but then his mouth filled with a lingering aroma. He was suddenly refreshed. The merchant gave him a bag of dried leaves from the magical tree, and Joru sent the roaming peregrine with the bag to Glingkar.

Now, Khrothung had lately fashioned a vulture out of a light wood and daily rode it haughtily across the sky, to demonstrate his powers to all of Glingkar. When he saw the soaring peregrine, he yelled, 'Dog of the sky, where are you going?'

'I am following Joru's command to fly to his elder brother, Gyatsa Zhakar,' the peregrine replied.

'What is that in your bill? Let me see.'

'You are not Gyatsa Zhakar,' the peregrine said.

Khrothung recited a spell to incite his vulture to snatch the bag. But Gyatsa Zhakar had witnessed this scene: he fitted arrow to bow to shoot down his uncle's wooden vulture. The peregrine landed on his shoulder and cried, 'Tea! Tea!' then flapped its wings and flew away.

Gyatsa Zhakar looked into the bag. It was not fresh cha from a green branch, so he said nothing when he returned to the fortress. Yet when the Han consort smelt the wondrous aroma her headache all but vanished. 'How lucky I am to smell the fragrance of cha!'

Gyatsa Zhakar was overjoyed: he had the right leaf after all. He presented the bag to his mother.

After the old steward had tasted the cha his wife brewed for him, he announced, 'From now on, my mind will be clear and my eyes bright. I will never again be deceived by illusions and my heart will always face in the right direction.'

The people began to murmur to each other: 'Joru is thousands of miles away, but he has changed leaves into medicine to send to Glingkar, whose people cruelly banished him.' And the good name of the son of the deities began to spread again among the people of Glingkar.

That evening a canker sore erupted on Khrothung's mouth and kept him awake. General Danma said, 'That is his punishment for spreading rumours.' Khrothung sent someone to the Han consort for some cha. But when her maid brought him a pot of the aromatic brew, he was suspicious: 'This may be a trick of Joru's. If he can change a leaf into medicine, he can change this bowl of cha into a magic potion to steal my powers.' So his maidservants shared the drink instead, and soon an exotic fragrance oozed from their pores. Grinding his teeth, Khrothung snarled, 'I could kill you all!'

Gyatsa Zhakar dreamed that same night of a world of white, covered with snow. Cows and sheep could not find grass to eat, shivering people could not find kindling and travellers could not find their way. When he awoke, he led a group of people to the mountaintop to pray at an altar made of nine layers of stone. They sacrificed an animal, but the shamans said they saw no sign from Heaven.

The Storyteller
Fate

His listeners looked up to the heavens.

Nothing except flickering cold stars showed in a sky that people had been gazing at for thousands of years. They felt someone should have been there to announce a miracle, so long had they been waiting for one. True, miracles did occur sometimes, but only for a handful of people.

It took the old storyteller a long time to look up, as though he were slowly awakening from his own story. People quietly approached and placed gifts on the blanket before him: coins, dried meat, flour cakes, dried apples, cheese, salt and snuff. Then they walked away, their shadows elongated in the moonlight.

Jigmed was the only one still sitting there; his shadow and his body remained together, a solid dark shape. He watched the old man put away his lute, pick up the money and tuck it away. Then, breathing hard, the old man rolled his blanket into a bundle so he could take the other gifts with him.

'Are you leaving now?' Jigmed asked desperately. 'I thought you'd come with me. What you sang was different from what I saw in my dream.'

A bright light seemed to burn in the old man's eyes. 'Maybe Heaven wanted to change the story and let you see that in your dream. So, tell me, young man, how are they different?'

'They're different from the beginning. The son of the deities didn't let himself be exiled. The people banished him because they didn't know who he was.'

'In your dream, who told you this?'

'I don't know.'

'Then tell me what he looked like.'

'It wasn't a person who told me. It was like seeing something in a film.'

'Tell me exactly how they differ.'

'I told you. They were different at the beginning.'

'Was everything the same after that?'

'After that . . . I haven't dreamed what happened after that. You sang so much in one night that you're already far ahead of me.'

The old man slung the rolled blanket over his shoulder and cradled his lute. 'The story will sprout new branches, young man. I'll return to hear your version if I don't starve or freeze to death on the road.' With that, he hobbled off into the moonlight, and just before his shadow disappeared, Jigmed heard him say, 'Why doesn't this story end? Then ill-fated people like me would not have to spread it for ever.'

His shadow splintered and vanished.

The old man's words pierced Jigmed's heart, like a gust of cold air. *Why has someone like him been chosen as a narrator for such a story?* The wind began to blow, and he began to shiver. *Storyteller.* The word rose in his head and startled him. Was he really going to be like that old man, wandering the land burdened with the ancient story of a warrior from Heaven?

When he got home, he looked at the moon through his window.

'Storyteller.'

I'm a fool. The deities made a mistake in choosing me, and now that they know how stupid I am they'll never let me see the extraordinary things in my dream again.

He looked at the moon, trying to stay awake. But as he did, it changed, and the shards of light became more solid than moonbeams and whiter than snow, drifting and settling from the deepest recesses of the sky. And then he heard a voice: 'The story, its main direction, has been settled, but there will be differences.'

'Why?'

Roaring laughter sent the snowflakes swirling, as if disturbed by wind. 'People always see things differently.'

The Story
Snowstorm

The son of the deities also dreamed about the snow. It was not the first time.

He put on a robe and walked out of his tent. There was no snow on the ground – it was summertime, and moonlight flowed like milk. He wondered if that was a manifestation of the will of the deities, a sign that one day this would be a blessed place, a place where livestock would thrive.

But what about the swirling snow in his dream? He received no response from the heavens. The celestial soldiers who were secretly protecting him ducked into the grey clouds with the moon, fearful of answering such a question.

Noisy migrating birds landed in the marshes at a bend in the Yellow river, on their way north. The wind did not change direction, but the south-easterly winds, usually warm and moist, brought the chill of the north-westerlies. Hearing the startled birdcalls, his mother put on her robe and came out to stand behind him. Joru was beginning to understand.

'Heaven is going to punish Glingkar,' he said.

'Will that incur more anger towards my son?' his mother asked, with a sigh.

'No, Mother.'

'Who made me come to this world to give birth to you and make you suffer so grievously?'

'Dear Mother, I no longer see it so. And I do love you.'

'That, it seems, is the only blessing Heaven has bestowed on me.'

Now he saw clearly. 'Mother, it is snowing in Gling,' he said sadly. 'We must prepare to receive refugees from Glingkar's disaster, it seems.'

It was indeed snowing in Gling. Danma went to tell Gyatsa Zhakar, who then went to the old steward.

'Snow in summer, an extraordinary sign,' the old man said. 'I know this is for the crime of banishing the son of the deities, a crime committed by all the people of Glingkar.'

They came out onto an open field where snow swirled in the air, turning the green summer grass yellow. In the evening, the blizzard died down a little, as a faint sunset appeared in the western sky. 'The snow is stopping,' the people said.

But the old steward knitted his brow. 'Yes, the snow is stopping. But even so, ignorant people, we must reflect upon our crime. This is a warning sign from Heaven.'

'Old Steward, don't frown like that. You will frighten the people.' Khrothung had appeared, and as he dismounted he spoke loudly: 'Fear not, citizens of Gling. When you get up tomorrow, you will see that the insects that fight for grass with cows and sheep have frozen to death. I sent the heavy snow with my magic.'

'I do not believe that your magic is adequate to such a performance. In any case, we will treat the snow as a special favour from Heaven,' snapped the old steward.

'What, then, is the reason for bestowing such a blessing on us?' asked Gyatsa Zhakar.

Unable to answer, the old steward walked back into the fortress with his hands clasped behind his back.

'The snow has stopped falling!' Khrothung shouted. It had indeed, and a great rent had opened in the thick clouds to the west, freeing the dying sun to send down its brightest light. With his hands raised,

Khrothung went on, 'The snow has stopped falling. Now do you see my powers? The snow killed the insects, which can no longer take grass from the cows and sheep.' The herders cheered. To them, this man was better suited to lead Glingkar than the fretful old steward.

The farmers, though, were worried. 'Our crops froze with the insects.'

'They will come back to life tomorrow.'

When the people of Glingkar saw how composed and resolute Khrothung was, they said, 'We have heard that Heaven is going to send us a king. Perhaps he is the one.'

But the crack in the west closed, and thick clouds darkened in the sky above them. Khrothung fled back to his own tribe on his flying horse. He knew that the people could turn away from him in an instant. As the saying goes, 'Good people believe that kind seeds are sown in people's hearts, while bad ones see only evil sprouts.' To a man like Khrothung, the people were sheep one moment and wolves the next.

A new snowfall began, and lasted nine days and nine nights.

Then the sky cleared once more.

The old steward said to Gyatsa Zhakar, 'I want to offer a reverential prayer at the mountaintop altar, for I believe that Heaven is going to send us a sign. But the heavy snow has covered the roads, and for horses it would be like falling into an abyss.'

Gyatsa Zhakar extracted an arrow from his quiver, drew his bow and shot. The arrow cleaved the snow on the ground, pushing it aside. He did it again and again, sending the snow rolling back in giant waves to clear a path. The old steward took a group of priests up to the altar. 'Deities in Heaven, I should have brought a human sacrifice, but my people have suffered too much. I shall be happy to offer you my old body. You may open up my chest with a sharp knife. Some people in Gling call me king, but I know that I am not a king. Please dispatch me and give them a king who will lead them out of the abyss of misery.'

The reflection from the snow was so blindingly bright that the people below could not see what was happening.

The deities sent a Buddha down with the bright light; it was Avalokitesvara, the Buddha of Mercy and Compassion. 'Heaven sent you a king, and he was among you, but you betrayed and deserted him. Now all of Gling must leave this place to follow him.' The Buddha and the light disappeared.

'May I tell the people?' the old steward shouted into the sky.

'The people must come to their senses for themselves. They must wake up.'

It was a loud, booming voice, audible only to the old steward. Even Gyatsa Zhakar, who was close by and saw the Buddha, did not hear a word, let alone the priests, who neither saw nor heard anything.

All the leaders of Glingkar's villages came to the old steward's fortress. Khrothung rode up on his wooden vulture. He circled the fortress three times before landing and, reciting an incantation, made sure that everyone saw his vulture cleverly tuck in its wings.

He asked the old steward if he had received a sign at the altar.

'The son of the deities, Joru, has found a new place for us,' the steward replied.

'Did the rocks on the mountain tell you so?' Khrothung said, with a sneer.

'We can take to the road once the snow begins to melt.' Then, turning to the crowd gathered outside the fortress, he called, 'Go back to your villages and prepare your people to follow you out.'

At this, even the steward's own people began to wail, for they loved this place, which they called home. Admittedly, there had been summer snow, but now that it had stopped, the grass would soon grow again. And, it was true, many cows and sheep had starved to death but not all of them. When spring came, the survivors would give birth to more. Only Gyatsa Zhakar and the great general Danma supported Rongtsa Khragan's plan; the others sat in blank silence like clay statues. Khrothung was among them, but he saw no need to speak since the silent people had done so for him.

The old steward realised he must describe what the Buddha had shown him, just as a booming voice sounded in his ears: 'Heaven can help, but the people must come to their senses for themselves.'

With a sigh, he said, 'Go home and talk it over with your people. You know that Joru has founded a new settlement along a bend in the Yellow river to the north.'

They had heard much about the banished Joru from caravans that brought tea. Now almost everyone in Glingkar drank it; their mouths no longer festered with cankers and their limbs had grown strong. More importantly, they were energetic and clear-headed all day long. On the caravans' return trips, not all the horses carried pelts and medicinal herbs, such as the blue flowers of rosemary. Some were loaded with slabs of shale from the rocky cliffs to pay Joru's rock tax on their return trip past the river bend. The merchants told them that Joru had built a tri-coloured fortress with the rocks he had collected so far.

'Three colours?'

'Rocks brought back by southern merchants are red, those by western merchants are copper-coloured, and those from the east are white.'

'What is the colour of rocks from the north?'

The merchants shook their heads. 'The north is still under the control of the savage leader of the Hor tribe, King Padrang, and the demon Lutsan, who has devoured countless people. We have no idea when King Joru plans to bring them under his rule.'

'That will never happen. He will pretend that he has already subjugated the north by using the green rocks from Glingkar.'

'Untrue. The king has said he will use them for the roof of the fortress as a sign that he never forgets his homeland.'

The girls, led by Brugmo, the prettiest, had something else in mind: 'He devotes himself to warrior activities so he must have grown into a handsome young man.'

The merchants shook their heads slowly and said, as if in defence of Joru, 'The greatest warriors are those who do not look like warriors.'

This was greeted with sighs of disappointment.

'But he was so clever and comely when he was newly born,' Brugmo said.

'But did he not turn himself into a monster?' Khrothung gloated.

Yes, he had cut a fine figure when he was first born, but by the age of three or four he had begun to dress in his strange rags, and in the end, his appearance had changed to match his odd attire and his nickname, Joru. People had forgotten that his real name was Gesar, although many were sure that he would one day regain his former looks. Gyatsa Zhakar said to the giggling girls, 'One day my brother will look like a warrior.'

The twelve prettiest girls of Glingkar, including Brugmo, said, 'If that is the case, then we twelve would willingly be his consorts.'

Stroking his oily black beard, Khrothung said, 'Do not wait for him. We men could not bear to see you waste your beauty and youth and wither like flowers. Why don't you all marry me? You will enjoy lives of wealth and glory, dine on delicacies and dress in the finest clothes.'

Like flickering fish that spot the shadow of a hawk, the girls fled.

The caravans left with their heavy loads of stone. As he watched them disappear, the old steward said softly, 'Son of the deities, why will you not show your true image?' A sense of powerlessness filled him, and he repeated his question. 'Son of the deities, why will you not show your true image?'

Khrothung came to the old steward. 'No one listens to you,' he said, 'because you are not the true king.'

'I am not the king. I am just a steward elected by the tribes of Gling. We are waiting for the king to appear.'

'If you cease to call yourself "steward" and replace it with "king", you will be the true king.'

'Return to your settlement. I am tired. Come back tomorrow when you have been able to think.'

'You are older than I, so you will be the king and I will be your steward. With your benevolence and my powers, Glingkar will surely prosper and grow strong.'

'Why don't you declare yourself king?'

'Why not indeed? Glingkar cannot go on without a king.'

The old steward waved his hand and said, 'We shall wait and see what Heaven has in store for us.'

Khrothung mounted his wooden vulture and flew off to tell the tribal leaders, who were travelling in different directions, 'Come back to the fortress tomorrow. We will not talk of moving. Instead, we will elect a king for Glingkar.'

As they trudged through the snow, the leaders followed the vulture with their eyes. 'Perhaps he *is* the king, the one who will lead us through the difficult days ahead.'

The next day the sky shone bright and clear, when the old steward stood on a dais in front of the fortress. The snowdrifts were silently collapsing under the heat of the sun, with water gurgling beneath the white blanket. It was nearly noon, but not a single person could be seen on the roads that led to the tribal lands. The old steward sent soldiers to find them, while he sat on the top tier of the fortress, neither drinking tea nor touching the cheese that was brought to him. Eyes closed, he could hear the snow melting, and when he opened his eyes, he saw steam rising in the sun's rays. Still no one came. The heat from the sun weakened and, battered by an icy western wind, the steamy vapours turned to grey mist and fog. He sank into gloom. Perhaps he had outlived his usefulness; perhaps he deserved to be abandoned by the people.

Suddenly, figures appeared on the road – Danma and Gyatsa Zhakar, who had suffered snow blindness on their return trip the day before and had lost their sense of direction. Then the soldiers returned with the tribal leaders, who had lost their way also after being blinded. The last to appear was Khrothung, who had ridden his vulture straight into a mountain and had had to limp his way back. The moment he entered the fortress, snow began to fall again.

The people, thirsty from their long walk, gulped tea.

'The caravans cannot get through,' the old steward said, 'and I have no more tea for you.'

'Are you saying that whoever has the most tea can be the king?' Khrothung spoke half in jest.

'You do not understand,' the old steward snapped. 'Listen . . . the snow is falling again. We have missed another chance given us by Heaven.'

The snow grew heavier, and its strange weight now seemed to settle not on the ground but in people's hearts. At last they pleaded, 'Old Steward, let us go to this other place.'

The old steward fell to his knees: 'Bodhisattva,' he prayed, 'they have come to their senses at last.'

On the fourth day, the blizzard eased, and the people of Gling left their snow-covered fields and villages, taking only their meagre belongings with the sheep and cattle that had survived the snow. As they walked they wept, until their voices reached the sky and changed the wind's direction.

It was late spring at the bend of the Yellow river. Lambs gambolled and wild strawberry flowers blanketed the roadside. The old steward knelt facing their homeland, which lay far in the distance beneath snow, and looked up into the sky. 'The people of Gling have arrived in their new home. I have brought them to the one you have chosen.' He hesitated, turning to his people. 'Yet you must go on alone. I am ashamed to face Joru.'

The Story
The Bend in the Yellow River

They travelled for three more days before the stone fortress appeared before them, its roof glistening with the dark green rock of Gling, laid like dragon scales.

Joru stood before the people, who touched their foreheads as a sign of celebration. He did not ride upon his stick, as he had done in his former playfulness, or wear the robe with those strange antlers on its hood. His eyes shone bright and clear in his unmarked face. After he had kissed the Han consort on the forehead, he and his brother embraced, tears streaming down their faces. Then he cast an admiring glance at the twelve beauties of Glingkar.

'Joru!' they called.

'Not Joru, it's Gesar.'

'His name matters little,' Khrothung said. 'Remember, he is just an eight-year-old boy.'

The girls retorted: 'But he's already broader and taller than you.'

'Already his glance makes our cheeks burn.'

'He has given us a new place to live.'

Danma led Joru through the crowd to the old steward, who was hiding in shame. Once he had made sure that the people were fed, Joru took his brother and the old steward by their hands and extended an invitation to his tent to all the tribal leaders, including his father, Senglon, the warrior heroes, priests, sorcerers and Buddhist monks who had recently been disseminating the Buddhist teaching in Glingkar. It was the tent that had accompanied Joru when he was banished from Glingkar, and the sight of it rekindled remorse in Gyatsa Zhakar, who fretted, 'How can such a small tent accommodate so many honoured guests?'

'The fortress is much larger and more impressive,' the old steward said.

As though he hadn't heard them, Joru parted the tent flaps to reveal an enchanting scene. It was roomy and airy, with a pleasant fragrance. Everyone was given a seat on a Persian rug, facing a table made of precious stones and sandalwood set with golden goblets, silver cups and long-stemmed red carnelian glasses filled with fruit. The people of Glingkar had never tasted such fruit, which came from distant lands.

Picking up his wine glass, Joru said, 'I thank the heavens for bringing my family and kinfolk to me. This is the happiest day of my life. Drink, all of you.'

They drank, all but the old steward, who approached him. 'I have a request on behalf of the people of Glingkar, and I will not drink until you agree.'

'Please speak.'

'A calamity has descended upon our beautiful land, owing to our many crimes, of which chasing you and your mother out was the most serious. I beg you, for the well-being of the people of Glingkar, let them spend three years on the land you have opened.'

'Why three years and not three days?' Joru was feeling mischievous.

The old steward bowed low. 'The severity of our crime was as deep as the snow at home. It will take three years for the snow to melt and for life to return to the land.'

A pain, as sharp as a pinprick, shot through Joru's heart as he heard the old steward shoulder the blame. He escorted him to the seat of honour and held out his own wine glass. 'Old Steward and tribal leaders, I, Joru, built this place because I wish to help Glingkar prosper for millennia.'

As he spoke, the top of the tent disappeared, and their seats seemed to rise. They heard Joru's booming voice: 'See for yourselves. This beautiful and broad section of the Yellow river is curved like a precious sword, its blade facing India to the south, its tip pointing at China, the sword plunging into Mount Nyenchenthanglha. I built the fortress here because Yulung Kulha Sumdo is the future centre of Gling. Once our nation has achieved great things, we will send some of our people back to our homeland.'

Overjoyed, the old steward picked up his glass and drained it three times. A banquet was served and when the people had eaten they began to sing and dance. All night long the thousands of bonfires lit outside their tents burned so brightly they outshone the stars in the sky.

The next morning Joru took the tribal leaders up a hill, where he pointed out their surroundings. 'Look at the river,' he said. 'The warriors have open spaces to gallop their horses, the people have a market for trade, and the herders have grassy plains to graze their flocks. I am giving the fortress, built with the rock tax, to our beloved old steward. It has a capacious meeting hall. When you summon us, Old Steward, the sound will travel far from the high tower.'

'It is your fortress and you are our king,' the old steward said.

'King Joru! King Joru!' the people cried.

'He is not Joru, he is Gesar,' his father shouted.

The people changed their chant: 'King Gesar! King Gesar!'

Joru used his magic power to stop the people's cheers before he brought the old steward into the fortress and set him on a throne that was covered with a tiger skin and had golden armrests carved with dragon heads.

'Sit here, Old Steward.'

'Heaven has shown its will. You are our king.' He struggled in vain to get up.

Khrothung walked up. 'He is right. Only you are qualified to be our king. Why don't you sit on the throne and give each tribe a new place to live? It makes us uneasy, dallying in your fortress and eating your good food.'

'I know that Uncle Khrothung wants to find land for farmers to till and pasture for the shepherds to graze their cows and sheep,' Joru agreed.

'Now, that is being a good nephew! I shall not fill your ears with pleasantries, as the old steward has done. My dear nephew, there are high places and low. Soil can be fertile or barren. You know that in Glingkar my Tagrong tribe occupied an area near a good river.'

'Not everyone can feel shame and not everyone can change from bad to good,' the old steward said, sighing over Khrothung's words.

'Old Steward, you can say these things because you are seated on the throne. I, on the other hand, have my people's livelihood and happiness to think of. I have no choice but to be candid.' He took Joru to one side. 'The people of Glingkar can no longer tolerate this steward. Since you have bestowed such favours on us, why won't you be our king?' Then he tugged at Joru's sleeve. 'My dear nephew,' he said, 'I believe you do not wish to be king because you are afraid.'

'I am not afraid, Uncle.'

'Child, you may not know it but you are afraid. You fear that with a child's intellect you will be unable to deal with people whose schemes are as vast as the ocean.'

'Enough, Uncle.'

'What are you afraid of? Do not be afraid.'

'I am not afraid. I am just weary.'

'That is fear!'

'Yes, it is indeed as you say. My dear uncle, I am truly afraid that, with the simple mind of a child, I cannot deal with an elder whose schemes are as vast as the ocean.'

Khrothung, of course, knew that his nephew's barb was directed at him, but he refused to give up. He continued: 'Remove the old steward from the throne, and I will be your steward. You can continue to vanquish evil spirits and demons, and I will resolve any troubles.'

Everyone heard him, and the old steward responded loudly, 'I will be the steward if Joru is king.'

The Tagrong people stood with Khrothung, but the other tribes supported the old steward. As their quarrel grew fierce, they forgot about Joru.

'Do not argue,' Joru said quietly. They reminded him of a flock of noisy migrating birds when they first land on a lake. He walked out of the fortress.

When his mother saw him, the sadness on his face sent sharp pangs to her heart, 'Do they want to take your fortress from you?'

'Oh, Mother. Why did you have to leave the Dragon fortress and give birth to me among these people?'

She wanted to tell him that they would have to ask Heaven, but held back from voicing words that might add to his distress.

The shouts grew so loud that the heavy stone slabs on the roof began to vibrate and the water birds feeding at the quiet riverbank were startled into flight. Gyatsa Zhakar and General Danma came out after him. 'Where is Father?' Joru asked.

'He is with the old steward.'

'Why does he not come to Mother? How can he help the steward?'

'Everyone has to declare which side he is on.'

'What about you?'

'Why don't you want to be king?'

'Why should I?'

'To build a nation, a real nation. At the moment, all the tribes, who have come from the same ancestors, are nothing but loose sand.'

'Everyone knows you were sent by Heaven to be King of Glingkar,' Danma joined in.

Joru looked up at the sky. 'No one has ever told me so. I only know that this argument is tiresome.'

Just then, they heard a pair of travelling monks claiming that Gling must wait for word from Heaven to determine who should be king. If the two sides could not reach agreement, they said, they themselves would take over. Without a king sent by heaven, only they could rule fairly and unselfishly. The monks offered further explanation. All under Heaven had been divided into separate worlds, each of which was to fall under the teachings of a different religion. Glingkar was placed in the realm of the Buddhist light. The son of the deities, who would be its king, had received blessings from accomplished Buddhists in the west, which was why he had magical powers and a clear mind. All this had been illuminated by Master Lotus and the Buddha of Great Compassion.

'Monks?' Joru's expression changed from solemnity to disappointment and from bewilderment to playfulness. He resumed the clownish form he had adopted when first banished from Glingkar. On his stick, he rode up to a mountain peak. Gyatsa Zhakar tried to follow, but could not catch up with him, so he returned to the fortress, and the crowd grew quiet, believing he had brought a message from Joru. He opened his mouth, but could make no sound. He tried again, and this time he succeeded, but the people were impatient. 'Louder!'

So he raised his voice: 'Since Joru does not wish to be king, whoever he puts on the throne will be our leader.' At that, he heard the sound of swords returning to their scabbards. If Joru heard it, Gyatsa Zhakar said to himself, he would be disappointed.

The crowd slowly dispersed. The old steward slumped on the throne. 'We have only just emerged from disaster. How has it come to this?'

Gyatsa Zhakar was quiet, but the quick-tongued General Danma voiced his anger: 'The old steward himself is the one who should answer that question.'

'How dare you?' Senglon roared.

'Hush, Father,' Gyatsa Zhakar whispered. 'You should go to our mother, Metog Lhartse.'

By then, the Han consort had already gone to look for Metog Lhartse, but in vain. Senglon also sought her, but he could not find her either. For the rest of the day, the people, who were once again feeling guilty, searched for Joru, but no one saw either mother or son. The tent by the fortress had disappeared; even the haystack fence around it had vanished in a gust of wind, as if nothing had ever existed on the patch of grass.

Joru had vanished again.

Two days later he reappeared. He was wearing his deerskin robe, with the crooked antlers on the hood; his face was dirty. Perched on the twisted magic stick, he descended from the skylight in the fortress roof and landed in front of the throne, where the old steward was resting. His eyes were tightly shut, but he could not stop sighing. Joru shook his shoulders and said, with a grin, 'Have they given you a headache?'

'Joru is back!' He nearly leaped off his seat.

'Come back in, all of you. Joru is here,' he shouted.

Joru waved his stick. 'Stop,' he said. 'I won't let them hear me.'

'Will you use heavenly powers?'

'I don't know, but they can't hear me if I don't want them to.'

'You are the son of the deities.'

A gust of wind blew through the window, fluttering the fur on Joru's robe and sending the stench of him to the old steward. He raised his hand to cover his nose, which made Joru laugh. 'Is that the smell of the son of the deities?'

The old man grabbed him by the shoulders and shook him violently. 'A Bodhisattva came from Heaven to give me a sign. He wanted all the Glingkar tribes to follow you, so I brought them here.'

'Bodhisattva?'

'The Guanyin Bodhisattva of Compassion.'

For an instant, an image flashed in Joru's mind, like the shadow of ripples on water. 'What is a Bodhisattva?' he asked.

'There are monks with shaved heads who came with us. You've seen them, haven't you?'

'Indeed I have. They also wanted to be king.'

'They are followers of the Bodhisattva and have come to spread Buddha's teachings.'

'Teachings?'

'They teach us not to fight and to be good.'

Joru was more confused than ever, so he said, 'I'm leaving now.'

'You cannot.'

'If I stay, you will continue to confuse me until my head explodes.'

'You cannot go, son of the deities.'

But Joru had drifted on his magic stick to the skylight, where he took out a parchment map and threw it down. 'I know the area around the river bend. I have divided the land for you.' Then he flew off. The crowd gasped as he turned into a roc, which spread its wings and flew towards the mountains.

The steward held high the parchment map. 'Let our hearts suffer late into the night in our shame. The one who has shown us his great image, the one we called Joru because we thought he was ugly, has settled everything for us.'

Joru's allocation of settlements for each tribe was logical: Tse Lhase Khado was suitable for the officials, so it would be the territory of the eight brothers from the senior branch; the prettiest canyon, Padma Rangshar, was the best place for brave men, so it was given to the six tribes of the junior branch; the Dradokyu canyon, south of the Yellow river, was assigned to Joru's father, Senglon; and Yulung Kulha Sumdo, where the tri-colour fortress was located, would belong to the old steward, Rongtsa Khragan.

'What about us, the Tagrong tribe?' Khrothung was upset when he saw that every other tribe had its place.

Downstream from the Yellow river, above Lugu, there was a narrow, throat-shaped gorge with an embankment like a blooming lotus, but it was not a peaceful place. If you called for a fellow human, a demon woman would respond, and if you called for a dog, a fox would answer.

It was the perfect place for an intrepid man, so naturally it went to Khrothung and his Tagrong tribe.

Other than Khrothung, who was unhappy that he had not been given the fortress with its golden throne, the tribes and their leaders were beset by shame for having driven Joru away again.

The Story
Bodhisattva

Joru left, in part because he was tired of the endless quarrels, but more because he desired to expand Gling's territory. Its only close neighbour was Hor to the north. A vast no man's land stretched between Glingkar and its other neighbours, India to the south, Persia to the west and the Han Empire to the east. Joru now travelled upstream along the Yellow river to a place called Mamed Yulung Sumdo. Like all other wildernesses, this land was overrun by demons and evil spirits, so Joru multiplied himself and chased the demons along the river and into the hills until they had nowhere left to hide. As the demons fled, they transformed themselves into animals. If Joru had been a little older, he might have felt some pity, but he was still a child, and one who had been banished from Glingkar at the age of five, then had exiled himself from Yulung Kulha Sumdo when he was only eight. For a boy, it was great fun to see what the demons would turn into after a defeat, or how his doubles would use their sticks to kill panic-stricken creatures that only pretended to be frail. It felt good. At first, his magic stick harmed living animals by mistake – if a fleeing demon changed into a flock of marmots, one or two might be actual animals that had come out of their burrows to sun themselves. But soon his stick was able to tell the real from the false. Real marmots would stare, wide-eyed and silent, when they saw the shadow of the stick coming their way. The false ones would release a shrill, bleak cry from their throats.

Travellers would gather wherever he had vanquished the demons, and caravans appeared on the new roads he built through snowcapped mountains and low-lying marshes. The merchants, no strangers to his accomplishments at Yulung Kulha Sumdo, had no qualms about coming forward. When they appeared in Mamed Yulung Sumdo, they asked, 'King of Mamed, will you still demand the rock tax when we pass through your territory?'

'I no longer need rocks to build a fortress.'

'Then what do you need?'

'I will think about it.'

Mounting his stick, he flew to a distant lake, in which lived a dragon that devoured caravan horses and demanded ocean corals, as if it wanted to turn its underwater den into a palace. Hovering over the lake, Joru commanded the dragon to stay below the surface and not to threaten the caravans. With a peal of laughter, the dragon spewed a giant column of water. 'Your stick is good only for killing foxes and moles in their burrows.'

'Then I shall take your life today without using my stick.'

'We'll see about that!' The dragon leaped high into the air.

Joru made three quick turns in the sky, then flung three thunderbolts from the palms of his hands. The dead dragon fell back into the lake.

'Why does he not wish to be our king?' the people and the merchants asked, when they saw what he had done.

But he had already flown off on his stick.

So they went to talk to his mother, who was teaching embroidery to a group of women. 'Perhaps he prefers to be a king without a throne,' she said.

When he was eleven, he came down the mountain, dragging his stick behind him in a flood of blood from three giant reptilian demons he had slain. He had to quicken his pace to keep his feet out of the gore, which made him a sorry sight. But he knew that what little power remained in the blood would die once he reached the far shore of the lake.

A wall of light suddenly descended between Joru and the flowing blood, and Guanyin Bodhisattva appeared in the light, seated on a lotus flower. Joru thought he knew who it was, but he still asked, 'Who are you?'

'I have come from a faraway place to see you.'

Involuntarily, Joru pointed at the sky.

The Bodhisattva smiled. Then he said, 'You have taken too many lives.'

'Of demons.'

'It is not that you should have spared them but that you should not have taken such pleasure in accomplishing it. You were like a merchant delighted by the sight of gold.'

'What do you mean?'

'It is hard to kill demons yet feel compassion for them.'

'What good would it do?'

'It would make the people do good.'

Joru laughed. 'You sound like the monks around the old steward. Are they your disciples?'

'Anyone can be a disciple of the Buddha and achieve enlightenment.'

'Then you should go now. I did not like those two disciples of yours, the ones who followed the steward around.'

'Why not?'

'Did you send them here to rule Glingkar?'

'They came to sow the seeds of compassion, like farmers tending the fields.'

'And yet they wish to be kings.'

As the Bodhisattva settled on the ground, Joru felt a fragrant breeze on his face. Sighing, the Bodhisattva said, 'That is why I am here. Come closer. I must speak with you.'

The two monks, who had pledged to spread the Buddhist teachings among the people of Glingkar, had turned their eyes on the throne because they had been received with such respect and veneration. The deities' original plan had been for their son to live among the people and, with the power given to him by Buddhist deities, vanquish demons. When the spate of killing had waned, the monks would be sent to sow the seeds of kindness. Now, it appeared, the monks had arrived too soon and, as they lived on a relatively barren land, the seeds they were sowing had not grown. Instead weeds had sprouted in the people's hearts.

'You must continue to collect rock taxes from the caravans,' the Bodhisattva said.

'I need no other fortress.'

'For a temple.'

'A temple?'

'For Buddha, as well as for the monks who spread his teachings. They should not mingle with common people, for they, too, are born of human flesh. And the temple should be far from the hubbub of daily life, so do not build it on a busy thoroughfare or in the king's fortress.'

'Why?'

The Bodhisattva did not answer, for it was hard to say why it was necessary to live a hermet's life in the mountains when the task was to cultivate human hearts and turn them into blessed fields.

As she was leaving, the Bodhisattva said, 'People usually understand something when they see me. The same is true for you, I hope.'

'I thought I remembered something from the past, but it was confused.'

'Have you achieved enlightenment?'

'Do you mean, do I understand what you have told me? You . . .'

'You may call me Bodhisattva.'

'I understand the Bodhisattva's meaning. In the future I will not laugh but weep when I slay demons.'

'You will indeed shed tears one day.'

Joru laughed. 'I was told that there was a powerful Master Lotus who came down to kill many demons, but that one day he left. Did you say something to him?'

Now the Bodhisattva felt that she had run into an intelligent opponent, but one who was impervious to reason. It would be pointless to continue arguing with him. So she returned to his lotus seat and rose up into the clouds. Her final words rang in Joru's ears: 'The right moment has yet to arrive. We will meet again when the karmic opportunity presents itself.' She faded, until there was nothing left but a rainbow above the lake.

As he gazed at the rainbow, Joru knew that something inside him had been touched by what the Bodhisattva had said. Suddenly his surroundings seemed unfamiliar. *It has been nearly twelve years since I came to Glingkar*, he thought. And then: *Why did I say I came here, not was born here?*

'You should ponder that question,' came the voice of the Bodhisattva from the sky.

The Storyteller
The Temple

Strange things were happening in Jigmed's dreams.

Until now he had always been a bystander. He would say it was like watching a film. But when he dreamed of the appearance of the Guanyin Bodhisattva, he saw himself in the dream. Even more astounding was that he ran up to Joru and shouted, 'Don't you recognise her? She's the Guanyin Bodhisattva.'

Joru stared blindly at the lake. The face of the Buddha had been familiar, though he could not recall where he had seen it before. He sat motionless. But the anxious Jigmed flew into the sky and caught up with the Bodhisattva in a patch of clouds. The celestial guards stopped him.

'Let him come to talk,' the Bodhisattva said.

Jigmed was so shocked that he prostrated himself on the fluffy clouds, which seemed to sink under his weight. 'You will not fall,' the Bodhisattva said.

The clouds supported him, as the Bodhisattva had promised.

'You've followed me a long way. Why are you so quiet now?' the Bodhisattva asked.

Jigmed heard himself say timidly, 'The Bodhisattva looks different from the statues of him in the temples.'

'I hear that not even all the statues are alike.'

'You hear? Don't you go to the temples?'

'They are smoky and hot. Why would I want to go to them?'

Jigmed had always been impetuous. 'Then why did you tell Joru to build a temple for you?'

The Bodhisattva smiled mysteriously, but said nothing. Instead, a solemn voice nearby roared, 'That is not something you are entitled to ask.'

The shepherd was so shocked he fell from the clouds and, with a startled cry, woke up. Around him everything was peaceful: the sheep were grazing and white birds soared above the blue lake. Slowly he came to his senses, but remorse filled his heart. How wonderful if he could be in his dream for ever, to be always at the Bodhisattva's side. But, like a bag of rubbish tossed from a house, he had been ejected from his dream world.

Over the next few days, he told everyone he met in the village, 'I've seen it.'

'What can a half-blind man see?'

'I saw the Bodhisattva.'

'Go to the temple if you want to see the Bodhisattva.'

'No! I saw the real one!'

What could people say to that? They shrugged their shoulders. 'That poor boy has lost his mind.'

Yet the madman did not stop there. 'I also saw the young King Gesar, like in the legend.'

Indeed the familiar melody from the story of the hero sounded in his ears. 'I hear it.' And he began to hum the opening tune, the one everyone knew.

'Lu-a-la-la-mu-a-la, lu-ta-la-la-mu-ta-la!'

People laughed, for that proved nothing. Anyone with ears on the Khampapa grassland knew by heart the opening lyrics of the heroic tale. Even woodpeckers made a string of similar notes by tapping their beaks against a tree trunk: tata – lala – tala – ta!

'That's not the same,' he argued, and his face reddened.

They laughed even more. 'Listen to him. He's telling us that woodpeckers are different from humans.'

A woodpecker in an old cypress tree was startled into flight, and, its wings like windmills, it flew towards a distant hill, an auspicious hill, with blooming flowers and sparkling stones buried beneath it, like the wealth of stories in a storyteller's heart.

Humming the first note of his tale, the storyteller looked up at the sky and called out the names of deities. Drifting clouds, stirred by air currents, were transformed into animals and deities. These images meshed in his mind, as a rainbow and a thunderstorm will sometimes appear together. The story! He saw it in his dreams, he even heard it, very faintly, yet he could not yet sing it. Of course the people should laugh at him; even in his dreams he could hear them. Then those who had laughed leaped onto their horses and rode along the bank of the Yalong and disappeared, leaving a sad emptiness in his heart.

He could not tell whether he had seen them in his dream or whether he had dreamed about them after they had disappeared. But they could not have been clearer – when they had hitched up their robes to leap onto their horses and gallop away, their clothes had billowed in the wind. But after a handful of notes plucked from a lute, nothing was left on the grassy plain but the flock of sheep and the sunlight reflected on the marshland. He lay in the grass and looked out of his good eye at the shifting clouds. Something stirred inside, so he sang the opening line of the ancient song: 'Lu-ah-la-la-mu-ah-la, lu-ta-la-la-mu-ta-la!'

He covered his strong right eye and, turning his blind left eye to the sun, he saw streams of light falling towards him. He fell asleep, his blind eye open, turning the shifting clouds into a thousand colours.

'Let me see you again, Bodhisattva.'

But the Bodhisattva did not appear.

Perhaps he could see her in the temple, thought Jigmed. The village had two temples to choose from. One, on the north shore of the river, was like a city in miniature, with sprawling buildings that took up the entire hill. The golden domes of the main halls – one for the Guanyin Bodhisattva, whose statue had a thousand hands that opened behind like a peacock's tail, each palm inlaid with a beautiful eye – towered over the monks' quarters. But Jigmed made for the temple on the south shore, a single building that most followers did not bother to visit. Two or three *li* to the east there was a ferry, but he knew that the ferryman would not make the crossing for him alone, so he walked a few dozen *li* west to cross at the highway bridge before doubling back east along the river to the ferry landing on the other side, where he spent the night.

The following morning he began walking up the hill, and by midday had arrived at a plateau. He glimpsed the red-ochre wall of the temple compound across a field of wind-blown barley, but when he arrived, he was met with silence. The main hall was locked. But the door to the monks' quarters was wide open, so he entered, calling a greeting. No one answered. He drank deeply from a stone basin of cool water before going back outside to sit beneath the wall. It was a serene place; lush green artemisia grew out of cracks in the wall. He snapped off a stalk and caught its subtle bitter scent, like that of new grass. Two magpies chattered in the eaves.

The place was called Guanyin Hall.

Many years before, a farmer had been tilling his field and his plough hit a rock; when he dug up the rock he saw that it was shaped like a Bodhisattva. It was about the time that Gesar, the son of the deities, was born into the human world, and Buddhism had not yet spread. One day a passing monk came through the field and, at the sight of the naturally formed image of the Guanyin Bodhisattva on an altar piled high with other idols made of clay and stone, prostrated himself. When the monk had finished his devotion, he arose and smashed all the clay idols with his walking stick. The people were incensed and ready to kill the monk when they saw how his stick had turned even their stone idols to dust. Fear sent them to their knees.

It was that monk who had built the temple with rocks from the old altar in the field. According to local legend, he had presented the people with it two weeks later.

The stone image of the Bodhisattva stood alone in the temple.

Unlike the chattering monks who would come after him, the first monk had spoken little. He had worn a faint smile, like the one on the face of the Bodhisattva, and his eyes seemed to see as clearly as a blazing fire, reflecting rather than absorbing the world. When he left he had told the people, 'Other temples will be extravagant, but let this one remain as it is.'

For generations, the monks had followed his instruction. But when the local Dharma prince, after receiving a rich gift from the Emperor of China, built a cluster of resplendent halls on the land across the river, even less incense smoke rose above the old temple. Its abbot travelled to the local villages, seeking alms. Eventually he had enough to buy a little gold, and encased the old stone statue in the precious metal. The lama even ground the remaining gold into powder and painted it onto the Bodhisattva's face, but still the incense smoke waned.

It was the shepherd Jigmed's first visit to Guanyin Hall.

With the bitter fragrance of artemisia still on his fingertips, he fell asleep in the warm sunlight, after praying, *Please let me see the Bodhisattva again in my dream.*

But he did not dream. Instead, he woke up to the tinkling of bells. The door to the hall was now open and, taking off his boots, he entered. As his eyes grew accustomed to the darkness, he saw a barefoot monk straining to push a prayer wheel that reached all the way to the ceiling. Bells hanging from the top rang clearly. And then Jigmed saw the silk-clad Bodhisattva in its niche. Over the years its golden face had lost its lustre.

'I would like to see the old Bodhisattva,' Jigmed said to the monk.

The monk held his palms together and smiled, but said nothing.

'I would like to see that Bodhisattva. I believe it was the one I saw in my dream.'

The monk's smile widened, but still he did not say a word.

'I think he wanted me to become a storyteller to sing the story of Gesar.'

Still silent, the monk pushed the heavy prayer wheel, the bells tinkling in the silence. The sounds settled on the storyteller's head, like dewdrops falling on half-opened buds.

Jigmed left the temple and walked back through the barley, enjoying the breeze on his face. A woman weeding the field spoke to him: 'Our lama cannot talk.'

'Is he mute?'

'During his spiritual contemplation, he will not open his mouth to speak.'

'I'll come back.'

The Storyteller
The Ferry Landing

That night Jigmed camped again at the ferry landing. When his fire died down he curled up under his blanket and watched the stars leap onto the curtain of night. He thought he heard bells from the temple on the hill, and wondered whether the Bodhisattva would show herself in the sky. He woke up once in the night and listened to the sound of the river water, as loud as though it were flowing next to his ears.

It was late morning when he woke again. The bright sun felt good. He had just rolled over to snooze for a little longer when a nearby clamour forced him to open his eyes. A group of monks and villagers were gathered at the ferry landing, and someone was calling to the opposite shore for the ferry. The ferrymen, a father and son, appeared. The old man carried a pair of oars on his shoulder while his son had a leather boat hoisted over his head, as though he were wearing an enormous cooking pot.

Jigmed sat up and saw that his fire, which had gone out during the night, had been rekindled. A kettle gurgled, and a pudgy lama was sipping tea. He smiled.

'Thank you for your tea,' the lama said.

Jigmed, whose brain was not quick, was muddled and half awake; he was at a loss for words. The lama spoke again: 'Wash your face. That will clear your head.'

Jigmed ran to the river, scooped up the cool water and buried his face in his hands. Then he drank deep and rinsed his mouth. When he returned to the fire he greeted the lama.

'I am a Living Buddha,' the lama said gravely, but then he smiled. 'Would a run-of-the-mill lama have that kind of retinue?'

'Is it . . .?' Jigmed looked towards the north shore, where the golden temple roofs were just visible.

The Living Buddha nodded. 'But not the biggest one.'

There were more than thirty Living Buddhas of varying ranks in the monastery across the river.

With nothing more to say, they gazed at the father and son, who had just launched the leather boat at the ferry landing. The leather skin had dried out, as the boat hadn't been used for a few days and had to soak before they could apply waterproofing grease in the seams. 'We must wait, so you may tell me about your dream,' the Living Buddha said.

'I went to the temple yesterday,' Jigmed said, adding, 'Not your temple, but the small one on the hill.'

The sunlight was bright, so one of the Living Buddha's attendants brought him a pair of sunglasses. The Living Buddha remained silent, staring at Jigmed from behind the brown lenses.

'I dreamed of the Guanyin Bodhisattva.'

'What did he reveal?'

'I've dreamed about her before. That was why I went up the mountain – to worship her. And I dreamed about her again just now.'

'Was there a revelation?'

'What's a revelation?'

The Buddha laughed. 'It's what she did or said.'

'She said nothing to me.'

'Of course she wouldn't say anything to you!'

'She was talking to Gesar.'

'What?' The Living Buddha lurched. If he hadn't been so plump he would have jumped to his feet. 'To Gesar? The Guanyin Bodhisattva?'

Jigmed was startled. He had been dreaming just before dawn, a dream like his earlier ones. The Living Buddha pressed him to continue, so he told him that the Bodhisattva had asked Joru to build a temple to separate the laymen from the monks who had arrived in Glingkar.

'To separate the monks from the laymen?' muttered the Living Buddha, clearly surprised.

'Well, it was because the newly arrived monks were fighting with Khrothung and the others over the throne.'

The ferry arrived at last, and the Living Buddha's attendants escorted him aboard. Jigmed gathered up his belongings and was about to set out again when he saw the Living Buddha waving him aboard. He squeezed in, despite the annoyance of the attendants. The Living Buddha studied him during the crossing, but waited until they reached the shore to say, 'Come to me at the temple. My name is A-wang.' He glanced at his attendants. 'Don't give him a hard time when he comes.'

The attendants had one expression on their faces as they listened to their master, but an altogether different one when the Living Buddha finished. This is the usual attitude of those waiting on a superior.

'The Bodhisattva has buried treasure in your heart and I will help you find it.'

The Story
The Temple

Joru once more began to collect his rock tax from the caravans. When the tribes who had come from Gling saw the rocks on the backs of caravan horses, they knew that he was building a temple and joined in to help.

The two monks, however, spent their time mingling with aristocrats, to spread the Buddhist teachings. One of the monks had come from China to the east, the other from India to the south. They said they shared the same Buddhist teachings as those propagated by Master Lotus, who was revered as a deity, but the people of Gling did not quite believe them. Master Lotus had travelled abroad, vanquishing evil spirits and demons, and it was said he soared on beams of light. When he wasn't fighting demons, he lived in a remote cave, where he faced the wall in contemplation, and only rarely accepted alms. But these two monks, who carried rolled-up sutras on their backs, arrived in Gling with their walking sticks. They were gaunt and emaciated, the colour faded from their hempen clothing. They spent their days teaching people how to recite the sutras, and since they claimed to follow the religious teachings of Master Lotus, most people recited the sutras with them in hope that the monks would teach them how to vanquish the demons.

But the monks said that most demons were born in human hearts.

What were these demons? The amassing of wealth, hunger for power, indulgence in satin clothes and fine food while the poor suffered – these were all brought about by the demons of the heart.

But a few years after their arrival, once the people had learned to recite the six true words that would help them maintain a clear mind, the two monks moved into the fortress and began to dress in silk and satin. The vessels they used for the rituals were now gold and silver. People were forced to bow to them and to agree with every word they said. And they spoke of strategy with the tribal leaders, who sometimes let them exert power directly.

The old steward, Rongtsa Khragan, asked the monks' opinion on Joru's plan to build a temple.

'Our mission is to save the masses, so we should be among them,' one replied.

The other added, 'How can a shepherd be away from his flock?'

The old steward did not like what he heard. 'According to you, then, I am a sheep.'

'Do not be upset, old steward. Everyone is a sheep before the supreme Buddhist wisdom, but not a sheep before us monks.'

The old steward was offended. 'We are only temporary inhabitants of Joru's land, so we must follow him.'

The monks wished to continue the debate, but the old steward raised his hand to stop them. He turned to Gyatsa Zhakar. 'Find your brother and ask him what he is doing – we never understand the reasons behind his actions.'

Gyatsa Zhakar mounted his horse and set off, thinking it would take him at least five days. On the way, he encountered a herd of gazelles and wondered if Joru, who enjoyed a prank, had transformed himself into one of them. He reined in his horse and said, 'Brother, if you have changed into a gazelle and are among them now, reveal yourself to me.'

But the gazelles saw the bow across his back and the quiver of arrows hanging from his saddle and galloped away. Later he saw herds of deer, wild oxen and horses, but Joru was never among them.

At last Gyatsa Zhakar found Metog Lhartse, who smiled and pointed to the broad bend in the winding Yellow river. Swans glided leisurely upon the clear water. When his horse reached the riverbank, one rose up and flew to his shoulder and he heard the bird's call turn into

Joru's happy laughter. The swan's wings became Joru's arms, which wrapped themselves around his shoulders. 'My elder brother has come to see me!'

The brothers pressed their foreheads together. Gyatsa Zhakar said to Joru, 'Take me to see the temple you are building.' The word 'temple' sounded strange on his tongue, for it was still a new idea. In Gling they had only an altar of piled stones.

The temple was nearly finished. In the main hall there were places for the two statues of the Buddha the monks had brought from China and India, as well as for an ornate loft to store the sutras.

Gyatsa Zhakar told his brother that the monks were reluctant to leave the fortress.

'They originally came from a temple,' Joru said.

'How do you know?'

'I don't know but I do. They will come, for a temple is where they belong.'

Those were the happiest days of Gyatsa Zhakar's life. The brothers raced up and down the hills on horseback. They explored a craggy hill with many caves; at one of the cave openings, they killed an ancient bear-demon that had slaughtered many sheep and their shepherds. Gyatsa Zhakar was a warrior, but while he had taken the lives of many of Gling's enemies, this was the first demon he had killed.

'I did not know that I could kill a demon!' he said.

'You can, as long as you believe you can overpower them.'

They rode to a barren plain where, with bows and arrows, they shot a king mole that had driven its followers to riddle the land with tunnels, killing the grass. When they returned three days later, the plain was like a desert after rainfall. The first lush sprouts covered the ground like a green mist. Soon shepherds would put down roots here, too. Gyatsa Zhakar understood now that this was how his younger brother had created a new land for the people of Gling. 'Little brother, you should be our king,' he said earnestly.

Joru turned a somersault. 'I am nobody's king.'

Gyatsa Zhakar dismounted, removed his helmet and knelt on one knee before his younger brother. 'I am unworthy to be your older brother.'

Joru helped his brother up. He pressed his forehead against his brother's and said, 'Let us bid each other farewell here.'

'Do you really wish the monks to come?' Gyatsa Zhakar asked.

'Yes.'

'But your temple is yet unfinished.'

Pointing to the distant mountains, Joru said to his brother, 'Turn to look when you reach that pass.'

Gyatsa Zhakar mounted his horse and raced across the plain.

Joru knew that celestial soldiers protected him at all times, though he usually pretended not to notice, since ordinary people could not see them. Now he decided it was time for them to show themselves. 'You mounted soldiers behind the clouds, come down before me.'

The celestial soldiers appeared, their helmets shining, their swords and spears glinting.

'The workers are exhausted. Since it was the Bodhisattva's idea to build a temple, I expect you to use your magic powers to finish it quickly.'

The celestial soldiers rose into the sky. Dark clouds shrouded the small hill. Thunder roared and lightning lit the clouds; rain like arrows and heavy hailstones chased the stonemasons and carpenters off the hill.

Gyatsa Zhakar did not look back until he reached the mountain pass. Then he saw the temple's red-ochre walls, standing sturdy and complete under a rainbow, the tips of its golden towers pointing into the blue sky. Joru had once again revealed a miracle.

Since the future king of Gling wanted the monks to come to the temple, he, Gyatsa Zhakar, must make sure they came. But how would he entice them into leaving the fortress? Although a brave warrior on the battlefield, he was by nature a gentle man, and the riddle gnawed at him as he rode home. But halfway along his journey, he met the two monks, who rushed towards him, trailed by new disciples carrying their statues of Buddha and their sutras. The monks had shed their silken robes, and sunlight glinted off the beads of sweat on the bald scalps of their disciples, who had shaved off their long hair. News of the celestial soldiers had travelled ahead of Gyatsa Zhakar, and now the monks spoke to him of the miracle.

'Buddhist teaching has shown its boundless power,' one monk cried. 'The world will know that temples will dot this land like stars in the sky and chessmen on a board. Their golden domes will sparkle on all its auspicious hilltops!'

The monks hurried on towards the temple.

The Storyteller
Sickness

From out of thin air a deity towered over him, dressed in golden armour. Gesar.

'It is you.'

'Yes.'

'King Gesar.'

Jigmed's immediate desire was to prostrate himself, but the power of the deity immobilised him.

Then the deity spoke again, in a voice that seemed to come from the depths of the sky, like an echo. 'You wish to sing.'

'I do.'

'But you have lost your voice.' With a snap of his fingers, the golden-armoured deity placed a small pill in Jigmed's mouth. It felt cool and moist, and fragrance filled his body, a fragrance that coursed through his veins as though he had been struck by lightning.

'Great King!' Jigmed cried, and he heard his own voice, clear and resonant, rising from his chest.

'Shepherd,' the king said, 'from now on you shall sing my story to the people.'

'But . . .'

'But your mind is not up to the challenge? It has been sharpened.' As he spoke, the deity vanished, and only his voice remained, as though he were still nearby.

The sky had cleared, and as Jigmed led his sheep home from the grassy plain, the scene before him changed. His sheep became ferocious lions, then snow leopards, and then indescribably terrifying demons. When he flicked his whip, lightning flashed and thousands of soldiers on horseback appeared. Some were motionless, their stern demeanour sending fear into his heart; others were like tidal waves churned up by a storm, swallowing and rolling into each other amid thunderous noise. Luckily the lead sheep knew its way home well enough and took the flock back to their pen, followed by the half-blind shepherd.

Jigmed groped in the dusk to close the gate, then fell to the ground, unconscious. At this the sheep set up a panicky bleat, and the rams began butting their horns against the pen. Even old men who had seen more than anyone else in the village had never heard so many sheep bleating at once, and the villagers hastened to the pen.

'Has he been bitten by wolves?'

'He's unconscious.'

'Did a ram butt him?'

'He's as hot as a piece of burning coal.'

The villagers took Jigmed home, laid him on his bed and left him uncovered; even the bearskin blanket on which he lay made his temperature rise. Two fast horses raced out of the village, one to get the doctor in the country clinic a dozen *li* away, the other to the temple to fetch the Living Buddha. The shepherd's fever was so high people feared he would not wait for the Living Buddha and the doctor to arrive. But there was nothing they could do.

And then the feverish patient woke. 'It's stifling in here. Take me outside.'

'Outside?' they asked.

'I want to be under the starlight.'

They carried him into the yard.

'Not the yard,' he said, 'the rooftop.'

They carried him up to a platform on the roof, a stone slab with a smooth surface on which he had worked leather. Stars filled the evening sky, the constellations sparkling. Stretching out flat, he felt the coolness of the stone seep into him. With a contented sigh, he said, 'Yes, I see the stars. Water.'

They fetched him cool, clean spring water. Though he was still only semi-conscious, he gulped it down, as if he was trying to put out a fire in his chest. He drank so much that more had to be brought from the spring. This time he took only a little. Someone dipped a cypress branch in what remained and sprinkled it on his face and chest, which rose and fell violently.

'I've seen it,' he said.

No one asked what he'd seen. No one pointed out that the one-eyed man could not see much when he was awake, let alone when he was sleeping. But they all echoed, 'He's seen it.'

Under bright starlight, the half-blind man had indeed seen the story that had been told by generations of storytellers over thousands of years. His body burned, but his mind was cool and refreshed. He saw how, many years before, the story had first been performed on the broad stage of the plateau of the black-haired Tibetans, which extends from the soaring cliffs above the banks of the Jinsha river to the boundless grassland through which the Yellow river meanders.

It was midnight; starlight shone like torrents of falling water, and the sound of horse's hoofs carried from the outskirts of the village.

The Living Buddha was first to arrive.

The shepherd sat up. His eyes shone with a light that had never been there before, and his normally lustreless face glowed. He opened his mouth and sang: 'Lu-ah-la-la-mu-ah-la, lu-ta-la-la-mu-ta-la!'

This time there was no mocking laughter. His once hoarse voice was transformed. What came out of his mouth stirred the people's souls. But his body was so weakened by the fever that he nearly passed out again and he could not continue to sing. Yet he smiled as he said, 'My heart is filled with stories of King Gesar.'

'There have always been stories of King Gesar in your heart,' the Living Buddha said.

Jigmed sat up again. 'It's different this time,' he insisted. 'Now my head overflows with them.'

'We are connected by karma. My ferry saved you one day of point-less travel,' the Living Buddha said. Then Jigmed realised that it had been this Living Buddha who had shared the ferry with him.

'I told you to visit me at the temple, but you did not.' There was a hint of displeasure in the Living Buddha's voice. 'As I said, there is treasure in your heart, and I would like to help you dig it out.'

True, Jigmed's head was crammed with so many things, with battles among deities, demons and humans in ancient times, that he could not make much sense at the moment.

'Do you need my help?' the Living Buddha asked.

'Please recite a sutra to clear my head.'

The Living Buddha laughed. He summoned a good-looking woman to come forward with her spindle and a handful of tangled raw wool. Taking the wool, he said, 'The stories in your head are entangled like this.'

It was as he said. Taking back the wool, the woman turned the spindle, and a thin thread took shape. Longer and longer it stretched, tighter and tighter it spun, until yards of thread were wound around the spindle. In a few minutes the raw wool had become a neat ball. Jigmed felt the knots in his mind begin to straighten, to take on a clear shape, with a beginning and an end.

The ball of yarn fell loose when the Living Buddha tugged at the end of the thread. 'Just like this,' he said, 'from beginning to end, you can now tell the story.'

Jigmed slumped to the ground. 'But . . . I lack energy,' he said.

'You will regain your strength.'

So he lay under a soft blanket, gazing into the starry sky and waiting for his strength to return. To the Living Buddha, who was compas-sionate but was also intimidating, Jigmed did not dare to say that, as a future singer, he would need nothing more.

So he closed his eyes.

But the Living Buddha commanded, 'Open your eyes and look at me.'

He opened his eyes to see that the Living Buddha was holding the loose sleeve of his coat in one hand, while the fingers of the other spread out and swept across the void three inches from Jigmed's face. He repeated the movement while chanting an incantation.

Finally the Living Buddha said, 'All is well now. Try, and you will see that your head is clear.'

But Jigmed's head now became muddled again, for he did not know how to test the strength of his own mind.

When the moon rose in the sky, the young doctor from the local clinic arrived. She took his temperature and checked his blood pressure: both were normal. His heartbeat, on the other hand, was a little slow.

'Of course it is,' Jigmed said. 'I lack energy.'

The doctor injected him with glucose.

'I can feel my energy slowly returning from some faraway place.'

The doctor told him to go back inside so she could hook up a drip, but he refused to leave the rooftop. The villagers set up an IV stand on the roof, while the Living Buddha was taken to the sutra room of a wealthy family to rest. The doctor stayed with her patient, watching the clear liquid in the moonlight as it slowly dripped into Jigmed's vein.

Everyone thought he had fallen asleep, when he abruptly laughed and said, 'The Living Buddha's hands are filled with heat, unlike this liquid, which cools me when it flows into my body.'

Not interested in talking about the Living Buddha, the doctor asked, 'Is your energy still far off?'

'It is closer now.'

'We'll wait then.'

So they waited. The villagers leaned against the base of the wall and shrank into their robes as they fell asleep. Even the doctor draped a blanket over her shoulders, tucked her head inside the upturned collar of her overcoat and slept. Jigmed lay quietly. With his good eye, he could see the north end of the village and the rolling hills above the flood plain. The moon travelled in and out of thin, drifting clouds and cast a mutable shadow on the hills below. Again Jigmed saw the story's mounted soldiers racing ahead like surging waves.

His lips began to move and he sang. To him it was more than singing – it was a new life. Tomorrow he would still be a shepherd, but different from yesterday.

The Living Buddha would say, 'I opened the door to wisdom for that man.' He meant that the stories had been congested in Jigmed's mind, their many tangled threads vying for attention. The Living Buddha had tugged at a thread and found the beginning, and a storyteller of the Gesar legend was born on the grassland, one chosen by the deities. Jigmed would sing because he had been asked to by the hero. In a world that was becoming increasingly prosaic, the hero's story needed to spread far and wide again. On that very night, the beginning of the story appeared before Jigmed's eyes.

The Story
The Beginning

In the distant, ancient past, three brothers, all demons, ran amok on the Tibetan plateau, which was fenced in by snowcapped mountains. They ate human flesh, drank human blood, swallowed human bones and wore clothes made of human skin. Ruthless and brutal, they committed so many atrocities that at last the deities subdued them. They were allowed to be reborn, and the deities even let them pray for their reincarnation. But they only pretended to repent, and were reborn as three crabs, then imprisoned beneath a cliff. The indescribable misery of their new life turned them against each other. Many years passed, but still they tore into each other, unable to separate themselves from their endless battles.

At last a deity passed by and took pity on the three crabs. He waved his iron staff, smashing the cliff and liberating them. They were reborn again as a nine-headed marmot. But the Maha Brahma Heavenly King in the Thirty-third Heavenly World thought that that was an unlucky sign, so he waved his sword and sent nine marmot heads rolling on the ground. Four of the heads prayed even as they rolled down the hill: *We are the best of all demons, and we wish to be reborn as mortal enemies of Buddhist teaching, in control of the lives of all living creatures.* The four heads prayed with such fervour and devotion that their wish was granted: they were reborn as King Lutsan of the North, King Padrang of Hor, King Satham of Jang, and King Shengkhri of Monyul, four demon kings who wrought havoc where they lived.

But one of the nine heads had been kind and gentle. He prayed to become a king who would vanquish the demon kings and protect the people. His wish was granted, and he rose to Heaven to become Thosba Gawa, the son of the Maha Brahma Heavenly King . . .

It was the time when domesticated horses had just been separated from their wild cousins. The primitive people had yet to be enlightened, and the world was filled with the cruelty of the demons. The life of the humans in the land between the mountains and the rivers was a boundless sea of suffering. The wealth was in the hands of an evil few, making it impossible for ordinary people to live a harmonious, peaceful life, to be kind and loving. They used hunting knives and spears to slaughter each other. And it was not just the people who suffered: even the veins of precious metals deep underground moved in an attempt to escape such a terrible world.

The lotus of enlightenment had already bloomed, but this rampaging evil set the land beyond the realm of civilisation. In rivers and on snowcapped mountains, on pastureland and in villages, visible enemies and invisible demons prompted the Tibetans to follow the path of evil.

Praying to Heaven remained the only thing the people could do.

Moved at last by the misery of the human world, the deities decided that the only remedy would be to send one of their own into it. They chose the one who had wished to rescue the human masses from their suffering – Thosba Gawa, son of the Maha Brahma Heavenly King, Korle Demchog, and Dorje Phagmo, the Heavenly Mother.

Thosba Gawa was called Joru in the human world. He would become the ruler of Gling, King Gesar, whose praises the people would sing for millennia to come.

Part II

THE HORSE RACE

The Story
Mother in Heaven

Joru had a dream in which a noblewoman descended gracefully from Heaven. When the clouds surrounding her dispersed, she was standing at the entrance to his tent. His mother, Metog Lhartse, was asleep. The moon was high in the sky, its misty light spilling over the Earth; the light around him was brighter than daylight.

This is a true deity, Joru thought, and he bowed at the waist, inviting her inside the tent, which was quickly suffused with an unusual fragrance. 'Please, sit down. I'll rouse my mother to make you some tea.'

'Mother!' The deity's body shook violently. She stood with her back to Joru for some time, then bent to look at the sleeping Metog Lhartse. 'Let her sleep. Tonight belongs to you and another mother.'

'Another mother?' Joru felt a stabbing pain in his heart.

The deity nodded. 'I am your mother in Heaven, Lhamin Dagmo.'

'Heaven?' Something stirred in his mind.

Seeing his confusion, Lhamin Dagmo wrapped her arms around him and, holding her own sorrow in check, said, 'You came from Heaven. The deities sent you to the human world to rid Gling of its demons, and eventually to become the king who will lead the people out of barbarism.'

The other deities, who were watching, made their presence known by imbuing that corner of the night sky with a rainbow and bright sunshine. They played enchanting celestial music; when they plucked their strings, the sound, which had the capacity to penetrate and open minds, soared like sunbeams.

The music awoke in Joru vague memories of the celestial realm and, as he thought of the dozen miserable years he had spent in the human world, resentment welled in him. 'If you are my celestial mother, how could you watch me suffer?'

Lhamin Dagmo nearly wept. 'You vowed to relieve the people's suffering. My feelings for you are the same as those of any human mother.' And then she told him of how he had vowed to free the humans from the demons and establish a just and compassionate nation.

The son of the human world asked his celestial mother, 'Did I really come from Heaven, and will I really return there?'

A string of gleaming tears hung on her cheek as her voice became solemn. 'We can see everything you do from Heaven, and it seems you have forgotten your mission in the human world.'

'I cannot remember, but I have killed many demons, and I founded a new home along the Yellow river for the people of Gling, who cannot tell right from wrong.'

His celestial mother reached out and brushed his eyes, and a clear light shone through his confusion. Again she reached out her hand, and this time brushed his face, smoothing his twisted features. 'You must show the people your true face,' she told him, 'for while you are among the humans you represent the celestial court.'

Joru wanted to call her 'Mother', but when he gazed at his sleeping human mother, at her ageing face, worn by suffering, he found he could not use the same word for the elegant woman who stood before him.

'They like me as I am,' he said.

'Perhaps. But you must keep in mind that they are your future subjects.'

'The old steward, my brother Gyatsa Zhakar and Danma wish the Gling tribe to form a nation, and they have asked me to be their king, but . . .'

His mother placed a soft fingertip on his lips. 'You were about to say, but there is Uncle Khrothung. My son, do not complain. A hero from Heaven should not behave as a pouting boy. You have let the people of Gling and those of us in Heaven wait too long. You must become king before the year is out.'

His mother then told him of a celestial horse that had descended to the human world with him. It lived with a wild herd that roamed the hills on the banks of the Yellow river.

'Find your horse and tame it,' she said. And with that his celestial mother vanished, with her attendants and the cloud on which they rode.

Joru awoke. The strange fragrance lingered in the tent, and beside his pillow lay a jade necklace, dropped by one of his celestial mother's attendants. He stepped out of the tent into the moonlight.

'But how will I know which horse it is?'

The celestial mother's stern voice sounded in his ears: 'Why do you dawdle? It is your horse and you will recognise him.'

'Mother!' he called, and the stars in the sky seemed to rush towards him.

His human mother, who had woken at his cry, came out of the tent with a robe to drape over his shoulders. He told her that from now on he would ride a fast steed instead of his uncle's magic stick.

His mother touched his forehead with hers and told him that that was what she expected her son to be: a warrior. Then he asked her if she wanted him to be a king, King of the Nation of Gling.

She responded with a grave look. 'If, and only if, the king can make Gling powerful and give the people a good life,' she said.

'Can I truly be that person?'

'You were not brought into the human world to do nothing.'

The Story
Khrothung's Dream

Khrothung also had a dream.

When Buddhism began to spread in Gling, Khrothung chose the powerful Hayagriva of Tantric Buddhism as his principal deity and studied his secret magic day and night, along with other witchcraft. What did the Hayagriva look like? He would have a ferocious, invincible face, Khrothung imagined. It was said that when a practitioner of magic reached the Hayagriva's level of power, he would be able to subdue *yaksa*s, ghosts and deities; to ward off spells by the eight non-human creatures, the demigods and semi-devils; to eliminate evils, plagues and sicknesses; and to avoid all curses and evil incantations. If he could somehow master this magic, Khrothung knew he, too, would be invincible.

Yet he made little progress. Or perhaps he had yet to see the results predicted by the monk who taught him. Naturally suspicious, Khrothung began to doubt not only the monk's skill, but also the existence of the powerful Hayagriva. And then the Hayagriva appeared before him in his dream.

He did not know that it was not the real Hayagriva.

Before Joru's celestial mother had left, she had told him to take the shape of the Hayagriva, whom she knew Khrothung revered, in order to set a time for a horserace, whose winner would take the throne. When Joru lay down to sleep again, he pondered whether he should lure his suspicious uncle into a trap set by Heaven. Yet he must have desired the lofty throne, for no sooner had he fallen asleep than he turned into the Hayagriva and entered his uncle's dream. The frightened Khrothung knelt before him.

'I will never again doubt your existence.'

'It is the Buddhist guardian Hayagriva who stands before you.'

Khrothung prostrated himself, trembling uncontrollably, and Joru flew out of his dream, singing a song that he made up as he went along:

> Gling must be a country soon,
> The chief of Tagrong should seek power.
> The warriors of Gling are great horsemen,
> A hero on horseback will be king.
> I know you have longed to be king,
> And I know you have studied my teachings.
> With my blessing, this race you will win.

When Khrothung awoke, the Hayagriva was gone, but his song lingered, and Khrothung was too excited to sleep again. The sun soon rose above the jagged snowcapped peaks to the east, and he rose, bowed several times before the Hayagriva's image, and described his dream to his wife, Danza, who offered tea to the deity.

'The heavens have spoken. I will become the king of Gling by winning a horserace.'

'But everyone says that your nephew was sent by Heaven to—'

Khrothung angrily cut her off. 'And the winner's prize will surely include the most beautiful girl in Gling, Brugmo. Only someone as beautiful as she should enjoy the honour of being the king's consort.'

Danza had not finished. 'An evil spirit, not the deity, must have been the source of that prediction, because Heaven has already—'

But Khrothung was convinced that he was Heaven's choice since, as everyone in Gling knew, he was not only proficient at magic but also his horse, Yusha, could outrun any of the warriors' chargers. So his ageing, faded wife Danza enraged him.

'Hold your tongue! A deity's prediction is like a precious golden pagoda. How dare you chip at it with your axe of evil words? If not for the fact that you have given me children, I would cut out your tongue so you could never again spew such foolishness. When I win the race and bring Brugmo into the Tagrong family, you will be fed only as long as you keep your mouth shut. Otherwise I shall drive you out of the house and you may follow Joru the clown, whom you believe should be king.'

Danza went to complain to her eldest son, but he parroted his father: 'How could a Tagrong woman not desire someone from our tribe to be king of Gling?'

Khrothung conjured up a great cloud of crows, which he sent to the other tribes. At each encampment, the crows cawed twice and dropped wooden invitations for the tribal leaders to gather at the Tagrong camp for an important meeting. As people picked up the pieces of carved wood, the crows cawed and flew off.

It took only two days for the tribal leaders to gather, even those who were furthest away. Khrothung had his retainers provide the best food and drink for the old steward, the tribal leaders and their warriors. But he himself stayed away.

'He did not invite us here just to ply us with good food and drink, did he?' the anxious leaders wondered.

Finally Khrothung appeared. 'It may have been years since we were exiled to the Yellow river plain, but we Tagrongs could treat you like this for three years without difficulty.'

'Tell us what you wish to talk about,' the old steward said.

With a glance Khrothung signalled for one of his retainers to relate how the Hayagriva had prophesied that the Gling tribe should hold a horserace, and that the winner, who would become king, would also be awarded the most beautiful girl, Sengcam Brugmo, and a vast treasure of gold, silver, coloured glass, giant clam shells, carnelian, pearls and trumpet shells.

It was clear to all assembled that Khrothung intended to rule. But they could not argue with him since he claimed that the idea for a horserace had come from Heaven. Danma glanced at Gyatsa Zhakar, who gazed anxiously at the old steward. But the old steward was calm: he had realised that the old prophecy was about to come true – Heaven would send one of its own to be king of Gling. He smiled. 'Indeed, we need a true hero to replace a useless old man like me. A horserace is a good idea, a fair and righteous way to give the throne, the beauty and the seven treasures to the winner. I do not think that anyone could find a reason to object. I have only one question for the honoured leader of the Tagrong tribe: as the land is sealed with ice and covered with snow, it is not an appropriate season for a horserace. Why would the Hayagriva make such a prophecy now?'

Everyone agreed that the old steward was right to ask. Their custom was to race horses in the warmth of springtime, when flowers bloomed, not in the depths of winter.

'From my divination,' said Khrothung, 'the fifteenth day of the first month, five days from now, is an auspicious day, so we will set that date for the horserace.'

'If the fifteenth is a good date, we must assemble all the important people of Gling to discuss a time for the race to be run,' the old steward said slowly. Everyone nodded in response.

Gyatsa Zhakar knew that the old steward wanted to delay long enough to find Joru so he could join the race, for no warrior in all of Gling had a charger capable of outrunning Khrothung's Yusha. He said, 'I do not object to the horserace, but we must not leave out my brother, Joru. We banished him and my mother for no good reason, yet he found for us a new place to live. If he is not invited to the race, I will leave this new nation.'

'Your mother has her own country,' Khrothung responded.

'Does that mean you will not let my brother race?'

Khrothung smiled. 'Who among you has ever seen my nephew ride a fine steed? I have no objection! But he may not use as a horse the magic stick I gave him.'

The fifteenth day of the first month was only five days away, but they were the five longest days of Khrothung's life. No greater prize could await the victor, not in this world: the throne, the beauty and the seven treasures were finally within his reach. In his view, the prize had been made for him, and winning it would be like taking it out of his own pocket. He did, however, try his best to suppress his enthusiasm, and he patiently planned the grandest banquet in the history of Gling, for unprecedented numbers of guests. This would be a prelude to his ascension to the throne, so the food must be sumptuous, the banqueting hall magnificent.

On the fifteenth day of the first month, Gling notables converged on the main road that led to the Tagrong fortress, like tributaries of a river. The mature men were as dignified as the snowcapped mountains and the young women as quiet as the ice on the lake, but the young men were like arrows on drawn bows. They assembled in a tent erected by the Tagrong for the banquet, where a master of ceremonies intoned, in a loud, clear voice: 'The seats of honour are of flowered satin threaded with gold. They are for the four princes, Gyatsa Zhakar, Nyibum Daryag, Anu Paseng and Rinchen Darlu.

'The middle seats are of soft silk. Those are for the four elders, Old Steward, Khrothung, Senglon and Langkha Sengzha.

'The bearskin seats are for the renowned seers, scriveners, doctors and astrologers.'

The last row of seats was reserved for the twelve beauties of Gling, led by Sengcam Brugmo. The others sat on the ground at tables laden with delicacies.

After the meal, Khrothung told again of how the deity had spoken to him in a dream of a horserace to select a king for Gling. He did not forget to mention the additional awards of the beautiful girl and the treasure. 'Since this is Heaven's wish, I have invited you here to the Tagrong tribal fortress so we may decide on a time and a route.' He then adopted a regretful tone, though his eyes were shifty. 'It is a pity that my beloved nephew, Joru, is not here. But he will appear on his magic stick if he wishes to join in.'

'Gling's future will be determined by this race, so the route must not be short,' said Khrothung's son, Tonggod. 'In order for it to be known all over the world, we must set the starting point near India and the finish line as close to China as possible.'

Senglon said sarcastically, 'If we really want everyone in the world to know of the horserace, then the starting point should be in the sky and the finish in the ocean, with the sun and moon as trophies. And the people of Gling should sit on the stars to watch the race.' A roar of laughter greeted this.

Khrothung's banquet had not only failed to win the people's support, but his son had been ridiculed. He was infuriated.

Then Gyatsa Zhakar stood up and said, 'The race will begin at Mount Ayu Te, cross the beautiful Yellow river and end at Mount Kure. The people will watch the race from the top of Mount Lute, while across the valley, on Mount Lahte, the shamans and monks will offer sacrifices and prayers. The time will be summer, when the grass is tall and the water is sweet.'

Everyone agreed that this was the best arrangement, so Khrothung had no choice but to wait for summer.

The Storyteller
The Hat

Day was breaking as Jigmed walked up the hill. He turned back to look down at the village, which was shrouded in mist. The villagers were still asleep, but he was already on the road, his few belongings slung onto his back. At the far edge of the village he could see a grey-green light glinting off the sheep pen.

The quiet village was about to lose a shepherd. They would have to find someone else to take the sheep out to the pasture when the sun rose. Jigmed smiled as he strode on, heavy dewdrops spattering his soft leather boots.

Three days later Jigmed arrived at a small town with one main street. A skilled maker of six-string lutes lived there. He was directed into the old man's yard and arrived just as the lute-maker was trying out a newly finished instrument. He blew air into the hole, smooth and round as a seashell, before holding it up to his ear to listen. He smiled.

'Come, try it,' the old man said.

One of his apprentices walked up to take the lute, but the old man said, 'Not you,' and handed the lute to the young man who had walked unannounced into his yard.

'Me?' Jigmed asked.

The old man turned to his three apprentices. 'This is the best lute I've ever made. This is the person who deserves to play it.'

'Him?' the apprentices said in unison, incredulous that such a fine lute would end up in the hands of such a man. Jigmed's blind eye was opened wide, his good eye a thin slit. As the town's livelihood depended upon business with shepherds, they could tell what he was without looking at his clothes or his face. They knew from his bow legs, which made him sway as he walked, and his pungent smell that he was a shepherd.

'Yes, him. I knew he'd come while you were oiling the lute.'

'The master is unschooled in divination. How would you know?'

Ignoring them, the master turned to Jigmed. 'Take it. You are the man I saw in my dream.'

'You saw me in a dream?'

'Yes, the deity told me that my lute would meet someone who deserved it, that my life of making lutes is coming to an end. Come, young man, take your lute.'

Jigmed clumsily took the lute, which emitted beautiful notes when he touched the strings. 'But I have no money.'

'Then why are you here? Will you trade your sheep for it?' One of the apprentices was losing his patience.

'I have no sheep. The villagers hired me to tend all of their sheep. I own nothing.'

'But aren't you here looking for a lute?'

'I'm looking for a lute and a storyteller's hat.'

'Then why don't you take it?' The master lute-maker was also becoming impatient.

'But – but I don't know how to play . . .'

The lute-maker picked up a stick and drove Jigmed out of the yard as if he was shooing away a stray dog, and that was how the new storyteller got his lute.

Three days later, he was strumming the notes he would need for his story. As he walked, it seemed to him that a tiny deity was hiding deep inside his ear, making rhythmic sounds for him to follow. He strolled along in time with the rhythm, and that was how he came to realise that the rippling of water and the rising and falling hills shared the same tempo. There were other tempos as well, of the wind making grass sway and of the birds flapping their wings. He also sensed more obscure rhythms: the wind whistling through rocky caves, water rising from inside a tree, veins of ore spreading underground. He found it took little effort to produce these on the strings of his lute.

By the time he reached his uncle's gate, which was hidden by trees laden with sour green fruit, he could string all those pieces together. He did not know when the deity drumming in his ears had disappeared, but he now detected the rhythms of the ancient song coming from the lute in his hands: the urgent beat of a battle drum, the light, springy pounding of a horse's hoofs, the angry thunderclaps from the heavens, the cracking of a whip by a siren who danced like the snaky ripples of lightning . . .

He came down to earth at the sound he made striking the knocker on his uncle's gate. Suddenly remembering he had gone without food for days, he fainted before the door was opened.

When his uncle saw the lute, he said to his unconscious nephew, 'Destiny has found you.'

Jigmed's uncle and his servants carried the young man to a low bed beneath a plum tree, where they fed him cheese, and burned incense, but he would not wake up, though his brow smoothed. His nostrils flared, the corners of his mouth twitched, and his ears shone with a faint glow. His face was undergoing a change: once rigid, it was now becoming mobile. A miracle had happened: the quiet, clumsy shepherd had become a *grungkan*, someone who carries thousands of lines of poetry in his heart, a storyteller chosen by the gods. Now, Uncle had been a storyteller of the Gesar legend, and one of some repute, but he had acquired his skill from a teacher. Everything was different for a storyteller chosen by the gods: he learned without studying, and when the right moment came, the lines of poetry poured from his mouth like water from a spring.

When Jigmed smiled, Uncle spoke to him: 'I won't ask you who gave you the lute, or how you suddenly learned to make it sing. But let me give you the two last things you will need as a storyteller.'

'A hat,' Jigmed said.

Uncle smiled. 'I thought you were awake. Which god told you to ask me for a hat in your dream?'

Jigmed held his tongue.

Uncle excused himself and put away the half-finished sutra plate he had been carving. He stuffed his various knives into their respective pouches, and as he walked inside, he said, 'A few days of needlework lie ahead.' There were no Buddha images in his house, only a line carving of Master Lotus, so fine he'd been unwilling to part with it. Lighting a stick of incense before the carving, he intoned, 'It was you who helped Gesar become a hero. Now I am sewing a *grungkan*'s hat for my nephew, Jigmed. If you agree, please help me sew a fine one. I have not touched a needle and thread in years.'

Over the next two days, Uncle sat by his nephew and made the storyteller's hat. First he cut up the finest gold-threaded satin, which the family had saved for years, and stitched the pieces together with fine silk to make a hat that looked like undulating mountains, with a large pointed peak surrounded by three smaller ones. Into each of the smaller peaks he inserted a hawk's feather. The larger peak represented a pagoda that reached into the sky, and the three small ones were the ears of battle horses on alert. He sewed a tiny mirror midway up the central peak to show that everything in the human world was under the gaze of Heaven's compassionate eye. It took Uncle only a single day to sew the hat together. Jigmed woke up as Uncle was brushing loose threads from his clothes. His face wreathed in joy, Jigmed cried, 'My hat.'

'Nephew, the gods have chosen you.' Uncle turned the hat so that the mirror was facing Jigmed. 'Even your appearance has changed.'

'I'm hungry,' Jigmed said.

'Look at yourself first,' Uncle insisted.

Jigmed turned his good eye to the mirror and cried out in shock, for in it he saw Gesar the hero, clad in armour and sitting astride a fine charger, with an arrow quiver over his shoulder. He prostrated himself on the ground in front of the hat.

'Why are you bowing to your hat?' Uncle could not contain his curiosity.

'King Gesar is in the mirror!'

Uncle knelt to look into the tiny mirror. 'I see nothing.'

'If you could see him, then I would be sewing a hat for you!'

Uncle arranged the hat to make the peaks stand up straighter. 'Are you sure you want to wear it?'

Without a word, Jigmed lowered his head.

Uncle put the hat on him, and tears came to his eyes. 'From now on, you won't be yourself any longer.'

'Then who will I be?'

'A special servant to the gods. You will wander everywhere to sing the story they have given to you, and you will never again have a home.'

Jigmed adjusted his hat. 'I also need to find a portrait.'

A storyteller had to carry, like a banner, a silk-framed picture of King Gesar as he roamed the land. When he arrived at a place destined to hear the epic story, he would plant the portrait in the ground and sit beneath it to pluck his lute and sing.

'You should rest a few days before going out,' Uncle said, 'since you will not come back once you leave.' The tears flooded his cheeks.

Adopting the natural tone of a storyteller, Jigmed said, 'Why should Uncle feel sad? Didn't you always want to do what I'm about to do now?' With that, he strummed his lute and left.

The Story
Brugmo

The people of Gling did not know that Joru had tricked Khrothung into proposing a horserace, so the old steward and Gyatsa Zhakar were anxious to relay the news to him. They had postponed the time of the race to the season of blooming flowers to give Joru enough time to prepare for the competition. There were many excellent horsemen in Gling, but no one had a horse that could outrun the wind-chasing steed Yusha.

'Joru's mount is a stick. Can we even call it a horse?' Brugmo asked anxiously.

The old steward pondered the question. 'What worries me,' he said, 'is not whether a stick will count as a horse, but how to persuade Joru to bring his mother back here and to compete.'

Everyone looked at Brugmo: she was one of the prizes in the race, but she had been outspoken in her support of Joru's banishment. And the lovely Brugmo would not want Khrothung to win, for then she would have to marry him.

As expected, she said, 'Old Steward and warriors, I have regretted my words ever since we arrived at this fertile land beside the Yellow river. If I could take them back, the pain in my heart would heal.' She left the meeting hall.

As she climbed onto her horse, she heard a good-natured jest from someone behind her: 'You see something new every day – this is the first time I've seen a pretty girl go to fetch her future husband.' Brugmo's face turned the colour of the morning sky at sunrise.

As she rode she came to an empty field. Dark clouds were sweeping across the clear sky. A man riding a black horse and holding a black spear emerged from the haze. He had a face like charcoal, eyes like brass bells. Lovely Brugmo paled at the sight of him.

'You are as alluring as a celestial fairy, and the jewels in your hair are like the stars in the sky,' the dark man said. 'Wealth and beauty seldom go together, they say – what virtues you must possess to have both.'

Though she trembled, Brugmo's voice was calm: 'Tall trees never grow in a swamp and great men do not make trouble for a woman. Please step aside for someone who must hurry.'

'I will make way for you, but you must choose one of three conditions. First, stay here with me.'

'No.'

'Or sleep with me, then give me your horse and your jewels before you leave.'

'Never!'

'The third choice is the hardest. Leave your splendid clothing with me and return home naked!' he said, stone-faced. 'I have no compassion, so do not cry or beg. Although, since I did not violate you at first sight, we must have a karmic connection.'

'You may have my jewels, but not the horse, and you may not take me as your lover. If you are a worthy man, you will not make trouble for a woman. I have an important mission: I am to bring home the future king of Gling.'

'Who is he?'

'The young warrior, Joru.'

'I will let you go then, since I have heard of his heroic deeds. But you must bring your horse and your jewels back to me once you have completed your task. Leave with me one of your favourite ornaments.'

Brugmo removed a gold ring and handed it to him without hesitation. The dark-faced man, his black horse and the clouds that hung over the field vanished. Urging her mount forward, she came to a place called Seven Sandy Hills and saw seven people on seven horses. She was glad to see signs of humanity after her encounter with the dark faced man, and she rode up to them. When she got closer, she saw they were boiling water for cooking. Their leader leaned in the shade of a rock. As soon as she saw him she could not take another step: it was as if a spell had been cast over her. She had never seen such a handsome man, of such ease and nobility. His skin shone as if he were cast in bronze, and his eyes were like deep pools. Brugmo was a woman who could make a man drunk with her presence, but this man seemed not to notice her. Offended, she turned her horse to leave.

Then the man spoke: 'I am a prince from India on my way to find a wife in Gling.'

Gling? A wife? Images of the girls she knew flashed through her mind, and she wondered who would be chosen. 'I am from Gling. Why have I not heard of this?'

'I have heard that a girl called Brugmo is an unsurpassed beauty,' the man said slowly. 'Could you be that girl?'

Brugmo felt as if someone had snatched her soul from her, but she shook her head vigorously, as a monk twirls a prayer drum.

'I have yet to make anyone an offer of marriage, so I shall take you back to India with me.'

His words aroused mixed feelings in her. She was happy she had made the man feel towards her as she felt towards him, but she was grieved, too – having heard of her rare beauty, he had come all this way only to change his mind as soon as he met another pretty girl. Yet he was so magnificent a man that delight trumped her sorrow, and she could not stop herself telling him that she was Brugmo. She drew out a bottle of the long-life potion she had intended for Joru. Its seal would prove her nobility. Taking the bottle from her, the man removed the seal without so much as a glance, and gulped the contents.

'You will not win the girl if you do not take part in the horserace,' Brugmo said.

'Then I will do so. I will take the beauty but not the throne.'

Brugmo's self-control abandoned her. Disregarding all decorum, she clung to the prince and emptied her heart of sweet words. He placed a crystal bracelet in her hand and she tied a white silk sash around his waist, knotting it nine times. They parted only after they had promised to meet at the horserace.

Brugmo could not know that the dark-faced man and the Indian prince were Joru in disguise.

The dunes disappeared and were replaced by low, rolling hills pocked with tiny holes. In front of each hole sat a mouse-like Joru. The sight so frightened Brugmo that she hid behind a boulder. Joru shouted, and the apparitions disappeared. 'Come out, fiend.'

'Joru, it is I, Brugmo.' She edged out from behind the rock.

Enraged by the memory of her talking so sweetly to the Indian prince, he threw a rock to the ground in front of her, and the pebbles at her feet flew into the air, knocking out her shell-like teeth and shearing the hair from one side of her head. 'Don't lie to me, fiend,' he said. Brugmo sank to the ground and began to wail. Joru's heart softened at the ugly sight, and he went to ask his mother to bring her home.

When Metog Lhartse saw that the girl, once pretty as a flower, was now toothless and half bald, she knew that Joru was playing one of his tricks. All she could do was try to console her: 'Come with me, and Joru will help you. He has the power to make you even prettier than before.'

Joru roared with laughter when he saw her. 'So you really are the proud and arrogant Brugmo. I thought a fiend had assumed your face. There once was one who did that and pretended to love me. She nearly broke my heart.'

'I was sent by the old steward to bring you and your mother back for the horserace. I have braved a long and difficult journey, only for you to turn me into an ugly fiend. How will I be able to face my family?' She began to sob, but all Joru felt was jealousy – surely she was crying because she could hardly show her face now to the Indian prince. But he felt better when he remembered that he himself had conjured up the prince.

'I can give you back your beauty, but you must do something for me first.'

'I'll do whatever you ask.'

'You say that the old steward wants me to go back for the horserace, but have you seen me with a horse? I have none.'

'My family has thousands of fine steeds. You may pick any you prefer.'

'Can any of them outrun Uncle Khrothung's Yusha?'

'Perhaps not. What should we do?'

'A celestial horse was born into a wild herd at the same time that I was born into this world. It is the finest steed Heaven could provide, but only you and my mother, working together, can catch it.'

'Me? Catch a wild horse?'

'It understands human speech, so you and Mother will be able to bring it to me.'

'Then I will go.' And as she spoke, her beauty returned. Yet she grumbled, *Since Joru knows how to catch this horse, why doesn't he go for it? And how shall I pick one horse from a galloping herd?*

She said to Joru, who saw that she hesitated, 'Why won't you tell me the shape, size and colour of the celestial horse?'

'It has nine special features,' he said. 'The head of a sparrow hawk, a wolf's neck, a goat's face, a frog's eye sockets, a snake's eyes, a rabbit's throat, a deer's nose wings, a musk deer's nostrils and, last and most important, a small tuft of condor feathers on each ear.'

'Why don't you catch it yourself?' Brugmo asked.

Joru smiled as he studied her face, but did not answer.

Metog Lhartse said, 'When the soil, the seeds and the temperature are right, crops ripen. We three were predestined to meet in this life. As the two of us have joined forces to make Joru King of Gling, you and I alone will partake in the glory of his kingship.'

Brugmo now recalled that she was one of the prizes of the horserace, and suddenly the way in which Joru was looking at her seemed familiar. His eyes, dark as deep pools, resembled those of the Indian prince. If only he had the prince's good looks, grace and elegance, and the prince had Joru's magical powers, she would be the happiest woman in the world. Joru sensed what was in her mind, and, without meaning to, assumed the image of the prince. Brugmo rubbed her eyes, disbelieving, and Joru was himself again.

Burdened with doubt, Brugmo went up the mountain with Metog Lhartse. They had just reached Mount Banne when they saw a herd of wild horses, their hoofs making the earth quake like a beaten drum. They recognised the celestial horse easily, though it mingled with wild horses that roamed the savage land. It was immensely powerful. As they drew closer, it raised its head and whinnied before galloping off, leaving a whirlwind in its wake. They tried many times to get close to it, but failed. At last they remembered that Joru had told them it understood human language, so Metog Lhartse began to sing:

> 'The long-tailed arrow of an archer,
> If not fitted with the bow in a warrior's hand,
> Stays in the quiver forever,
> And cannot be used to vanquish an enemy.
> What then is the use of being sharp?
> Magical, precious horse,
> If you are truly a celestial steed,
> Why do you not help your master succeed?
> What is the use of running on a deserted grassy plain?

When it heard the song, the horse left the herd and trotted towards the singer. It stopped half an arrow's flight away from the women and spoke in a human voice that sounded almost aggrieved.

'I am Rkayngkar Perpo. I have indeed come from Heaven. When my legs feel strong I can gallop through the air above the wild mountains. It has now been twelve years, and I am looking forward to my master's call. But all I have heard is the cold wind sobbing in the hills. A horse's life is shorter than a human's. A twelve-year-old steed is already beyond its prime. Its mouth can no longer hold the bit, and its back cannot take the saddle. I await the time when my soul will return to Heaven.'

Brugmo fell to her knees. 'Celestial Horse, it was because the people of Gling were ignorant of Heaven's will that you have wasted the best years of your life here. Knowing the harm we have done, we are here to ask you to come down from the mountain and help your master finish his work.'

'The wild horses did not know my origin because they are mere animals. The people of Gling could not recognise a warrior from Heaven because they chose to follow evil ways. What else is there to say?' With that, the horse rose into the air and hid its powerful body in the clouds.

Brugmo cried in despair and fell to the ground. Metog Lhartse knelt and called to Heaven. Gods appeared above the cloud with Joru's celestial brother, Donkhyung Karpo, who gently waved his arm to extend the lasso in his hand. When he pulled back, the celestial horse was standing beside him.

'I have spent twelve useless years in the human world,' said the horse.

Donkhyung Karpo did not respond; rather, he lovingly caressed the horse's neck and fed him a magic pill. 'Go. You and your master have just reached adulthood.' He let the lasso fall through the clouds and land in Metog Lhartse's hand; the horse followed. It stood before the women with its head held high.

Brugmo leaped up and wrapped her arms around the horse's neck, so startling it that it rose up in the air again to gallop through the moist clouds and cascading sunlight. When it heard the women's frightened cries, it said, 'Don't close your eyes out of fear, but look at the world far below.'

So the women opened their eyes, and saw vast, open fields, bright lakes, rivers and winding mountain ranges that slowly spiralled and opened up. They saw Gling, high in the snowcapped mountains, between China, India and Persia. China lay in the direction of the sunrise, Persia in the direction of the sunset and India to the steamy south. All three great countries had imposing cities, linked by grand thoroughfares, but to the north were desolate plains, where whirlwinds raised columns of sand and water from salt lakes dried to shiny crystals under the sun. Moonlight flowed over the glazed roofs of China's imperial city, while the first rays of sunlight lit the Persian palace dome.

'Now you have seen it. Gling is not the whole world, not even the best of the worlds.'

'Let us down now. If you will not help Joru, then so be it. But we want to be with him.'

The celestial horse laughed. 'I cannot return to Heaven until the son of the deities completes his task. I brought you here so you could see both the good and bad in Gling's future, as well as the happiness and suffering that have already played out in the world of the humans. You must look hard, for the sake of Gling's future.'

The horse soared through the sky, and the women's clothes fluttered in the wind. They saw mountains rounded and jagged, waters fresh and salty, countries benevolent and evil. They crossed not only extraordinary distances but also through magical time, and saw all the beginnings and endings, good and evil. And they saw chaos and ignorance, where a beginning was the same as no beginning at all, and an end showed no sign of ending.

The horse spoke to them again: 'When we are back on land, I will become just a horse and I will lose the ability to speak. But now that you have learned things from Heaven, it is up to you to help Joru whenever his mind is confused.'

'But he is the son of the deities. Why would he listen to ordinary people like us?'

'He may be the son of the deities, but he is also a mortal, like you. Brugmo, I know that you have nine herds of fine steeds, so you must be a good judge of horses. Now, I have seen my young master ride a stick for enjoyment on the grassy plain but I have never seen him astride a good horse. You must tell him of my virtues.'

When Brugmo returned to Earth, she handed the lasso to Joru. 'This celestial horse will enhance your magic powers, and will help you to rule Gling.'

The Story
Love

Brugmo knew that Rkayngkar Perpo would bring his master victory:
Joru would be her husband and she would be Queen of Gling. Yet,
though elated by this prospect, a secret bitterness occasionally entered
her mind, and she wished that Joru and the prince could have been the
same person, either Joru with the prince's good looks or the prince with
Joru's courage – and magic powers. The thought made her blush, and
she had to press her hands to her chest to stop her heart thumping like
a rabbit's. But she would not allow her thoughts to run wild, like a
horse with a free rein, since she had accomplished only half of her
mission. She urged mother and son to set out without delay.

On the auspicious day they had chosen, they gathered their belongings and rode for home. Joru nearly fell off his horse at the sight of
Brugmo, who was more beautiful than ever. She slapped her horse's
rump and it galloped ahead. Reminded again of the Indian prince, he
was stung by jealousy, as if his heart were being pinched. At the crest
of a hill, she stopped and turned to him with a smile. He reached out,
but as he touched her willowy waist she cracked her whip to urge her
horse on. Joru's face clouded. He knew how foolish he was being, since
the Indian prince had been his own transformation, but she had been
coy with him by abandoning all decorum to run into the arms of a
handsome stranger.

When she saw him pause at the side of the road, she rode back. 'Can
your celestial horse not keep up with mine?'

Joru decided it was time to stop sulking.

'My horse is wild, and has neither bridle nor saddle. If we want to
move fast we must share a mount,' he said, and leaped astride her horse.

His warm breath on her neck made her blush. 'Get off! What would people say?'

'My horse needs a saddle.'

'I'll give you a gold saddle from my father's treasure house.'

'The celestial horse is hard to control without a bridle.'

'You know there are fine bridles in my father's treasure house.'

'I know everything about this land, if I care to.'

Brugmo felt as if the sharp teeth of a mouse were gnawing at her heart. But Joru continued, 'The celestial horse needs two more things before it can compete. Since the old steward sent you to fetch me, I am sure you will help me get them.'

'Go to the steward for what you need.'

'A celestial horse must have the perfect saddle and bridle.' And then he held her tightly to his chest. She stiffened, to make him feel as if he were holding a stick of wood. As the Indian prince he had been allowed to feel her supple, delightful body. He jumped down from the horse and anger rose in his chest. 'Very well. Have your horserace. I shall return to Heaven with my celestial horse. Let Uncle Khrothung be your king . . . or whoever else may win.'

Brugmo could not help but wonder if he knew of the Indian prince, so she hastily agreed.

'Tell me what you need.'

'The saddle must be secured with a fine strap and rest upon one of your family's checked felt saddle blankets.'

He was demanding a set of her father's most treasured riding gear. How could a son of the deities be so greedy? How was he any different from Khrothung? And Joru was so mysterious, while Khrothung was open at least about his greed. And then there was the Indian prince to consider. If not for the great trust the people of Gling had placed in her, she would have left Joru behind with a flick of her whip. But he knew exactly what was on her mind, so he waved his magical stick and her horse flew over two hills before she could halt it.

The horse stopped at the very spot where she had met the Indian prince.

Fingering the crystal bracelet the prince had placed on her wrist before they parted, Brugmo could not help thinking of the loving tenderness he had shown her. The cool, smooth crystal reminded her of his skin, and of the bright unfathomable look in his eyes. She thought about how the people of Gling had turned her into a trophy, and of how the fair-skinned Indian prince would never be able to defeat Khrothung, and sadness welled up in her. Then, suddenly, the crystal bracelet became a coil of dry vine, which broke apart and fell to the ground. When she looked up, Joru was sitting in the shade of the same boulder as the prince and his eyes were those of the prince, full of love and of mystery. She was so ashamed she lowered her head.

'Brugmo, the sun is blazing down on us. Come down from your horse and rest awhile. We'll wait till after midday to ride again.'

She did as he said, and sat next to him.

'Where is your mother?' she asked.

'Her horse is so slow she has fallen behind.'

'Why did you not stay with her?'

'Your horse ran too fast. What would I say to the old steward and to the warriors if the most beautiful girl in Gling were to be stolen by bandits? But let us not speak of that. You look thirsty. What would you like? Yoghurt? Barley wine? Tea? Or fig juice from India?' Without waiting for her answer, the prince's servants, whom she had seen before, appeared and offered her drinks.

Now she knew what he had done.

'Why have you tricked me, Joru?' she asked tearfully. 'Because I spat at you and spoke venomous words when you and your mother were banished?'

He beckoned to the sky and a thrush, with the nine-knot white silk sash she'd given to the prince in its beak, landed on his shoulder. The gold ring she'd given to the dark-faced man sparkled in the leaves of the cinquefoil at their feet. Brugmo felt she would die of shame.

'You conjured them up to embarrass me.'

He put his arm around her and this time her body was soft and yielding.

'After the horserace you will be my queen, and you have yet to look at me properly.'

'I was already a young woman when you were born. You had a round, moon-like face and you were very calm. But then you chose to be ugly – and vicious.'

'You think I am too young. My strength and wisdom are greater than those of all the warriors of Gling, including my brother, Gyatsa Zhakar, yet your beauty sends thunder and lightning to my heart.'

'But you lack Gyatsa Zhakar's temperance and tolerance.'

'And you think I am ugly.'

'A man whose reputation reaches far and wide should have a noble look.'

'Do you like this? Or this?' And he transformed himself into a series of handsome men, each of whom pleased her beyond words. The final face he assumed was regal. Brugmo embraced him, and said, 'Joru, a king must have a valiant look.'

And then he was Joru again, not *ugly*, exactly, but a little oily and certainly not noble. Brugmo did not move away, but sadness clouded her gaze.

'These are such grave matters. Why do you insist on looking like this?

He laughed, but she could see that his eyes were solemn, and his sorrow touched her deeply.

'Your eyes are the sea of your heart, Joru, and I will drown in that sea.'

'Lovely, gentle girl, you are right. And I am like a bird that has been shot by the arrow of your gaze.'

'I am so happy when you look at me like this, but I feel as though I were the very lowest of creatures. Am I, dear Joru?'

'You are a woman of nobility and your beauty is incomparable. How can you feel that way?'

'I think anyone you looked at would feel so. Is that the expression all who gaze down from Heaven at us in the human world display? . . . I know what it is – you have the eyes of the Guanyin Bodhisattva in the temple you built.'

'The Bodhisattva's eyes. Perhaps. I cannot recall.'

'Did you really come from Heaven?'

Joru looked up at the sky. 'That is what they tell me.'

'Who are *they*?'

He waved his hand, and the celestial soldiers made themselves visible, some in white helmets and armour, others in gold. Their weapons glinted in the light and the red tassels on their helmets fluttered in the wind. Joru waved again and they faded into the clouds.

'You are a god.'

'I am not.'

'You are like a god.'

'Yes.'

'I love you.'

'If you did not, my celestial powers would vanish.'

When Metog Lhartse finally caught up with them, they were entwined like a pair of geese. She wept as she spoke: 'My children, let me be the first to wish you happiness.'

The Storyteller
A Horserace

In just two years Jigmed had become the most renowned storyteller in Khampa.

A storyteller will usually give himself a new name, as a storyteller chosen by the gods is no longer the same person brought into the world by his parents. A storyteller is – to use a popular metaphor – a loudspeaker. The real loudspeakers, of course, are the mouths of those in government, but a storyteller is a loudspeaker for the gods.

Lamas from several sects offered to give Jigmed a new name, but since his parents had died when he was young, the name they had given him helped him to remember them. One day, as he stood under the loudspeakers mounted on a pole in a market town, he tried to recall what his parents had looked like. But their faces were blurred with time. Sitting down, he wiped the mirror in the middle of his hat, but could see nothing clearly. 'Blind man,' he said, and smiled.

His eyesight had worsened as his storytelling skills improved, and he stumbled on the smooth streets as if he were walking on roads treacherous with potholes. Old women who saw him said, 'Poor man,' while young women covered their mouths and giggled at the sight of him. Children shouted, 'A blind man.'

'That's what people call me, but I can see you. I'm not completely blind.'

'He's the storyteller.'

'Yes, I am the storyteller.' He had got used to his name travelling before him, and this small town had heard of him before he arrived. The school bells had just rung to signal the end of the day, and swarms of children rushed through the gate to follow him.

'Are you that blind man?'

'Tell us something about King Gesar!'

'Blind man, what will you tell us today?'

His lute was still in its velvet bag, slung across his back, for he had not planned to sing the story in such a dusty place. Although he had bad eyes, his voice, which had once been hoarse, was loud and clear, and he believed it would be a sin to let dust damage a voice that had miraculously gained a rich timbre.

'Are you going to the horserace? The county-wide horserace?' the children asked him.

Slapping his bag, Jigmed said, 'But the race is over and Gesar has ascended to the throne.'

The town chief came to greet him. 'This is a new race, sponsored by the government to commemorate King Gesar.' And he added something about how 'culture erected the stage and economy was putting on the show', which Jigmed did not understand. Then the chief opened the door of his Jeep and said, 'Get in, blind man, and sing for us at the horserace.'

But the blind man hesitated, so the chief said, 'Can it be that your talent does not match your reputation?'

'If that were so, I would have stayed at home to tend sheep.'

'Several other storytellers are to be at the race. You're not afraid to compete with them, are you?'

Jigmed had no choice but to climb into the Jeep, and they bounced over the rutted mud roads across the grassland. Cradling his lute, he said, 'Don't call me the blind man. I have a name. It's Jigmed.'

The chief laughed. 'I attend meetings at the county seat of government, and the Party secretary there, who can't remember my name, calls me Bandy Legs.'

They had left town around noon, and Jigmed fell asleep as the Jeep swayed and bumped along. When he awoke, they were chasing a gorgeous sunset. He grew anxious: the last of the setting sun was clinging to a snowcapped mountain.

'Hurry,' he said, 'hurry.'

The chief stopped the Jeep on a small hill facing the open grassland, where thousands of white tents had been thrown up to form a temporary city. The westering sun lent it a steely blue, dream-like quality. They were like the tents pitched by soldiers in Jigmed's dream. But then the Jeep started up again, veering off the road towards the racecourse, which was flanked by colourful flags and banners. Coming to an abrupt stop in front of the command post, Jigmed was thrown forward and banged his face on the headrest of the seat in front. He was still seeing stars when the murmuring began.

'He's here. The storyteller is here.'

'That man is here, after all.'

Cradling his lute, Jigmed walked along the racecourse, following the banners, until he came to the crest of a hill, just as the sun was about to pull in its last rays. A shadow loomed over him. A man was squatting at the top of the hill, the light of the setting sun draped over him like a cloak.

'Everyone is talking about the arrival of a man. You must be him.'

'I don't know what you mean.'

'A man who sings better than anyone else.'

'I don't know if I sing better than anyone else, but I am a storyteller, a *grungkan*.'

'Ha.' The man snorted. 'You don't *act* like a talented storyteller. But who knows? If the gods want you to be a storyteller, that's what you'll be.'

By now Jigmed had moved from under the shadow and was standing on the hilltop, face to face with the man. He was old, with a gaunt face, hawk-like eyes that glinted sharply and a white beard that fluttered gently in the evening breeze. He was just what people would imagine a storyteller to look like, and this alone won over Jigmed.

'Old sir, how could I think of out-singing you?'

The old man laughed. 'You say that because of how I look. But I shall sing only praise of the fine steeds and their riders before the race begins.' He was an artist. He did not tell stories, but praised the horses, the weapons, the warriors' appearance, the holy mountains, the sacred lakes and even the storytellers' hats, with their many symbols.

'What are you doing up here?' asked Jigmed.

'The sunset is so splendid, yet there are no fitting expressions of praise. I am pondering which words might best express this dazzling view.'

'What have you come up with?'

The old man replied sadly, 'The scene keeps changing, and no words can capture the sight.'

'Is that because there aren't enough words?'

'Maybe there are too many.'

The sun seemed to have burned up its energy, for the red sky quickly faded into darkness.

'The night curtain has descended. Now, go and sing for the people at the festivities.'

From the hilltop the tents looked like small squares, each with a fire before it. Jigmed bade the old man farewell and headed for the bright spots. Custom required anyone eating and drinking beside a bonfire to make room for newcomers, then give them mutton legs and drinks. Jigmed sat between two taciturn men to enjoy his dinner. He soon felt tipsy. He looked up at the sky and saw that the dark clouds that had followed the burning sunset had vanished. Clusters of stars now glinted on the curtain of night. Without putting on his storyteller's hat or raising his banner, he took the lute out of its bag and, gazing at the stars, began to pluck the strings.

The people quietened, listening to the lute and to the crackling of the bonfires in the wind. The melody became lively. 'Is that him?' they whispered among themselves.

'Is he the blind man?'

Jigmed heard them. He smiled and stood up to be closer to the sky. He strummed his lute, moved near the bonfire and began to sing:

'The lion on the snowcapped mountains
Must show its dark mane when fully grown.
The fierce tiger in the forest
Must show its stripes when fully formed.
The golden-eyed fish on the sea floor
Must show its six fins when fully developed.
The son of the gods among the humans
Must show himself when the moment comes.'

Cheers erupted, and Jigmed paused. When he played again, he no longer heard the notes, only the sound of the stars as they fell from the sky to his strings. When he closed his eyes, he saw the galloping chargers of long, long ago.

The Story
The Race for the Throne

The Gling horserace began.

Tents pitched by the Gling tribes turned the grassland along the Yellow river into a city that did not sleep.

Khrothung, the leader of the Tagrong tribe, his sons, Tonggod and Dongtsan, and all the tribe's warriors arrived, heads held high, eyes turned skyward. Khrothung's horse, Yusha, was so peerless an animal that they believed they were there not for the race but for the celebration when the Tagrong tribe claimed the throne.

Warriors from the senior branch, headed by nine brothers, had also arrived. Dressed in yellow silk robes and perched on saddles with gold saddlecloths, they were magnificent in the sunshine. They thought the throne should go to the most senior of the nine branches, and they were eager to compete.

When the middle branch, led by eight warriors, rode to the site, they were like falling white snow, dressed all in white – white helmets, armour, robes and saddles.

Warriors from the junior branch were also there. In their blue helmets and robes they lined up in formation, with the old steward, Rongtsa Khragan, in the middle. He knew that the race was to help Joru ascend the throne of Gling. Unlike the presumptuous Khrothung, he did not believe in the prophecy of the Hayagriva. Neither did he behave like those in the senior and middle branches, who were burning with eagerness. They had lined up at the starting point long before the race was to begin, and they were growing restless. The old steward called Gyatsa Zhakar to him: 'You seem less anxious than they.'

'I *am* anxious – Joru is not here yet.'

'Has the idea of becoming king ever crossed your mind?'

'I believe there is someone who could bring more happiness and well-being to the people of Gling than I.'

The steward sighed. 'Gling is about to become a nation. When Joru ascends the throne, it will enjoy Heaven's favour and endless blessings, so long as all warriors share your belief.'

'But where is he?'

The old steward was concerned, though he did not sound so when he spoke. 'He will be here when the time comes.'

His words were barely out when a shout arose, 'Joru is here!'

Khrothung's true competition had arrived. So too had Yusha's.

Reunited with the eleven other beauties, Brugmo was sure that this time Joru would not appear in his usual bizarre attire. He would be riding his celestial horse gorgeously caparisoned. Indeed, when it showed itself, everyone applauded. But the cheers were followed by sighs, for Joru, who led the horse, had put on the filthy clothes he had worn when he was banished. He looked nothing like a king.

The warriors who supported him lowered their heads in disappoint-ment; the other contestants, on their way to the starting line at the foothills of Mount Ayu Te, refused to ride beside him. Only Khrothung welcomed him, convinced that he himself would win the race. And while Brugmo knew that Joru had his reasons for dressing thus, the other girls knew that she was fond of him and his appearance caused her a great loss of face. Joru, who had transformed himself into a bee, flew up to hum in her ear, but she was so upset she reached out and slapped at him. The dispirited bee flew off, reeling.

Once all the competing riders were lined up beneath Mount Ayu Te, the trumpet shell sounded, then a monk and a Taoist priest released the smoke from a burning mulberry branch. Guardian deities and moun-tain gods descended to watch over the race. Drumbeats sounded, not from the human realm but from above the clouds, as an arrow from on high struck the ground with a clap of thunder. The Gling warriors loosened their reins, and a cloud of yellow dust rose behind them. Before it had settled, the horses had disappeared along the road that wound around the mountain.

Khrothung and his horse Yusha shot ahead. Gyatsa Zhakar whipped his horse on, searching for his brother among the other riders. He spotted him at the back, gazing up at a dark cloud the size of a lamb as if he were not in the race. The cloud grew bigger, and by the time the horses had reached a distance of three arrow-lengths it covered the sky. Thunderclaps followed snaking bolts of lightning. It seemed that monks performing magic on the mountain to seek protection from the gods had neglected to offer a sacrifice to the local demons, and three – Tiger Head, Leopard Head and Bear Head – were offended.

'The people of Gling are holding a horserace in our territory,' seethed Tiger Head. 'They spur their mounts forward, sending dust flying throughout the mountains, without offering us any tribute.'

'We cannot let them run amok in our land!'

'We must show them what we are made of!'

They summoned a giant hailstorm to chase the racers away. But Joru knew what was about to happen, and before the sky filled with hailstones he tossed his magic lasso and dragged the three demons to him. When they saw the son of the deities they begged his pardon for their mistake.

'Today is a happy day,' Joru said, 'so I will not take your lives. Just draw back your dark clouds and hailstones.'

The dark clouds vanished and were replaced by dazzling sunlight as a mountain goddess drifted over and gave a key to Joru. He smiled. 'When I win the race,' he said, 'I will have the throne and a queen. How could I think of using a key to your back door?'

'A king needs great riches, but you have nothing,' the goddess said. 'This key gives you access to treasure in the mountains.'

Joru, serious now, thanked her.

'You are falling behind,' she said. 'Already you are at least ten arrow-shots behind the others.'

Without raising his whip, Joru patted Rkayngkar Perpo's neck, and the celestial horse was soon galloping among the thundering herd of horses. When he spotted the tribe's fortune-teller among them, Joru slowed to ride alongside him.

'Has the master fortune-teller divined for himself? Can it be that the golden throne has called out to you?'

The fortune-teller whipped his horse twice and panted, 'Whoever casts a divination for himself will go blind. If not for that, I would truly like to see what my fortune is.'

'You think a fortune-teller can compete with warriors to rule a nation?'

The fortune-teller laughed. 'You are one of the competitors. Why, if not for the golden throne?'

'As far as I know, neither the Indian Karma Dawa throne, the Chinese emperor's dragon seat, nor the throne of any other nation is decided by a horserace. But in our land, the one with the fastest steed will be king, while those with slower horses will be his ministers. Is this not strange?'

'Have you never heard the Chinese saying that one may not be able to *rule* the world on horseback, but one can definitely *own* the world in that way?'

'Do you wish to own the world? You cannot divine that for yourself, but you could for me.'

The fortune-teller roared with laughter. 'Before an arrow leaves the bow, you can ask if you will hit the target, but once the arrow is out, even the best fortune-teller cannot see the result.' He whipped his horse and galloped off. Joru smiled and, when the fortune-teller was an arrow-shot ahead, flicked his reins; Rkayngkar Perpo quickly overtook the fortune-teller, and as he passed him, Joru said, 'You are a good fortune-teller, for you did not lie. If I win, I will make you the official fortune-teller.'

Then Joru saw a famous healer on horseback, though the healer's horse was tiring.

'Healer, you dropped your medicine satchel,' Joru called.

When the healer reined in his horse, he saw that his satchel was still securely fastened to his saddle. But Joru grinned at him and said, 'I could tell that your horse was exhausted, and I thought you should let it rest.'

The healer smiled and slowed his horse to ride alongside Joru.

'I think you are ill,' Joru said.

'To say that a healthy person is ill is the same as casting an evil spell.'

'Then it must be me who is ill.'

'You do dress . . . oddly, but your eyes are bright and clear. You are not ill.'

'I am.'

The healer began to talk as if he had forgotten about the race and the throne. 'Joru, there are three types of illness, those associated with the wind, the gallbladder and phlegm. They are caused by greed, anger and senselessness. The three intertwine to afflict humans with four hundred and twenty-four illnesses. You, however, show no sign of illness, so spur your horse forward and win the throne that you deserve.'

'Why do you whip your horse, if you know you will not be king?'

'I am well known in Gling. I must race to win. How otherwise shall I hold up my head?'

As he spurred his horse on, Joru shouted, 'If I become king, you will be my royal healer.'

Rkayngkar Perpo was clearly the finest charger in the race – all Joru had to do was flick the reins and the horse would run like lightning. They caught up with the old steward.

'Uncle,' Joru called out, using the honorific befitting an older man of the family.

The old steward would not let that pass. 'I may be your uncle, but you may call me that only in private. On public occasions like this, you must address me as "Steward".'

'I know what I say. The old order in Gling is broken. Only after someone wins the golden throne can we make a new order. That is why I called you "Uncle".'

'You are a son of the gods,' the steward said, with a nod. 'That is why your thoughts are both rational and profound. Go and win the throne: obey Heaven's will and fulfil the people's wish.'

Joru was about to say that the steward would be his chief minister when he won the throne, but Rongtsa Khragan whipped Joru's horse, and it shot forward like an arrow. Effortlessly they passed Khrothung and his horse Yusha, which was so fast it seemed to carry the wind on its hoofs.

Mount Kure, the finish line, rose up like a helmet before them. Khrothung had felt as if a golden throne had been placed there for him; he and his horse were beyond anyone's reach. The prophecy of the Hayagriva was about to come true: the rare beauty, Brugmo, would soon be his, and the door to the treasure in Kure mountain would open for him. He felt as if his body flew while his mind ran ahead into the future where he was king. And in that moment he heard someone breathing hard, and turned to see Joru behind him, looking as though he would fall off his horse.

Khrothung laughed. 'Even if you used every bit of your strength, you would be far from the throne. But, my good nephew, since you have surpassed all those others, I will let you walk ahead of them when I hold court.'

Khrothung saw a light shoot past him. Joru and his celestial horse were suddenly in front. His gloating vanished and he nearly coughed blood in his despair and anger. He cast obstacle magic at Joru, but the celestial horse turned into a bright light and pierced the dark wall he had created to block them. The bright light blinded him and he saw darkness; his body swayed and he nearly fell off. He whipped his steed forward. The golden throne was so close: he had only to sprint the short distance and leap from his horse onto the throne. But he could not see Joru, who had raced ahead. Maybe the boy was not such a good rider after all and had failed to rein in his horse when they reached the throne.

Khrothung swallowed hard and gripped his horse with his legs, but the animal reared. The throne was moving away from him. Khrothung could not halt Yusha, so he jumped down, the horse whinnying pitifully behind him.

'Dear Yusha, there is nothing I can do for you now. When I am on the throne, I shall return for you.'

The horse's legs gave out, and it collapsed on the ground.

Khrothung crawled towards the golden throne, but again it moved away from him, forever at his fingertips and forever beyond his reach. When he heard Joru's laugh, his embarrassment turned to anger.

'Are you laughing at me, lowly beggar?'

'My noble uncle, are you talking to me?'

'Why did you use magic during the horserace?'

'You used the obstacle magic on me. I used none on you.'

'Then why could I not reach the throne even though I ran hard?'

'The gods are punishing you, Uncle. Rkayngkar Perpo and I have circled the throne twice already, but we dare not sit on it.'

'The little beggar is frightened by the golden throne,' Khrothung said to himself, but he poured honeyed words on Joru.

'My dear nephew, you are wise. To be in power means shouldering the concerns of many people – it is nothing less than unbearable suffering.'

'I must ask Uncle's opinion of the trophy – the girl.'

'She is like wild fruit on the mountains, red and enticing, sweet as honey, but if you eat it, you will die.'

'What about the treasure in Kure mountain? Uncle must have lost sleep over that.'

'Good nephew,' Khrothung said, ignoring Joru's teasing, 'please step aside, so I can sit on the throne and assume the people's suffering, while you continue to lead a carefree life.'

'It is a hard seat – let me take it, Uncle. Eight years of roaming the floodplain along the Yellow river has taught me to endure hardship. And, Uncle, you should see to your horse.' He held up his whip, and Yusha got to its feet. Khrothung took the reins and tried to mount the horse, but its front legs buckled.

Khrothung wrapped his arms around his horse's neck, and began to sob. 'Good nephew, help my horse. Heal him.'

Joru was touched. 'Abandon the throne that is not yours, and the horse will run like the wind again.'

But Khrothung was still unwilling.

'The Hayagriva prophesied that the throne would go to the Tagrong tribe.'

Joru took off his hat and wiped his brow as if mopping sweat. His face assumed the ferocious features of the Hayagriva. Khrothung rubbed his eyes, but Joru was himself again. No – not quite the same. His face had undergone a subtle change. His narrow forehead was broader, the bridge of his nose higher, and his brows more clearly defined. Freckles from the plateau sun vanished to leave his skin as clear as a gemstone. Khrothung could only cry plaintively. 'Heaven gave me great powers and intelligence, so why send a son of the gods to the noble throne of Gling?'

Joru walked up to the golden throne, and examined it carefully. He wondered why one had to sit on it in order to have the power, wealth and beautiful women that others envied. Did the throne mean only those three things? He looked up, but the blue sky was silent as usual. Then he gazed at the endless stretch of grassland that ran to the horizon, and suddenly felt relief, as if he had come home after a long journey. The snowcapped peaks sparkled, a hawk spread its wings. For an instant, everything between Heaven and Earth held its breath. It had all been predestined, but it had taken Joru twelve years to reach this point. Perhaps he could indeed transform the grassland into a place where people felt at ease, a homeland for the tribes of Gling.

Joru sat on the throne.

The people who had gathered on Mount Lute to watch the race went silent. But then they understood what had happened, and a thunderous cheer broke out at the sight before them.

The Story
Winning a Horserace to be King – II

Joru sat on the throne, and the sky filled with auspicious clouds that parted like water as the gates of Heaven opened. His celestial mother, Lhamin Dagmo, holding a quiver, rose into the sky.

Rkayngkar Perpo, the celestial horse, whinnied three times, and Joru tossed the key that the mountain goddess had given him to Mount Kure. The mountain roared, boulders rolled like an avalanche, and the crystal gate to the trove of seven treasures opened. Attendants to the mountain goddess came forward to lay the treasures before the throne. Warrior gods emerged, in black iron armour and helmets like snowy mountain peaks, with red rattan shields and tiger-skin sheaths for their bows. They dressed Joru as a warrior: a bow over his back, a sword on his hip, a spear in his hand. And as they did so his face changed from that of an ugly clown into that of a man of dignity. A rain of flowers fell from the heavens.

Since his birth, Joru had been like the sun behind clouds or a lotus in mud, its sweet smell buried. Yet the hardships with which Heaven had showered him had made him feel the people's suffering keenly. And now he sat on the throne. Above him the heavenly gate was slowly closing. A stern voice came from behind it: 'From now on Gling is a nation, and Gesar is its king.'

As if they had awoken from a dream, the people of Gling now swarmed down the mountain, calling out joyously to Joru, to Gesar, the son of the deities.

Gesar rose from the throne and gazed down at his people. He began slowly: 'All you warriors who raced today and all you citizens of Gling, it has been twelve years since I pledged to come down to the human world to kill the demons and relieve the people of their suffering. Over the past twelve cycles of summer and winter, you have seen what I have done. Now I have ascended to the golden throne of Gling, as Heaven ordained. But I still do not know one thing: are you willing to accept me as your king?'

'Heaven has blessed Gling!' the old steward shouted. 'He is our hero, King of the Nation of Gling!'

King! The people of Gling had never dared to say the word before, although they had hoped for it for a long time. Now their thousands of hearts and thousands of mouths cried out together, 'King! King! King!'

'Gesar! King! King Gesar!'

The word shone more brightly than any treasure.

To show their allegiance, the leaders of the tribes, led by the old steward, offered up their tribal records of ancestry and their flags. Gesar accepted them, and the people's heartfelt cheers. With a wave of his hand, he began to appoint his officials.

First was the old steward, who was made chief minister, then the centiarchs and the chiliarchs, contingents of a hundred and a thousand families, who were responsible for keeping order in each tribe.

Of the thirty Gling warriors, Gyatsa Zhakar, Danma, Nyibum Daryag and Gnyatsa Aten were installed as the four great generals. Then came the civilians, the high monks and the doctors. Everyone praised his choices. Even Khrothung could do nothing but congratulate the new king.

'Great King,' Khrothung said, 'we still need a palace for the golden throne. I invite the king to use my fortress – there is no grander castle in Gling.'

Chief Minister Rongtsa Khragan offered his advice: 'A king must stay at the centre of the country. Tagrong is on the borders.'

The two men began to argue.

Gesar smiled and said, 'Let us all go to the big tent and celebrate. We will discuss this there.'

The warriors mounted their horses and raced down the hill to the tent, where a feast had been laid out. Brugmo led the girls of Gling in singing to greet them. She danced gracefully up to Gesar and knelt before him, raising a bowl of wine over her head.

'My king, may your brilliance shine like the sun and let my happiness bloom like a flower. I will be as your shadow in all your deeds, and hold your reins and steady your stirrups.'

Gesar raised her up, and offered her the seat beside him. People came up with well-wishing *hadas*.

Thus in one day a loose cluster of tribes became an orderly nation, an ugly boy became a mighty king and took the prettiest girl in Gling as his bride. And as the people celebrated, a palace rose out of the ground like a mushroom until it stood gleaming by the Yellow river, with its nine twists and turns. They had all been sitting together on bright cushioned seats, but now a jade staircase ran the length of a grand hall lined with one hundred and twenty fragrant cypress trees. The king's throne stood above all else, and the king's voice, as he repeated his pledge to the people, to his officials and generals, and to the heavens, to reconstruct the land and subdue all the demons and evil spirits, reverberated as if someone had struck a bronze bell.

Groups of artisans, half god, half human, arrived – although it is more accurate to say that they began as humans and became the gods of their trades in Gling.

The one among them who knew how to smelt metal was the father of iron, the head of Gling's armoury. He became the god of blacksmiths. And then there was a carver; a potter, who could turn clay into glazed tiles; a lutemaker; a geomancer, who knew how to break rock to build roads without incurring the anger of the mountain gods; a seed magician, who made flowers love each other like humans to produce more fertile seeds and who became the god of harvests, worshipped by crop farmers; and a spice master, who collected the scent of flowers and became a secret god in the boudoirs of women who wished to look beautiful.

King Gesar invited them to sit and share the feast, saying, 'I will have great need of you in the future.'

All sat down, all but one, the lutemaker, who said, 'The wine is good but the music grates on the ear. These forlorn drums and trumpets are not suitable for a palace. Let me teach these musicians how to play elegant music.'

Gesar gave his consent with a smile, but the crowd waited to see how the man would teach a cohort of fierce warriors, used to playing drums and trumpets, to play his refined music. The man placed his finger to his lips, and the band stopped playing. Then he strummed his lute strings, and the music that flowed from his fingertips was like fine spray above a waterfall, like sunlight dappling the surface of a lake. His music seemed to travel far away, and when it returned, the musicians' faces became peaceful. The lutemaker ran his hand over a drum, and the congealed blood of sacrificed animals fell away, replaced by a lotus flower. He strummed his lute again, and trumpets made of human leg bones fell to the floor and smashed.

'Here are your instruments,' he said, and lutes appeared in their hands.

They began to play, and the music blew through the people's hearts like a fresh wind. Tears streamed down the faces of men who had been warriors and shamans, and in that moment they became musicians instead, known as the 'men who were born twice'.

Many women fell in love with the lutemaker. But there were many who gossiped, and one woman, hiding by the lake to watch him bathe, discovered that he was in truth a woman. Yet still they longed for him. When he played that first time, even Queen Brugmo, sitting next to Gesar, prayed for the strength to resist the lutemaker, for the music invoked a sweet emotion in everyone's heart.

The Storyteller
A Fine Charger

The horserace in Khampa began.

There were so many horses with so many riders competing that if they were to set off at the same time the starting line would have had to be at least two kilometres wide. So they set out in heats. At one end of the line a man held a starting gun, while at the other a man held up a pennant. The riders grasped their reins and waited. Such throngs of spectators crowded in that it took a police line to keep the way open for the horses. When the starter fired his gun and the pennant was waved, the first heat raced towards the finishing line, where a judge with a stopwatch sat on a high stool under a large parasol. He recorded the time of every horse.

Jigmed had to shove his way through the crowd. He largely ignored the horses. He had never seen so many people in one place in his life. A man in sunglasses whispered to him, 'The true charger has not yet appeared and the moment has yet to come.'

Was the man speaking to him?

'Yes, I'm speaking to you. Will you come to my tent for tea and a little rest?' He turned and squeezed through the crowd. Jigmed followed and saw him wave from a distant tent.

Outside, the sun was scorching, but inside the tent it was cool. Jigmed drank a bowl of tea as the man spoke.

'You sing the praises of horses, so you must know them.'

Jigmed shook his head — he merely followed the will of the gods when he sang.

'Anyone who sings about horses must know them,' the man said obstinately.

Jigmed remembered the old man who had appeared on the hilltop at dusk. 'I know someone who does know about them. He specialises in singing their praises.'

The man, who, despite the shade of the tent, was still wearing his sunglasses, sighed. 'Let's go, then.'

Jigmed followed the man through the tent city to the foot of a small hill, where several men were standing around a horse in a grove of willow trees by a river. The horse looked exhausted, but it was an exceptionally beautiful animal.

The man in sunglasses said, 'A horse like this will appear and win the race.'

'It . . . doesn't look very happy.'

'How can a horse not be happy to race? If not for racing, what is the point of having fine steeds in this world?'

'Is it sick?'

'How can a fine steed be sick before a race?'

The man then told Jigmed that the horse had been cursed – by the old man who sang the praises of horses. They believed that he was, in fact, a powerful shaman who had been asked by the owner of this horse's opponent to cast a spell on it. A rider in suede boots embroidered with cloud patterns was caressing the horse's mane and sobbing. They asked Jigmed to cast a spell on the other horse.

'In your story, Gesar knew plenty of incantations, so you must know a few.' They told him that their horse was like Gesar's Rkayngkar Perpo and that his opponent was Yusha. The man in sunglasses said he had heard a storyteller sing about the horserace: on the night before the race, Joru and Khrothung had tried to curse each other's horse, but Heaven had stopped them. This storyteller had sung that Gesar became King of Gling as a result of the race. But Jigmed did not tell the story in that way, so the man lost his temper.

'How could your story not have this passage? Do you not deserve your reputation?'

'Have I ever done anything for ill-gotten gain?' Except for his hat and his stick, he was alone and penniless. 'Have I ever gained anything?'

'Food and drink!' The man was still upset.

'There was no need for me to walk such a long way for food and drink when I tended sheep at home.'

The rider pleaded, 'Will you sing a song of warriors for my beloved horse?' He removed his satin coat and spread it out in the shade of a willow for Jigmed to sit on as he sang. Moved by the young man's grief, Jigmed chose not to sit; instead, he stood in front of the horse and smoothed its mane as he began to sing. He saw that the shadows of the willow gathered, as if they, too, were listening to him. The horse pricked its ears and its dull coat grew lustrous as Jigmed sang. The sight sent the young rider to his knees before Jigmed.

'If my singing was all the medicine the horse needed, then come to me again if you need me.' Jigmed walked out of the willow grove and down to the riverbank. He sat on the grass to think – not about anything in particular, just to get a feel for the world around him. Asters bloomed nearby, and crisp birdsong seemed to drip on his head like rain and go straight into his heart. When the evening sunset again burned the sky bright red, he went up the hill behind him.

'I went to listen to you sing last night,' the old praise-singer said, when he arrived.

'I didn't see you.'

'A true artist usually replies with polite words like, "I welcome your comments."'

'The gods taught me how to sing. Only they can comment on what I do.'

'Why don't you sing about the curses that Joru and Khrothung cast on the eve of the horserace?'

'Do you love curses?'

'You're not bad with them yourself.'

Jigmed did not want to make another enemy, and the prospect of using magic to turn an adept shaman into one was terrifying. Although by now he was a well-known *grungkan*, at heart he was still a simple shepherd. The thought of harming others never crossed his mind.

'They asked me to sing for a sick horse and its hair regained its lustre – that's all that happened.'

'Really?'

Jigmed held his tongue.

'You don't look like a liar.'

'Why would I lie?'

'Don't sing for that horse again.'

Jigmed shook his head slowly; he had liked the animal and he had also liked the rider, who had wept for his horse. He had not liked the man in sunglasses.

'Are you still living in your story? Do you honestly believe that the horserace was run so that an upright person like Gesar could take the throne? Do you know the fate of a winning horse? It is sold to the highest bidder!'

Of course – the man in sunglasses.

'How much is he offering?'

The number was simply too large for Jigmed to comprehend. He never had more than two hundred yuan.

'Do you know why I did what I did?' the old man asked.

'You mean, why you cursed the horse?'

'I want to keep the truly great steeds on this grassland. They are the soul of the grassland, but that man wants to sell the best horses to the city for races. I've heard there are people who bet a lot of money on those races. So you must promise not to comfort that horse with your singing.'

Jigmed did not reply.

'Did you hear what I said?' The man raised his voice. 'And the next time you sing, I hope you will include the part about the curses.'

At this, Jigmed was outraged. He was sure that his story was the true one, chosen by the gods. He spat on the ground and turned to walk away. Though it was still bright on the hill, the valley was submerged in shadow. As he went into the deepening dusk, he began to worry about what he had just done. But the spit had soaked into the grass and could not be retrieved, so he decided to sing again for the horse. But the rider would not let him, saying that the horse would be unable to hold back its explosive energy till the day of the race. Jigmed wanted to ask if it would be sold after it had won, but he could not find the right words.

Jigmed left before the day of the race, though he later heard that the horse had won. But before he left, he met a man with a camera around his neck and a tape recorder in his hand. Jigmed was singing for a crowd when the man came up and placed the recorder before him. 'You're a national treasure,' the man said.

Later that day he was dozing against a pole at the racetrack when he thought he heard himself singing. He woke up and looked around; the singing voice did not stop. It was nearly identical to his own; even the way the lute strings were strummed to fill the pauses was the same. He could see no one singing, but a crowd of people stood around the pole, so he shouted to them, 'Am I dreaming?'

They burst out laughing, and the man he'd seen earlier pointed to the loudspeaker on the pole, where the sound was coming from.

'Who's that?' Jigmed asked.

The man said, 'It's you.'

Jigmed closed his mouth tightly and said, with his eyes, *I'm not making any sound.*

So the man took him into a tent filled with machines and removed a cassette tape from one of them. The singing stopped. He reinserted the tape and the singing resumed. Now Jigmed understood. 'I see. You have a camera for sounds.'

The man, a scholar who specialised in the Gesar song series, put his arm around Jigmed's shoulders and said, 'Let me take pictures of all your singing.'

'Here?'

'Come to the city with me.'

'Now?'

'We'll wait till the horserace is over.'

The scholar took him into the command post tent, where he shook hands with several men. Unable to contain his excitement, he introduced Jigmed to them. 'My biggest reward this time was discovering a national treasure at your race.'

'National treasure?'

'An artisan chosen by the gods.'

'Oh, one of your singers.'

Indifferent looks all around.

'They hid like mice during the years when singing was banned,' one said. 'Now things have relaxed a little, they're emerging from everywhere.'

Jigmed felt he was no longer a man but a mouse; he shrank in front of them.

'Let's ask him to sing before the race, the part about winning the throne,' the scholar persisted.

One of the men laughed, and, walking out of the tent with his arm around the scholar's shoulders, said, 'We respect you as a true scholar, but we're about to hold a meeting. Come and see us another time.'

Jigmed followed them out. The scholar decided they would leave the next day, but before they did, he took his camera to the willow grove with Jigmed, and watched the man he called a national treasure sing to a fine horse, smoothing its mane as he did so.

The Story
The Consort

After the founding of Gling, Gesar realised that there was little for a king to do. The new authority was far more efficient than the loose connections between the tribes had allowed in the past. Did kingship mean simply listening to refined music, drinking wine from golden goblets and jade cups and basking with beautiful women in perfumed robes?

He held court each day, but all that was presented to him was news of favourable weather for crops and peaceful borders. Yet he felt that there should be more.

'Is this what it means to be a king?' he asked.

The ministers, who worked hard in carrying out their duties, were stung by his question, especially Rongtsa Khragan.

'The king should be happy that the nation enjoys peace and prosperity.'

He realised that a king must choose his words with care. When he returned to his private rooms and Brugmo helped him change out of his court attire, he asked her, 'How can everything be perfect so quickly?'

Surprised, she replied, 'Didn't Heaven send you to be a wise king and to provide the people of Gling with a peaceful, comfortable life?'

Weariness crept over Gesar's face, and although Brugmo offered herself to him, hoping he would forget his worries, a strange lethargy continued to flicker in his eyes, like dark clouds drifting across the sky.

She sent for the royal doctor, who prescribed a love potion. When the chief minister heard of it, he said, 'Our king has come from Heaven. Why would he need your trifling skills?'

Khrothung, of course, thought differently. 'The consort is the beauty of all beauties, but she sings the same song night after night. The king's senses are dulled from spending every night with the same woman. All kings have several consorts.'

Rongtsa Khragan could not suggest this to Brugmo, so he led a contingent of high-ranking ministers to the king's mother, Metog Lhartse, who nodded her agreement: she had come from the strictly run Dragon Palace.

'Brugmo has always been proud and competitive, so she will not easily accept a princess from another country. Before my son became king, she and the other eleven prettiest girls of Gling were as close as sisters. We should bring the others into the palace and call them the twelve consorts.'

A great festival took place, with musicians showing off their skills and warriors competing in horsemanship and archery. The eleven girls displayed their most dazzling smiles to the king. Brugmo shed her tears in secret, and nurtured her kinship with them. Indeed, now that the king and his consorts were living together, he no longer appeared burdened by worries.

When Gesar thanked his chief minister for his efforts, Rongtsa Khragan, taking his long white beard in hand, replied, 'I am in my eighties, and I hope to serve the king for another eighty years. The country enjoys peace and prosperity because the king has followed the will of Heaven. Long may the king reign.'

One night it was Meza's turn to serve the king. When he awoke the following morning, he asked her the question he had asked Brugmo: 'Is this what it means to be a king?'

The ministers entered a new round of debate: should they find new consorts for the king? If so, they would have to search outside the country, for he already had the twelve loveliest girls of Gling. The next day Khrothung sought permission for a delegation to travel to other countries with gifts to seek out prospective consorts. Thinking that this was what a king must do, Gesar agreed, as he had for other official matters.

When he returned to his quarters, he found Brugmo weeping. He did not know that the news of his seeking consorts outside the country had already found its way to his private quarters, so he asked why she was crying. She told him that there was dust in her eyes, and he did not press her. And then she asked him the question he had asked her: 'Is this what it means to be a king?'

He lay down, and soon he was dreaming. His celestial mother, Lhamin Dagmo, stood before him.

'Why is my son idle?'

'I have nothing to do.'

'You should not waste your days in indulgence. Your magical powers will diminish, and then how will you fight if the demons rise again?'

Gesar said he would travel to a cave in the mighty Mount Kure, without his consorts, for spiritual renewal.

'Take Meza with you.'

'Why not Brugmo?'

'I am here to tell you Heaven's will. You must stay there for twenty-one days.'

Gesar's celestial mother had come for a reason. To the north there was a country called Yarkam, whose demon king, Lutsan, had heard of Gesar's twelve beautiful consorts. Travelling upon a cloud, Lutsan had come to see them for himself, and now he could think of nothing but Meza. So Lhamin Dagmo had been sent to tell Gesar that he should take Meza with him to keep her out of sight until the demon's obsession faded, and that he should practise Great Anger Magic in case Lutsan attacked. But she did not tell him all of this – just that he should take Meza with him to the cave.

Waking from the dream, Gesar found his room shrouded in the unusual fragrance his celestial mother exuded. Enchanted by it, Brugmo begged him to tell her if the fragrance master had invented a new scent. But Gesar simply told her he was taking Meza to the cave in Mount Kure. Brugmo was distraught.

'I am first among the twelve girls. Why Meza?'

He told her that it was Heaven's will.

Brugmo went to Meza. 'The king is to undergo spiritual renewal in a mountain cave. He wants to take you with him, but you should stay here to look after Mother Metog Lhartse, since you are the most thoughtful of us all.'

Meza nodded. As the gentlest of the twelve, she was no match for the bewitching Brugmo, who went to tell the king that Meza would rather stay to take care of the Mother Metog Lhartse. So, Gesar took Brugmo up the mountain.

The first seven days passed quickly, but on the seventh night Meza had an ominous dream and woke up frightened. She went up the mountain to see Gesar, thinking that, as the king was protected by Heaven, no evil could befall her.

She met Brugmo fetching water at the mountain spring near the cave. 'Sister Brugmo, I have had an ominous dream. Please let me stay near the king.'

'He must not be disturbed,' Brugmo said, 'but I will tell him about the dream.' She left and quickly returned, saying, 'The king says that dreams, particularly women's dreams, are caused by confusion. You may go now.'

Meza had no choice but to go back down the mountain, after asking Brugmo to present to the king some sweetmeats she had made for him. Brugmo offered them to him, without telling him of Meza's visit.

'Hmm,' he said. 'Only Meza makes these so well. Has she been here? Has something happened at the palace?'

'Can I not make them as well as Meza?'

Gesar knew that Brugmo was not telling the truth, but he did not pursue the matter. 'You are all so close,' he said to Brugmo. 'Why must you quarrel? Is it because you are women?'

'If the king wanted no one but me, we would never argue.'

'I am to blame?'

Brugmo lowered her eyes. 'You are not.'

Gesar felt a pain in his heart when he saw her face, for he still loved her the most.

As his spiritual renewal continued, he lost track of time, for he had told Brugmo not to enter the cave before the twenty-first day. But one morning she came to the entrance, hung her head and told him that Lutsan had stolen Meza. Now Gesar understood his celestial mother's request. He was unsure whether to blame himself or Brugmo but he suspected that Khrothung had been involved: not only had Gesar won the race, become king and kept the prize, Brugmo, but he had taken the other eleven girls as consorts. This had made Khrothung angry, and when Gesar had left for the mountain cave, Khrothung had sent a raven to Lutsan with the news.

'I wanted to bring Meza, but you would not let me,' Gesar said to Brugmo.

'If you had brought her, I would have been taken by the demon.'

When Gyatsa Zhakar heard of Meza's plight, he brought his soldiers to help his brother.

'Lutsan came alone to take my consort,' Gesar said, 'without the help of a single soldier. I will have no one with me to rescue her. Elder Brother, please return to camp and work with the chief minister while I am gone.' Then he sent for his horse.

Brugmo prepared a farewell drink for the king, who thought it was meant to bolster his courage, but she had laced it with a potion that made him forget his purpose. When Rkayngkar Perpo was brought from the hills to be saddled outside the palace, his master did not come out to him. The horse whinnied. At this, Gesar was roused.

'I believe I should be making a long journey,' he said.

'The king need not worry,' Brugmo said. 'Go back to sleep. You have been dreaming.'

Again Gesar's celestial mother came to him in a dream, but this time with a severe countenance. 'So, your vow to eliminate the world's demons was all for show. Your true intention was to come to the human realm to enjoy its wine and women,' she said.

He jolted awake, though he still could not remember what he had to do. He left the palace, and found Rkayngkar Perpo. He climbed into the saddle and held the reins, but did not know where to go. Brugmo came with another drink, but this time he poured it on the ground, drenching the flowers and grass, which immediately failed to turn with the movement of the sun.

Ashamed, Brugmo told Gesar what he must do. He spurred his horse and soon he was beyond Gling's borders, in Lutsan's land. By dusk he had reached a city near a heart-shaped mountain. The walls were hung with banners made of corpses. *So this is what the demon's land looks like*, Gesar said to himself. As he dismounted at the gate to the city, a group of little demons drew their bows. He pounded on the bronze gate so loudly that all the little demons' arrows fell to the ground, making them screech. The gate opened, and out walked a dazzling girl, with a wild and rugged air.

She reached out to touch his broad shoulders. 'A general with no soldiers. But you are so handsome that I will spare your life.'

Lutsan was unusually powerful, but how, Gesar wondered, had he made such a remarkable transformation? He pushed the woman to the ground, and placed the tip of his crystal sword to her chest. 'Are you human or demon?'

'Tell me your name so that I will not forget your face, even after I die.'

He told her.

'My name is Atag Lhamo, and I am the younger sister of the demon king, Lutsan. I am responsible for protecting our borders.' She added, in her melodious voice, 'I've long heard of you, since we live so close to Gling. They say that pretty peacocks fall for true dragons. Great King, you have stolen my heart before your sword has even pierced my chest.'

'I will spare your life if you help me kill the demon king.'

'I will do your bidding.'

'Even if it means killing your brother?'

Atag Lhamo led Gesar into the palace and ordered her attendants to wait outside.

'Great King,' she said, 'I was born to this place because I took a wrong turning during reincarnation. My brother has betrothed me to one of his warriors, a man with a frog's head. Great King, I would rather spend the rest of my life with you, so take the city if you wish. If you are thirsty, I will offer you good tea. If you are too hot, I will shade you with a white silk curtain. If you are troubled, I will comfort you.'

Gesar, already drawn to her beauty, was now moved by her sincerity, and they spent the night as husband and wife. Compared to the twelve beauties of Gling, she was gentle and submissive, but with a wild streak that brought him great pleasure. With her he felt as if he were returning to camp in victory after a great conquest. The next day they rode their horses together, galloping freely, calling up wind and rain, and ordering the mountain god to chase out fierce animals for them to kill in the foothills.

But Gesar's knitted brows told Atag Lhamo that she would not be able to save her brother, no matter how much pleasure Gesar took in her. So she ordered a sumptuous feast, and when Gesar asked her why, she said, 'It is to bid my husband farewell.'

'But will you not return with me to Gling?'

'Great King, you will never return to Gling unless you kill Lutsan and rescue Meza. You should leave tomorrow, and I will wait for you to return in victory.'

After the feast, they retired behind a white silk curtain, where she took a ring from her finger which she gave to him. 'My king, since I will not take you to kill my brother, I can only guide you to his palace. I lack the heart to tell you how to despatch him.'

Her candour increased his affection for her. If she had pleaded on her brother's behalf, he might have spared the demon's life.

In a single day Rkayngkar Perpo could travel a distance that would take a mortal horse half a year. So they soon reached a place where, as revealed by Atag Lhamo, a ridge shaped like a sleeping white elephant appeared. A slithering black snake of a bridge spanned the river before the mountain. On the far side of the bridge lay a body of water that was as white as milk; Gesar and Rkayngkar Perpo drank from it before they galloped on to a mountain that resembled a wild boar with its hackles up. In front of the mountain lay another body of water, black as pitch. When the sound of Rkayngkar Perpo's hoofs reached the lake, a black dog as big as a bear leaped out. Everything was as Atag Lhamo had said, so Gesar took out Atag Lhamo's ring, and the dog retreated into the water at the sight of it.

They continued on to a maze created by the demon king. At each junction, the white path let them live while the black path led to death. The white path took them to another city, where the eaves of the houses were made of bones. There, a three-headed demon turned its deadly gaze on Gesar, but he met it with a light of his own, then took out his sword, lopped off its heads and rode on without a backward glance. Atag Lhamo had told him that the three heads would grow back if he turned to look.

It dawned on him that he had seen nothing but black and white after entering the demon country; everything, the mountains, lakes and plants, was either black or white. No wonder Atag Lhamo left. The next demon he met had five heads and was herding a flock of sheep. It turned out to be a hard-working farmer named Sheng-ngon from the country of Rong. He had been snatched by Lutsan with many of his countrymen, but as Sheng-ngon knew a little magic, the demon king had chosen him to grow extra heads and guard an important pass. He told Gesar that, if he could change back to human form and become a farmer in Gling, he would help him.

'Then you must discover where the demon is and tell me what my consort, Meza, is doing.'

Sheng-ngon agreed and went to Lutsan's nine-spired palace.

Lutsan detected an unusual odour on him. 'Have you met a stranger?' he asked.

'One of the white sheep was sick, so I slaughtered it. Its blood must have spattered me. That will be what the king smelt.'

Lutsan was not convinced. 'Let Meza give you food. I must go out to see for myself that no stranger is close at hand.'

He mounted a cloud and left the palace, giving Sheng-ngon the chance to speak with Meza.

'Yesterday I met an Indian merchant from Gling who was passing through our land.'

Meza had not wanted to talk to Lutsan's five-headed demon, but mention of Gling aroused her interest. A bright light shone in her eyes. 'Did he bring news of Gling?'

Lutsan had showered affection on her, but no pretty clothes or fine food, no songs or dances, no banquets or merriment could smooth her brow. All in the demon country knew that she missed Gling.

'I could bring him here and you may ask him yourself.'

'Bring him to my private apartments tomorrow, but do not let the king see him.'

The next day Sheng-ngon disguised Gesar as an Indian merchant and brought him to Meza.

Something about the man's face seemed familiar to her. Her hair ornaments could not hide the sorrow on her face, and beneath the extravagant clothes her once full body was wasting away.

'Are you really from Gling? Have you ever been to the court and met King Gesar?' she asked, in a trembling voice.

Now Gesar knew that Meza had not ceased thinking of him even though she had been forced to become the demon king's consort, so without a word he took off the Indian merchant's clothes to reveal the armour he wore beneath them. Then Meza took off the costume of the demon king's consort to reveal the white skirt she had worn with Gesar in Gling. As tears streamed down her face, he took her into his arms.

'Great King, please take me home to Gling.'

'I must first kill the demon who stole my consort.'

Then Meza took him to see Lutsan's rice bowl, his bed, his iron cannon balls and arrows. Gesar lay down on the bed, which made him look like an infant. He could not pick up the rice bowl, let alone lift the cannon balls and arrows. He was abruptly reminded of the Great Anger Magic his celestial mother had wanted him to practise, for she had known he would need it. He had failed to master it. Now Meza urged him to leave.

'And I will not go back until I have killed him.'

'I have heard that by eating one of the demon king's yellow cows one grows more powerful.'

They killed one of the cows, and as Gesar devoured it, he grew taller. Then Meza told him that the demon king stored his soul in several places: in a bowl of blood, in a tree that could be felled only with a golden axe, and in a cow that would die only if pierced by a golden arrow.

Gesar emptied the bowl of blood, cut down the tree and killed the cow, then returned to the palace to challenge the demon king. Without his soul, Lutsan was quickly vanquished.

Gesar did not return to Gling until the waters were clear, the mountains green and the flowers blooming, until even the cows, horses and birds in the woods became brightly coloured again. Sheng-ngon travelled with Gesar and Meza to the lake with the mirror-smooth surface, and as the king walked away, Sheng-ngon shouted, 'Great King, you did not remove my demon heads.'

Gesar called, 'Look at yourself in the water.'

So Sheng-ngon did, and saw that he was once again the farmer from Rong, and that he wore the feathered hat of a minister of Gling.

Gesar and his consort soon arrived at the border fortress guarded by Atag Lhamo, who ordered a banquet for a three-day celebration, saying that she wanted to give herself a grand wedding: once they returned to Gling, she would be simply another consort. The banquet lasted not three days but three years. Song and dance never ceased in the palace, while the fragrance of meat and the aroma of wine travelled many *li* from it. What Atag Lhamo had disliked most about the demon land was that everything was in black and white, and now she was reluctant to leave. Meza, still ashamed at having become the demon king's consort and knowing that many more women were waiting for the king's favours in Gling, was happy to stay. Here only outspoken Atag Lhamo shared the king with her. The two women knew what the other was thinking, without a word uttered between them. And so they stayed, for three long years.

The Storyteller
Romance

The scholar took Jigmed to a Tibetan radio station. Jigmed was happy in the studio with the lights dimmed. When the young programme announcer, Asang, was on air, she spoke to him in an intimate voice, though she would not look at him outside the studio. He wondered if Brugmo, the consort, had spoken in such a voice, bewitching yet serious.

'Before the storytelling begins, I'd like to ask Master Jigmed two questions.'

He straightened, his body tense, as if an electric current ran through him.

'Master Jigmed, how does it feel to be the first person to sing this epic story on air?'

'It makes me happy.' He heard his voice go hoarse.

Asang laughed. 'I believe that Master Jigmed means he feels honoured.'

'I feel happy.'

'Now please tell our listeners something about your time in the city and at our station.'

'I feel happy.' His voice was stubbornly croaky.

She was growing impatient. 'Master Jigmed means that he enjoys his life here. Now, let's hear some songs.'

She left him alone, though through the glass partition he could see her joking and flirting with the sound technician. He began to sing, and was Jigmed again. The walls disappeared and he returned to open grassland below snowcapped mountains. Powerful gods, humans and demons travelled back and forth between Heaven and Earth, scheming, praying, fighting. In his stories the prettiest women were also the strangest, for they cried like village women, fought for favours, and became entangled with humans and demons. Yet somehow they were always the most important characters in the story.

When his singing ended, the host returned. 'Listeners, it is now ten o'clock. Please remember that tomorrow night at nine we will play a live performance of the epic song of King Gesar. Be sure to tune in.'

Then Asang stood behind him and bent over, and he felt as if a large bird had descended from the sky to cover the pitiful creatures below with its shadow. He was trembling. He could smell her perfume as, her lips nearly touching his neck, she said, 'You sang well tonight, but you don't understand women.'

He nearly fainted.

When his head cleared, he was alone in the recording studio. On his way out, he took a wrong turn in the maze of hallways and ended up in a much bigger and more complex area, the one for Chinese broadcasting. There, he told everyone he met that he was looking for Asang. But no one knew who she was. Somehow he managed to walk out of the building and into dazzling sunlight.

In the hostel, he felt hot and cold all over as he lay down on his bed. He dreamed that Asang, wearing Brugmo's splendid clothes, was pacing back and forth on a green hill, casting her worried gaze to the north. He tried to tell her to run, for danger lurked, but could not find his voice.

That afternoon, the scholar from the research institute came to see him, and when he saw that Jigmed had not touched the food sent up from the cafeteria, he said, 'You're sick.'

Am I? Jigmed wondered. But his head was filled with the girl who had hosted the programme, and he was afraid. 'I want to go home,' he said.

The scholar said seriously, 'A true storyteller, a real *grungkan*, has no home. The world is his home.'

'I want to go back to the grassland.'

'But the government will give the best performer money, a house, expenses.'

He wanted to argue that a house was not a home. Destined to wander, why would a *grungkan* need a house? But he was, after all, Jigmed, and he did not know how to argue.

'I'm afraid,' was all he could say.

The scholar smiled. 'Maybe that's your sensitivity as an artist, a people's artist.'

A new storyteller came the next day, a coarse, middle-aged woman who had been struck by lightning while out grazing cows. When she had come to, she had known, without instruction, how to sing the Gesar epic. Jigmed bumped into her that afternoon in the hostel corridor. He was on his way back to his room with a bowl of cafeteria food when the woman stopped him. 'They tell me you're a good singer.'

He nodded.

Shyly, she said, 'My name is Yangcan Drolma.'

He laughed. Drolma, which meant 'celestial fairy', did not suit her loud voice and fierce eyes.

'Let's see what they're feeding us,' Yangcan Drolma said. 'Oh, my, soup. And steamed buns. That's all I was given the last time I was here.'

'But you're back.'

'Come with me.' She took his hand, and they went to her room. 'They said I could cook my own meals, but I'm not allowed to use firewood or electricity.' She had two rooms, the inner one for sleeping, the outer one for cooking and drinking tea. A hotplate rested in the middle of the room. She touched his shoulder to guide him to a cushion. 'I'll make you some tea.'

The water boiled quickly, and she added milk powder to make aromatic milk tea. She laid out cheese and poured out his soup, with the thin greens floating on top. Then, with a smile, she said, 'Now you can eat your steamed buns.'

He finished enough cheese for three meals, and Yangcan Drolma seemed pleased as she watched him.

★

The next day, as Jigmed left to sing, Yangcan Drolma put a Thermos flask into his hand. 'Some tea for when you're thirsty.'

'I'm not supposed to drink anything when I sing.'

'Nonsense. They can, so why can't you?'

'They do it outside.'

'Then go outside to drink.'

'She won't let me.'

'And who is she?'

'The girl, Asang.'

Yangcan Drolma gave him a knowing look. 'The government pays for our singing. You don't have to listen to her every word.'

He did not drink his tea that day. Not because he didn't want to, but because Asang would not let him.

'We finally managed to get rid of your pasture smell,' she said, 'and now it's back.'

He had to leave the flask outside the studio, and took it back, untouched, to the hostel that evening.

Talk began to spread about the daydreaming shepherd who had fallen in love with the fashionable radio host. When Asang came to the recording studio she refused to speak to him. He wanted to say, 'It's not true. How could I dare to think of loving you?' But when the lights dimmed in the studio, and she spoke in her rich voice, he was thrown into confusion. Her voice was magnetic, and her skin gave off a sweet perfume.

One day she said, 'If you want to sing again, you must tell those gossips that it never entered your head.'

'What never entered my head?'

She began to cry. 'You dirty, ugly thing! Tell them you've never been in love with me.'

He lowered his head, but he could not hold back the truth. 'I dreamed about you at night.'

With a shriek, she stormed out of the studio.

The others rushed in. 'What did you do? Tell us!'

He hadn't done anything. Could it be that his words carried poisonous barbs, like those of a sorcerer? He seemed even to have hurt Yangcan Drolma, who spat at his shadow. Earlier, when they had gone into and come out of the station together, people had joked that the two singers were a couple made in heaven. Drolma had smiled sweetly when she heard that. But now she spat at his shadow.

A few days earlier, they'd argued over the story.

'It wasn't entirely the fault of Atag Lhamo and Meza that Gesar stayed so long in the demon country,' Yangcan Drolma insisted. 'If he hadn't fallen in love each time he met a new woman, and had stayed faithful to Brugmo, there wouldn't have been so much trouble.'

'We should not criticise a story created by the gods,' Jigmed replied.

'The story came from male gods. It would be quite different if it had come from goddesses,' Dolma retorted.

Frightened, he spread out the banner with the embroidered image of the god and knelt to show his obeisance. Yangcan Drolma fell to her knees beside him to ask for forgiveness.

But now Jigmed was too ashamed to show his face at the radio station, and this time he really did fall ill. He heard the door creak, and Yangcan Drolma walked in.

'What are you doing here?' he asked weakly.

'Now you know who treats you well, who is the right woman for you.'

She bent down and kissed his forehead, then his hands, covering him with hot tears. But the heat from those tears could not enter his heart.

'Please go back to your room,' he pleaded. 'I'll come for tea tomorrow.'

She kissed him again. 'My poor man, my poor, suffering man.'

After she had closed the door behind her, he wiped away the tears she had left on his face, and the memory of the scene in the recording studio flooded his mind. So he left without saying goodbye, disappearing from the city. No one knew where he had gone.

The Story
The Weapons Tribe

Something troubled Gyatsa Zhakar, something he had planned for a long time. He was waiting for Gesar to return from subduing the demon country to ask his permission to carry out his scheme. But Gesar had been away for three years, and rumours flew that he was entertaining himself in the demon land to the north with Meza and his new consort Atag Lhamo, and had no thought of returning. People began to doubt that he should be their king, for even though he had powerful magic, he was wilful. Metog Lhartse repeated that Heaven had sent him to be their king: there could be no alternative. The chief minister, Rongtsa Khragan, shared her view.

But Gyatsa Zhakar was burdened with anxiety. He said to the chief minister, 'My mother says that in China an emperor loses his people's support if he indulges in banquets and merrymaking while ignoring his duties.'

The chief minister replied sternly, 'Our king is a son of the deities.'

'Mother tells me that the Emperor of China is called the Son of Heaven, meaning that he, too, is a son of the deities.'

'You are Gesar's brother, the king's favourite warrior. You speak like the devious Khrothung. Are you not aware that we have instituted a new law that makes slanderous talk of court matters a crime?'

'I wish only that you would send an envoy to urge the king's return.'

The chief minister sighed. 'Before he left, the king told me to continue as usual, collecting taxes and mediating disputes. He ordered you to guard the borders.'

'It is in regard to the borders that I must report to the king. Who would have thought I would need to wait three years?'

'Return to the border region for the time being. We cannot question the king's authority. We must not doubt him.'

Gyatsa Zhakar had no choice but to bid his mother farewell, though he repeated his complaint to her.

'Gling has become a country, but in many ways it has not yet achieved perfection,' his mother responded. 'If following your orders can help move it in that direction, then that is what you should do.'

He then told her that Uncle Khrothung had invited him to a banquet and that he did not know how to respond.

His mother shuddered. 'Get on your horse, my son,' she said, 'and return to the border region at once.'

It was a moonless night when he rode back to his camp. As he left, he saw, by the light of the stars, a figure that resembled Brugmo, standing on the roof of the palace, gazing to the north. Unlike many people of Gling, who were proficient in all sorts of magic, Gyatsa Zhakar had gained his reputation through hard work, and could not see her clearly from a distance. Brugmo, though, had enough magic to see him. She sent an owl to him, which alighted on his shoulder and spoke in her voice.

'I heard that you had returned, and assumed you would come to see me tomorrow.'

He dismounted and, facing the palace, answered respectfully, 'Honourable Consort, I came to report to the king, but he has been delayed in his expedition to the demon land in the north. I must return to the border region. The chief minister, who adheres strictly to rules and orders, did not have the courage to send someone to fetch him. Would it please the honourable consort to come forward and request the king's return?'

All Brugmo could do was sigh. Her own selfish design had caused all of the trouble, and she could only suffer silently. But Gyatsa Zhakar knew nothing of the palace intrigues, and misread her. He mounted his horse and prepared to ride on, but Brugmo stopped him.

'I have been uneasy over the past few days, as if some calamity were about to befall us.'

'If the honourable consort stays in her palace and awaits the king's return, what is there to be afraid of?'

'The fortune-teller has said that an evil aura threatens my constellation. When that happens . . .'

'I will protect the honourable consort with my own life, if necessary.' With that, he spurred his horse and disappeared into the night. The owl had flown from his shoulder, but he could still hear Brugmo's sighs in his ears, and they filled him with foreboding. He could no longer wait for the king's return to carry out his plan. Who knew when, or even if, that would be?

In the old days, the outcome of battles between tribes had been determined by the leaders' skills. Nearly every one of the thirty Gling warriors had had special powers, and gods and demons had joined the struggle, so the common soldier had not been useful in battle. But Gyatsa Zhakao had heard that once a nation was established, the gods would return to Heaven and its people would lose their magical powers. *Well*, he thought, *the gods have certainly disappeared from Gling.*

Now Gyatsa Zhakar wanted to turn his soldiers into an army that did not rely upon magic. He had trained them from a book of tactics his mother had given him. When he returned from the palace, he moved an entire tribe from the grassland along the Yellow river south into the mountains. Of course they were no longer called a tribe: they were a chiliarch. Gyatsa Zhakar told them that they would go south until they reached the homeland they had been forced to leave because of the snowstorm. When they reached the familiar river, the thousand families were to settle in a deep mountain valley or along the steep riverbank, wherever they could smelt copper and iron.

Their leader said, 'We will set out in three days, but I hate to hear people weep over leaving their homes.'

Gyatsa Zhakar suggested composing a song to replace the weeping, and when the tribe left, they were indeed singing a travelling song. Gyatsa Zhakar and his soldiers walked ahead, and when they reached a forest too dense even for the wind to blow through, he told them that this was the time to practise their sword skills and to build their muscles. So the soldiers opened up a broad, bright path in the forest with their swords. When boulders blocked their way, the junior officers said, 'Come, this is a fine opportunity to practise wrestling with giants,' and they rolled the boulders down into mountain streams. When wolves and tigers appeared, the soldiers declared they would improve their archery. Now the best archers were draped in striped tiger pelts.

They finally stopped at the banks of the great Jinsha river, where the valleys were arrayed like lotus petals, and the surrounding mountain peaks were shaped like valiant swordsmen. The severe winds and snowstorms of March had the grassland in their grip, but here a warm wind blew through valleys that opened up to the south-east. Groves of chestnuts, roses and peaches bloomed in the valleys. A few days after their arrival, an old man woke up early one morning after a spring rain and discovered that his willow-cane, which he had stuck carelessly into the ground, had sprouted new leaves.

The site had one more advantage: they did not have to worry about building houses, at least not straight away, for they could live in caves. They found ore in rocks that seemed to know the magic of transformation. Piled high on the smelting ground in the rain and wind, the rocks turned red or green. They had copper and they had iron. The tribe was known for its many artisans: stone masons, furnace builders, smelting experts and weapons makers. Now they had knives, swords, spears, arrows, horse fittings, maces and armour, all of which shone a dark green when Gyatsa Zhakar's soldiers stood in proud formation. He was convinced that no enemy could withstand a charge by his troops.

When autumn arrived, they heard that tribes from further south were planning to steal their harvest, but Gyatsa Zhakar would not allow his army to meet them in battle. Instead, when the harvest had been gathered in, he made them drill on the barren fields. The barbarians spied on the troops for three days and three nights, then came to surrender. Gyatsa Zhakar sent these new subjects to the palace. The chief minister had never heard of the places these people came from. As he bowed to the north, he said, 'King Gesar, your ageing minister sends his congratulations. Thanks to your reputation, even uncivilised southern tribes have come to pledge their allegiance and offer their vast lands.'

The Story
The King Forgets to Return

North-east of Gling, where a desert, a grassland and a salt lake converged, lay the country of Hor. This vast territory was ruled over by a king who called himself the Emperor of Heaven and had installed his three sons as kings. Since these sons lived in yurts of different colours, they were called the Black King, the White King and the Yellow King. The White King was the most skilful in the art of war, and was aided by an indomitable warrior, Shanpa Merutse, who was both straightforward and ferocious.

The same year that Gyatsa Zhakar moved a tribe to the Jinsha river to smelt iron, the White King's favourite Chinese consort died. Believing that only a foreign woman could ameliorate his sorrow, he ordered a parrot, a dove, a peacock and a crow to search for a foreign beauty.

Inauspiciously, the four birds flew towards Gling.

When they arrived at the border between Hor and Gling, the parrot said, 'We are like arrows shot by the White King – easy to fly off but hard to return. Finding the woman he seeks is beyond us. Besides, even if we find her, he will want to take her by force, and who knows how many lives might be lost? Why not flee before that happens?'

'Flee to where?'

'Dove came with the Chinese consort so he can return to China. Peacock will return to India, and I will go back to Monyul in the south. It is even easier for you, Crow. The world is filled with your kind, so you can go wherever you wish.'

As the three other birds soared into the clouds, the crow remained on the tree. It had been wondering who would take credit for finding the king a beautiful woman. Since it was not a pretty bird, the White

King had never given it even a sidelong glance when bestowing awards for merit. Now was its chance: if it found the beauty the king sought, it would not share the praise with anyone. That thought sustained it through hunger as it circled the sky above Gling; but after forty-nine days it had still failed to find a beauty to meet the king's ideal. It was not that there were no pretty girls in Gling, but the news of the White King's search had spread, and without King Gesar, their protector, the people were frightened when the crow circled the skies above Gling. Brugmo alone went to a high place to gaze into the distance, but the crow, skirting the palace and its warriors' arrows, never spotted her.

Khrothung had been out of sorts since Gesar had taken the throne. That day, he got out of bed feeling especially irritable. He used his magic to change into a hawk and fly into the sky, since the hawk's brain was too small to contain his human worries. When the crow appeared, the hawk pounced and would have torn off its wings if the crow had not squawked, 'Spare my life. I was sent by the White King.'

'One of the White King's underlings. Did he send you in search of pretty women?'

'Yes.'

Since the hawk's brain was too small to develop a nascent idea, it flew over a hill and landed behind some trees, where it changed back into human form and thought hard for a minute. Then Khrothung reassumed his hawk form and flew back, sending the crow into a flutter.

'Don't be afraid. The most beautiful woman of Gling is standing on the roof of the palace,' the hawk said.

The crow spotted Brugmo. Her beauty was beyond words, and her eyes, tinged with sadness, were very like those of the late Chinese consort. It dived down to her and snatched a string of turquoise hair ornaments, then flapped its wings and cawed, 'The brave White King of Hor will soon be here to make you his bride.'

The crow flew straight to the White King, and complained of the other three birds' desertion. But the king was impatient. 'Have you found a beauty to my liking?'

The crow gloated as it flew up to his throne and gave him the hair ornaments.

'After Gesar subjugated the demon country, the new consort lured him into her arms, and he has not returned. Brugmo is left alone in the palace.'

'I shall send troops to bring her to me.'

When the king's senior general, Shanpa Merutse, received the order, he said, 'Great King, Gling may be small but Brugmo is the king's consort. We cannot fetch her without causing a war that brings suffering to the people.'

Naturally the White King would not listen, but he sent for Princess Jetsun Yeshe to cast a divination.

Jetsun Yeshe, daughter of a Hor prince, was one of the country's true beauties. When the Chinese consort had died, some had suggested that their king marry her, but he refused. A gifted girl, she had received instruction from an unusual teacher, and was accurate with her predictions. The most powerful king is the one who can keep his secrets; the aura of power as he sits on the throne is enhanced when no one knows what he is thinking. The White King knew that his authority would be compromised by the princess, which was why he had suppressed his desire for her and was looking for a consort among the foreign tribes.

'The signs point to danger,' Jetsun Yeshe said. 'The king must not send his troops for such a trifle.'

The king's laugh was cold. 'You say that because you do not want me to marry this woman from Gling. If not for your youth and beauty, I'd have you beheaded and your body tossed to the hungry mountain wolves that disturb my sleep every night.'

Jetsun Yeshe left with a sad smile, showing no sign of alarm.

Seeing that the king would not budge, Shanpa Merutse mustered his soldiers and set out with the White King.

Unaware that troops from the north-east were advancing on them, the people of Gling placidly awaited their king's return. Khrothung, who alone knew of the impending attack from Hor, flew to see Gyatsa Zhakar in the south.

'My dear nephew,' he said, 'Gling has had no leader for three years. The chief minister is ineffectual, so you must come forward as regent.'

Gyatsa Zhakar objected: 'If you mean me no harm, do not say that to anyone else.'

'You have been smelting iron, making weapons and training your soldiers. People are wondering about your plans.'

'I am doing this to make Gling truly strong. When the king returns, I shall turn over my commander's seal and return to China with my mother to visit her homeland.' This he had written in a letter to the chief minister. But he was not unaware of the rumours and remained uneasy after Khrothung had left, so, with two attendants, he returned to the palace to see the chief minister.

The chief minister said, 'What you have done is good, but you should have waited until the king returned.'

'What if someone were to attack us now?'

'Dear nephew, who would be so foolhardy? Besides, King Gesar's intelligence is as vast as the ocean. Would he sit by and watch war break out at the border?' He changed the subject. 'I hear that you built an iron wall for the fortress.'

'A border fortress must be invincible.'

'Should an official's residence surpass the palace?'

'You seem different from the steward I once knew.'

'Dear nephew, did we not wish for a country? That is what we have. You should not return to the border. Stay here to guard the palace, and set my mind at rest.'

So Gyatsa Zhakar did not return, which made Brugmo happy. But she found it difficult to bring up the White King's intentions, so she said only, 'I have had bad dreams every night. Something terrible may happen. But I feel safer now that you are here guarding the palace.'

The White King, whose army had reached the border, sent a messenger to demand Brugmo. She wept when she heard, and Gyatsa Zhakar begged to be allowed to go to the demon country to fetch the king, but his request fell on deaf ears: he had no magic powers, so who knew how long it would take him to cross the high mountains and deep rivers? If war broke out, a brave general like him would be indispensable to Gling.

In the end, they decided to send the white crane, Gling's soul-bird, north. But when the bird arrived, Gesar had been drinking with his consorts. 'I think I know this bird,' he said.

The bird spoke: 'I am the soul-bird of Gling and you are the King of Gling, so of course you have seen me before. But Gling has missed its king for many years, and now Hor has sent an army to take Brugmo by force. The people of Gling desire their king's speedy return.'

Gesar declared that they would set out early the next day. But when he awoke shortly after daybreak, he drank the spirit offered by his consorts, and forgot about his departure, asking Meza why so many people were gathered there. Recalling that Brugmo's jealousy had caused her to be trapped in the demon country, Meza told Gesar that they were rehearsing a great play for the king, and his departure was delayed for another year.

Imperilled Gling sent a magpie to him, but it perched on the city gate and chirped anxiously. Before its departure, Brugmo had told it that the king's magical powers would ensure that he understood it, but strong drink and women had dulled his senses.

'Is that bird trying to tell us something?' Gesar asked his consorts.

Knowing that Brugmo had sent it, Meza replied, 'Why should a bird make all that noise when the King is trying to enjoy himself? The king has not used his bow and arrow for a long time.'

With a single arrow Gesar killed the messenger magpie.

Another year passed.

Brugmo pleaded with the chief minister to send a third messenger to the king, but Rongtsa Khragan replied, 'We have sent two already. The king must have his reasons for not returning to us.'

People began to complain that the chief minister was no longer the same wise old steward of earlier days. He retorted, 'You must not doubt the king's wisdom.'

No one could respond to that, so they held their tongues.

Brugmo's last resort was the fox. Since it could not speak, she gave it her ring, believing that the king would remember her when he saw it. Avoiding the consorts, the fox found the king and spat out the ring in front of him. It reminded him of something, so he went to the top of the fortress and gazed into the sky, believing that his celestial mother would tell him if something important was happening. But he saw only clouds blowing across a sky as blue as the ocean. Then he recalled that he carried a crystal mirror, so he took it out and peered into it. What he saw shocked him: Hor soldiers and their horses had massed at the border and were ready to attack Gling. He looked to the palace, and saw Brugmo's haggard face. He sent an order to leave before the moon rose and mouted his horse. But then he drank two cups of farewell wine and climbed off his horse.

Gesar did not know this, but the wine in the demon country brought on forgetfulness. Since the demon land had no subjects of its own, Lutsan had taken people from other lands and installed them there; he gave them the wine to make them forget their homelands.

The Story
The Death of Gyatsa

The senior general, Danma, who was guarding the northern border, climbed a hill with his trusted soldiers and saw the powerful troops of Hor in tight formation. The Yellow King was stationed in the middle; to his left the Black King's troops were arrayed like the wing of a hawk, and to his right the White King's troops comprised the second wing. Densely packed reinforcements brought up the rear, while Shanpa Merutse's advance guards were in front, the arrowhead of this formidable army.

Devoid of evil air, Gling was bathed in an atmosphere of peace and prosperity. Danma had only a few dozen soldiers with him as he inspected the border, and he had been ordered to take no rash action. Yet he recalled his pledge of loyalty to Gesar, and knew he would miss an opportunity to serve his country if he did not act in this moment of national crisis. Having sent back his soldiers to report to the palace, he resolved to fight the Hor armies on his own.

His horse spoke: 'They are as numerous as the hairs on an ox. If you and I ride out against them, they will stop us with one volley of arrows as dense as a swarm of locusts. If we are to have a chance at victory, we . . .' And the horse whispered its plan to Danma.

Danma dismounted and limped towards the Hor camp. His horse followed slowly, as though it were lame. When they reached the camp of the advance guard, Danma leaped back on the horse and fought his way into the middle formation. There he found the battle horses of the Hor soldiers grazing in the valley and took advantage of the chaos he had created to herd them into Gling territory.

Shanpa Merutse, who had not been eager to fight a battle, used this opportunity to advise the White King: 'If a limping soldier and a lame horse from Gling are so formidable, we will not be able to withstand Gesar at the head of a large army.'

But the White King would not be dissuaded: 'You have undermined the soldiers' resolve in the face of battle. If it were not for your previous victories, you would now suffer the sting of my whip.'

No worthy warrior could take such a slight, so Shanpa Merutse led twenty thousand of his troops into Gling. On the way, they met Gyatsa Zhakar with his army, coming to Danma's aid. Soon blood flowed like a river and the sky grew dark. But the people of Hor could not take the upper hand, and turned back to their border, while the Gling army, having suffered heavy losses, gave up the chase. If the enemy had launched their full attack at that moment, Gyatsa Zhakar could not have held the line.

The two sides remained at the border, gauging each other's strength, and for the next year Rongtsa Khragan, attired in bright clothing as befitted his station, travelled back and forth between the armies with messages of truth and falsehood to confuse the enemy. The White King was duped by this strategy, and the citizens of Gling were glad to see that the old steward was himself again. But the situation unnerved Khrothung.

One day, Rongtsa Khragan sent another letter to the White King, suggesting that they withdraw their respective troops before the harsh winter descended. They could then decide whether to fight or negotiate the following year. But the White King was reluctant to give up and decided to launch another large-scale attack. If he failed, there would still be time to discuss withdrawal.

Unexpectedly, the White King encountered no resistance for the first thirty *li*. But at sixty *li*, the Gling army counterattacked. After days of fighting, the Gling forces showed signs of weakening – their defeat seemed imminent – and the chief minister agreed to let Gyatsa Zhakar bring up his troops from the south, but by then it was too late.

Brugmo knew that she had been the direct cause of this war, and that it was also her fault that Gesar had remained in the demon country for so many years. Since she was the cause, she decided, only she could be the solution. She would have to eat the bitter fruit she had grown. The king had not returned after she had sent the fox, which could mean only that he had tired of her. So be it. She would go with the White King, and sent him a letter, asking him to withdraw his troops.

The White King sent Shanpa Merutse to bring her back.

'I will leave in three days,' Brugmo said.

'Why three days?'

'I am the consort, yet I was as jealous as a village woman. I must repent.'

Three days later, Shanpa Merutse came again.

'Wait another three days. I must repent for having lost the favour of a son of the deities.'

Another three days passed. Shanpa Merutse returned. 'The king is not a patient man,' he said. 'He will launch another attack if Brugmo does not leave with me now.'

'Please ask him to wait just three more days.' She reflected that she had learned how to be a virtuous and graceful consort, but Gesar had yet to learn to be the true king of a large nation, with wisdom and keen insight. She needed three days to mourn the loss of him. She placed a ruby before her, and when the pain in her heart was at its keenest, the gem broke into splinters. She turned to her maid. 'Even Heaven knows how I repent and suffer, but the king does not. When he returns, tell him that my body is gone and that my heart was broken here in Gling.'

The maid knelt in front of her and said, 'I ask the consort to recall how I came to be your personal maid.'

She had been a shepherdess but resembled Brugmo in face and figure, and for that she was selected to be her maid.

'Because you are like me.'

'I could not possibly possess your grace but the White King has never met you, so I ask to go to his court in your place.'

Brugmo replied, weeping, 'Then I must ask you to suffer for my sake. When the king returns, I will ask him to send an army to bring you home.'

Brugmo hid in the palace on the third day, and her attendants dressed the maid in the consort's clothes. When Shanpa Merutse came for her, she left with him, looking graceful and delicate; but she could not stop weeping once she was on horseback. Shanpa Merutse was suspicious: the woman before him looked like Brugmo yet she wailed like a commoner. However, he was angry with the White King for going to war over a woman, so he did not attempt to determine the truth.

The White King's armies withdrew like the ebbing tide, and he and his new consort made merry in his palace. But she lacked the fiery passion of her predecessor, and wept often, so he was not entirely satisfied. Thinking of Brugmo's shattered ruby, she told him, 'My heart was broken by a man. Will the Great King have the patience to wait for it to heal?'

Moved, the White King began to treasure the false Brugmo.

Gyatsa Zhakar asked the chief minister's permission to bring his troops to protect the palace, but the chief minister rebuffed him.

'With the king away, people would think you coveted the throne.'

With a heavy heart, Gyatsa Zhakar returned to the southern border.

Khrothung was angry. Without Gesar, none of Gling's warriors would have been a match for Hor's three kings or for Shanpa Merutse. He had been hoping that when Gesar's men had been killed, he could take the throne. He decided to reveal to the White King that the consort had been replaced by her maid. He transformed himself into a peregrine falcon and circled the border region, looking for a Hor crow. The White King had handsomely rewarded the crow that had found Brugmo, bestowing upon it the title 'King of All Birds', while the pigeons, parrots and peacocks were all killed. Emboldened crows now flew around the borders of the neighbouring countries, noisily looking for secrets they could carry back to the White King.

The falcon frightened them at first, but finally they mustered the courage to come close.

'Bring to me your King of All Birds.'

The King of All Birds remembered the hawk that had pointed out Brugmo, and came as quickly as it could. It wore heavy strings of gemstones around its neck and gold shields on its claws.

'An old friend.'

'I—'

'Get back, further back, until I can't see you any more,' the King of All Birds shrieked at the other crows, then turned to the peregrine.

'The White King has married not Brugmo, but a maid who resembles her.'

'What do you expect to gain by telling me this?'

'I want the great king to attack again.' And then Khrothung told the crow that Gesar had not returned from the north.

The White King was not convinced, and told the crow to gather more intelligence. It found the falcon lingering at the border, hoping to see Hor soldiers launch an attack.

'Our great king says that, without knowing your true identity, he cannot be sure that your intelligence is accurate. He also asks why you would betray your country if you do not ask for a reward.'

Khrothung ground his teeth. 'If not for Gesar, I, the leader of the Tagrong tribe, would have won the horserace and become king. Tell your great king that I will send him a pretty woman every year if he helps me now.'

When the news reached the Hor palace, the maid slit her throat before the White King could stop her. Furious, he sent forth his army, and soon the golden dome of Gesar's palace was in sight. The chief minister sent messengers out for help, but the Hor soldiers had surrounded the palace like an iron barrel.

As the White King prepared a final attack, Shanpa Merutse spoke.

'Great King, if you marry Brugmo, the country of Gling will be as your father-in-law. The last time I was here, the woman chosen by the king was so dazzling that I did not dare to look at her too closely. Let me go again to her.'

The White King laughed. 'You are right. How could I visit my consort's kin if I had destroyed their palace? You may go.'

So Shanpa Merutse went to the palace, and spoke once more to Brugmo. 'This time you cannot escape.'

'I shall slit my throat here in front of you.'

He snickered. 'No one in Gling will die if you live, but thousands of people will be trampled by our horses if you die. And if Gesar is unwilling to come to you . . .'

Two drops of bright red blood rolled from her eyes as she said, 'So be it, then. If you promise not to slaughter the people or ransack the palace, I will go with you.'

Later, people argued as to whether or not she had looked back as she left the palace. The chief minister said she had, but many said she had not.

She was long gone by the time the warriors arrived from the border regions.

Gyatsa Zhakar, with several thousand men, gave chase. But those on foot soon lagged behind, and such was his haste that he soon left the cavalrymen behind as well. By the time he caught up with the Hor troops, who were spread across several grassy hills, he was alone. He raised his sword, but there were so many soldiers it would have taken forty-nine days to finish them off, even if they had stuck their necks out for him to lop off their heads. Besides, no true hero would kill unarmed soldiers as if they were melons. He reined in his horse on a hill, and shouted for the White King to come out and fight. It was dusk, and the moon had not yet climbed into the sky, but its bright light was already at the horizon, and Gyatsa Zhakar cast a fearsome shadow.

The eight princes of Hor answered his challenge. They fought until the moon was high in the sky, and he had taken the lives of seven with his sword, his spear, his bow and arrow. The youngest prince, standing before him in the moonlight, was paler than a moonbeam. 'Where is your courage?' Gyatsa Zhakar yelled. 'Raise your sword!'

'I will not kill my brother.'

'How could you and I be brothers? But I will not kill an unarmed man, so draw your sword and fight.'

'Has your Han mother never mentioned her younger sister? I am the son of the Hor king's Han consort. My mother often spoke to me of a sister from whom she had been separated for many years, and told me of her sister's son, the great hero of Gling, Gyatsa Zhakar.'

Gyatsa Zhakar lowered his sword. 'I have a brother?'

'I am that brother.'

Gyatsa Zhakar saw tears sparkle in the young prince's eyes. 'But my mother never spoke of this.'

'Go back to her and ask.'

'So you can flee and your father can steal Gesar's favourite consort?'

More soldiers had arrived and their horses' pounding hoofs were like war drums. Gyatsa Zhakar's veins pulsed.

'Raise your sword if you will fight, or hide behind me and watch me kill every last one of your Hor soldiers.'

'Brother, why do you not leave? You are brave and strong, but you killed my seven brothers and the king will never let you live.'

'You pretend to be my brother because you are afraid to die.'

The prince's face darkened, and he said hoarsely, 'You may not insult me, even if I am not your match, even if you are my brother.' He grasped his spear and leaped onto his horse. 'Gyatsa Zhakar, I will not win, but behind my horse lies my country. Before I die, I make this vow. If I am your brother, my blood will be white. If not, it will be black.'

Then the prince rode at Gyatsa Zhakar. With a flip of his hand, Gyatsa Zhakar ran the prince through with his sword, knocking him to the ground. The prince smiled and said, 'My brother is a fine warrior.'

Then blood the colour of milk poured from his mouth.

Gyatsa Zhakar stood up and howled at the sky. The soldiers saw him take off his armour and say to the brother who lay dead in the moonlight, 'I will not return alive. Your soul must wait for me. We will be true brothers in the underworld.'

With that, he jumped into the saddle and charged at the soldiers.

Shanpa Merutse rode to face him, stopping an arrow's shot away.

'Send me the White King.'

Shanpa Merutse said, 'Today is the first day of the full moon. On this day, our king wraps his hands in white silk and will not engage in killing in order to cultivate good karma.'

'Enough! Tell the White King to come out.'

'I am no common soldier. May I not compete with a hero?'

'If you lose, the White King must come out.'

'If I lose, I will tell him.'

'Swords or bows and arrows?'

'The fallen heads of our soldiers are proof of your skill with the sword. Let us try arrows.'

Gyatsa Zhakar took up his bow. 'I am aiming at the red tassel on your helmet.'

Shanpa Merutse felt the arrow shoot past his head. When he turned to look, the arrow with the tassel was lodged in the trunk of the cypress tree behind him. Shanpa Merutse fixed an arrow to his bow and, without warning, sent it straight for Gyatsa Zhakar's face. It hit him between the eyes, and with a yelp, he fell from his horse. The upright and brave Gyatsa Zhakar lay dead, killed by a base trick.

With the new consort Brugmo, the soldiers returned to Hor that night, blaring victorious trumpets and beating drums. By the time soldiers from Gling arrived, Gyatsa Zhakar's righteous heart had stopped beating. His tall figure would never again be seen on horseback at the head of the armies of Gling.

The brightest, purest moon of Gling had fallen.

When Gyatsa Zhakar's body was carried down the hill, the chief minister knelt on the ground and, heartbroken, shouted towards the demon land to the north: 'Great King, in my loyalty to you, I have caused the death of Gyatsa Zhakar. Great King, do you still remember Gling? Do you still need our loyalty?'

Above him the full moon rose, no longer a rich, pale yellow but a cold, ashen white.

The Story
The King's Return

The chief minister's cry of grief travelled to the sky above the demon country and sent stars raining down on Atag Lhamo's fortress.

'Are stars falling from the sky?' Gesar asked.

Minister Sheng-ngon, replied, 'Yes, stars have fallen.'

Light gathered in Gesar's misty eyes. 'I felt a spasm in my heart. Some catastrophe has taken place in Gling. We must go home.'

'Great King, you should begin your travels when the sun rises in the morning. Only demons sneak away in the middle of the night.'

'You are right. But tomorrow . . . if I forget, you must remind me.'

The consorts promised they would.

'I have been here for nearly a year, have I not?' he asked.

They exchanged a look, but no one answered him. A servant brought wine, which Gesar refused. 'When I came to rescue Meza,' he said, 'Brugmo gave me wine that made me forget to leave. I shall not drink today.'

'Then have some tea,' Atag Lhamo and Meza said together.

But in the morning he had forgotten what he had said the night before, and no one came to remind him to leave. There was a well of forgetfulness in the demon land, and in the night Gesar had drunk the water from it; he had forgotten the sign of the falling stars, and his duty as king. Three more years passed.

At the beginning of the third year, Brugmo bore the White King a son.

After the death of the great warrior, Gyatsa Zhakar, the chief minister lost the people's trust, for he could no longer give orders in Gesar's name. Khrothung named himself king and asked his own brother, Senglon, Gyatsa Zhakar and Gesar's father, to be the steward of his increasingly splendid fortress. And the father of the great warrior Gyatsa Zhakar and King Gesar submitted to this humiliation. Each year he respectfully delivered the tribute that Khrothung had collected from the countries up to the border with Hor.

The celestial horse, Rkayngkar Perpo, had also drunk from the well of forgetfulness so his body was limp and his mind weak. While Gesar rejoiced with his consorts, the horse was surrounded by pretty young mares. But he was uneasy, and often ran to the top of a hill to peer into the distance. He would run to a second hill, then a third, and still find no answer. He had, after all, a horse's brain. Sometimes the king came to see him, lost in thought as he patted his head and slapped his flank. Clearly the king, too, was trying to remember something.

And so Rkayngkar Perpo stopped wondering, and expended his energy in the conquest of the prettiest mares in the herd. His reputation travelled far among his kind, among both domesticated and wild horses.

In Hor, Shanpa Merutse was ill at ease. He knew that he could not have bested Gyatsa Zhakar in a fair fight and that the people of Gling hated him. But now the beautiful Jetsun Yeshe sneered at him. 'You say you are Hor's finest warrior, but you stabbed your enemy in the back. You are nothing but the White King's dog.'

The princess's words pierced his heart.

'Tell me, Princess, how can I atone?'

'The consort you abducted has given birth to a new master for you. Why are you not tending him with the maidservants?'

'Your tongue spews poison!' he said. 'Just tell me how I can atone for my crime.'

'By awakening Gesar.'

'But I dare not go to that land.'

'Then go to the salt spring and herd all the wild horses that live there into the demon's territory.'

So he went north into the desert with his soldiers and herded the wild horses away from the salt spring. It took them nine days to reach the borders of the demon land, and there he opened a silk purse that Princess Jetsun Yeshe had given him. In it she had placed a message instructing him to herd the horses for three more days, deeper into the demon country.

When he returned to Hor, she said, 'You have atoned for half of your crime.'

'And the other half?'

The princess did not reply.

Among the herd of wild horses some striking mares caught Rkayngkar Perpo's eye and those of the demon country complained that he was fickle. Within a few days, the horses from Hor, missing their salt spring, moved back towards the border, Rkayngkar Perpo among them. These horses never drank fresh water from the springs that gushed everywhere, but lapped the dewdrops from the grass at dawn. Puzzled, he asked the mares why, but they were silent. When they reached the sandy area near the border, where there were no more springs, Rkayngkar Perpo's head began to clear, and he realised he was far from his master.

'Why would you return to him?'

'To help him rid the land of demons.'

'Think carefully. How long has it been since your master last saddled you?'

A breeze blew from deep in the desert, and he cried out, 'It is six years since we left Gling!'

Then the wild horses bade him farewell, saying that the taste of the salt spring called to them. But before they left the most beautiful mare turned to him and said, 'Return to Gling.'

He did so, and what he saw broke his heart.

He galloped back to the demon country. Like the wild horses of Hor, he drank only the dewdrops, ignoring the cool water that gurgled up melodiously from the springs. The desire to pour out his heart to his master grew with each hoofbeat. He wanted to ask why they had come down to the human world, why the springs of forgetfulness were invested with such indomitable power, why his master would let himself fall victim to the springs even though he had the power to fight off evil spells. Had there been no warning sign from Heaven?

Wherever the celestial horse shed tears, new springs emerged, and the old springs of forgetfulness dried up. So Gesar's head was clear even before Rkayngkar Perpo reached the iron fortress. He saw the fog of misery over Gling, the arrogant tyrant Khrothung and his own earthly father collecting tribute. He saw the long-suffering Brugmo in the White King's palace, smiling at her newborn baby.

Rkayngkar Perpo wept when his master began to weep. Neither could speak until Atag Lhamo and Meza came towards them.

'Will you try to stop me again?' Gesar asked.

The two women hurried to help him onto the horse.

Gesar rode straight to Hor where, with the help of Jetsun Yeshe and Shanpa Merutse, he killed the White King and his two brothers. He took Jetsun Yeshe as his consort, and Shanpa Merutse became his minister in charge of the Hor territory. And then, with a single sweep of his sword, he killed the child of Brugmo and the White King.

'Great King,' Brugmo cried, 'that child may have been the White King's flesh and blood, but he was mine too.'

But Gesar's heart was devoid of pity.

If he killed Khrothung, he would incur the wrath of the Tagrong tribe, and Gling would be thrown into chaos. So when he came to the palace, and Khrothung knelt to beg Gesar's forgiveness, the flame of anger in Gesar's heart was replaced with disgust. He stripped Khrothung of his titles and banished him to the borders as a horse herder. But Gesar knew that in a few years he would have to allow him his titles.

The order of exile had been given, but before Khrothung reached the border, Gesar's father, Senglon, came to him to plead for Khrothung.

'The senior and middle branches of our family are watching us. If the junior branch is caught up in struggles, there will be trouble.'

Before leaving the celestial realm, the son of the deities had had a simple view of the human world. He had thought he had only to subdue the demons. He had not expected that, once he took the throne, he would have such trouble. It had begun with the consorts' jealousies, and now bloodlines made it impossible for him to reward and punish fairly. Rongtsa Khragan, Senglon and Khrothung were the three elders of the junior branch, and Gesar hoped that the chief minister would not agree with his father. But the chief minister nodded.

The young king said coldly, 'You tell me that the junior branch of Gling has always been united, and that I bring disunity. I came to Gling to bring peace, but you have brought forth so many troubles that I shall return to the celestial realm.'

The two old men knelt before him. 'Great King!'

The Storyteller
On the Road

'How embarrassing! How disgraceful!' Jigmed muttered, as he hurried away from the radio station.

He did not believe that he had fallen in love with the woman in the recording studio: how could two people from such different backgrounds be in love? Had her suggestive voice or wanton fragrance beguiled him? Was that why he felt drugged?

As he walked along the road, he thought of Yangcan Drolma, of how, with hands that were rougher than his own, she had taken him to her room for tea.

'Hmph!'

Tiring, he lay down in the grass by a stream. Two Jeeps arrived at around noon and drove straight into the water. The passengers, well-dressed men and women, climbed out. They washed the vehicles, then, using the same buckets, had a water fight. Their cheerful banter made Jigmed feel as if he'd been cut off from the world. When they sat down to rest and to dry their clothes, they behaved as if they hadn't seen him. He heard someone ask one of the drivers to put on a cassette. The driver asked what they wanted to hear and someone answered, 'Gesar.'

'This is the new section – I recorded it from the radio. It's Jigmed singing "The Country of Jang and Its Raid on the Salt Lake".'

The song began. Jigmed had sung of Gesar's confrontation with the demon king of Jang, Satham, when they had reined in their horses in the middle of battle and asked each other riddles about mountains. Even Jigmed was captivated as he listened to himself playing the interrogator and, in the next line, the respondent.

'*Om* –

The nearest mountain,

Like an acolyte standing before a table holding incense,

What is the name of that mountain?'

'*Om* –

The young acolyte holding incense is the Sandalwood Mountain
  of India!'

'*Om* –

The flat rocky surface rises into the sky,

Like banners flapping in the wind.

What is the name of that mountain?'

'*Om* –

Where banners dance upon each other is Wayiweigelama Mountain!'

'*Om* –

Fairy wearing an apricot-yellow hat,

Draped rosy sky standing among the clouds,

What is the name of that mountain?'

'*Om* –

Fairy wearing hat is Mount Chomolungma,

Which is as high as the sky!'

'*Om* –

Steep hills backed by a gentle rising slope,

Like a king who has just taken the throne,

Stairs spiral upward.

What is the name of that mountain?'

'*Om* –

It is the Nianqingtanggula mountain that divides east and west!'

'*Om* –

Between mountains are many smooth rivers,

A steep peak towers into the clouds and the sky,

Like an elephant on the plain.

What is the name of that mountain?'

'*Om* —

Like an elephant roaming the river plain, that is Mount Emei of
    China!'

Jigmed laughed. The two did not behave like the leaders of armies
about to engage in battle, but like lamas showing off their learning.
Only an extraordinary man could tell the story so well – so that it was
as real as a film – and that thought intoxicated him.

The Jeeps drove off, and the singing grew fainter, until Jigmed was
again shrouded in silence. He tried to make the vivid pictures continue
to play, but they lost their colour and outline.

'No,' he heard himself say, in a terrified voice. 'No.'

Then even the still pictures in his mind disappeared. Confused, he
remembered the words of the Living Buddha: 'You should not look
outward,' he had said, 'but inside. That is where the stories originate.
Imagine it as the mouth of a spring with a continuous flow of water.'

Jigmed gathered his consciousness to illuminate the dark inner world.
But the light shone into chaos, like a traveller who sees nothing but
mist.

As he set off again, he thought, Black Jang seizes the salt sea. But
that was all that came to him.

Further down the road he met an old man with a friendly face who
was sitting by a spring and patiently polishing the blurred lenses of
his glasses. 'You look troubled,' the old man said.

'I'm finished.'

The old man stood up. 'Finished? You can't be finished.'

He led Jigmed to a rocky cliff by the roadside. 'I can't see without
my glasses, but tell me what that looks like.' An impression of something as long and as thick as an arm was worn into the rock.

The impression looked like a man's sex, but Jigmed did not say that.
'It's too vulgar to mention,' was all he could manage.

With a loud laugh, the old man said, 'The gods would love to hear something vulgar for a change. Look, this was left by a big penis! A huge one.'

Then he told Jigmed a story. When Gesar was on his way back to Gling after all those years in the demon country, he thought about the time he had spent drinking and in carnal pleasures and wondered if his manhood had lost its prowess. He took out his penis to test it, which was how this impression had been made. Taking his hand, the old man guided him to feel the life-like shape of the indentation. So many people had touched it that it was worn very smooth.

'Now go home and you'll be as potent as a stallion,' the old man said, and sat down again at the mouth of the spring to polish his glasses. Jigmed smiled helplessly. The problem was not down there but in his mind. He went back to the spring. 'Old gentleman, I want to go to the salt lake.'

'Salt merchants travel in teams, but you're alone, and there are so many salt lakes. Which one do you wish to visit?'

Jigmed heard himself say softly, 'The one Satham, the demon king of Jang, wanted to take from Gling.'

The old man had bad eyes, but his ears were keen enough. He told the storyteller that they were at the place formerly guarded by Gyatsa Zhakar, far from the salt lakes north of Gling. There, salt lakes dotted the land like a chessboard, and no one knew exactly which one the demon king of Jang had wanted. He sighed. 'If Gyatsa Zhakar hadn't died, the King of Jang would never have dared try to seize Gling's salt lakes.'

'The old gentleman knows so many tales of Gesar. You must be a *grungkan*.'

Instead of replying, the old man got up and walked off. Jigmed followed him to where one of the Jinsha river's tributaries roared through a valley. The ruins of an old fortress, with crumbling mud walls, marked the site of Gyatsa Zhakar's border camp. The ground was littered with lumps of a dark red substance, as heavy as rock. The old man told

Jigmed they were from the fortress's foundations. Expert craftsmen had poured the foundations using smelted iron and fritted iron ore.

From the hill where they stood in a briar patch, they could see a wall winding down to a depression before rising again to a higher hill opposite. At the top of that hill stood the ruins of another, taller, fortress, buffeted by strong winds. An ancient road had once traversed the valley between the two hills, but the land had long since been turned over to crops. The old man said that these ruins comprised two wings of Gyatsa Zhakar's fortress, while the main part occupied the lowland between them, though not a single stone or timber remained. Sitting down, the old man said that now he had polished his glasses with water, he had to polish them with wind.

'I know you are a *grungkan*, which is why I brought you here to see these relics. Tell me, young man, what do you think?'

Jigmed said, 'The Gling of the story sounds like the whole world, but now I see that it was not very big.' He had travelled from the Ashug grassland, where Gesar was born, arriving finally at this place after stopping several times along the way. It had taken less than two weeks.

The old man said sternly, 'That was when Gling was first established. The Gling army travelled south along the Jinsha river, to conquer Jang, ruled by Satham, the southern demon king, and then Gling's border extended much further south, where flowers bloomed on the grassland even in the winter.'

'By then Gyatsa Zhakar was dead.'

'Yes. He was Gling's finest strategist and most loyal general.'

'So who led the soldiers when they went to conquer Jang?'

The old man glanced sharply at him. 'Aren't you the *grungkan* who sings on the radio? You are a wonderful singer.'

'But my mind is confused.'

Putting on his polished glasses, the old man said, 'I see. Have the gods left you? Have you done something to displease them?'

'I don't know.'

'What did you just ask me? Oh! Who led the soldiers to conquer Jang. Let me tell you, the Jang people were afraid of our hero, Gyatsa Zhakar. If he'd been alive still, they'd never have had the courage to seize Gling's salt lake.'

'But where is the salt lake?'

The old man was not interested in geography but in who was most loyal to Gling.

'Next to Gyatsa,' the old man said, 'Danma was the most loyal. It was he who killed Jang's last general, Tserma Kherkye.'

The old man took Jigmed to his home in the valley, where every house was shaped like a fortress and the Jinsha river cascaded down a cliff outside his window. On the land around his house, potato and broad-bean plants were in bloom. They found his family outside. There were three children with dirty faces and bright eyes, a quiet middle-aged man and a sallow, middle-aged woman.

'This is my younger brother, and this is the wife we share, and our three children. The eldest son left home to be a lama.' Seeing Jigmed's face, he said, 'You are a Tibetan, why are you surprised?'

Jigmed was embarrassed – even though there were families in his own village in which brothers shared wives. But the old man did not pursue the matter, and opened a door to reveal a workshop with a coke-fired blast furnace, bellows made of sheepskin, a sturdy workbench, tongs, hammers and rasps. The room was full of steam from dousing red-hot metal in water, and the smell of sparks from sharpening knives and swords. Half-finished objects were scattered throughout the room; knives and swords, arrayed by size, glinted on a wooden rack, facing the window. Again the old man guessed what was on Jigmed's mind.

'My family has been in this line of work from the time of Gesar. And not just my family, but every family in this village and in every village along the river – we all do the same work. His eyes expressed a sense of loss. 'But we no longer make arrows and our knives are not used on the battlefield. The people of this noble tribe have become blacksmiths, serving farmers and herders. And, of course, we fill special orders from the tourist bureau.' The old man gave him a dagger with a curved handle and a blade slightly longer than an adult's middle finger. He told Jigmed that it imitated the style of Gesar's crystal dagger.

'I thought he used real crystal to make a dagger,' Jigmed said.

The old man laughed. 'I like you, Grungkan. You question the story you tell and don't pretend to know everything.'

'You don't look like a blacksmith.'

Jigmed spent the night at the blacksmith's house. As he listened to the river outside the window, he had another dream. He'd wanted to meet Gyatsa Zhakar in his dream, but instead he saw King Gesar. Shanpa Merutse, the general of vanquished Hor, had just defeated the Jang army at the salt lake in the north and had taken Jang's valiant prince, Yulha Thoggyur, hostage.

The waves on the lake cast shiny salt crystals to the shore, and at the sight the hostage sighed. 'Salt is very valuable in our country, but here it is as plentiful as sand.'

Shanpa Merutse said, 'Salt not only gives the people of Gling boundless strength, but also endows us with limitless wisdom. If you surrender and make Jang part of Gling, your people can have all the salt they want.'

'Is this what King Gesar desires?' the prince asked.

'Yes.' It was King Gesar who answered.

The prince surrendered on the spot. But his father held out, so the Gling army gathered at the southern border, where Gyatsa Zhakar's fortress was located. Brugmo led the twelve consorts in offering a farewell drink in a jade bowl to King Gesar, reminding him of how he had lost his elder brother as a result of drinking and dallying with women in the demon land. Suspecting that the drink might be laced with a potion to make him forget, Gesar flung the bowl at a cliff.

★

The next morning Jigmed told the old man about his dream.

'It seems that the gods want you to sing that tale,' the old man said. He walked with Jigmed for a while. 'This is the spot where Gesar bade farewell to the consorts who came to see him off to battle, and this is where I, too, will say goodbye.'

The valley was cut in two by a tributary of the Jinsha river, and a road ran between the water and the rocky cliff. The old man pointed out an indentation on the cliff: according to local legend, that was where Gesar had smashed the liquor bowl.

Jigmed stared at the fork in the road. One road led to the old Hor land to the north and the other to the old Jang land to the south. Eddies formed and disappeared in the water below him, just as the story appeared and faded in his mind. The lost story had returned.

'I remember it now!' he shouted, and turned, but the old man had left without a word.

Sunlight shone on the road, and tiny flecks of quartz glittered, like salt crystals pushed by waves to the lakeshore.

The Story
Solitude

After Jang had been conquered, the territory, population and treasure of Gling increased many times. Intimidated by Gling's power and King Gesar's reputation, the neighbouring countries were content to live peacefully side by side and enter into trade agreements, which further increased Gling's wealth and power. Her people enjoyed a decade with no wars and no scourge of demons. Gesar's palace was filled with rare treasures from all over the world. Temples, houses, workshops and shops rose up around the palace, like mushrooms after summer rain. The capital city was now called Tagste khar and its fame travelled far and wide. Girls learned to weave and embroider from their mothers, while the young men, dressed in purple robes, used stone tablets to practise reading, writing and reciting the sutras with teachers in the temples. The scholars named this situation 'prosperity'.

While Gesar enjoyed the affection of the consorts in his palace, he often set out by himself to see the country, and what he saw could be summed up in a word created by scholars to describe a situation in which nothing happened: 'stability'.

Of course, he could not stop wolves eating sheep or people falling sick. Neither did the idea of leaving this world enter his head when he encountered old age, sickness and death – he was not from this world, so how could he leave it? The monks came into the palace to spread their teaching, and some even tried to instruct the king, although they knew that he had no need for their counsel. But ruling a prosperous, stable country had not been part of the original plan, and Gesar would sometimes wonder if it was time for Heaven to recall him. It seemed he had accomplished what Heaven had sent him to do and now had nothing with which to stave off idleness.

This thought, of course, was immediately known to the Supreme Deity, who said that after humans solve one problem they create another, and there is no end. It seemed that Thosba Gawa had contracted the human affliction.

'Then why not recall him?' someone said.

'Not yet. Since he complains about peace and idleness, let us find something for him to do. We will have to ask Lhamin Dagmo to go to the human world once more.'

That night, when Gesar went to bed after feasting and merry-making with his consorts, his celestial mother, Lhamin Dagmo, entered his dream, and told him of a country called Monyul, to the west of the old Jang territory, a demon land ruled by Shengkhri Gyalpo, one of the four great demon kings, who also included the vanquished Lutsan, the White King, and Satham of the Jang. Shengkhri Gyalpo had a seven-year-old demon horse called Misen Marpo. The demon king and his demon horse were working on their magic, and by the following year, humans would be incapable of subjugating them.

'Has Shengkhri Gyalpo ever harmed Gling?' Gesar asked his celestial mother.

'Before you were born into the human world, and when your brother, Gyatsa Zhakar, was very young, armies from Monyul penetrated deep into Gling to loot the Tagrong tribe, killing many people and seizing cattle.'

Then she turned to go back to the celestial realm, but Gesar had caused the rainbow she would use to vanish.

'Does this mean the Supreme Deity wishes me to remain here?' she asked, concerned.

Gesar laughed. 'The rainbow would return if Mother did not always come and go so quickly.'

'So, it was one of your tricks.' She relaxed. 'Son of the Deities, you seem sombre. Is something wrong?'

'I came to destroy the demons for these humans but . . .'

'Not all are grateful for what you have done?'

Gesar did not reply, for that would mean he was disappointed in the people of Gling. Changing the subject, he said, 'I have rid Gling of all its demons – how can there be another I have never heard of?'

'Were you not restless in the palace? Have your monks not told you that demons come from one's own heart?' His mother stopped herself. 'Son of the Deities, I have said too much. Show me the rainbow again.'

He did so, and his celestial mother returned to Heaven.

He woke in the early dawn, the dream still clear in his mind. He looked at the consort beside him, a pretty woman who wore a foolish expression when she slept, and felt lonelier than when he had been banished to the Yellow river bank, though his palace shone in the dark like a giant gemstone, and his consort was warm and sweet-smelling.

He dressed and went up to the roof. The moon had set, but Venus was bright on the horizon. The consorts woke, too, and came to his side.

'The Supreme Deity wishes me to go into battle again,' he said to them.

Brugmo would not stop him this time. 'After the king leaves, I will go to the temple to recite sutras for you every day.'

Meza was concerned. 'Are the good days coming to an end?'

Atag Lhamo said valiantly, 'I shall be the king's advance guard.'

He asked if any had heard of the demon Shengkhri Gyalpo in the southern land of Monyul. They had not. Jetsun Yeshe said, 'It seems that the enmity between Monyul and Gling was formed in the previous generation, with the Tagrong tribe. Why not ask Uncle Khrothung?'

The Story
Gralha the Youth

On the day of the next court session, Khrothung, who had been reinstated as leader of the Tagrong tribe, was the only person summoned by King Gesar to appear.

'Is there a lingering dispute between the Tagrong tribe and Monyul?' Gesar asked him.

Khrothung came forward. 'Their king, Shengkhri Gyalpo, not only killed our people but also stole the brocade robe, a symbol of the power of the junior branch of Gling.'

'Why has no one told me of this?'

Chief Minister Rongtsa Khragan replied, 'Once the king descended to Gling and his influence reached all corners, the demon king no longer dared to trouble us. Besides, the brocade robe failed to unify our people and led to disputes among the three branches. Now, with the great king leading us, there is no more use for the brocade robe.'

Khrothung, his eyes shifting, said, 'Many years ago, Shengkhri Gyalpo wished to marry his daughter, Metog Drolma, into our Tagrong tribe. I hear that she is twenty-five years old but still as pretty as ever.'

Everyone laughed when they saw Khrothung lick his lips at the thought of a beautiful woman.

'You think she is too old for you? But you are sixty-two,' Danma said.

Khrothung's self-satisfied air made Gesar wonder if it had been a mistake to reinstate him so soon.

'If Gling wages war against Monyul, the Tagrong tribe should be the vanguard in order to settle old scores,' Gesar said.

Khrothung had no choice but to say, 'If the king gives the order, I will obey.'

It had already occurred to Gesar that since Shengkhri Gyalpo was skilled in magic, the advance guard must be the Tagrong's soldiers under the leadership of Khrothung, who was equally adept in transformation. But he changed his mind when he saw Gralha, his elder brother's son. The boy had just turned sixteen, but was handsome and valiant, with a bright face and clear eyes. He had rushed to the capital from the border region the day before the court session, and Danma had brought him to see the king that same night. It was as if Gesar's brother stood before him again, and he felt a tightness in his chest.

Although he enjoyed the favours of Brugmo, Meza and other consorts, all of whom were beautiful as flowers, as well as Atag Lhamo and Jetsun Yeshe, the Hor princess, Gesar remained heirless. The consorts all wanted to give him a son so they could consolidate their position in the palace; his father, Senglon, and the chief minister wished him to have a son to inherit the throne of Gling. But as a king sent down from Heaven to save the people, he was unsure whether he should leave a son to become the next King of Gling. Neither the Supreme Deity nor his celestial parents had offered any guidance on this. None of the consorts had borne him any children, even after sharing his bed for ten years, and he took that as a sign from Heaven.

Gesar had planned to bequeath his throne to his loyal brother, Gyatsa Zhakar, after he had accomplished his mission, but Gyatsa Zhakar had ended his earthly life too soon and had left for the Pure Land of the Buddhist realm. Now his nephew stood before him.

Tender feelings welled inside Gesar. 'You remind me of my brother.'

Tears shone in Gralha's eyes when he heard the king speak of his father.

'I shall love you like a father and treat you as my own son,' Gesar told him.

The youth knelt before him. 'I came here today to ask the king's permission to be the advance guard for the expedition to Monyul.'

Gesar's heart stirred. This youth may indeed grow up to be Gling's future king, he thought. But Gesar composed his face as befitted a king and made only a questioning grunt. 'Oh?'

Under the encouraging gaze of Danma, the prince slowly made his case: Gling might have tens of thousands of soldiers and horses but it conducted warfare in a way passed down from primitive times, when a battle was won solely upon the generals' magical powers and individual combat. But in powerful countries like India, they knew how to deploy thousands of elephants. In China, fine horses wore armour into battle, and tens of thousands of warriors in chariots raised their swords. Like wind piling snow, or waves pushing sand, their swords met no resistance wherever they were pointed. The prince's father had built such an army, in which tens of thousands of soldiers moved in unison, turning a thousand swords into one sword and ten thousand arrows into one.

Gralha said to the king, 'I have followed my father's methods and trained daily. I would like to try a new battle strategy.'

Gesar said, 'You may go now. I will consider your request carefully.'

Before they left, Danma knelt before the king.

'Revered King, I, Danma, pledge absolute loyalty. I will do my best to help Gralha.'

Gesar paced the palace halls for a long time, thinking about Prince Yulha Thoggyur of Jang, who had joined him after the salt-lake battle. The Jang prince was also a trustworthy young warrior. Why not give the heroes of the younger generation a chance to display their talent in a battle with Monyul? At court the next day, he gave the order to let Gralha lead the army trained by Gyatsa Zhakar, and he sent a messenger to tell Yulha Thoggyur to take his troops to the border.

Several days later Gesar left with his army, heading south. Along the way, he was joined by troops from Hor, led by Shanpa Merutse, and from the demon country, led by Atag Lhamo. Deep valleys marked the border between Monyul and Gling, but Gralha's advance guard had already built broad plank roads and floating bridges. The troops passed as if across flat land.

They entered a forest where the sun could not shine, and a thick mist made the horses and their riders so sleepy that they fell to the ground as if drugged. Gesar rose up into the sky on his celestial steed, and saw that great glaciers like mirrors covered the mountains and reflected the light to the south. But the valleys were in shadow. Gling's men and horses were falling asleep on the soft moss under the ancient trees, their faces and bodies turning green. Mushrooms sprouted on them. Still astride his steed, Gesar summoned the mountain gods.

'Let the sun shine into these valleys,' he said. 'It will drive away the poisonous fog and dry the muddy road.'

The mountain gods shrugged. 'Let the sun shine into the valleys? Why would we do that?'

Gesar laughed, and sent thunderclaps from his hands, cracking two towering mountains in half and causing the mountain gods to bleed from their noses and ears. Sunlight burst through the fissures and into the valleys, and the soldiers caught in the fog shouted for joy. Valleys that had been dark for thousands of years were filled with light, and the fog slowly dispersed. Tangled vines in dank places shook themselves free, and the muddy road dried. The sleeping soldiers rose up and the army set out again.

Gralha and his men had crossed the river to the south and were encamped along its banks by the time Gesar arrived. Shanpa Merutse led his soldiers to the south bank, while Senglon and Khrothung guarded the middle troops. Warriors of the senior and middle branches spread out like the wings of falcons. Atag Lhamo's soldiers brought up the rear, in case the Monyul mountain demons and water sprites attacked from behind. And, indeed, when night fell and the other camps slept, demons attacked. They had been hiding along the route the Gling soldiers had traversed earlier. Atag Lhamo and her warriors fought hard until the red sun rose and chased away the demons.

Gesar smiled when he saw her. 'The general looks exhausted, probably because she did not sleep last night.'

Atag Lhamo said, with pride, 'The demons troubled us, but my warriors dealt with them.'

Gesar invited his consort to sit by him. 'Our mission is not only to conquer a country but, more importantly, to destroy demons and bring peace to the people. You have made a great contribution to our goal.'

'It was the effective battle formation arranged by the great king. My troops are the strongest against demons.'

'I did not create the formation.' Gesar pointed to Gralha. 'This time I followed his orders.'

Monyul occupied a vast land, with thirteen large river valleys and a population of millions. The people were favored with plenty of rain, a short winter and a long summer. The mountainsides were covered with flowers and fruit. Yet the people did not have a good life: their king, Shengkhri Gyalpo, was a demon and so was their chief minister, Kulha Thoggyal. Neither of them concerned himself with managing the country, but feasted on human flesh and drank human blood. The people of Monyul lived in constant fear.

Gesar said, 'The four demon kings have terrorised the world for too long. The other three met their destruction at the hand of Gling, but Shengkhri Gyalpo has survived because Monyul is so far away and he has caused no trouble for many years.'

Yulha Thoggyur said, 'Shengkhri Gyalpo is at the most critical stage of his training, which is why he has given strict orders to his underlings to be alert. He hopes to pass this year in peace and, when he finishes his training, he wishes to rule the world. This is why he has avoided us so far. There are two rivers to ford before we reach his palace, where his army waits to wage war with us.'

Gesar summoned Gralha and, touching the young man's shoulder, said, 'Tomorrow the troops will take your orders as you put my brother's tactics into practice.'

But the next day all was quiet, and the drawbridge to the Monyul camp was up. At noon a single horse rode out to meet Gralha.

'May I ask the name of the young commander in chief? I am Kulha Thoggyal, chief minister of Monyul.' He told Gralha that the fields along the river were where the king's consorts came to pick flowers, and where his officials held contests in magic and horsemanship. Flowers bloomed, cuckoos sang; it was a blessed land. How could they sit idly by and watch a foreign army fill the air with a murderous atmosphere?

Gralha smiled. 'Wherever the warriors of Gling point their swords, we turn a place overrun by demons into a blissful land such as you have just described. Now get off your horse and surrender.'

Kulha Thoggyal responded calmly, 'I, Kulha Thoggyal, treat my family and friends as gently as Chinese silk, but I can be a sharp arrow and powerful thunderclap in battle. So, I warn you, your troops must be gone from the riverbank before sunrise tomorrow.' He turned his horse and rode at a leisurely pace until he rounded a grove of trees, when he spurred it into a gallop. He was drenched in sweat when he reached the palace.

'We must delay,' Kulha Thoggyal told his king. 'We will placate the Tagrong tribe by giving back twice as many people and livestock as we seized, and returning their brocade robe. Then, once the king has perfected his occult practice, we shall make them pay a hundredfold for what we must do today.'

With a stony look, the king said, 'Have you agreed on a price?'

Kulha Thoggyal said, 'Your humble official would never do that. This is only my suggestion. Besides, Gesar will not leave without a victory – he would never negotiate with me.'

'Then what are you trying to tell me?'

'I have had dealings with Khrothung, the leader of the Tagrong tribe, and he knows what we are capable of.'

'That old man has been coveting our beautiful princess. Would you have me give her to him?'

Kulha Thoggyal knelt before the king. 'I will prepare our army for a battle with Gling tomorrow.'

Shengkhri Gyalpo smiled and left his seat to help Kulha Thoggyal to his feet. 'You receive the desired results from negotiation only after you have dealt your enemy a severe blow. Let us fight first. Their blood will flow like a river, which will save your tongue some effort.'

The Story
War between Monyul and Gling

Early the next morning, Kulha Thoggyal rode out with Shengkhri Gyalpo to look over Gling's troops. He could not conceal a disdainful grin.

The king asked if he was sure of victory.

'Great King, they will be defeated. We hear that Gling has many heroes, but that is a rumour spread by the faint-hearted. When we attacked the Tagrong tribe, they put up little resistance – and look at their formation. Hordes of people crowding into each other. What creature needs to crowd together to bolster its courage? The sheep! If a tiger or a leopard walks alone, its majesty make you take notice.'

Yet the king felt a sense of foreboding. 'But see how their tens of thousands of soldiers move as one man. We must be careful.'

A command banner had been raised in Gralha's camp, and now ox horns sounded. The troops crossed the bridge and advanced into the open space between the armies, foot soldiers in a square, cavalrymen in snake and hawk formations. The two young warriors, Gralha and Yulha Thoggyur, rode ahead, holding a spear and a bow respectively. Gralha, who led the advance guard, carried a spray of brightly coloured flags on his back. When he waved the green flag, the soldiers who had green tassels on their helmets – some with spears and shields, others with bows and arrows – quickly occupied a hill in the field between the two armies. After they had taken cover, Gralha waved a yellow and white flag. The cavalrymen, with white and yellow tassels on their helmets, spread out like the wings of a hawk, then rushed forward, stopping behind the green-tasselled foot soldiers. Gralha waved a red banner and spurred his horse forward, and the red-tasselled middle troops moved behind him. Many thousands of boots rose and fell in unison; thousands of horses stamped down the earth with their iron shoes, and the land of Monyul trembled. The green-tasselled soldiers marched forward in neat rows, their spears and swords glinting, and bore down upon the gate of the Monyul camp.

When they stopped, the mountains, rivers and people held their breath, in the presence of a force they'd never encountered before.

'They don't look like sheep,' Shengkhri Gyalpo said.

Kulha Thoggyal shouted for bowmen. A rain of arrows filled the air, but the soldiers raised their shields. Unscathed, they lowered them and lifted their weapons. Outraged, Kulha Thoggyal shot an arrow with lightning at one end and thunder at the other. It sped into the middle of the formation, smashing shields and killing thirteen of Gling's soldiers. Like a plough turning the soil, it left a bloody furrow. Untrained soldiers would have hidden behind the horses of their generals, but after a brief commotion, the formation quietly moved forward again, shields protecting the front, sharp blades showing between shields. The space torn open by the arrow closed. Kulha Thoggyal rushed forward with a shout and opened another small space with his magic, but when the soldiers behind him tried to follow, they were blocked by the shields. Gralha waved his banners, and the foot soldiers advanced, the cavalrymen rushing to join them, like breakers tumbling onto the shore. Used to fighting on their own, the Monyul generals were swept up in the torrent and their camp was overrun.

The survivors retreated thirty or forty *li*, fighting all the way. It was not until dusk, when the Gling army stopped to prepare the evening meal where a row of hills rose up out of the grassland, that the Monyul army could re-form.

The next day Shengkhri Gyalpo came out and sent thunderbolts among the enemy, killing hundreds of soldiers and creating chaos in the formation. Standing on a hill, he spoke to his generals. 'I have heard that Gesar cherishes life and for that I once respected him, but see how, instead of using his magic to subjugate his enemies, he drowns them in the blood of his soldiers I will send a few more thunderbolts – his troops will trample all over each other. And then you may kill at will.'

He summoned a black cloud as he rose into the air. But this time the thunderbolts failed to appear – Gesar, astride his celestial horse, had taken them and was wielding them like whips.

'The wind delivered your words to my ears,' he said, with a grin. 'Are you ashamed now?' Gesar cracked the thunderbolt whips and turned the Monyul flag into a fireball. 'Show me what other magic you have,' he said.

Shengkhri Gyalpo fitted an arrow to his bow, but Gesar stopped him before he could shoot it toward the Gling army. 'Let the soldiers fight. You and I will have an archery contest, using that red rocky peak as our target.' He pointed to the cave on the red rock mountain where Shengkhri Gyalpo studied his black magic.

Ignoring him, the king unleashed his arrow of thunder and lightning at the Gling army.

Danma rode out and fired three arrows, knocking Shengkhri Gyalpo's arrow to the ground. A cheer rose, but the young warrior fell from his horse and coughed up bright blood. He was carried by his men into the tent where, quietly reciting the Heart-protecting Golden Incantation that Gesar had taught them before the battle, he gradually recovered.

'You laughed at my generals for being afraid to die,' Shengkhri Gyalpo said. 'Why do you use so much weak human flesh to protect you from swords and spears?'

'I want the people to save themselves.'

'They have no magic – they cannot.' Shengkhri Gyalpo laughed.

Beneath the clouds, the Gling army advanced again. No single soldier in it was the equal of a soldier in the demon army, but their fragile bodies moved in unison, and, like a floodtide, they surged up the hill.

'You see? They are like water. But mere water cannot flow to a higher place. This is their power.'

As he spoke, Gesar shot three arrows towards the secret cave. The top of the mountain was sliced off, and Shengkhri Gyalpo's power dimmed. Now Gesar laughed. 'Go home and rest. Tomorrow you will see how those whom you call weak can fight.'

In the days that followed, Gralha's army penetrated deep into Monyul territory. At first, the rivers they crossed flowed from west to east; later the rivers and mountain ranges moved north to south. The rivers became rapids, and mountains that had resembled lions, crouching to observe their surroundings or running with their heads held high, now seemed more like elephants.

The soldiers grew fearful, not of the elephants but of the great distance they had travelled from home. They worried that if they died their souls might not find their homeland. Yet they were still fervent in their desire for battle.

The Story
War between Monyul and Gling – II

Early one morning, when sunlight began to gild the snowcapped mountains, Gesar summoned his generals.

'The sun has yet to rise into the sky,' he said, 'but we can see its light on the mountain peaks. Since we launched our attack, Gralha and Yulha Thoggyur have given us one victory after another. This is an auspicious sign that Gling will stand as tall and strong as those mountains.'

The generals were sure that this meant the young warrior, Gralha, would be king one day. Shanpa Merutse came forward. 'We rejoice, Great King, that Gling now has an heir to continue the undertaking.'

Khrothung's frustration was to be expected. 'We have yet to take their city or disturb a single hair on the demon generals' heads. I will go alone and bring their heads back for the king.'

Gesar said patiently, 'The evil black fog has not dissipated, and the sun has yet to rise. The time has not come. I summoned you today because I wish you to avoid such rash moves. When the sun dries the dew on the grass, the Monyul army will launch an attack. We will have no trouble in repelling it, for I have found a spring in this overheated country from which sacred water flows. And my celestial mother has given us protective amulets that will make us invincible in battle.'

Days later, they had still not found victory over the demon generals.

Khrothung sought out Gralha. 'You are of my grandchildren's generation. Allow me to give you some advice.' Khrothung had told himself that Gralha, the future king, would be in his debt if he won, but if he lost, Gesar would have to find someone else to inherit the throne.

Gralha said politely, 'An elder's wisdom is wider and deeper than the ocean. It will be my honour to hear the advice of the powerful leader of the Tagrong tribe.'

'Some of the king's generals were unhappy with you, so the king made you the rearguard. They have gone into battle, and you can see how they have fared. Now is the time for a young warrior like you to make a name for himself. You should ask the king to send you into battle again.'

'My soldiers are exhausted. Besides, I follow the king's orders. When my father was alive, he told me to trust in our king's wisdom.'

Khrothung stamped his foot. 'You are stubborn, as was your father. Do you know what it would mean if you led your troops into the Monyul palace city?'

'I do not.'

'It means you would be the king's heir.'

Gralha stood up and told his attendants, 'See Minister Khrothung back to camp.'

Khrothung returned to his tent, where he nursed his anger for a long time. Then, donning his armour, he went to Gesar. 'The heroes of Gling have done their best, but none of them is Kulha Thoggyal's equal. It has fallen to me, the only one who truly cares for Gling's honour, to defeat him.'

Unperturbed, Gesar asked, 'Who will go with Khrothung?'

No one answered. So Khrothung rode alone to the front line where, without a word, he fought Kulha Thoggyal. In the third bout, Kulha Thoggyal swung his sword with the force of a crumbling mountain. Khrothung's weapon flew out of his hand and his armour was breached. He felt a chill bore into his very marrow, turned his horse and fled. Kulha Thoggyal gave chase, but two arrows shot by Danma, who had followed Khrothung at a distance, stopped him.

Khrothung returned to camp, greeted by raucous laughter from the other warriors. 'Enough,' Gesar said. 'The day will come when we will take the demon country.'

The demons' last day dawned.

Guided by his celestial mother, Gesar travelled to the Jade mountains in the south, above the Gungi plain. There he found a giant horse-shaped boulder upon which sat an iron statue sent from Heaven. It looked like a yak, and on it someone had placed a skull encircled with human intestines. Gesar knocked on the statue and a small door opened. Inside it was darker than the darkest night, and Gesar had to strain to see a nine-headed scorpion. This was where Shengkhri Gyalpo stored his soul. To his left was a nine-headed monster. Here Kulha Thoggyal's soul lay. Gesar killed the scorpion with an arrow and slashed off the monster's nine heads. He did not turn back as he left the statue.

Strange things began to happen. Flowers with human faces, the souls of young women devoured by the demons or offered as sacrifices to evil spirits, had bloomed on cliffs and in river valleys during the day and were abused by the demons at night. Now the flowers freed the souls inside to float up the path to reincarnation. The sky was so crowded with souls that the path did not clear until daybreak.

All that night Shengkhri Gyalpo and Kulha Thoggyal dreamed that power was leaving them. Shengkhri Gyalpo dreamed that he was a bellows with a small hole gnawed in it by an insect; no matter how hard he tried he could not gather enough wind to make his life burn brightly. Kulha Thoggyal dreamed of a sack of grain that poured out like falling rain, no matter how hard he tried to seal the tear. His heart filled with despair. The next day, inauspicious signs were everywhere. Owls laughed, fires sprang up in the forest, copper pots splintered, a python curled around the central pillar of the temple, and the deep sacred lake turned into a giant block of ice.

Princess Metog Drolma also had a dream. She dreamed that four suns appeared in the southern sky, where the snowcapped mountains melted. Women were taken north by troops wearing metal armour, while weeds in the fields of Monyul seemed to hiss as though they were jeering at defeated warriors. When she awoke, troubled by the dream, a crow circled above her head three times, then dropped a letter with a wax seal. It was a marriage proposal from Khrothung.

Metog Drolma went to see her father. 'If by marrying him I could bring peace, I would do so . . .'

Shengkhri Gyalpo mustered the spirit to say, 'I will never let you marry into Gling.'

Metog Drolma saw her father's weakness, and knew that Monyul was doomed. But she could not go against his will, so she despaired in silence.

The Gling army had arrived at Monyul's palace city.

Shengkhri Gyalpo asked Kulha Thoggyal, 'Will they use the soldiers or the generals to fight?'

Kulha Thoggyal answered, 'No matter what they do, I will employ the same tactic as before.'

'It is time for me to show my strength,' said Shengkhri Gyalpo, as he cast a dense fog into the clear blue sky.

When it dispersed, a great army stood before Gesar's troops, like Gralha's army, but many times larger. The soldiers lined up neatly, filling the land as far as the eye could see, even the mountains and the river. The ground beneath Monyul rose and fell as if it were breathing heavily. The mountains melted, the lakes congealed. There was nothing to see but soldiers in tight formation – no villages, no herds of cattle, no mines, no meditation places, no snowy peaks, no rain. Lightning snaked across the grey sky. Gling's army was locked in. Soldiers who broke formation vanished with their horses.

Gesar told them not to panic: it was an illusion created by the demon king's magic. He summoned the wind, and the Monyul army began to flutter, like draperies. His soldiers yelled, 'Stronger wind.'

In less time than it takes to burn an incense stick, the vast Monyul army faded in the early-morning sun, turned into a thick mist and disappeared. The Gling soldiers who had been lost reappeared on the battlefield, unharmed.

The Gling army engulfed the enemy like a floodtide.

After the flickering of swords and spears, only Kulha Thoggyal and his attendants still sat astride their steeds. Shanpa Merutse spurred his forward and spoke to Kulha Thoggyal.

'Our great king knows you are a magnificent warrior. He cherishes your skills, so if you will come over . . .'

'Damn you,' Kulha Thoggyal cursed. 'You betrayed and abandoned your master, and now you ask me to follow in your footsteps. Heed my arrow!'

But the arrow he shot lacked his old strength. Incensed, Shanpa Merutse returned the shot, smashing Kulha Thoggyal's armour. Kulha Thoggyal looked up into the sky and let out a long sigh. 'So be it!' He raised his sword to his own neck, but fell to the ground when his horse was speared and stumbled under him.

'Will you surrender?' Shanpa Merutse shouted again.

'Never!'

The word hung in the air when a dozen spears were thrust at him. He let them pierce his chest.

From his palace, Shengkhri Gyalpo saw Kulha Thoggyal and his remaining soldiers sucked down with the force of a whirlpool. He saw Kulha Thoggyal's soul run towards him, and gathered his last breath in a sack he carried with him.

'Everything has turned into flying dust and dying ashes. We will go together to another world and resume our training. You and I shall return!'

The palace was engulfed in a blue flame. From the sea of fire rose an ever-lengthening ladder, and at the top stood the demon king. The fire could burn away every trace of him in this world, but he could fly safely to another.

Gesar poured water from a nearby lake onto the palace, but the fire burned on.

Shengkhri Gyalpo laughed. 'I see that you are unskilled. Heaven has not helped you.'

Then thunder roared, as if to say, 'We are indeed coming to help him.'

It was not rain but a red fire that came down to douse the blue flame.

Shengkhri Gyalpo scrambled towards the top of the ladder. Gesar took out his sun-moon magic arrow and shot down part of it. He fired two more arrows, and Shengkhri Gyalpo was back on top of his palace. When Gesar took out a final arrow, Shengkhri Gyalpo yelled, 'I will not die at your hands!'

He leaped up, but instead of flying towards the heavens, he plummeted earthwards. Mustering all of his strength, he crashed into the rocky ground and destroyed himself.

The Storyteller
Salt Lake

Jigmed was on the road. He had come back to the plateau, and when he saw cows and sheep among the grasses, he stepped off the bus and began to walk, singing the story from the beginning. But he had yet to see a single salt lake. In his hometown and wherever he had travelled, he drank from lakes at the feet of snowcapped mountains, and had not been convinced that lake water could be as salty as tears. But he still believed that the lakes must exist.

He continued on, singing of the battles between Jang and Gling, as he travelled north. The first salt lake he reached was dry. Shepherds told him that it had begun to shrink more than a dozen years ago, and it had completely disappeared during the summer of the same year, when the last drop of water was burned off by the sun. Down at the lakebed, Jigmed scooped up a greyish-white crust and touched it with the tip of his tongue. It was salt.

Was this the lake that the country of Jang once tried to seize? he asked those who lived nearby. They had planted highland barley and herded cows and sheep.

They told him it was.

Pointing at a rocky cape that had once been part of a peninsula in the lake, they said that hoofprints from Gling warhorses could still be seen on it. There were even boulders that had been cloven by swords. So he walked towards the centre of the lakebed. But the soles of his boots began to dissolve in the salty soil and the soles of his feet stung. He retreated to the shore, near a village. The people who lived there had been salt-gatherers before the lake dried up.

They gave him a new pair of boots and rubbed his feet with an ointment made of animal fat, which soothed them.

These villagers were descendants of the people of Jang, who had surrendered to King Gesar and stayed to gather salt by the lake. They did not have land to farm, like those living on the southern or eastern shores, or pastures, like those on the northern and western shores. For generations they had remained on land south-west of the lake to gather salt and send it south. Their ancestors had worked in the water, which was why it was said they had webbed hands and feet. It was said also that the eyes of the salt-gatherers were not black but dusty grey from a lifetime of sorrow. In fact, no one in the village had webbed hands, though their eyes were indeed grey, the colour of mourning.

Now the lake had dried up and the land had turned to sand.

Those living off the lake blamed the salt gatherers for draining its vitality by removing the salt. They said that Gesar had had a deep love for Gling and, if he had known how it would end, he would never have let the Jang people gather salt from the lake. But he had not known. Neither could he have predicted that others would later conquer the Gling he had established. Thousands of years after the disappearance of Gling, the lake, too, had vanished. Land where demons had once run amok had turned into grassland for humans during Gesar's time, but now the people were forced to find a new place to live.

A wind raised a cloud of dust over the village, and made a mourning sound. Tears streamed from the salt-gatherers' eyes. 'Where can we go?' they asked.

'Back to where Jang used to be,' the storyteller said.

An angry young man shouted, 'Can anyone return to their homeland a thousand years after they have left it?'

Humiliated, Jigmed left the village and the dry lake.

The further north he went, the stronger the suffocating dusty wind became. The grass had gone, with the thin soil where it had grown.

Now when a gust of wind blew over, the rocks on the ground rolled about. It was at such a place that Jigmed saw his second lake.

He had found shelter from a gale behind a boulder. Away from the whistling wind, he saw the sparkle of a lake amid the sand, and heard a voice inside him say, *Gesar, am I seeing an illusion created by your magic?*

But it was a real lake, and its unnaturally green water shimmered before him. A giant steel boat sat in the middle, dredging up salt with a metal scoop big enough to hold a cow. Jigmed sat down on the road between a pair of ruts, near a grove of wormwood covered with salt dust. He was disappointed when the boat reached the shore, for the salt, piled on the rusty steel deck, was grey. It did not smell of salt but of decomposing fish. When the people jumped down from the boat, they waved him away, not giving him time to ask whether two ancient countries had fought over the salt in this lake.

He was in the way of the truck coming to transport the salt.

'But, but . . .'

'Get out of here.' They were very brusque.

So he went to a distant spot, where he turned back to look at the lake. He saw many more boats and trucks. Nothing grew beside the water, but there seemed to be plenty of salt in the lake. He thought that perhaps no one had lived near this lake in ancient times. And what about grass? He decided that the grass had been blown away by the wind. Gesar surely had never been to this place; if he had, the wind would not be so savage.

Turning to the south-west, he headed for places that people believed Gesar had visited. A faint glint from snowcapped mountains cooled him. He had met too few people in the desolate fields to do much singing and was hoping to catch up on the story as he walked on.

When the soles of his boots were worn out again, he reached the foothills and stepped onto a grassland nourished by streams rushing down from the peaks. There were no villages, but he came upon a couple of shepherd families in a valley. He spent the night with them; they gave him milk and a leg of mutton. 'You look like a storyteller,' they said. 'Can you sing the Gesar legend?'

His mouth was stuffed with meat, so it was impossible to speak; besides, the stories were now hidden in his heart, and he was no longer as eager as he had been to tell them. Secretly he feared that the tales would leave him: they had been at their most vivid the first time he had told them. When he sang them for the second and third times, the colours had faded. So he kept quiet.

Though the grass was sparse and short, he was happy to be on grassland again. One day he sensed the green deepening before his eyes, and thought that he had at last found grassland worthy of the name. But it turned out to be a lake.

By the time he reached the shore, the grass had been replaced by smooth sand and pebbles. The lake was long and narrow. He saw the light from a fire and heard the muted sound of a flute coming from the southern shore. He walked towards the sound.

At the southern end of the lake the water was a deep blue. Waves rolled in, pushing sparkling salt crystals with them. On the shore he met a group of salt-gatherers. 'Is the country of Jang your homeland?' he asked them.

They stared at him.

'Which country?'

'Jang, a place in the south.'

'To the south there are India and Nepal, nothing else.'

An old man stepped out from the group of salt-gatherers. 'I may know what you're asking about.'

Jigmed repeated his question.

The old man laughed. 'No, we're not.' He added that they did not know if they might have come from the ancient kingdom of Gling. 'We're shepherds, so who knows where our ancestors lived a thousand years ago?'

'But is this place a part of ancient Gling?'

The old man laughed again. 'We know only that there's salt here.'

They came to gather salt every year at this time. 'Are you here for the salt?' the old man asked him.

Jigmed shook his head.

'Then why are you here?'

'I'm looking for the salt lake that the country of Jang tried to take from the country of Gling.'

'We've heard that story, but we don't know if this is the same lake.'

'I think it must be. I heard someone playing a flute on the other shore, so I came over.'

They called to a shy youth and told Jigmed that he was the flute-player. But he could not play for Jigmed, since his music was meant for the lake god on the night before they began gathering salt. If it made the god happy, he would be generous. As they talked, waves continued to push salt to the shore with a shushing sound, like the murmuring of grass when the wind blows.

Jigmed stayed for three days and gathered salt with them. They strained it, dried it under the sun, and put the crystals into sacks woven from yak hair. The people rose late in the day when they gathered salt, and at night they told smutty stories. Legend had it that the lake god was lecherous, so such stories pleased him, and when he was happy, he pushed the finest salt from the depths of the lake to the shore. But Jigmed was not interested in the stories: they reminded him of what had happened at the radio station.

The night before the salt-gatherers left, the young man played his flute again, to thank the lake god. Then Jigmed told them the tale of the battle between Jang and Gling.

Jang, to the south of Gling, had a mild climate that allowed for abundant produce but no salt. So the King of Jang sent his army, led by Yulha Thoggyur, north to snatch one of the salt lakes scattered across

Gling's territory. One night on their way north, camped by a lake that did not produce salt, Yulha Thoggyur could not sleep. He got up, threw a cloak over his shoulders and went for a walk. His boots were wet with the dewdrops that hung from the grass stems and glistened in the starlight. He sat down wondering why this lake and those in his country did not produce salt. The stars, sparkling in the sky like the dewdrops, were unlikely to give him an answer. He sat there for a long time. By the time he left, the dew on the grass had turned to frost. He broke off a stalk and took it back to his tent, where, in the light of a lamp, he studied the beautiful crystals. They were so bright, so sharp, and they seemed to whisper to him. He thought of calling the sorcerer to interpret the mysterious sound, but the frost melted under the lamplight. A drop of limpid water slid down the thin blade of grass and disappeared into the ground.

On the day the soldiers found the salt lake, so many rushed forward and stuffed so much salt into their mouths that no one in the army could shout a decent battle cry the next day when the fight against Gling began.

Yulha Thoggyur sat in full armour near the lake, watching the wind make waves that pushed salt crystals towards the shore. He saw the salt change colour in the sun, at dusk and under moonlight. At midnight, the wind died down and the surface of the lake was calm, but his ears were filled with the sound of salt crystallizing.

On the battlefield the next day, he came close several times to knocking Shanpa Merutse off his horse. But each time a deity came to the old general's aid. Yulha Thoggyur wondered if this meant that Jang should not have sent an army to take the salt lake by force. He wanted to ask his father, but the king was not there, so he went to his military adviser.

'Besides war, how else can we obtain the salt?'

'Trade.' The military adviser became agitated. 'But it is not a fair bargain. To obtain it we give up our treasures: rare gemstones from deep in the mountains, fabrics woven by hard-working women, and elephant tusks that take more than a decade to grow. That is what we have to trade for this substance. Salt appears on its own – the people of Gling do not have to work for it, yet we must offer up so many of our precious things to have it!' Raising his hands to the heavens, the military adviser shouted, 'Heaven! You are unfair.'

The outburst frightened Yulha Thoggyur, who thought he felt a tremor in the sky.

'You are afraid, Prince.'

The man's voice still echoed on the surface of the lake when a thunderbolt came from the cloudless sky and struck him dead. He fell to the ground, his mouth buried in salt.

Now the prince was truly frightened. It seemed to him that Heaven indeed helped some people but not others, and he was afraid that omniscient and omnipotent Heaven would hear his thoughts. But they kept rising from the depths of his mind, like bubbles to the surface of a dark swamp. He fought them through a sleepless night; they refused to leave him the following day, when he donned his armour for battle. As he faced his opponent, he looked up into the sky.

'Do not appeal to Heaven,' Shanpa Merutse said. 'The gods will not help you, because they are on the side of Gling.'

That enraged the prince, who spurred his horse and came at Shanpa Merutse with his sword, but the old warrior reined in his horse and successfully dodged the blow.

'I came on King Gesar's orders to talk to you,' he said.

'Gesar is not your king.'

'He is now.'

'You are a traitor,' the prince said, and charged again.

This time Shanpa Merutse did not move out of the way. 'We shall see who Heaven will help now, you or me.'

Heaven could see that Shanpa Merutse was no match for Yulha Thoggyur, so two mountain gods came to help subdue the prince. In the end, it took three more mountain gods and the weight of five towering mountains. As he tied up the prince with a rope that was as thick as his arm and as long as a goat's intestine, Shanpa Merutse apologised. 'You are a great warrior, and I will not harm you. I will take you to see King Gesar.'

The prince cried to the sky, 'Soaring falcon, fly south and tell my father that his son Yulha Thoggyur has failed and that he will soon die at the hands of Gling.'

But Gesar liked Yulha Thoggyur from the moment he met him. Yet he needed to test how brave he was. 'You are a prince, but you came to take my salt lake. Therefore I am going to sacrifice you to Heaven.'

'I am a prince so my life does not belong to me. I die for the people of Jang with no regret.'

Gesar smiled when he heard this. 'The people of Jang are fortunate to have such a gallant prince. You are a valiant man. With a prince like you, the people of Jang will enjoy even more blessings.'

He untied the prince.

'Will you really give the Jang people salt?' Yulha Thoggyur asked.

'The path you have opened on your way north will become a salt road,' Gesar said. 'And I will make you the leader of this country.'

'What about my father?'

'He must give up his throne in atonement to his people.'

The Storyteller
Salt Road

It was late at night when Jigmed finished his story; the constellations that had been high in the sky were sinking towards the horizon.

The young folk wanted to hear more, but Jigmed lay down by the fire and pulled the blanket up to his chin.

'Go to sleep,' one of the elders said. 'We have to be on the road tomorrow.'

'Was this really the salt lake they wanted?'

A subtle fragrance rose from the creeping cypress that had been laid over the dying fire.

When day broke, the salt-gatherers set off. They had travelled the same route for many years, but it seemed different that day. Few among the black-haired Tibetans had not heard the story of King Gesar, but how many had heard it from a real *grungkan*, beside the salt lake that featured in it? It was a new experience for the storyteller as well, for it had never occurred to him that the story he told would so vividly unfold before his eyes. People in his homeland no longer gathered their salt in the lake, or travelled to a distant place to get it. The government sent salt to them: it would not let anyone touch the salt business. Government salt was of the highest quality and did not have the acrid taste of lake salt, for it had come from under the ground. It was as white as snow, unlike the dark grey lake salt with its bitter taste.

Was this the same salt road as in the story? Sheep formed a winding line through the deserted fields, carrying sacks brimming with salt on each side. They looked as if they might buckle under the weight.

'Those poor sheep,' Jigmed said, but no one paid him any attention.

Three days later a lama joined them on the road.

'Look at those poor sheep,' Jigmed repeated.

'You are carrying their burdens in your heart,' the lama said. 'But you can only carry them there, not on your body.' Lamas were always making meaningless statements that sounded profound.

Jigmed's heart ached when he saw how the sheep stumbled along with the salt on their backs.

The lama struck up a conversation with Jigmed to divert his attention.

'They tell me you're a *grungkan.*'

'I wasn't before, but I am now.'

The lama laughed. 'I wasn't always a lama either.'

'Did you become one after a Living Buddha enlightened you?'

'Clearly a Living Buddha has enlightened you.'

Jigmed changed the subject. 'You're a learned man. Can you tell me if this has always been a salt road?'

The lama turned to an old man who had earned the respect of everyone in the salt caravan.

'Maybe this will be the last time.' The old man sighed, and told them that for generations they had been coming here to gather salt to sell in farming areas further south. They exchanged the salt for the grain and pottery they needed in the pasture. But now the government, using aeroplanes and trucks, brought them salt of much higher quality. It was as white as snow and as fine as milled flour. The shepherds no longer needed to collect and transport salt with their sheep. He went on, 'Rows of towering snowcapped mountains border the far end of the farming villages, and I think that Jang must have been located beyond them.'

'I have heard that Monyul was also beyond the snowcapped mountains.'

'I don't know about that. I know only that our people will no longer come here to gather salt. We'll be the last group to travel on the salt road. Heaven has given us the salt, but we don't need it now.'

'Is that bad?'

'Maybe Heaven will be reluctant to give us things in the future.'

The lama knitted his brows. 'You must not guess at Heaven's will.'

The old man quickly brought his palms together in front of his chest, as he recited a Buddhist phrase. 'I'm afraid that Heaven will take back the salt in the lake and that there will be none left if we need it again.'

The lama said, 'Oh, you ignorant people. You may doubt yourself, but how dare you question Heaven's will?'

The old man slowed his pace and fell behind. The lama, on the other hand, led the way in high spirits.

'They are unhappy about the salt,' Jigmed said.

'Are you defending them?'

'How could a salt-gatherer know Heaven's will?'

'So,' the lama stopped and turned to him, 'do you think you do?'

'I didn't . . .'

'You don't know it either!' The lama flew into a rage. 'You think you know Heaven's will because you can sing the Gesar legend. Well, you do not. You don't even understand the stories. Heaven let you sing them, not understand them. Heaven didn't want you to understand. If it had, it could have had a parrot sing it!'

'I just wanted to know if the story was true. I wanted to know if there was really a salt lake or a salt road.'

'You want a true story? You want what happened in the story to be true?'

'Is that wrong?'

'If you keep at it, Heaven will turn you into a mute. Heaven does not need a storyteller like you.'

Jigmed wanted to continue the discussion, but the lama was ready to leave the caravan to visit a sacred relic on the rocky peak just ahead of them.

'Then I won't be able to learn from you,' Jigmed said.

'I shall catch up with you later, if I wish to.'

True enough, a few days later the lama rejoined them. He said he'd meditated facing the cave wall for five days.

'But we've been on the road for only three days since you left,' Jigmed blurted.

Their road slanted downwards and cut into a deep mountain valley, where fields and a farming village appeared. But the sky darkened before the caravan reached the village, so they spent the night halfway down the mountainside, where they could see lights below.

The young flute-player begged Jigmed to finish the story, but with the lama present, Jigmed was reluctant to begin.

'Did King Satham surrender after the prince had done so?' the young man asked.

'He, King Lutsan, Hor's White King and the King of Monyul were the four demon kings, whom Gesar had come to the human world to destroy. So Gesar would not accept his surrender, nor would he admit defeat.'

'So how did King Satham die?'

Taking out his lute from its bag, Jigmed sang again for the salt-gatherers sitting around the fire.

> 'There was a King Satham in the country of Jang,
> A devil incarnate, he had great magical powers.
> He opened his mouth and roared like a thunderclap,
> And he stood tall, as high as the sky.
> A poisonous fire shot from a point on his head,
> His queues were coiled poisonous snakes.
> Thousands of soldiers and horses could not subdue him.
> Gesar put on his armour to take up the fight,
> His celestial horse turned into a sandalwood tree,
> Three hundred arrows with hawk feathers
> Changed into ten thousand low brushes,
> His armour and bow into leaves,

Conjuring up a forest to block out the mountain valley.
Satham, who came to repel the enemy, saw the beautiful
   scenery,
Freeing his flying steed by the lake,
Putting down his weapon to bathe in the water.
Gesar turned into a golden-eyed fish,
Boring into the demon king's guts,
Turning into a wheel with a thousand spokes.
With magic power the wheel twirled like the wind.
The poor King Satham,
Heart, liver, intestines, lungs all now mushy porridge!'

They were quiet when he finished, but it was not the kind of silent reflection Jigmed had been hoping for. Instead, it was the silence of disappointment. Sure enough, the flute-player asked, 'So King Satham just died? That's it?'

'Yes, he died.'

'Why didn't Gesar engage him in a fight to the death?'

The question made Jigmed unhappy. 'No one ever asks a *grungkan* a question like that.'

'I was hoping they'd fly into the sky and burrow into the earth, wielding eighteen different kinds of weapons to have a good fight,' the flute player muttered.

Jigmed put away his lute.

'But weren't you asking questions too?' said the lama. 'You should not have asked if this was the salt road from Gling to Jang. Heaven will punish you.'

Jigmed was frightened but unrelenting. 'How will Heaven punish me?'

'It will take back the stories. What did you do before?'

'Herded sheep.'

'Then you can expect to become a shepherd again.'

'I just thought that the stories I tell should be true.'

'So you're saying that this isn't a true story?'

Jigmed dared not answer. He was simply curious. He had wanted to see the salt lake and, after seeing it, had wanted to see the salt road and the two ancient countries, Jang and Monyul. But now he was apprehensive. He wondered if the gods would appear in his dream with a warning. But he did not dream that night, and when he got up the next morning the lama was gone, leaving only the vague indention of a human form on the grass.

Following the salt-gatherers, Jigmed entered the village at the foot-hills, where the first person they met said, 'You're five days late this year.'

'What would you like to trade?'

'No one needs salt these days. But I have an extra pot, so why don't I trade it for a little salt?'

'We can buy our own pots. We'd rather have grain,' the flute-player said.

Feeling sorry for the grassland shepherds, who had travelled thousands of *li* to trade, the farmers exchanged a few things for the impure salt they no longer needed: a few pecks of beans, an earthenware jar, barley, dried vegetables, oil lamps (the villages now had a water and power station) and hempen ropes.

They kept moving south, passing through three villages in three days. They exchanged salt that the farmers no longer needed for things they could easily obtain in front of their tents at home: walnuts, dried apples, flour, anise seeds, homemade barley wine and factory-brewed beer. They planned to drink all of the wine and beer

Villagers invited the shepherds, with whom they had been trading for generations, to their homes for dinner or to spend a night. 'You're not likely to come next year,' they said.

'We should not have come this year,' the old man said, 'but we want our young to know the route. If you need salt again, send them a note and they will come straight away.'

They spent the night outside the village in an open field. But the villagers sent over food, a vast quantity, worth far more than their salt. They could not take it all with them, so on the morning they left they lined it up neatly under a walnut tree at the village entrance. The village, shrouded in a thin fog, was still asleep. They set off southwards, where the land became lower, the open valleys more crowded. Jigmed, who had been quiet for a few days, could no longer contain himself. 'Was this place once the country of Jang?' he asked a farmer, who had come to trade.

Unnerved, the farmer turned to the old man in the salt caravan: 'Why did he ask me that?'

'He wants to know if this place relies upon salt from the north.'

'It did, but no longer.'

They would finish trading salt that day, so Jigmed felt he had to ask the old man something that had been on his mind. 'Did you always come only this far?'

The old man told him that in the past they had gone much further, all the way to where the valley sank and disappeared, and to places where the land began to rise. They would not turn back until they saw undulating snowcapped peaks rising above the horizon. But this was a farewell trip for them, so they had not carried much salt.

'Then you must have been to the former Jang territory.'

'I'm old enough to have heard many *grungkan*s sing, but none has ever asked us, their audience, that question. It is just a story. And now we're turning back to our grassland. It's time to say goodbye.'

As the salt-gathering shepherds walked away, a keen sadness gnawed at Jigmed's heart. He would keep going south, following the salt road. But he had to hurry, because the story had raced ahead of him.

The Storyteller
Reprimand

After traversing the open valley, Jigmed began to climb the snowcapped mountain range in the south, which he was sure must have been the territory of the old Jang or Monyul nation. He carried a small sack of salt the shepherds had given him.

Tired from walking, he drank at a spring, before looking up at snowcapped mountains that rose above the horizon. They were higher, steeper and brighter than their northern counterparts. He took out a pinch of salt and placed it on the tip of his tongue; its bitter taste filled his mouth. He looked thoughtful, searching for the truth behind the story, like the scholar who had taken him to the radio station.

He'd seen farmers store hay in trees for their oxen the following year while they tilled the land and sowed the seeds. So he climbed a tree and buried himself in the hay to spend the night, during which he dreamed about the scholar. But he woke up before he had a chance to ask whether he would be in the Jang or the Monyul territory once he entered the mountains. He wondered if the scholar had looked for him after he had left the radio station. He did not go back to sleep until Venus rose over the horizon. In the morning, he decided that the scholar was probably not looking for him: it could not be difficult to locate a travelling storyteller who sang the Gesar legend. Jigmed was beginning to weary of roaming the land. He wanted to return to places where people congregated.

But the next day he entered the mountains.

A foaming stream surged down from the peaks and merged with a river not far from the giant dragon spruce in which he had spent the night. It took him two days to follow the stream to its source, only to see more peaks rise before him. He was still above the snow line. Far below, canyons shimmered with the green of a forest.

He spent the night in a cave.

And that was where the gods reprimanded him.

Waking at midnight, he put another pinch of salt on his tongue as a way of filling the emptiness in his heart, and that was when he realised he was in an ice cavern. Moonbeams shone through cracks in the ice walls. In the glow a god appeared, tall and august. Jigmed was frozen by the light from his eyes.

'Are you . . .?'

The god remained silent.

'You *are*!'

'A *grungkan* should be singing among crowds,' the god said.

'My audience wanted to know where the salt lake was, and the palaces of Jang and Monyul. They will believe my story if I can find these places.'

'They already do.'

'These are all true stories?'

'If they want to believe, they will not care if the stories are true. Why must you ask?' The god was growing impatient.

'But I have travelled a long way.'

'You were chosen because you were ignorant of worldly affairs. Would you become someone who knows everything?'

'Should I remain a fool?'

The god smiled coldly. 'Do you wish to offend me?'

Jigmed knew he was shaking, for the salt at his belt was trickling onto the ground.

'What is that noise?' The god had sharp ears.

He wanted to tell the god that it came from the falling salt, not from his bladder; he did not lose control of that. But before Jigmed could open his mouth, the god began to glow, then stretched his bow and fitted Jigmed to it as an arrow. Jigmed shot out, his body smashing through the ice walls and tearing apart the clouds. Rushing past stars in the blue sky, he lost consciousness, but not before he heard the god's voice. It still echoed when he awoke: 'You need only open your mouth and the stories and poems will fill it. Do not tax your brain.'

'Please don't be angry with me. I promise to stop thinking,' he said, his eyes closed. But the god did not respond.

A fly crawled onto his face, buzzing, and Jigmed opened his eyes to find himself in a pen where pigs wallowed in filth. He crawled out, but the flies followed him, and the wind could not blow away either the stench or the anger inside him. Raising his head, he shouted: 'You should not have done this to me!'

But the sky was empty, except for the wind-shredded clouds.

He quickened his pace until he encountered a pair of itinerant monks, one old and one young, resting by a small lake. They asked where he was going.

'I don't remember,' he said.

'Uncle is a joker,' the young monk said.

Jigmed gave him a stern look. 'I never joke. I know I'm looking for something but I forget what it is.' Pointing to the sky, he added, 'He's unhappy with me, and has made me forget.'

'Those who know how to tell a joke always say they're not funny. They make others laugh but do not laugh themselves.' The solemn old monk's face creased with a smile. 'Since you do not know where you are going, may I ask where you come from?'

He whispered in the old monk's ear, 'I've forgotten where I slept last night.'

The old monk laughed. 'You are indeed funny, just like Aku Tonpa.'

Aku Tonpa! Jigmed had heard people mention that name. Aku Tonpa had no status, no property, no wealth of knowledge, yet he was the clever hero of countless stories. 'Take me to see him if you know him,' Jigmed said, clutching the old monk's arm.

He brushed away Jigmed's hand. 'No one knows Aku Tonpa.'

Clouds whipped through the sky and water gurgled in the spring, portents that something was about to happen. Nothing did. The young monk put the teapot and bowls into his knapsack.

'I must meet Aku Tonpa,' Jigmed said.

Slinging the bag over his shoulder, the young monk said, 'Stop, or you'll lose your wit and begin to talk nonsense. Ah, I see that my master has left. I won't be able to catch up with him if I stay any longer.'

The old monk disappeared around a bend in the road, the young one hot on his heels.

It dawned on Jigmed that he could never meet Aku Tonpa, for he was an ordinary human, not a god. Aku Tonpa would not want others to tell his story, since he was neither a god nor royal. But almost everyone loved to tell stories about him.

When he was a shepherd Jigmed had once glanced at his reflection in the waters of a lake. His face had been full and dark, with a serene expression. Now he went to the lakeside and looked again. The face in the water was gaunt and stern, with a straggly beard. He was shocked by its cynical, distrustful air. The man in the water did not resemble the person he believed he was. He sat by the lake for a long time, listening to the water flow over grass and seep into a nearby ditch. At long last he detected a faint smile in the melancholy eyes, which made him happy. Then sun set, and the evening chill forced him to set off again, though he still could not recall where he'd come from or where he was going.

That night he asked a family to give him a bed, and as he was a travelling storyteller, they asked him to sing. But even without seeing the disappointment in their eyes, he knew he'd done badly. The god had left him the story but had taken back the rich language and cadence. To make up for it, he offered to tell the story of Aku Tonpa, but his host said, 'You're tired and must rest. Anyone can tell the story of Aku Tonpa. The legend of Gesar requires a special storyteller.'

He got up dejectedly and was following his hostess to his bed when the family's youngest son blurted out, 'He looks like Aku Tonpa.'

'Nonsense!'

'But he does.'

As he lay in bed, Jigmed wondered if Aku Tonpa had a gaunt face, low spirits and a straggly beard. As he fell asleep, he heard his own self-mocking laughter.

The Story
Aku Tonpa

Gesar's reputation reached its zenith after the victory over Monyul. There were banquets, singing and dancing, parades and hunting trips. The moment his horses raised dust on the horizon, people roasted cattle and slaughtered sheep for a feast. The chief minister, afraid that the king would be exhausted from his travels, ordered a sedan chair, carried by brawny men and attended by handsome young ones with gigantic parasols. Wherever the magnificent procession passed, people knelt on the ground, earnestly kissing the shadow cast by the parasols; they dared not lay eyes on the king.

Gesar was puzzled. 'Why won't they look at me, their king? I would if I were them.'

'They're afraid that their lowly gaze will offend the noble king.'

He did not know that his ministers had forced the people to suppress their curiosity. 'I'd want to see my king.'

'Everyone knows how handsome and powerful you are.'

'How, without looking at me?'

'From paintings, songs and stories.'

'Really?'

'Great King, you founded the nation of Gling, you vanquished the four demon kings, and you have given the people a happy and prosperous life. Is that not worthy of praise?'

'Then find me a good storyteller. I wish to hear how people tell my story.'

'The best storyteller would have nothing to say in front of you.'

That was so. At least a dozen storytellers were led up to the king that night, but after they stumbled in, they knelt on the floor to touch his boots with their foreheads. 'I wish only to hear how you tell of what I've done,' he told them gently.

No one dared to tell the stories about his background, his romances, his treasured horse, his archery, his wisdom, his bravery or, least of all, of how he had lost his way.

Prince Gralha came forward. 'Great King, the gods sent you to the human world, so naturally they will let people tell your story.'

'They should love me, not fear me.'

Without answering his concern directly, Gralha repeated, 'Great King, since Heaven has sent you to the human world, it will not object to the people telling stories about you.'

'Are they afraid of me because I am not human, because I came from Heaven?'

'Perhaps.'

'Then you will listen to the stories and report back to me.'

Gralha left and returned a few days later. 'I did not hear stories about you, but I did hear stories about someone else,' he said. 'A man called Aku Tonpa. Everyone tells stories about him.' Prince Gralha began his tale.

There was once a wealthy aristocrat who spread the news that he had more barley seeds than anyone else in all of Gling. Many of Gling's destitute people came to pledge allegiance to him, even citizens of Jang and Monyul, since he could lend them barley. But when autumn arrived, the aristocrat sent his people to collect the debts, which were now ten times what he had lent them. Aku Tonpa was one of those who had been forced to borrow seeds. But the newly reclaimed land had yielded a small crop, and there would be little left after the borrowers had paid back the aristocrat tenfold. So Aku Tonpa fried the barley seeds before delivering them to the aristocrat. The seeds were lent again the following spring, and of course the fried barley would not grow. In the end, Aku Tonpa took the people with him to other, more compassionate, aristocrats.

'What a clever man!' The king laughed.

Gralha had hoped that the king would want to know which aristocrat had been so heartless, but he did not. He was simply amused by how a clever, resourceful person had tricked the man – who had been none other than Khrothung. In fact, Khrothung was not the only Gling landowner engaged in such dealings. So Gralha did not smile when the king laughed. Neither did the ministers.

'I want to meet this man,' the king said.

Khrothung tried to stop him. 'Why would you want to meet such a lowly, ordinary person? A king has many more important matters to occupy his time and energy.'

'But I have nothing to do.'

When he came to Shanpa Merutse's fiefdom on a northern inspection, he met the man. Aku Tonpa swayed when he walked, like a sapling rocked by the wind.

'Why are you so thin?' The king was shocked.

'I'm fasting – no food and no milk.'

'Why?'

'So that the common people, like the immortals, will not worry about food, and will be convinced that they live in a blessed country.'

The king had hoped to meet a light-hearted, witty man, but Aku Tonpa was cynical and bitter. Unsure whether he liked him, Gesar said, 'I have had a tiring journey. Perhaps we can talk some other day.'

With a look of indifference, Aku Tonpa bowed and left.

Shanpa Merutse wanted Aku Tonpa to stay at the palace so he could be presented to the king at any moment, but the man said, 'I shall go home now. I will leave my hat here. When the king wants to see me, tell the hat and I shall know.'

Shanpa Merutse saw him to the entrance of the palace. 'So you also know magic.'

'You could say so,' Aku Tonpa replied. He did not, but he sensed that the king would not want to talk with him again. Sure enough, the king left Shanpa Merutse's palace, and dust began to cover the hat that hung in the hall. One day it disappeared, stolen by a weasel to make a nest under the floor. Then the master of the palace realised he had not seen Aku Tonpa for a long time, and when the king heard of his disappearance, he summoned him to be his minister of parables, but by then no one could find him.

Khrothung appealed to the king to arrest this man, who despised wealth and power.

'He is already an immortal,' the king said. 'You cannot arrest someone who lives only in stories.'

Still, Khrothung flew off on his magical vulture to search for Aku Tonpa, but all he found was the latest story about him.

'It is refreshing to hear that you are trying to find a character in a story,' the king told him. 'Sit on a hill and think about it.'

Khrothung travelled from one hill to the next, but none felt like the right place, and the wind whipped away his ideas the moment they formed in his head. So he returned to the palace. The king had tired of Khrothung. 'Aku Tonpa's stories are in everyone's mouth and head,' he said, 'so he lives in the mouth and head of every storyteller. You cannot catch him, so don't waste your time.'

Khrothung had hoped to get closer to the king by arresting Aku Tonpa, the man who showed no respect for rich men, aristocrats or monks. But the cunning Aku Tonpa had found a perfect hiding place in stories, where he could travel around the world without having to move his feet, and there was nothing anyone could do about him. Khrothung gave up and set off for his own fiefdom.

On the road home, Khrothung's soldiers came upon a caravan of Persian merchants come to trade in Gling. They had fine steeds and luminous pearls, as well as a secret code that would take them to a great treasure in the mountains. The caravan had stopped for the night, and, using two large pearls to light their camp, they made dinner, then prayed in the direction of home. Weary from their journey they fell into a deep sleep, without putting away the pearls. In the strange light of the pearls, Khrothung and his soldiers seized the riches of the caravan. The two leaders of the Persian caravan awoke to find themselves tied up, swaying back and forth on horseback.

After vanquishing the four demon kings, Gling had enjoyed an era of peace. Now Gesar received a report that a large army was massing at the western border, claiming to protect the trading caravans. He commanded the warriors of the tribes to prepare for battle.

Prince Gralha thought that as Khrothung's greed had prompted the invasion, he should be bound and taken to the Persians, along with the Tagrong tribe's property, which would compensate them ten times over for what they had lost.

'What good would that do?' the king asked.

'The prince has put forward an excellent idea,' the chief minister said. 'First, we would be rid of a treacherous official, and second, our people would continue to live in peace.'

But Gesar said, 'Gling's tall mountains and broad rivers in the east serve as a border with China. We defined the northern and southern borders by conquering the four demon countries. But I have never had a clear sense of our western border. This expedition will make our territory complete. Say no more, and wait for my orders to march.'

The expedition lasted a year. Gesar's armies continued their conquest in the west until a towering mountain range blocked their way. The surviving Persian troops crossed the mountains and disappeared into the deep, dark valley beyond.

Gesar surveyed the mountain peaks that surged westward, like waves, and as he did so, someone said that the mountain gods had fled west, away from Gling's armies.

Gesar plucked a magical arrow from his quiver and shot it deep into the rock at his feet, halting the flight of the mountain gods. The mountains straightened and paused in their westward movement. Dark shadows of Persian troops lingered in the spaces between the peaks. Khrothung asked to continue the chase, saying that he knew the secret code that would lead him to the treasure.

'We stop here,' Gesar said. 'Gling will be bordered by mountains on all sides.'

One of the attendants wrote a poem for the occasion, using the newly invented writing system. In his poem he compared the mountains that surrounded Gling with fences.

'Fences?' Gesar pondered this. 'They are like fences, but I hope that the people of Gling will not be fenced in. Why say "fences" to describe mountains that soar like ferocious lions?'

Prince Gralha laughed. 'Our horses can sweep through the mountain passes like a storm.'

'Perhaps for now, but what of the future?'

'Gling armies are invincible. The king should not worry about the future.'

'You may feel as I do when you are king.'

'That thought has never crossed the mind of your humble servant,' Gralha replied. 'You will be our king for ever.'

'No one can be a king for ever.'

'Then when will the king . . .'

Gesar gave him a sharp look. 'Ask Aku Tonpa,' he said.

'The man in the story?'

'I have met him but once, when he hid from me. Perhaps I displeased him. But you are a likeable young man, so perhaps he will not hide from you. If he neither mocks nor teases you, you will be a good king. You need not worry about me. It's him you should fear.'

'Will you be in the stories too?'

'They will tell stories about me for thousands of years to come. Do you believe that?'

'I do. The king is a deity and a deity can predict the future.'

'I shall not select all of the storytellers, perhaps just one, someone who looks like Aku Tonpa.' The king laughed. 'He must look as if the world owes him something, as if he has been wronged but has no idea why.' The king was pleased by this thought. 'You may go now. I shall sleep, and I sense I may meet him in my dream.'

'Aku Tonpa?'

'No, the one who will come in a thousand years, the one who looks like Aku Tonpa.'

The Story
Dream Encounter

Gesar had his dream. He dreamed about the grasslands of Gling more than a thousand years hence.

The scene was familiar to him: the position of the mountains, the movements of the rivers. But there were new trees – fruit-bearing trees in orchards, other trees flanking newly opened roads, like soldiers. On the roads strange vehicles trailed long columns of smoky dust into a clear blue sky. The houses were different, filled with strange objects. But when the people emerged to look into the sky, they mumbled words Gesar understood. Drivers stopped for water from the stream, cupped their hands to drink and spat mouthfuls into the air, in a fountain, making tiny rainbows in the bright sunlight, just as his soldiers did when they dismounted to rest by the river.

Jigmed looked as he had imagined, like Aku Tonpa, who had disappeared into stories. But his figure flickered, as if it would vanish at any moment. 'Come in,' Gesar said.

'There's no house, no tent and no door. How shall I come in?' the man replied.

'Come into my dream.'

'You come in and out of my dream freely, but I dare not enter yours.'

'I may come often in the future, but I have not been there yet. The idea has just occurred to me.' He laughed. 'It must be something I will do after I return to the celestial realm. So, tell me, what did *that* Gesar do in your dream?'

'You put your Gling stories into my belly.'

'How did I do that?'

Jigmed told him about the god in golden armour who had opened his belly and stuffed a book inside.

Gesar laughed again. 'That is how lamas put treasures inside the Buddha. But you are a living person!'

'It didn't hurt, and when I woke up, I knew how to tell the story of the lion-like King Gesar of Gling.'

'Are you afraid?'

'No. He was just looking for someone to tell his story.'

'But are you afraid now?'

'Afraid of what?'

'You are in my dream. Are you not afraid that I shall not let you leave?'

Jigmed had never been particularly courageous, but he was not afraid. Instead he laughed. 'I've offended you, but I only wanted to know if the countries of Jang and Monyul in the stories were real. I went looking for them, and the god was upset. He shot me with a single arrow to stop me searching.' Jigmed felt at his waist and found the arrow that had pierced his belt and gone up along his spine to his collar. He turned to show it to the arrow's owner, wondering how Gesar could see an object in his dream that existed only in Jigmed's mind.

Touching the arrow, Gesar said, 'It is my arrow but I did none of the things you say I have done to you.'

'Then what have you been doing?'

'I have conquered the Persian troops and set up Gling's western border. Now there is no more war and I have nothing to do, so I thought someone should record all of this. I tried to find a man who resembles someone else I have met.'

'Do I look like him?'

'Yes, very much.'

'Who is it?'

'Aku Tonpa.'

'You know him?'

'He still exists?'

'Yes!'

'Have you seen him?'

'No one has seen him. He lives only in stories.'

'Ah. Obviously, finding someone to tell *my* story is the right thing to do.'

'I'm doing that already, even telling of things you haven't done yet. And the story will go on until you return to Heaven from Gling.'

Gesar grabbed Jigmed's arm. 'Tell me, what other great feats must I accomplish before I return to Heaven? And will Gralha become the new king?'

'I cannot tell you.'

'You must.'

'I cannot.'

'Perhaps I shall keep you in my dream.'

Jigmed sat down comfortably. 'I won't leave. At least I won't have to trudge through the wind and snow any longer.'

'You should go.'

'You won't change your mind, will you?'

Gesar was displeased. 'You will not address me as *you*. I am the king. If the chief minister were here, he would have someone slap your face.'

'You are the King of Gling, but you are not my king.'

'But you must be a subject of Gling.'

'The land is still here but there is no more Gling.'

'No more Gling?'

'Not now.'

Seeing the disappointment on the king's face, the storyteller reminded himself that every king believed that the foundation he had laid would last a thousand years. He decided not to tell him that scholars studying the Gesar legend were debating whether there had ever been a country called Gling on the plateau, and whether the half-god, half-human King Gesar had been a historical figure. He simply stood up, bowed and withdrew from the dream. The last thing he heard the king say was, 'No wonder you failed to take off your hat when you came in.'

Jigmed found himself in an empty field. He took off his hat and held it to his chest, saying, 'I'm sorry. I forgot I was wearing a hat.' Then he got back onto the road. Yet the idea that he knew things that the king did not, and that he would now roam the land as a storyteller, taking alms from the audience, left him feeling melancholy.

The last thing Gesar heard from the man who would sing his stories a thousand years later was, 'I'm sorry. I forgot I was wearing a hat.' Then he left his own strange dreamscape, and fell asleep, satisfied, knowing that someone would sing about him centuries later.

But he woke up out of sorts: the storyteller had said that Gling would one day disappear.

At court that day, the ministers brought only good news: a new tribe had come to pledge allegiance; a small country had sent an emissary with tribute; a scholar had written a book on the inevitability of Gling's greatness; the soul of a heretic lama had been subdued. In short, the weather was favourable for crops, the country was prosperous, the people lived in peace, and the wise king's influence reached all corners of the world. But he said softly, 'How long will this last?'

'Ten thousand years!' came the ministers' response.

The king abruptly stepped down from his golden throne and walked out of the palace alone. His attendants followed at a distance as he climbed a hill. He told himself that the next time he was in the dream he would take note of what the palace looked like and if the rivers still flowed to the south-west. His attendants heard him mumble, 'What is the meaning of it all if it is destined to vanish?'

His question was as meaningless as the roar of the river. Of course, there were some clever people who believed that even the river noise had meaning, but it brought them no peace of mind. None at all.

As he came down from the hill he passed through the crowd that waited for him – ministers, generals, consorts, palace guards, personal maids, a sutra instructor – as though he was crossing an empty field. The monks claimed that the king had reached enlightenment and now regarded what ordinary people considered solid as 'empty', which meant the triumph of Buddhist teachings. Everyone else was worried.

But a king cannot allow himself to be mired in thought for too long, for something is always happening. Now, Gesar and his army had established the borders of Gling, but there were small countries still where Gling's towering peaks divided the land. They offered yearly tribute and showered it on Gling, but wars were constantly breaking out between them, and when war clouds rose, Gling's peace was disrupted.

On this day, Gesar felt the malevolent air of battle rising above the mountainous south-east. He told Prince Gralha to ready the troops and prepare an expedition. Sure enough, a messenger from a small country called Guchen came seeking help. They were being attacked by another small country, Brugku.

'Why would Zhugu attack you? Has the king taken a fancy to your princess or some other rare treasure?' Gesar asked.

The messenger knelt. 'If we had a lovely princess, we would have offered her to Gling long ago. And if we had any treasure, we would not consider ourselves worthy, and would have presented it to the throne of the great king.'

Gesar nodded. 'So, Brugku has started a war without reason. Go back and tell your king that Gling will set matters right.'

The Storyteller
Cherry Festival

There were now two Gesars in Jigmed's mind. One was the hero of the stories he sang. The other was the Gesar whose dream he'd entered, the god born into the human world. Yet though the dream was not quite real, and he could remember only blurred grey images, he preferred the Gesar of the dream.

He awoke thinking about the arrow in his back. But when he took off his clothes, he found no trace of it.

If he ever re-entered that dream, he thought, he would ask Gesar to give him the arrow as a souvenir. But Jigmed had never been the sort of man who hoped for the impossible, so he said to himself, *Very well. Let the arrow become part of my back.*

He carried it with him as he walked to a town where he had been invited to perform at a new festival named for its major export – the cherry. An arborist familiar with the area's unique soil and climate had convinced the government to order the farmers to grow cherry trees rather than barley in the poor soil of the dry riverbed. As predicted, the trees produced fine cherries.

The town was crowded: cherry merchants, journalists and officials who outranked local officials. Even so, Jigmed was put up in a room of his own at a hotel, where they had laid out promotional brochures with pictures of him singing in his storyteller outfit. He was pleased. That day during the opening ceremonies he'd sung only a brief passage, barely finding his voice before applause carried him offstage, where he'd had to press himself to a wall to make way for a group of girls, made up like bright red cherries. But that night he was invited to sing in a banquet tent set up in a riverside orchard. 'Which passage will you perform?' the mayor asked.

'The one about Gesar helping Guchen defeat Brugku.'

With a broad grin, the mayor said, 'With that battle, Gesar opened the treasure trove in Brugku's mountains and returned to court in triumph. That's exactly what we want for our cherry festival. Let's have a toast. Cheers!'

Jigmed left before the cherry festival was over. Along the road, when asked where he'd come from and where he was going next, he said he'd come from it. The people laughed and told him that when the cherry festival was over, he could go to the apricot festival or the plum festival. He wasn't sure if their sarcasm was directed at the festivals or at him for singing at them. But he just said, 'If you don't want to hear me sing, I'll go to the apple festival.'

'Do you know any new passages?'

The ancient story could not have new passages: it was just that some *grungkan* sang lots of passages while others sang fewer. Jigmed could sing them all, the only storyteller of his era who could do so, and this he told them.

They said that that was what they had thought, and that before they would have asked him to stop and sing for them. Now, though, someone had come along who could write new passages.

Jigmed did not miss the fact that they had said 'write', not 'sing'.

Yes, there was someone who could write but not sing the stories, a lama called Khontag. The villagers near Khontag Lama's temple were proud of him, which was why they refused to invite the most famous *grungkan*, Jigmed, to sing for them.

'I'd like to see this man,' Jigmed said.

The villagers who supported the lama had also become wordsmiths. 'You should not say *see* him. You should say *pay him a visit*.'

'Not *pay a visit*, but *ask his advice*,' another said.

'Very well. I'll pay the man a visit.'

He was quickly corrected, 'Not *the man*. It's His Holiness Khontag Lama.'

'Oh, a lama. What did you say his name was? Khontag Lama?' He used the word *name*, though well aware that it was the lama's *fahao*, his Buddhist appellation. But, after all, the wordsmiths had only a very small vocabulary and didn't catch his error. So it was with authority that he said, 'Take me to him.'

A guide was summoned, and they walked to a large pasture, where they had yoghurt and grilled bread for lunch. Then, following the valley, they reached another village, where a river surged through a forested canyon. Here the water made eddies that swirled and disappeared and swirled again. Scarecrows in tattered clothes swayed in barley fields.

A bridge spanned the river, and his guide told him that the temple was on a hill on the far side. He looked for it, but saw only cypresses and dragon spruces against the setting sun. They crossed the bridge and climbed a steep path and, as they rounded a corner, a lovely little temple appeared amid the trees. Wild bees hummed among the blooming burdock flowers, but otherwise the temple was quiet. A yellow silk curtain hung at each window. A barefoot young monk of seven or eight sidled from behind the door and, without waiting for them to speak, put a finger to his lips and led them to a tree not far from the temple. Another silent monk came to offer tea.

'Return in ten days,' the boy whispered, 'when Khontag Lama emerges from his retreat. He is writing the new legend of King Gesar.'

'He's really doing that?'

'He had stopped writing for a long time and only began again when he was inspired by Dakini. Then new stories poured from his head.'

'Dakini?'

The boy gave a knowing smile and pointed to a window in the monks' living quarters. A round-faced woman was peering at them through the curtains.

'Is that her?'

'Yes.'

The woman was gone from the window when Jigmed turned to look again.

The Storyteller
Digging up the Treasure

Jigmed spent the night in a riverside village. When he awoke the next day, he complained to his host about the noise from the river. A voice from the far side of the room spoke. 'The river isn't noisy,' it said. 'The village is too quiet.'

The morning sun streamed through the window and the man on the other side of the fireplace was in shadow. He could see Jigmed but Jigmed could not see him, which made him uneasy, as the stranger's gaze felt like ants gnawing at him. Sensing his discomfort, the man laughed and said, 'Just pretend you're singing under stage lights, where everyone is looking at you but you can't see them.'

'Yes,' Jigmed replied absently, and quickly added, 'But there may be some hidden meaning in what you said.'

There was no response – the man was gone. Having had frequent unusual encounters, Jigmed was not surprised by this. He asked his host about him, and was told that he, too, was waiting to see Khontag Lama.

'Are there many people who wish to see Khontag Lama?'

'Not so many. But you're a famous *grungkan*, and you're here, aren't you?'

'How do you know I'm a *grungkan*?'

'We knew that before you came. Everyone has been saying that the most famous *grungkan* of all is coming to our village for the new stories written by Khontag Lama.'

Jigmed scowled. 'I didn't come here for the stories. I sing what the gods want me to sing.'

It was a quiet village. One family was repairing its animal pen and another was adjusting the solar panels blown over by the wind; a mill-stone rumbled near the village entrance. Leaves shushed the wind, *Soft, soft, soft*, and the wind whispered, *Listen, listen, listen.*

It was a quiet that augured a serious event, such as when someone is ready to tell you something but hasn't yet begun, or the moment just before fledglings break out of their eggs.

Jigmed could not keep the sarcasm out of his voice when he spoke to the man fixing the solar panel. 'Are you afraid you'll miss important news on the TV?'

And to the old man making new gears for the millstone: 'Be quiet. You'll frighten the fledglings back into their shells.'

They just smiled. They knew who he was but would not invite him to sing or even talk to him, which offended him. At last he walked up to a wooden post. 'The villagers refuse to talk,' he said, 'so maybe you, who can't talk, might want to speak with me.' The post swayed and fell slowly to the ground, as if pushed by an invisible hand. Jigmed was so frightened that he ran back to his host's house and stayed inside. That night, before he fell asleep, he prayed to Gesar, hoping to meet him again in a dream. But he slept so soundly that he did not even see the faint, greyish glow of the dream world. At breakfast time, the same slanting sunshine lit his half of the room, while the other was in darkness. He had barely sat down when a hand reached out from the curtain of light that blocked his view.

'Let's introduce ourselves properly.'

Jigmed raised his hand, then hesitated. 'I can't even see you.'

Laughter erupted from behind the curtain of light. It was not one person, but three, two men and a woman.

One moved into the light. 'Don't you recognise me?'

It was the scholar who had taken him to the radio station.

'Come, shake hands. How long has it been?'

'I wanted to see you, but I couldn't find you,' Jigmed said.

'Yet I hear about you. You're famous now.'

The scholar introduced his two students to Jigmed. The woman was studying for an MA, the man a PhD. The woman held a tape recorder while the PhD student carried a video camera, like TV journalists. They, too, were here to see the lama who wrote new Gesar stories. Turning on her recorder, the woman asked for Jigmed's thoughts.

'These stories came from King Gesar many years ago, and were not written by a lama.'

The scholar laughed. 'You're seeing it all wrong.'

'He's not writing it, he's discovering it. It's called digging up treasure,' said the PhD student.

Jigmed knew that sutras hidden by Buddhist masters had been unearthed. The PhD student told him that the lama was doing something similar in writing stories, delving in his heart and mind.

'So you, too, were digging up a heart treasure when you wrote your book?' Jigmed asked the scholar.

'No, I was just writing a book.'

'Then what makes Khontag Lama's writing different?'

The scholar did not offer a view. Instead, he looked at Jigmed, waiting for him to say more. Jigmed wanted to tell him that the Gesar legend had been in circulation for thousands of years and there were no new stories. But all he said was, 'What is the new story about? That new countries have appeared on land where old countries had already been conquered by Gesar?'

'Maybe.' The scholar was unsure.

'Do you think that establishing a new country is as easy as growing a mushroom? In my stories, countries that opposed Gling were all annihilated!' Jigmed was shouting now.

The three scholars laughed, which enraged Jigmed so much that he left the village. He completed two days' journey in one. On the second mountain he crossed, he came upon a temple under construction. He learned that Khontag Lama had been one of two abbots here, but that Khontag Lama did not command the same respect there that he did in the village; in fact, the monks referred to him casually.

'Khontag Lama is somewhat eccentric.'

'Khontag Lama may have managed profound Taoist skills, but his followers enjoy no benefit from them and have no say here,' said a young lama wearing thick spectacles, who seemed to be engaged in diligent study of sutras. He went on, with a shy smile, 'That is why I switched to my current master.'

His master was well known, with acolytes there and abroad. Whenever he went on a journey, he returned with substantial donations. The nearly completed monastery had cost tens of thousands of yuan.

'What about Khontag Lama?'

'Things aren't so good with him. He concentrates on his own skills and few people know of him. He has never collected much money. He complained that this place was too noisy, so he left and built a small temple for himself.'

'And he never came back?'

'He kept saying he'd return the key, but we've yet to see him.'

'A key to the monastery?'

'The monastery is not locked. It's the key to the room where the treasure is stored.'

The treasure was a suit of ancient armour supposedly left behind by Gesar. Jigmed asked to see it, but could only detect its outline through a small window in the door, which had several locks. Each abbot had one key, and the door could be opened only when all the abbots were present. They had not all been present for several years.

Jigmed felt no excitement as he looked through the window. He beseeched the void, 'Deity, please let me know if you wore this suit of armour and if it glistened on you as you went into battle.'

The setting sun painted the sky a bright red, and the stars leaped onto the curtain of evening, but there were no celestial signs. He did not dream that night.

When the sun of another day rose, Jigmed walked to the slope across from the temple to watch craftsmen decorate the golden dome.

He was not thinking of the dome's burnished beauty but of Khontag Lama, who had been digging a treasure trove of legend from his mind. Suddenly he strode back along the road. He said to himself that he did not care if he heard new stories, but he wanted to meet a lama who had been unhappy in a temple that was growing more splendid by the day.

By the time Jigmed reached the village, Khontag Lama had completed his meditation. He lived in a small two-storey building, with three rooms on the ground floor and a staircase that led to the single room upstairs. Someone led Jigmed to the bottom of the flight, and shouted, 'The *grungkan* has returned.'

'Tell him to come up,' came the response.

Jigmed took off his boots and left them at the foot of the stairs among a clutter of other shoes. The room's low ceiling forced everyone to hunch, and a group of people was already crowded inside, among them the scholar and his two students. The scholar had his notebook open, the MA student handled the tape recorder and the PhD student had set up his video camera. Jigmed saw several people he'd not noticed before; they looked like officials.

'Please ask him to come forward.' Everyone got up to let him squeeze to the front, where he came face to face with Khontag Lama.

The bright sunlight of the plateau came through a small skylight to fall on him, the lama and the little square table between them. Khontag Lama had a gaunt, pale face, and sat on a meditation bed with his legs crossed. He gave Jigmed a fleeting smile. 'It must be springtime now,' he said, in a weak, hoarse voice.

'Summer will soon be over, and the burdocks have nearly finished blooming,' Jigmed said.

'Winter had just arrived when I began my retreat. The other night I heard ice cracking on the river and thought that spring was on its way. So, summer will soon be over.'

'Yes.'

'Oh.' The lama heaved a long sigh and closed his eyes. Everyone held their breath; the room was quiet but for the video camera.

When the lama opened his eyes again, Jigmed said, 'I've been to your temple. The new monastery is almost finished. I'd like to go into that room and touch Gesar's armour, but they lack keys. Do you have one of the keys to that room?'

As if he hadn't heard him, Khontag Lama extended his little finger and, with his long nail, dabbed oil from the Buddha lamp and rubbed it into his chapped lips.

'The Buddha revealed through my *khandroma*, my sky-dancer, that the treasure in my heart has opened. Last night I dreamed about the person who will spread the treasure from my heart to every corner of the world. I feel that person must be you.'

Jigmed opened his mouth, but before he could tell the lama that he would not add to the stories given him by the deities, the lama put a finger to his lips, then turned and placed a stick of burning incense on an altar. From under the altar he drew out a bundle wrapped in yellow silk and placed it on the table. Layers of yellow silk unfurled to reveal a manuscript in the form of a Pattra Sutra. Several cameras clicked, with blinding flashes.

'What story is this?' Jigmed asked.

'Gesar conquered another country and opened the treasure trove guarded by a demon, giving Gling more wealth and blessings.' Khontag Lama offered the top page of the manuscript to Jigmed. 'I dreamed of you, so I believe the Buddha wants me to give you the treasure I found for you to spread it to the world.'

Jigmed touched the page with the tips of his fingers and quickly withdrew his hand.

Khontag Lama froze.

With a laugh, the scholar broke the silence. 'Lama, he can't read, so he cannot understand what you have written. Here, let me look.'

The lama's hands withdrew with lightning speed, leaving the scholar's hands suspended in mid-air.

'If this *grungkan* is not the predestined person,' the lama said, 'I shall wait for a revelation from the Buddha.' Although he was usually devoid of a sense of humour, he managed a small joke: 'I shall even go myself if the Buddha wants me to sing.' His hoarse voice sounded even more gravelly when he added, 'If you hear about a lama *grungkan* singing a new story, you will know it's me.'

No one laughed.

The hint of a smile creased his face. 'I mean it. I will go if the Buddha wants me to sing.'

From a dark corner came a woman's sobs, and a middle-aged woman with a dark red face appeared.

'My wife,' the lama said.

Jigmed heard the scholar whisper an explanation to his female student to the effect that Khontag Lama belonged to the Nyingma or 'Ancient' School, which allowed its monks to be married and have children.

The PhD student turned his video camera from the woman to the lama. 'Is she your Dakini?'

The lama nodded. 'She is crying because she's afraid I'll start roaming like a *grungkan*. I have told her I am not a *grungkan*, that I am a lama who digs up treasure, but she won't believe me.' He spoke gravely, yet the people began to laugh softly, which broke the solemn atmosphere.

Kneeling down, Jigmed touched the pages of the new Gesar stories with his forehead.

'Will you sing these stories?' the lama asked hoarsely.

'I can't read.'

Everyone laughed again, the lama also. 'And I don't know if you have a predestined connection with the stories, so I need a further revelation from the gods. You have travelled a great distance to be here, so perhaps there is a bond between you and the stories, but I cannot teach them to you until I am instructed to do so.'

'My stories were given to me by the gods. They were not taught to me,' Jigmed said.

The lama cocked his head. 'Don't move. There is something unusual about you.'

'What is it?'

'I do not know. Let me try to feel it.' The lama lifted his closed eyes towards the skylight, where the sun shone straight down, and stayed in that position for a long time. The scholar, his students and the county officials all felt that the lama was trying too hard to be mystical, so they stretched out their crossed legs and began to whisper among themselves. They coughed softly to clear their throats and spat phlegm into the corners of the room. Finally the lama opened his eyes. 'There is nothing I can do if you do not believe me.'

'We believe you.' But their laughter held a hint of doubt.

The scholar, his students and the local officials began to converse with the lama, so Jigmed walked outside and lay down in the grass, surrounded by flowers that swayed in the breeze. He tried to imagine how the lama had received his revelations through his Dakini – but all he saw in his mind's eye were men and women copulating. Angry with himself, he got to his feet and, once again, left the temple.

As he walked away, he silently reproached the heavens. 'Deity, do you really have other stories that you did not tell me?'

At that moment, the lama sat up and looked straight into the video camera. 'I will meet that *grungkan* again.'

'He'll come back now,' the scholar replied.

'No, he's gone.'

Part III

THE LION RETURNS TO HEAVEN

The Story
Puzzlement

Once again Gesar had nothing to do.

He asked his consorts, 'What should I be doing as king?'

The other consorts looked to Brugmo.

'The king should look after his ministers. It has been a long time since the chief minister last came to report. Perhaps he is ill.'

So the king went to see the chief minister, bringing gifts as well as the palace physician. The chief minister accepted the gifts, but refused to see the physician. 'I am not ill, just old,' he said.

'What happens next?' the king asked.

'Honourable King, I would like to serve you for ever, but I will die. One day I shall fall asleep on this bed and not wake up again.' He reached out his hands. 'These hands are as withered as tree roots.' He opened his eyes wide. 'My eyes are no longer as bright as a clear spring.'

'Why must it be so?'

'We are humans, not gods. All humans die. The king has seen it himself.'

'But you are a hero. I thought that heroes were different from the common people, that they die only on the battlefield, like Gyatsa Zhakar.'

'Dying in battle is the best a hero can hope for, but not everyone can be so fortunate. The same will happen to your beloved consorts. They will grow old and lose their beauty before they die.'

Tears streamed down Brugmo's face; grief-stricken, she covered her face and left.

The chief minister said, 'You may all go now. I have something to say to the king and I do not know how long my strength will last.' When they were alone, he continued: 'It has been a boundless blessing for the people of Gling to have a king from Heaven, but you will find it hard to watch so many warriors die before you, and to see your consorts age. But Gling has a solid foundation. One day you, too, will leave and return to Heaven.'

'Is there nothing more for me to do here?'

'There is one thing, but . . .'

'Go on.'

'You must kill Khrothung. That is the only way to ensure that Gling's prosperity will last ten thousand years. If you do not, civil unrest will ensue as soon as you leave.'

'I thought he had changed for the better.'

'The king has a compassionate mind, and believes that everyone is like himself. You cannot imagine how evil Khrothung is. You must promise me that you will not return to Heaven until he is dead.'

'You are making me lament the transience of human life.'

As he rode back to his palace, Gesar was in the thrall of sorrow. He told his attendants to drop back from him, even those who held the parasols, teapots and teacups, and those in charge of his clothes. Brugmo could not stop weeping. 'Perhaps the king should return to Heaven,' she said sorrowfully.

Her words pained him, but he feigned cruelty when he said, 'Why should I feel sad if this is Heaven's will?'

'Your wisdom and power come from the celestial realm, but you gained a human heart when you came to our world – you will suffer in watching us age and die.'

Her words were like a curse. 'Brugmo, my heart aches,' he said softly.

That night his consorts' tenderness only made him feel their fleeting beauty more keenly, so he climbed into his big bed alone. 'Lhamin Dagmo, dear mother,' he heard himself call.

His celestial mother appeared amid stars that flickered like gemstones.

Her cool fingers caressed his forehead, and she quieted him when he asked about life and death in the human world. 'Do not trouble yourself with such questions. They are for humans. You are a god who serves as their king, so you must be concerned only with Gling.'

'When should I return to Heaven?'

'When you have turned Gling into a paradise.'

'But if I cannot recall what a paradise is, how can I create one?'

'What is the matter with my son today? Are you ill?'

'Must I leave them all behind when I return to Heaven?'

'Them?'

'The chief minister, my human parents, Brugmo and the other consorts.'

'My child, how could you fill your mind with such thoughts? I have been sent by the Supreme Deity to tell you that another war is about to break out, and you must be careful.'

Although she had more to say, the hem of her robe began to drift upwards, taking her into the sky. She spoke her final words to him: 'Someone is planning a mutiny by collaborating with the enemy.'

Who was planning a mutiny? Who would invade? Even in his dream these practical concerns drove away all thoughts of life, death and ageing beauty. Gesar went directly to the chief minister. Several monks were saying prayers for the old man, but they left when the king arrived. Gesar told him excitedly of the coming war.

'You are happy because you have something to do.'

Gesar did not miss the sarcasm: humans hoped for peace, while the deity dreamed of missions and great victories. 'When the war is over and I have quashed Gling's enemies, the people will enjoy a lasting peace.'

'Is that so?' The chief minister continued, 'Great King, I know you have a good heart, but that will never happen.'

Aches and pains have rendered the chief minister a sentimental old man, Gesar said to himself, and forgave him for it.

But the old man said, 'Great King, you may choose not to forgive me, but you should not consider me sentimental. You are a deity, and cannot truly understand the sufferings of the human world.'

'I came here to help rid you of demons,' Gesar replied.

The monks emerged from behind the heavy curtains. With his head lowered, one said, 'The king is talking about one kind of demon, but there is another – the kind that grows naturally in the human heart.'

The king asked a question of his own: 'What can you do about them?'

'We teach humans to overcome the demons in their hearts.'

Gesar laughed. 'I've eliminated many demons outside the human heart and will vanquish the rest before returning to Heaven. But when will you eradicate all the inner demons?'

'Humans will never die out.'

'So the demons in your hearts will never die either.'

'We do not tell the people so because we wish them to remain hopeful.'

Gesar turned to the chief minister. 'We must mobilise our army and prepare for war.'

The chief minister sat up. 'Who would dare attack us?'

'I cannot say, but they will launch an attack soon – with the help of a traitor.'

The chief minister nearly blurted out the traitor's name, but Gesar held up his hand. 'Any traitor who collaborates with the enemy is burdened with inner demons,' he said, 'so the esteemed monks should be able to recognise him.'

One of the monks protested: 'Even a king cannot demand that this be done by those who spread the Buddha's teachings.'

Gesar's stare was severe.

The protesting monk was silent.

Gesar turned to the chief minister. 'Come to the palace as soon as you can. And before you come, find out the location of the country with Khridan Gyalpo.'

His vigour renewed, the chief minister ordered that a red flag be raised above his fortress, calling back his scouts from the four corners. They all made the same report: 'The king of Khache Yul, Khridan Gyalpo, is about to attack Gling.'

'Khache Yul? It is a tiny country in the west.'

The scouts told him that Khache Yul had changed after Khridan Gyalpo ascended the throne. He was a *rakshasa*, an unrighteous spirit, who had conquered Nepal shortly after taking the throne. At eighteen, he had defeated Weikha and Mukha, then conducted aggressive expeditions against small neighbouring states, all of which pledged allegiance to him. His ambition had grown with his wealth, and he claimed that only the sun and the moon commanded a higher position than he. When he had heard of King Gesar, he had vowed to conquer Gling.

'Well, well!' the old warrior shouted. 'Our warriors' joints are rusty. Prepare my clothes. I am going to see the king.'

Throwing on his black cape with the red lining, Rongtsa Khragan, his pale face now aglow, set out for the palace.

The Story
Gyatsa Zhakar Shows Himself

For some time Gesar had been having dreams from which he awoke tired and lethargic. His consorts thought he had lost interest in them. 'Our husband is weary of idleness in the human world,' Brugmo said to others.

They listed many activities with which he could fill his days.

'Hunt.'

'Practise Ati Yoga.'

'Learn about medicinal plants.'

'Visit the poor, the sick and the aged.'

'Discover underground treasures.'

'Study painting.'

'Teach Prince Gralha the art of transformation.'

'Give new designs to the potters.'

'Help the weapons tribe smelt stronger iron.'

The king's laughter emerged from behind the heavy bed curtains. He had been listening to them. 'I am worn out by my dreams, and now you wish me to work harder.'

'The great king can learn how to interpret dreams.'

'I have just woken from another dream. Of iron weapons that were sharper than those smelted by our weapons tribe.' As he spoke, the chief minister entered. The king showed no sign of surprise at the change in him. 'Sit so that we can talk. I was telling my consorts that I dreamed of iron weapons.'

'That is a sign of the king's prescience.'

'What do you mean?'

'The scouts have come with news.'

He told the king about Khache Yul. Gesar asked why this was the first they had heard of it. The chief minister replied that it was because Gling and Khache Yul were separated by a black iron mountain, beyond which was a red iron mountain. A day's journey through these mountains wore down the hoofs of horses, and when lightning struck the mountains, their power increased a hundred times; travellers rarely escaped with their lives. Gesar asked how Khridan Gyalpo would dare cross the mountains to attack Gling, and was told that Khache Yul used the iron from the mountains to make shoes for their horses to protect their hoofs. Moreover, Khridan Gyalpo was a *rakshasa* incarnate, who could banish thunderclouds to make way for his troops.

Gesar smiled. 'Now I understand my dream. When I conquer Khache Yul, the iron mountains and blacksmiths will be ours, and they will make Gling invincible.' He summoned his armies.

All of his warriors showed willingness to fight. Only Khrothung objected, saying that, unlike other countries, Khache Yul had no treasure. The iron mountain made it powerful.

'I summoned you here not only to crush Khridan Gyalpo but because, with our vast territory, I hardly see any of you and I miss you all,' said Gesar.

Convinced that Gesar would soon leave Gling, Shanpa Merutse and others of his generation wept. But their younger companions, led by Gralha, clamoured for a fight. Gesar filled their wine cups and told them to drink to their hearts' content tonight and enjoy the company of their king. Meanwhile, the arrogant Khridan Gyalpo had sent his troops to Gling, but Gesar asked the gods to send a snowstorm to trap the Khache Yul army in the mountains.

The ministers and the king enjoyed a vast feast.

Meanwhile Brugmo and the other women performed songs and dances that were even more exquisite than usual. Their dances were no longer imitations of war, love or work: they expressed the blowing wind, the flowing water, the current of energy that flows down from the head, along the spine and into the belly. When Brugmo sang, one man said he saw a mountain bend at the waist, while another said he felt the water in the river flow backwards. The passage of time had left its mark on everyone, including Gesar, the son of the deities, but Brugmo's grace was unchanged from when she had first become the Gling consort. Her gaze was innocent, passionate, and she looked as though she had never fallen for the Indian prince, as if she had never been abducted and borne a son by the White King. She could stir anyone's deepest desires. It was hard to tell if she was a fairy or a demon: she could make the pure of heart more virtuous and evildoers more iniquitous.

When Khrothung had dreamed of becoming king, he had coveted Brugmo. Now he had the homage of tens of thousands of his own tribespeople, and he lived for the most part in peace. But, seeing Brugmo again, he became keenly aware that only a true king could possess her. The flames of desire, which had never died, burned more fiercely within him than ever.

When he returned to his tent, he set up an altar. *Great King of Khache Yul*, he prayed, *in a display of your invincible power, send the army at once. If you are truly powerful you will sense my wish.*

Khridan Gyalpo, trapped in the snow at Black Iron Mountain, sensed Khrothung's prayer and told his shaman that an old man, with a pointed beard, who dressed like a king, had entered his dream.

'Have you seen his eyes?'

'They were crafty.'

'This man would have been King of Gling if not for Gesar, who came from Heaven. Our armies will return in victory.'

In the dream, Khrothung had told Khridan Gyalpo that the snow would not last long, as the sky was running out of water. Sure enough, the snow soon disappeared and the sky cleared. The Khache Yul army stormed down the mountain, like a floodtide. Gesar had arrayed his troops with their backs to a range of small mountains. In front were Prince Gralha, Khrothung's two sons, Dongtsan and Tonggod, and other young warriors, along with the old generals Shanpa Merutse and Danma. Over the next three days, battle raged. Gesar sat in his tent playing dice with the chief minister, while Khridan Gyalpo grew agitated, wondering why Khrothung had not revisited his dream.

Khrothung had not been idle. He had been strengthening his invisibility skill, and he was ready to put it to a test. He walked, invisible, through the fighting, and saw his sons, Dongtsan and Tonggod, battling a great Khache Yul general. Back and forth they went, locked in stalemate. Khrothung spread his cloak of invisibility like the wings of a bird, and swept his sons and their clamouring troops from sight. The enemy general twirled his sword like a dazzling halo as he fought his way into another regiment. He beheaded two commanders, and their formation returned to order only when Danma came up to fight.

Elated, Khrothung mounted his horse, Yusha, and galloped towards the command tent.

'Are you so afraid my warriors cannot withstand the enemy that you have come to conceal me with your magic?' Gesar asked.

'I am here to ask permission to infiltrate the enemy camp. I will kill Khridan Gyalpo, and the leaderless Khache Yul troops will withdraw.'

'The arrogant king started this war,' Gesar said. 'I will crush him.'

'Over the past days, the warriors have fought bitter battles, but none has returned in triumph. If it is victory the king seeks, I can prevail.'

The chief minister signalled that the king should not agree, but Gesar said, 'As you wish.'

Khrothung mounted his wooden vulture and flew straight to the enemy camp.

The chief minister stamped his feet with displeasure. 'Does the king really believe he will kill Khridan Gyalpo?'

'I believe he will surrender to him, so I shall make use of his own plot to defeat him.'

'You should have killed him.'

'I was sent to this world to kill demons, not humans.'

'So we can do nothing about him?'

'That is something you humans may do.'

The chief minister was shocked to see the son of the deities' friendly expression replaced by a look of hard indifference.

'So demons can be eradicated but we humans must live with his like?'

Gesar shook his head. 'You have been well again, but now you are pale. You must stop questioning me.'

'If this is truly the state of human affairs, what is the use of my regaining my health? Longer life means more suffering. If I tell the warriors so, they will lose the will to fight.'

'That is why I speak of these things to you only.' Gesar's smile returned. 'Now, let us discuss how to turn Khrothung's scheme against him. Without him, our victory would not come so quickly.'

They decided to send their army to a different place.

Khrothung's wooden vulture had barely landed when Khridan Gyalpo spoke to him. 'This is the first time I have met someone from a dream.'

'If you win this war, you must install me as King of Gling. If you will not agree to that, kill me now.'

'I have asked about you. You are not a brave man but you risked death to come here, and you will do anything to be king. I agree to your demand.'

'Swear it to Heaven.'

'I am Heaven. How should I swear to myself? Khrothung, you must tell me your plan.'

'Tomorrow you will leave a few units here as a decoy. I will cloak your best troops with my invisibility magic and lead you to the palace.'

'Invisibility magic? When an army travels, the soldiers must cook and relieve themselves – there will be traces of them.'

'Have no fear. My magic lasts two days, and by then you will be on Tagrong land.'

'How can I know that this is no trap?'

'You must believe me. It is the only way for you to win.'

The following day, no battle cry was heard from either side. Khache Yul's élite troops stealthily set out. The Gling banners flapped in the wind, and by noon, under the intense heat of the sun and swirling vapours, the illusion of an army that Gesar had created shimmered and rose into the sky. Khache Yul troops panicked, thinking that Gesar had employed celestial soldiers. But their sorcerer saw through the illusion, and cried out in alarm when he saw that the enemy's troops had vanished and his king had been duped. He sent out the remaining troops to search for Khridan Gyalpo, but he was so securely cloaked by Khrothung's invisibility magic that no trace of him could be found. One of the search parties fell into a swamp and was sucked under; another was caught among a herd of wild oxen. On the fifth day the sorcerer saw a black war cloud rising into the sky. He urged his tired troops onwards to alert the king.

Gesar said, 'Let us have more magic.'

That night, the sorcerer and his men encountered a lake so vast they could not cross it. They spent most of the night trekking around it, but when the moon rose, the lake vanished. Then the party arrived at a cliff guarded by hungry ghosts. At this the soldiers sat down and refused to go on. The sorcerer began to wail, 'Great King, your arrogance has sealed Khache Yul's doom.'

Hearing this treachery against Khridan Gyalpo, the general who led the party raised his sword and killed the sorcerer. At that moment, the sun rose and the cliff crashed down on them in the morning light.

The rocks had been an illusion, and did not harm a single man, but many died of fright, and the rest fled in the direction of Khache Yul. The general, left alone, could see nothing but grass waving in the breeze and the dewdrops dripping onto his boots. Birdsong surrounded him. In despair he cried out the king's name, then slit his own throat.

The Khache Yul troops set off under the early-morning sun, no longer cloaked in invisibility. Khrothung assured the king that in two more days they would see the golden dome of the palace. But the king sensed war in the air. 'Bind this man!' he shouted, and several lassos dragged Khrothung off his horse. The king told Khrothung that he would be King of Gling if his plan succeeded, but if it did not, Khrothung would die.

In an hour they came to a low hill covered with rocks that resembled beasts squatting in the dead grass. The slanting sun made it impossible to see clearly. They unleashed a hail of arrows, but afterwards all was quiet, except the wind whistling over the grass. At a wave of the king's hand, they began to cross the hill but suddenly there was a loud noise, followed by arrows, like a plague of locusts. The Khache Yul soldiers cried out as they fell; the king was hit by two arrows. One smashed his armour, the other pierced his neck, its feather buzzing at his ear, like a bee. He pulled out the arrow, and a stream of blood spurted from his vein.

'A trap!' he screamed. 'Kill Khrothung!' But it was not time for Khrothung to die, not yet, for he lay hidden beneath a fallen horse. Another storm of arrows rained down, and the king was forced to lead his troops into the foothills. By the time Gling banners rose around them, the King of Khache Yul had lost more than half of his army.

Gling came down like a flood upon them. Khrothung's sons, Dongtsan and Tonggod, humiliated by the rumour that their father had surrendered to the enemy, redeemed the family name by leading the first wave. But Dongtsan heard Khrothung call and dismounted to find his father, who shouted, 'If you untie me I'll be a dead man. Take me to Gesar like this.' Dongtsan had no choice but to shield his father and watch his younger brother, Tonggod, wield his sword as he rode down the hill to face Khridan Gyalpo. The young Tonggod thrust his sword three times but failed to strike the king. Then Khridan took a dagger from his waist and stabbed Tonggod, who fell to the ground. Danma and Gralha came forward to fight off Khridan so that he could not inflict on Tonggod the final thrust.

Before he had left for battle, Shanpa Merutse had cast a divination that showed it was an ill-fated expedition for him. Gesar told him to stay back, but he refused to heed the king's advice. Redemption for his part in the death of Gyatsa Zhakar would come only in battle. He fought fiercely now, but silently he said to himself, 'Great Warrior Gyatsa Zhakar, let us be brothers in Heaven if I redeem myself.'

Time seemed to stop, and the vast land twirled. A rainbow stretched across the clear blue sky, and upon it Gyatsa Zhakar, long dead, appeared. He raised his arms and sent a thunderbolt from his palms, which knocked Luyag, Khridan's brother, off his horse as he was about to slay Shanpa Merutse. The enemy lay scorched to death, green smoke curling up from his armour. Shanpa Merutse gazed up as Gyatsa Zhakar faded into the blue sky, along with the rainbow.

Prince Gralha heard the Gling troops call his father's name. He looked up, only to see his father disappear. Tears burned his eyes. He spurred his horse towards the hilltop, calling his father's name. His father reappeared, and said, 'Come.'

Prince Gralha rose into the air, and everyone saw how he pressed his forehead to his father's chest and how his father adjusted the red tassel on his helmet. Then Gyatsa Zhakar told his son three things.

First: 'The name of Shanpa Merutse must be included among those of Gling's heroes.'

Second: 'I thank my brother, King Gesar, for making Gling strong.'

Third: 'My son is an upright hero, a great comfort to me.'

Then he faded.

The appearance of Gyatsa Zhakar's spirit inspired the soldiers. Gralha felt invincible. 'My father gives me strength!' he shouted, as he wept. 'Death to whoever stands in the way of the son of Gyatsa Zhakar!'

Khridan Gyalpo, who thought himself peerless and who had sought to become king of the world, was distracted, leaving himself open to attack, and his chest was pierced with Gralha's spear. His last view of the world was of a blank blue sky that darkened until eternal night shrouded him.

The victorious Gling warriors rushed into the command tent, where Gesar was tending Tonggod. He sighed and put his arm around Dongtsan's shoulder. 'Untie your father.'

Danma was outraged. 'Shall the king free the traitor?'

Gesar said sternly, 'He has lost a son. Is that not punishment enough?'

Khrothung threw himself at Gesar's feet. 'Save my boy.'

With a shake of his head, Gesar left the tent. 'I did not see my brother,' he said to his generals. 'Now I must wait to see him in Heaven.'

Khrothung curled up on the ground and wailed.

The Storyteller
Statues

Gesar entered the storyteller's dream again, not as a god but as the king.

Jigmed had never met anyone who cared what Thosba Gawa looked like. There were a few portraits depicting him as a celestial being, but he never seemed any different from other deities. People remembered his human form. Wherever he had waged war, the government had hired sculptors to create his image in clay, stone, black iron, stainless steel or bronze. He was always on his horse, sword in hand and quiver at his waist, no matter whether the sculpture was in a museum, a town square or even the hall of a hotel.

Jigmed had recently been invited to sing at a sculpture unveiling in a new hotel. The owner had a dark, red face, and an oily sheen on a moustache that resembled the one on the statue. 'The leaders attending the ceremony today are busy,' he said, 'so sing briefly. Choose the best part.'

Jigmed felt like asking which part, in his view, was the best. But he forbore and chose a passage at random to sing while the VIPs removed the red silk that covered the statue. It was not his best performance – he was not used to such perfunctory renditions and he did not care for the golden statue. But he liked the thick wad of money in the envelope that the hotel owner stuffed into his hand.

After the ceremony, he strolled around the bustling plateau town. In a display case in a bookshop, he saw a CD of himself singing the Gesar legend. On the cover there was a picture of him wearing a *grungkan's* hat, sitting on the grassland with his lute, lost in the story. He asked the young woman behind the counter several questions, hoping that she would recognise him. But she did not, although her jaw moved incessantly. His last question was: 'Miss, what are you eating?'

The girl blew a huge bubble and let it pop in his face.

An old man who was flipping through an almanac answered one of his many questions. If Jigmed went outside and walked to the end of the street he would reach a building where some young painters had a studio on the second floor. Downstairs a tourist shop sold the paintings. Jigmed found the place and enquired about a portrait of Gesar. The assistant pointed to a ladder, telling him they had just sold the last; a new one was not yet finished. He climbed upstairs and found several painters working in a spacious, sunlit room. One was kneeling on a rug and carefully applying brushstrokes to a canvas. From a distance Jigmed recognised the hero of the story – his horse, his helmet and his armour. The painter was adding colour to the sword, but the face was just an empty circle where the weave of the canvas was still visible. 'Why have you left the face blank?' he asked.

The young painter did not speak until he had added a glint to the blade and let out the breath he had been holding. 'I'll do that tomorrow, after we have held a sacrificial rite for the face.' He switched to another brush and a different colour to paint the arrow's feathers.

'Do you know his story?' Jigmed asked. The painter turned to him but said nothing. Jigmed went back downstairs and looked around the shop, where he found another kind of Gesar, carved on a dark green stone tablet in shallow relief. It was the same image of him, on horseback wielding a sword, but he liked this one better. 'Was this done upstairs?' he asked the clerk.

'On the mountain.'

'Who works on the mountain?'

'These portraits are piled up on it, but no one knows who carves them.'

He left the shop and, on the outskirts of the town, hired a tractor, whose driver at first refused to take him when he learned that he wanted to go to the mountain where the Gesar images were to be found.

'I want to meet the person who carved them.' He couldn't remember when he had begun to think of everyone related to Gesar as his own kin. To be sure, there were good relatives and bad ones. The girl selling CDs was not so good; the young painter worked hard but was haughty. Jigmed hoped that whoever carved the images would be a good relative, and he was not disappointed. In a row of tall fir trees that ringed the edge of the grassland, he heard clinking sounds. A windblown man was carving a portrait of Gesar in stone. The finished pieces formed a long wall along the mountain ridge.

Jigmed asked only one question: 'Are you carving them to sell in the city?'

The veins in the man's face were red from long exposure to the elements. He said, 'In this town someone in every generation carves images of the hero of Gling. I am one of them.' Then he asked Jigmed, 'Have you come to take the portraits to sell? You don't look as though you have.'

Jigmed walked down the mountain, convinced he had found a good relative. He went back to the hotel, where he had free room and board for two nights, in addition to the fee for his performance. It was the softest bed he had ever slept in, and it was to him in this bed that Gesar the king appeared in his dream. Bewildered, Gesar said, 'I thought I had cowed all of the demon countries. Where did Khridan come from?'

Jigmed could not tell him.

Gesar continued to mutter: 'Which country will be my next enemy?'

'I'm just a storyteller. You tell me what you've done and I turn it into song.'

'But what happens next? You claim to know my story – what will I do next?'

'Your celestial self would be angry if I told you. Perhaps you should visit the man who is writing new stories about you.'

'How can I do that? I don't even know how I appeared in your dream. Perhaps you should see him for me. Then I will return to your dream and you can tell me.'

At that moment the telephone by his bed rang. He heard the King of Gling ask, with childlike curiosity, 'What was that noise?'

But Jigmed was awake. He spoke once more to the king. 'If you can hear me, when will you remove the arrow from my back?'

He was answered with silence. The glass over a portrait of a pretty woman on the wall sparkled in the bright sunlight that streamed through the window.

He closed his eyes. 'Are you still here?'

Nothing. So Gesar could appear only in dreams. Jigmed laughed. 'You want to know what you'll do next. Well, I'll tell you. You'll subdue more countries and find more treasures. You once said, "The strength of a fine steed is not inexhaustible, and one enemy can be vanquished, but another will appear, as if there were no end."' Lying on his bed, Jigmed recited a long list of countries, all of which appeared in stories he knew. But now someone was writing a new story.

'Are you listening?'

He opened his eyes and looked at the portrait of the pretty woman. With her expressive eyes, she looked as if she wanted to speak. If she were to speak, she would probably sound like the radio-programme host. The memory propelled him off the bed; he got dressed and frowned at the portrait. 'Pah!'

He spent only one night in that comfortable room.

He came next to a beautiful valley where people led a hard life. It occurred to him that he did not know what had happened to all the treasure Gesar had collected. What if Gesar asked him in a dream? He stopped everyone he met and asked, 'Do you know what happened to Gesar's treasure? Have you seen Gesar's treasure?'

He repeated the question as he travelled, and many lamented, 'The poor *grungkan* has lost his mind. He's asking about the treasure of the Gling from many years ago.'

But Jigmed just wanted to know why so many people suffered hardship on the land of the former Gling.

The Story
Inspection or Farewell

The king woke up, and so did Brugmo, who was sleeping beside him.

'I had a dream.'

Brugmo might not have been completely awake, but her laughter was like water in a mountain stream. 'Is dreaming unusual?'

'I dreamed that I entered someone else's dream.'

Brugmo propped herself up. 'Tell me.' Her half-naked body glowed like a pearl in the dark night.

'I could not see clearly – it felt like a mountain valley in fog.'

Her slender fingers traced a path over his chest. 'So you cannot tell me what you saw?'

'It was the dream of a strange man, who seemed to know everything I have done in Gling. And he knows what I have yet to do.'

Brugmo put her soft arms around him. 'Will the king and I always be so tender and loving together?'

She was holding him too tightly, and the king moved a little, saying, 'I asked him how many more countries had to be conquered and why they appeared like mushrooms after rain, one here, another there. And why they are all ruled by evil kings.'

Brugmo rolled over, pretending to be angry, but the king was oblivious. 'He said he knew but could not tell me. My celestial self does not allow him to reveal anything to my earthly self.'

Brugmo turned back to him. 'Will I return to Heaven with you?'

Knowing what his favourite consort wished to hear, Gesar said, 'You will.'

'Then what worries the king?'

'I wish to know how much more I must do.'

'It pains me to see you like this.' Brugmo took him in her arms, and her burning body, the body that had stopped ageing once it reached maturity, drove all thoughts of enemy countries from his mind and set his own on fire. 'Let Prince Gralha lead the warriors into battle so I can be with you every day,' she said.

The man whose body was also burning did not speak.

At daybreak, the strange night world returned to normal. The king stood by the window as Brugmo's maids helped him dress, and said, 'I should see if the weapons tribe have learned the smelting method from the Khache Yul artisans. And then go to Shanpa Merutse, who has fallen ill. And perhaps also to Tagrong, where Khrothung may need comfort. Tonggod's death may have changed him.'

Brugmo asked to accompany the king, but he said, 'Meza has a calming effect on people, while you make men burn with desire.'

She was unhappy, but he pretended not to notice. 'Mother is not feeling well, so please visit her often while I am away.'

And so the king left.

Since he rarely inspected the vast territory he had created, his people did not recognise him. They assumed he was a high-ranking aristocrat and, afraid that he and his contingent would demand a feast when they saw all the fat cows and sheep, the shepherds hid their livestock when his colourful banners appeared on the horizon. Only the old, the frail, the sick and the dim-witted remained on the road-sides, holding up their thumbs to beg. Gesar told his attendants to toss food to them, and let the servants add precious stones, such as coral, turquoise and tourmaline. The children in tattered clothes were overjoyed when they found the gemstones; they leaped and ran like ponies. The aged, their faces weathered by the elements, prostrated themselves in devotion to Heaven. Some sobbed as they tried to kiss the boots of a compassionate official.

'Can a gemstone really make them happy?' Gesar asked Meza.

'Great King, it is not the gemstone but good fortune. These people have been strangers to it all their lives,' she replied softly, her eyes lowered.

Gesar thought of the countries he had conquered, where magical incantations had overcome demonic spells and opened heavy doors to reveal gold and silver, rock crystal, rubies, sapphires, clam shells and more. Treasure had flooded out. 'I gave out so much treasure. Why was it not shared with the common people?'

Meza was quiet for a while, then said, 'I recall that the king once told the chief minister that he came to the human world to rid it of demons, not to interfere in human affairs.'

'Has this occurred long in the human world?'

'I am not learned, but I recall that the world was like this when I was born.'

The king's spirits were low for the rest of that day.

Riding alongside him, Meza sensed his gloom. 'My honourable respectable husband, everyone says you know everything. But I know that you have many questions about this world.'

'This woman knows how I feel,' Gesar said to himself, and he was glad he had brought her with him.

A few days later they arrived at the former border with Hor. Several decades had passed, and the wood that the troops from both sides had used to build their camps had rotted away. On the ancient battlefield, a stone altar marked the spot where Gyatsa Zhakar had sacrificed his life. Gesar got off his horse and walked around the altar, his boots crushing decaying horse bones and rusty arrowheads. A faint path had already been worn into the ground. 'I know who has been pacing this area,' Gesar said. 'Come out.'

Shanpa Merutse, bent at the waist, appeared from behind an old cypress. The king exclaimed with shock at his pallor.

'Remorse gnaws at my heart like a poisonous insect,' Shanpa Merutse explained. 'Now that Gling is safe, let it swallow me.'

Rain sluiced from the clear sky.

Gesar gripped Shanpa Merutse by the shoulders. 'I know your loyalty to Gling. When you torment yourself so, even the heavens shed tears.'

'Why did the spirit of Gyatsa Zhakar save my life? His nobility diminishes me.'

'As a righteous man, he came to the aid of another righteous man,' Gesar said. 'He wanted you to help me build a solid foundation for our nation, one that will last thousands of years.'

Tears and rain streaming down his face, Shanpa Merutse looked into the sky and shouted, 'Is this so, Gyatsa Zhakar, god of war?'

Thunder rumbled, and the sky cleared to show a bright rainbow.

'Are my sins forgiven?' Shanpa Merutse asked.

Another roll of thunder sounded in the clear blue sky.

'Then I can die in peace. I will die happy if the king will deign to visit my fiefdom and accept the respect of the people of Hor.'

'Can you be sure that the people will cheer my arrival?' Gesar asked, with a frown.

'They will.'

'But those we met along the way hid from me.'

'That was because they did not know it was you.'

'I also saw many beggars, who had nothing,' Gesar said. 'They were happy to pick up the gemstones I scattered. Why was that? Were they given none of the treasure we took from the countries we defeated?'

'Great King, the soldiers and generals who participated in the battles were rewarded.'

'So some remains?'

'Not much, at least not here in Hor. We spent what we took from the wars on new wars.'

'What about the women and children begging on the road?'

'They are the mothers and children of dead soldiers.'

'Why weren't they given help?'

'We will be able to help them when there is no more war. At least,

I will help them. Not every high-ranking, powerful hero or Gling official is compassionate.'

In Hor, Gesar was welcomed by cheering crowds. He saw that these people felt fortunate and proud to be living in a country built by a great king. On the night before he left Hor, he and Meza enjoyed a passionate interlude after the banquet. He said to her, 'It seems the time has come to return to Heaven.'

Pressing her cheek against the king's chest, Meza said, 'Have you the heart to abandon us?'

'It appears that wars will never end if I am here.'

'But you slew the demons that plagued the human world.'

'Yet soldiers continue to die and their wives and sons wander the earth like stray dogs.'

After leaving Hor, they went to Prince Gralha's fiefdom. From the top of his fortress, on a night that twinkled with stars, they saw the mountains lined up from east to west and a mighty river running from north to south through a deep, dark canyon. They saw, too, the flames from the iron-smelting. Gralha told the king that they would go the next day to see how artisans forged new weapons from techniques they had recently acquired.

'There is no need to go,' the king said. 'We can see it from here.'

'But the presence of the great king will be an immense honour to the artisans.'

Gazing at the flames, Gesar said, 'Much wealth must have been spent on making these weapons.'

'The treasure we obtained from the wars has been sufficient.'

Gesar spent three days in Gralha's fortress, but he made no mention of the weapons. He either kept quietly to himself or instructed Gralha on how to be a king who cared for the old and the poor, the king Gesar had wanted to be but had failed to become.

'Gyatsa Zhakar's blood flows through your veins,' he said to Gralha, 'so you must be as open as he when you become King of Gling.'

Prince Gralha paled when he heard the king's words and knelt before him. His courtiers had told him that he must not give the king the impression that he was impatient to succeed him. The king helped him up and said, 'You are the son of Gyatsa Zhakar. Do not let such thoughts enter your mind.'

As they were leaving, Gesar said to Meza, 'I've left Prince Gralha with an impossible dilemma. He will not know whether to give all the treasure to the people or to continue making powerful weapons.'

'Perhaps he will begin to learn how to be a great king.'

Gesar laughed. 'A troubled king.'

'If a king can never be happy, why does Uncle Khrothung seek the throne?'

The king told her to ask Khrothung in person when they reached the Tagrong tribal area.

But she did not dare to ask at the extravagant banquet held in their honour by the Tagrong. Khrothung was still sunk in grief, but when the king tried to console him, Khrothung reverted to his old self, and the grief left his face. After the banquet, Khrothung took Meza by the hand and asked her to present to the king a nine-foot piece of coral and a bronze Buddha statue that had formed naturally in the mountains.

Meza asked if there was something he wanted in return.

'News of the king's inspection tour has spread far and wide. Everyone is saying that he is about to return to Heaven. Only, I, Khrothung, have magical powers like him.'

'Does Uncle mean . . .'

'He will know that only Khrothung should inherit his throne.'

Meza had thought that the king would refuse such lavish gifts, but he did not. He simply said, 'If we are living in a story, then everything has already been settled, and if that is the case, what good will it do him to give me these things?' He told Meza to have them sold to the Persian or Chinese merchants who were always eager for rare treasures. The money from the sale would be distributed to the poor people they had met along the way. 'We will be returning to the Tagste khar palace soon, so if we meet someone without a house, we will give him one. If we meet a girl who is about to be married without a coral necklace, we will give her one. We will give the sick medicine, the barefooted sturdy boots, the helpless a pleasant surprise.'

Then he sighed. 'I have been in that man's dream again. I entered it in his body, but I could see his face.' He described Jigmed to Meza: a tall, gaunt man with a weatherworn countenance. The dust on his boots was a sign that he was always on the road with his lute. His eyes were lacklustre. 'Since my celestial self chose him to spread my story in Gling, why is he not of noble lineage?'

The Storyteller
Rejection

Jigmed sang in a village. After the performance, the villagers did not follow the custom of compensating him with food and a little money, believing that the village chief should pay for the performance, since he had arranged it. The collective account should not be used exclusively for official inspectors: a performance like Jigmed's qualified. But the village chief insisted that a traditional activity should be conducted in the traditional manner. 'A fine horse will always follow a familiar route for its master,' he said. Neither side relented, and in the end a young man stepped forward and gave Jigmed a hundred yuan. He asked to be Jigmed's disciple, but Jigmed responded that as Heaven had given him the stories he could not teach them to others. The young man said he wanted only to learn some lute techniques and tunes, not the stories. Taking his own lute out of its bag and holding it in his arms, he played a few notes.

'I want to use this lute to play your tunes.'

Jigmed assumed that it would take a long time to teach him, but he learned in three days. When they were tired from walking through deserted fields, they sat down and played together. Jigmed would strum a few notes; the young man would follow. Soon they did the same with longer passages. The young man quickly mastered them. One day they arrived at an autonomous prefecture reputed to have been part of the former Gling. Steady winds pushed them as they came down into the city, helping them maintain their stride even after a long trek. The wind was blowing north, but the airy clouds above drifted nimbly to the east. The city had a large square, and there the two men sat by a fountain to watch vehicles and people pass by.

'Teacher, here we must say goodbye.' The young man tried to pay, but Jigmed refused.

'The tunes go with the stories, so why do you want only the tunes?' Jigmed asked, for he had changed his mind and would be happy to teach the long narrative to the cheerful young man.

'I want to give the tunes new lyrics,' the young man said.

He began to sing of love, with a sorrowful look in his eyes. At first he sang softly, but then the melody surged. It was Jigmed's tune, yet somehow different. Jigmed felt his heart swell, stretching beyond the square. When people heard the young man singing, they gathered, and as the crowd grew, women shouted and men whistled, for they knew who he was. Jigmed realised he was a famous singer. Amid cheers from the audience, the singer introduced his 'teacher' to the crowd, who granted him a round of polite applause. Then, tossing their hats and headscarves into the air, they begged the young man to sing another song. He did so. Jigmed got up to leave. The singer could not stop, so he bade Jigmed farewell with eyes that were in tune with his love song, forlorn and emotional. Jigmed wept as he left the square and the crowd.

'This wind is hurting my eyes,' he said. Then he said to himself, 'I'm crying.' And he wept again.

He spent the night in a pasture that reminded him of his home. As the cow-dung fire died down, he fell asleep; but during the night he awoke. A woman who smelt like sheep and fresh leaves slipped under his blanket. Holding her in his arms, he groaned.

'You don't sound like a *grungkan*,' she said.

'Oh! Oh!'

Then he was alone again under the blanket.

He fell asleep to the sound of a baby nursing from the woman who had just left him, and starlight falling on the dewy grass.

Gesar appeared in his dream. 'I wish to see your face, since you will tell me nothing,' Gesar said. 'You are different from how I imagined.'

'What should I look like?'

'You are not handsome.'

'I was an illiterate shepherd before the gods stuffed your stories into my belly.'

'Has life been good to you?'

'Sometimes, but at other times it hasn't.'

'Have you a home?'

'I had one, but then I began singing your stories across the land. The four seas are home to us storytellers.'

'Us? Are there others?'

'Yes, quite a few, but they all say I'm the best.'

'What about your wife?'

'I don't have one.'

'You seem to have no money either.'

'I made some a while ago. A hundred yuan!' Jigmed pointed to the notes in his pocket.

'But those are just pieces of paper.'

'Paper with writing from the bank is money.'

'So for you writing is magical. You know that here writing is just words on paper. I am in Khrothung's fiefdom.'

'He presented you with gifts because he wanted to be king after you.'

'Will he become king? You will not tell me. But I will not let him. I saw many suffering people on my inspection trip. I am king, so why are so many people hungry and homeless? Do many people suffer where you are?'

'Many.' Jigmed wanted to say that he himself was one of them, but he didn't. Instead he said, 'There are also many prominent officials and eminent persons, as well as rich people.'

'So the world has not changed.'

'No.'

'Are there still wars?'

'The television says that many countries in the world are at war, but there are no more battles between demons and deities. People fight other people, black people, white people, people of our colour.'

'Then I shall go back.'

The king vanished.

When Jigmed woke, he was at a momentary loss as to where to go next. Then he recalled the lama who had been writing the story of Gesar, the one mining for the heart treasure. So he took that road and arrived two weeks later. Amid the rustling of the trees, he waited for the lama to emerge from his meditation.

'I told them you'd come back,' the lama said, when he saw him.

'You've been waiting for me?'

'Yes. I want to teach you the new stories I have found in my heart so you can sing them.'

Thinking of the king in his dream, Jigmed lowered his head.

'You don't want to?'

Jigmed came straight to the point. 'What have you written about?'

'There have been many *grungkan*s, but none has ever told a complete story. Now I have been inspired by the gods to unearth all his heroic deeds.'

'What else has Gesar done?'

'He vanquished several demon countries no one had ever heard of.'

Jigmed was quiet for a moment. Then he said, 'I won't do it. And I want to ask you to stop writing. King Gesar is tired. He wants to return to Heaven.'

The lama was taken aback, but then said, 'You, an ordinary man, lecture a lama?'

'Please, I beg you. He is so tired of war.'

'It was war that brought him glory!' The lama looked haughty. 'It was your good fortune that the gods chose you to be a *grungkan*. How dare you criticise the stories? Those of us who have been chosen by him should be his humble servants.'

'I think . . . I think he will forget the human world once he returns
to Heaven.'

'Gods! Hear what this crazy man is saying!'

'Please . . .'

'Steward! Send this man away!'

'Am I wrong?'

'You are.'

'I'm not.'

'Steward!'

The Story
News from China

Three pigeons took to the air in the distant land of China while King Gesar was inspecting his territory. They flew from the Fragrant Orchid Pavilion, where the Chinese princess lived alone in the golden palace. One carried a letter from the princess to King Gesar; the other two carried gifts, a piece of fine jade and the seeds of exotic plants from the princess's garden.

The pigeons had first to cross a mountain country called Minyag, which lay between China and Gling. Minyag had lent assistance to King Gesar in the past, but the Dharma King of Minyag, Yutse Tonpa, had become disenchanted with Gling and levied heavy taxes on Gling's caravans. Before long he had closed the border and severed communications between the two countries.

On this day, as the pigeons flew over Minyag, Yutse Tonpa was practising ascetic contemplation in the mountains, calling forth wind and rain to increase the power of his magic. Seeing the pigeons, he summoned snake-like clouds, leaving only a small patch of clear sky above his head, and transformed a magic stick into a fruit-laden tree. When the pigeons landed on it, it turned into a giant sack and caught them. Roaring with laughter, Yutse Tonpa said, 'Messengers from China, my country is not your destination. Where are you flying to in such a hurry?'

'We can no longer carry out our duty, so kill us.'

'You are too small, and after such a long flight, you have used all the fat and meat on your bodies. Would I kill you just to crunch your bones? I shall not.' Then the king read the letter. 'Loyal pigeons of the Chinese princess, you must deliver this letter to Gesar of Gling.'

He treated the messengers to a hearty meal to restore their strength. 'Now, fly away. And ask Gesar on my behalf how he expects to lead his troops to your country if I do not let him pass through mine. Your princess will have to ask for my help.'

'Will you help her?'

'If she will marry me.'

The pigeons flew on to Gling, but when they arrived at the Tagste khar palace, they found only Brugmo, who, on hearing of their news, grew jealous. She told them of the king's inspection trip with Meza, so the pigeons flew to Hor, but the king had already left. When they reached Prince Gralha's fiefdom, they were nearly killed by artisans of the weapons tribe who were testing their arrows. Prince Gralha comforted them, then pointed the way to the Tagrong tribe. Before the pigeons disappeared in the sky, he ordered his troops to prepare for an expedition to China.

When the pigeons came to the Tagrong tribe, they were welcomed by Khrothung, who told them he was the famed King of Gling. They gave him the letter and the gifts from the princess. 'You may return home to tell your princess that Gesar will send his Gling armies to China without delay,' he said. Then he gathered his army and set off for the Chinese palace.

When Gesar at last returned to his palace, Brugmo kept from him the Chinese messengers' request for help, fearing that he would set off on another long journey. Then, one fine, sunny day not long after his return, as Gesar was resting in a tent in a meadow filled with flowers, drinking with his ministers and listening to the latest songs, columns of yellow dust appeared in the distance.

'No summons has been issued,' the surprised king said.

The chief minister gazed at the horizon. 'The dust is rising above the public road from the Tagrong area. You don't think that Khrothung . . .'

Messengers were sent to all corners with an urgent call for troops from all tribes to protect the palace. A dozen or so miles outside the fortress city, Danma's palace guards stood in the path of Khrothung's advance.

'Honourable leader of the Tagrong tribe, why have you left your territory? Where are you bound, looking so proud?'

'I have an important matter to report to the king. If it is delayed, Danma, you know you have only one head.'

'You are taking a large force into the fortress city without having been summoned.'

Danma's words, like a breath of air rekindling a dying ember, sent flames burning through Khrothung's heart. 'Those few men of yours are no match for my army.'

'So you are planning a coup.'

Khrothung had set out to deliver his message and follow the king to China, but if they thought he was planning a coup, why not do so? 'And if I am?'

Enraged by Khrothung's arrogance, Danma charged.

It grew dark, but Khrothung continued to fight until his son Dongtsan rode up to separate the two warriors. 'Danma would not block our way without the king's consent,' he said. 'The king is probably concerned about your intentions. There is no need to force the issue, Father. I'll deliver the letter myself.'

'Gesar!' Khrothung cursed. 'I have come with good intentions, but instead of treating me with fine wine and good tea, you send your general to block my way. You think I am rebelling? Very well, I shall rebel!'

Dongtsan said, 'The palace may not be heavily guarded, but everyone knows that Gesar has immense powers.'

'He uses magic, and so do I! Are you really my son? How can you be so willing to submit to him?' Khrothung continued slowly: 'I am making the best of a mistake. If we succeed, this is a Heaven-sent opportunity. If not, I shall tell Gesar that Danma insisted upon fighting me. Ready the troops for a battle tomorrow morning. If we win, we make straight for the palace. If not, you will still have time to deliver the letter from China.'

But a heavy fog rolled in at midnight. The Tagrong soldiers were forced to wait for the red sun to rise before they could launch their attack. But Gesar had used his magic to call up the fog, and high noon felt like dusk. Khrothung could not attack. Try as he might he could not disperse the fog, for the mountain gods and water-dragon kings had come to help the king. On the third day, Khrothung called off his challenge, and his son Dongtsan showed Danma the letter from China and sought permission to see the king.

The king accepted the letter from Dongtsan and rewarded him. 'The tribes will gather here in a few days and then we will decide what to do.'

Dongtsan leaped to his father's defence. 'It was simply because Danma forced . . .'

'I have treated you hospitably. Go now, but return in three days with your father,' Gesar said.

Three days later, Khrothung came to ask the king's pardon.

'You would probably be sitting on the golden throne now if not for Danma's bravery,' Gesar replied. 'What would you do to me if you became king? Kill me? Put me in a dungeon? Or banish me to the wilderness, as you did so many years ago?'

Banging his forehead on the floor, Khrothung said, 'Read the letter from China before you decide how to punish me. If you do not need me, you may kill or torture me, and I will not complain.'

The king ordered that the letter be read.

The envelope was opened to reveal three sheets of thin silk crammed with words. No one in the court, neither ministers nor warlocks, could read the foreign script. So Gesar ordered Khrothung to the dungeon; he would decide what to do with him after the letter was translated.

'If Gyatsa Zhakar's birth mother were alive,' the chief minister said, 'understanding the letter would be easy.'

The king knitted his brows. 'Gling has been trading with China for years and yet, it seems, we have no one whose tongue can speak two languages and whose eyes can read two scripts.'

Wordlessly, the old general Danma pushed Prince Gralha forward.

Gesar laughed. 'Have you learned the foreign tongue?'

'No. But the lamas who translate sutras in the temple, and the merchants who travel between our two countries know it.'

'Bring them to the palace.'

A wise lama and a shrewd merchant arrived in the palace, and each produced a translation of the letter in his own style. The lama's version was elegant, with embellishments, while the merchant's text was plain and straightforward, but both told the same story.

The chief minister hurried to the palace. As he made his way through dark, winding passageways, he glanced out of a window that faced west. The red sun was a full horse-length away from the mountaintop.

The Story
A Demon Consort Wreaks Havoc

'The Princess of Great China tearfully bows at the throne of the great King Gesar, the hero and lion from Heaven. Please allow me to tell you respectfully what has led to my request.'

The princess had poured out her story in the letter.

The Chinese emperor Gela Genggong ruled a vast and populous territory. But none of the fifteen hundred palace consorts pleased him completely, so he had not selected any of them as empress. A search had been conducted among the neighbouring vassal states, but still no one satisfied the emperor. The ministers had at last received news of a princess, Ngima Khrice, from the Dragon palace in the Eastern Ocean, who had reached marriageable age. Her beauty was described as beyond compare, and it was clear to all that she would please the emperor – if a match could be made. Without telling the emperor, the ministers had sent a delegation on a ship laden with gold, gemstones, silver, bronze and sandalwood, as well as elephants, peacocks, flying dragons and phoenixes.

But there was no princess of marriageable age in the Dragon palace. It had been a trick devised by a demon who wanted to rule China. After nine days on the ocean, the ship had arrived at a palace created by the demon. The false Dragon king had agreed to the marriage proposal from China and promised a dowry that included treasures from the deep sea. Three days of feasting had been staged, after which a princess, her personal maids, and the rare ocean treasure floated to the surface of the ocean and were gathered into the Chinese ship. With a tailwind filling the sails, it took less than three days to return home.

The princess had fair, smooth skin more delicate than a conch shell, a face like a flower about to bloom, and she moved like a breeze that caresses the ocean waves. The emperor was dazzled.

Spring arrived, and painted green the willows outside the palace walls. It was time to offer sacrifices to the gods of earth and the five grains, but Ngima Khrice refused to leave the palace.

'Am I beautiful?' she asked the emperor.

'The word does not do justice to your grace and loveliness.'

She began to cry. 'Dear lord and husband, my beauty, which cannot be described in words, is for your eyes only, not for those of your subjects. Their gaze would be a curse, their words a blasphemy. Exposing me to those eyes and tongues would be to abandon a delicate flower to the wind and the frost.'

So the emperor went alone this time, but never went again. He began to ignore court matters and left the princess's personal maids to convey his edicts. Most of the time they turned his words to their own purpose, and disaster soon followed disaster. Lakes dried up; cranes migrated, taking their loud cries with them, even those painted by court artists on silk; towering mountains broke off at the waist; rivers changed their course. Some people lost the source of water that supported their lives; others had too much, and their roads and villages, even their cities, were flooded.

When Princess Agon-tso, the child of the emperor and his demon empress, came of age, the country was nearly beyond salvation. The ministers had realised that Empress Ngima Khrice had not come from the Dragon palace but had been formed from the blood of nine female demons.

Three gods, disguised as a lame man, a blind man, and a mute, were sent to help. They arrived in the capital city with an ox and a donkey. In the square in front of the palace, they tied the two animals' tails together and began to perform. The mute danced, the blind man sang and the lame man did conjuring tricks. The people greeted them with excited cheers. At dusk, unable to suppress her curiosity, Empress Ngima

Khrice covered her face with a silk scarf and climbed a watchtower that looked over the square. But as the sun, nearing the horizon, gave out its last bright rays and lit the tower, a gust of wind loosened her scarf and her beauty was exposed to the masses. Their eyes feasted on her, praise spilled from their mouths, and so the beautiful siren was cursed.

Upon returning to the palace, she fell ill. She refused to see anyone. No one but her daughter was allowed to visit her, and she saw only heavy curtains draped around the bed. From behind the curtains she heard her father speak: 'I have summoned the most famous doctors in the country and have spent much of the treasury's gold to pay them. Why has your health not improved?'

The empress sobbed and said, 'I cannot be cured even if you used all of the nation's wealth.'

'Can nothing be done?'

'I have been cursed by your subjects' mouths and eyes, so I must die. But I will come back to you.'

'Will you be reborn? I will not love another woman after you.'

She told him that she would return as long as he did exactly as she said: after she died, her body must be wrapped in the finest silk and placed in a sealed room that no light entered. 'You must order the sun to be shut up with the gold in the vault, the moon with the silver and the stars with the conch. There must not be a bird in the sky or a fish in the water, and no wind may stir the air.' Nine years she would spend in this dark silent space. Afterwards she would be even more beautiful and, better yet, immortal.

'You will gain immortality,' the emperor said, 'but I will die.'

'I will help you to reach immortality,' the empress replied weakly.

Knowing that was impossible, the emperor was overcome by sorrow. But she knew that her life hung by a thread, so she went on, 'After my death, you must order all bridges leading to Gling to be destroyed, and the ferry landings closed. News of my death must never be known in Gling.'

'Why?'

'Gesar will come to burn my body, and I will be unable to return to you. Remember this.'

Princess Agon-tso heard every word.

A few days later the empress died, and the princess was immersed in sorrow, but her father was a hundred times more stricken. He spent every night in the sealed room, sleeping beside the empress to warm her body. The sun, the moon and even the faintest starlight disappeared from China, and the country was plunged into darkness. Birds no longer sang, flowers stopped blooming and the people did not sing. At last the princess understood that her mother was a female demon, come to wreak havoc in the human world. If she were reborn, who knew what calamity would befall the country? The kind-hearted girl decided that the demon must be eliminated, and that light must return to the country. She talked it over with the girls she had grown up with, and they settled upon using the pigeons as messengers to ask for King Gesar's help.

And so the letter, embroidered in gold thread on black silk in total darkness, came to Gesar's court. What was puzzling was the method of killing the demon: a braid woven with green, white, red, yellow and dark green gemstones, worn by a *yaksa* called Asal Lokhra. Everyone knew of his existence but no one knew where to find him.

Then they heard Khrothung singing in the dungeon: 'You must ask the clouds if you want to know when the rain will fall. The clouds fly higher than the wings of hawks, but the one who knows Asal Lokhra's whereabouts is imprisoned in the king's dungeon.'

They chuckled when they heard him, but their smiles faded under the king's stern gaze. Khrothung continued to sing.

Gesar laughed. 'I almost killed the prisoner, and now I discover that he is still useful.' He ordered that the prisoner be brought to him.

'Condemned man, does the *yaksa* really wear a gem-studded braid? Where is he now?'

'Honourable king, my hands are tightly bound and my tongue is very nervous.'

'But your tongue is still glib, even with Death looming over you. You are a coward. Why are you not afraid now?'

'Fear is useless when one is about to die. And my nephew still needs me to subdue the demon in China.'

'Untie him.'

As soon as the ropes were off, Khrothung knelt before the king. 'I thank you for sparing my life.'

The Storyteller
Dajian Lu

Dajian Lu was the ancient name of a place the Manchu armies used as their base for an expedition into a foreign land. They built furnaces – *lu* – there, to make arrowheads, giving the place its name. Later it was renamed Kangding. Another century, then more passed, and the place grew into a bustling border city, where travellers came and went freely and mountain climbers restocked their equipment one last time at outdoor supply centres. Farmers came to town to sell mushrooms and medicinal herbs, herdsmen cheese and butter.

Now a red cloth banner hung from the large hotel in the city centre: 'Congratulations on the Opening of the Gesar Scholarly Conference'.

Jigmed, who had been roaming the grassland, was brought to the hotel in a Jeep. There he saw the scholar who had first discovered him, and that night he sang the story of how the demon in China was subdued, called 'Consort Meza Steals Magic Implements with a Trick', the old scholar translating it into Mandarin and English.

The next day he attended the morning sessions, but could not understand what they were talking about. Over lunch, he stared at the chandelier above his head, but stopped when, to his embarrassment, he noticed that people were looking at him.

'What were you gaping at?' the old scholar asked him.

'So much glass . . . I was afraid it might fall,' Jigmed replied.

'Young man, that's not glass. It's crystal.'

His eyes widened. 'So much crystal?'

'You're surprised? In your songs, you sing about the great quantities of crystal that Gesar wins from the treasure stores of his enemies.'

'But that is just a story, and this is real . . .'

His words were overheard by an expert in the Gesar epic who sat nearby. 'Does the *grungkan* believe that crystal and other treasures exist only in stories, that they could not exist in such quantities in real life?'

A professor sitting at another table moved over. 'Apparently, I am not alone in questioning the credibility of the story, if even a famous *grungkan* has his doubts.' With his arm around Jigmed's shoulders, he continued, 'Master Storyteller, tell me why you don't believe that the story is true.'

Jigmed's face reddened. 'I didn't say that.'

'But you suggested that such things could happen only in stories.'

'I wasn't talking about stories. I was only saying . . .' He looked up at the crystal and stammered, 'I – I – I am not saying the story . . .'

His friend stepped in. 'We should let him sing.'

The old scholar led him away from the table, down the wide staircase and out to the river that ran through the city centre. It was fast-flowing, and the breeze from it helped to clear Jigmed's head. 'I don't like those people,' he said.

'You didn't expect us to be arguing over whether the story is true at a Gesar conference, did you?' The old scholar laughed.

Jigmed made a noise deep in his throat to show his agreement.

'I should not have involved you in these matters. I suggested that we invite you only so that you could sing for the experts.'

'I want to go back now.'

Jigmed's gaze turned westward, following the path of the river. He knew that behind the peak at the end of the canyon was the open land of Khampa, with its grasslands, snowcapped mountains and lakes as blue as gemstones. At the mountain pass, the main road branched like a tree, each small road leading to a village in the valley or a pasture on the highland. A storyteller was like a bird, flying between these branches before settling on one to sing its beautiful song. For generations, that was how stories had travelled among the people.

'You know all those places,' he said to the old scholar. 'On the other side of the mountain is Minyag, and if you keep going west, you'll reach the Ashug grassland, Gesar's birthplace, with the lake where Brugmo bathed. Then you'll be at the site of the weapons tribe. Northwards are the salt lakes, and if you travel down the wide river, you'll see the steep ridges and tall mountains of Monyul.'

The old scholar told Jigmed that this time he had not invited him there simply to sing. An artist of the people was a national treasure, and at the conference the committee of experts would name him a Master of the People's Art. The title meant that the government would give him a house, monthly wages and health care. 'Almost like a cadre.'

'Me? Like a cadre?'

'Our government places a great emphasis on our non-material cultural heritage, so we treat people like you as rare treasure,' the old scholar said, becoming emotional. 'I'll say no more. But I want you to know that I've been thinking about you ever since we first met.'

'You took me to the radio station and you recorded my voice for me to hear.'

'And you ran away.' The scholar laughed.

Jigmed was quiet at the thought of the incident. 'Why did she talk like that in the recording studio? I thought maybe that was how Brugmo talked.'

'She would be very happy if she heard you say that.'

'She hated me. My lowly background was an affront to her status.'

'She was remorseful and told me to apologise if I ever saw you again.'

'Did she really?'

'All this belongs in the past. I'm old and ready to retire. Anyone who roams the land will one day lose the strength in his legs and should settle down. Would you like to?'

'I don't know.'

'Come, I'll take you to see someone.'

They crossed a bridge and walked down a winding street to a dimly lit staircase inside a big grey concrete building. At the ringing of the bell an old woman fingering a string of Buddhist beads opened the door. She broke into a broad grin when she saw it was the scholar; Jigmed saw her gold teeth shine in the dark hallway. She turned and called, 'We have important guests. Make some tea.'

Jigmed recognised her once they were in the brightly lit living room. It was Yangcan Drolma, with whom he had performed at the radio station. She had grown into a plump old woman. When she recognised him, she pulled a long face, her lips pressed together over the sparkling teeth. But then she laughed, and called to her husband, 'This is the fellow who ran away from the radio station.'

She turned to Jigmed. 'I told him all about you.'

That dissolved the tension.

'What an outstanding *grungkan* you've become. We hear about you, singing everywhere.' The old man bowed, respectfully touching his forehead against the lute Jigmed was carrying. 'You're still singing the hero's story. That shows how much the deity likes you.'

'The deity likes everyone.'

'I've never heard Yangcan Drolma sing, except on tapes.'

'I sang for you once,' Yangcan Drolma said.

'A few segments, not a complete story. The deity has taken back the stories in your head.'

Jigmed knew that the deity did not always give an artist a complete story, and even if he did, he might let the storyteller remember it for only a little while. Jigmed asked Yangcan Drolma if that had happened to her.

'After coming back from the radio station, I stayed in the Museum of Culture and Arts, where I sang into the tape recorders of story collectors every day,' she said. 'I sang the story from start to finish, making many tapes. But one was ruined. A cat knocked a cassette off the shelf and pulled out the tape to play with it, dragging it over to the stove, where it burned. So the story collectors decided to remake that part, but when the moment came, my mind went blank, not a story to be found. For three days my head felt like an overcast sky – no humans, horses, mountains or lakes in it. The deity who had given me the stories had taken them back. The collectors returned three months later, but left empty-handed. They came back the next year and the year after that, but each time they were disappointed.'

Yangcan Drolma smiled, revealing her gold teeth again. 'The deity loves me too. Otherwise how could a farmer's daughter be paid by the government to sit comfortably at home and drink tea without having to do anything? Jigmed, see how fat I've become. I don't have to worry about feeding or clothing myself. That's no way to stay trim. The doctor tells me to walk more, to climb mountains, but I don't listen to him. If I'd wanted to do that, I'd have stayed in the village to work in the field and raise livestock. The deity wants me to have a good life. He loves me.' The monologue had tired the old woman, who continued, from an easy chair, 'Drink some tea. I need to rest.' She fell asleep.

Jigmed and the scholar sat for a while before getting up to leave.

The old woman's eyes snapped open as they moved to the door. 'No goodbye, Jigmed? Are you trying to sneak away from me again? Give me a kiss. No need to be shy about kissing an old woman.'

They touched foreheads.

The strong smell of boiling tea filled the room.

'The deity is still with you. I smelt him again,' she whispered to Jigmed.

After two more days at the conference, Jigmed asked the scholar, 'Will I be like her in the end?'

'I don't know.'

'I don't want to be like her. I *won't* be like her. Gesar came into my dreams many times.'

'That is what many *grungkan*s say.'

'I don't mean the deity, but Gesar the king.'

The old scholar mulled that over. 'So you believe that those stories will never leave you?'

'Gesar even asked me in my dream what he would do next.'

'So you're quite pleased with yourself.'

'I didn't tell him that the story is also a kind of secret.'

'To me, your experience is the true incomprehensible secret.'

'It happened.'

'But why did it happen as it did?'

'The deity wanted me to know his stories.'

'Why in this manner? It would sound like nonsense to most people.'

'You shouldn't say that.'

'We're old friends, so I can tell you of my doubts.'

Jigmed sensed that if they continued talking in that way, he would offend the story. He felt it get up to leave. 'I'm sorry, but I must go. The story is upset with me.' He walked away, calming the story in his head, then turned to see the old scholar, with his salt-and-pepper hair, watching him go. 'I should have said a proper goodbye to him. Well, I'll roam the ends of the earth as long as you don't leave me. I cannot live to make tea in a house every day.'

'Where are you going?' the old scholar shouted.

'To Minyag.'

After walking along the highway for a while, he stepped onto a small path that wound through azalea bushes. The clustered buildings had disappeared by the time he stopped to look back. It was as though he'd entered a new world – the live smell of trees mingled with that of dead branches and fallen leaves. The bright world, lit by a sparkling crystal chandelier, was gone. Which world was real? He did not know. But this winding path flanked by unbroken lines of trees felt familiar.

He roused a skylark making a nest in the grass, and it shot up into the clouds. The wind began to blow, over the trees and over the grass, sending waves of green light surging into the distance.

The Story
Minyag or Meza

At last Khrothung spoke. 'Honourable King, the magic braid of gemstones is worn by a *yaksa* called Asal Lokhra, who hides in Minyag.'

'That must be a distant country.'

'No,' Danma said. 'Minyag is a neighbour to the east, between Gling and China.'

'Why do I not know of this country?'

The chief minister mustered his strength, and replied, 'It was I who stopped them from telling you.'

Enraged, Gesar said, 'So the king still does not know everything, which means that the king does not have the country completely under his control. Years ago, I did not know that many people were living in poverty, though we had opened the treasure stores of many enemies. And now a country called Minyag is on my doorstep.'

'A very big country.' Khrothung took the opportunity to add fuel to fire.

The king ordered that a parchment map be unfolded, and saw that the country called Minyag was missing.

Kneeling on the floor, the chief minister pointed out a blurred area between Gling and China. Gesar had seen the map countless times; after each military victory, he would order someone to scrape off the original border of Gling and draw out a new one to include his new territory. Tapping his finger violently on the inky line that snaked from north to south between Gling and China, he smashed the coral set in his ring, but managed to suppress his anger long enough to ask, 'What is this?'

'That is a river. The northern part of the river is the border between

Gling and China, and the southern part, well, the king already knows about that.'

Now Gesar saw a particularly blurred section on the map, where a misty fog rose and spread before his eyes. 'Tell me, how much more have you concealed from me?'

Khrothung shouted, 'The king is wise. They hid this country because they are planning to collaborate with outsiders to usurp the throne.'

'Then why did you not report their scheme to me?'

The king's finger had been cut by the broken ring and his blood dripped onto the map, soaking into it where Minyag was located. 'I am going to send my armies to level this country that has been hiding in plain sight.'

'I will be the king's vanguard,' Khrothung cried.

'The king must not start a war so casually,' the chief minister counselled. 'Gling and Minyag have agreed to remain friendly towards each other. Let me tell you everything. There will be plenty of time for you decide on a course of action. When Gling was first established and you delayed your return after vanquishing the demon country, Hor sent a large army to invade Gling. Minyag, to the east, had stationed its troops at the border with the same intention. At that time Minyag was ruled by two brothers, the Dharma King Yutse Tonpa, and the Worldly King Yu-ngog Tonpa. The former's heart was as hard as black steel, while the latter's as soft as white jade. The Dharma King normally made all the decisions, and Yu-ngog Tonpa took over only when his brother was sequestered in contemplation. When Hor began its invasion plan, Yutse Tonpa told his brother that they had to send their troops at the same time as Hor to destroy Gling. Otherwise, Gling would become like a tiger at one's pillow, and no one would be able to sleep soundly or eat in peace. The young King of Gling, it was said, indulged himself in women and drink, so much so that he had forgotten to return. Gling had thirty heroic warriors, but without a leader, they could do nothing. It was the perfect opportunity for Minyag to join forces with Hor to annihilate Gling. Reluctant to start a war, the younger brother replied that everyone said that Gesar was a deity sent from Heaven to save humans from suffering. They should not eliminate a good country only to help the rise of a country of tigers and wolves. But in the end, he listened to his brother and an army was sent to the border, their weapons pointed to the west as they waited for the perfect moment to attack.'

The chief minister banged his forehead on the floor. 'At that time, the king was detained in the demon country and Khrothung was plotting with the enemy. Gyatsa Zhakar was in the northern borderland fending off attackers, so I was left with no choice but to take a few attendants to the eastern border to negotiate with Minyag. Fortunately, Yu-ngog Tonpa knew that our king was a deity sent from Heaven to help the people, and he convinced his brother to sign an agreement of peace, ensuring that our countries would never attack each other.'

The king was ashamed. 'Then why did you not tell me the truth when I returned?'

'The king had orders from Heaven to eradicate demons, and would never tolerate the king of a neighbouring country practising his magic in the mountains – and there are many people in Minyag with demonic powers. That is why I hid the truth from you. Now the king knows everything.'

The king sighed. 'Humans are so complex. How can I know what is right and what is wrong?'

He returned to the royal harem. But Meza, full of remorse at her part in the matter, chose not to spend the night with him, and when the morning star rose, she decided to travel to Minyag alone to bring back the magic braid. She rose, and began to prepare for her journey.

Brugmo did not spend the night with the king either, for she was worried about the long journey to China, the high mountains and great rivers that must be crossed, and about the pretty Chinese princess. With the flame of jealousy burning in her heart, she dressed and went to the central courtyard in the faint moonlight. There she saw Meza, in a dark cloak.

'May I ask where Younger Sister Meza is going?' Brugmo called.

'To Minyag to bring back the braid and atone for my crime,' Meza said, tears streaming down her face.

Brugmo sneered. 'You bewitched the king once, when you kept him in the demon country. Now you are going to wait for him in Minyag.'

Meza knelt before Brugmo. 'I know that my wilfulness in keeping the king to myself has had serious consequences, and I have repeatedly shown my remorse before the Buddha. But this time I am truly going to redeem myself. Dear sister, please let me go. If I return alive, I will shave my head and live apart from this world as a nun. If I do not return, that will be just retribution.' Then she stood and flapped her cloak, as though she were about to fly off like a crane, her wings spread.

Meza's tears doused the fire in Brugmo's heart. 'I will go with you,' she said.' I have magic that will help you. And if you are going there to wait for the king, then you shall not have him all to yourself.' Quickly she wrote a letter and placed it by the king's pillow, asking him to send an army to rescue his two consorts if they did not return within ten days. Then they turned their capes into wings and flew towards Minyag in the first light.

With the rising of the sun a tall mountain appeared before them, and astride the mountain stood Gesar, giantlike, the golden rays of the sun behind him. They folded their wings and knelt before him.

Gesar helped them to their feet. 'I know what you are doing, and I grant you my permission.'

The women kowtowed.

'But you must not be so rash. You should prepare properly for your journey to Minyag.'

The three flew down into the foothills, where a large tent had been pitched in a grove of trees. The consorts, all but Atag Lhamo, who was stationed at the border, gathered for a banquet, at which Gesar taught the women some transformation magic. Khrothung told them how to take the magic braid of gemstones from *yaksa* Asal Lokhra's head: they would need the root of a particular kind of bamboo that grew naturally in the shape of a human palm, with claws that looked like human fingers. If an incantation was spoken, the claws could be made to open and close like human fingers. Only this root could grasp the braid.

The two consorts, in the guise of white cranes, flapped their wings and flew off. But when they arrived above Minyag, they could see nothing, for the Dharma King, practising his magic in the mountains, had created a dense fog that blotted out the land. Using the magic they had learned, they made their wings very wide and flapped them as hard as they could. The clouds and fog blew away to reveal a clear blue sky and open land below, surrounded by mountains with serpentine rivers. Tidy rows of houses dotted the riverbanks.

After briefly circling in the sky, the women spied the place where three mountains met two merging rivers, and where a grove of bamboo gave off a green glow. They glided down on an air current and took the bamboo claw.

'Change!' They recited the incantation, and the claw moved, just like a human hand.

As they returned to the sky, Brugmo laughed and said, 'If the king had come for it, who knows how many passes he would have crossed or soldiers he would have killed?'

But Meza, who was more cautious, wondered aloud: 'It is strange that we have so easily taken this from the King of Minyag, who commands such powerful magic.'

Below them, a lake surrounded by a grove of bright green trees appeared. On it were flocks of brightly coloured birds, and the scent of flowers rose into the sky.

Brugmo said, 'We have been flying for a long time, and I am tired. Let us rest awhile by the lake.'

They gathered flowers and made wreaths to wear, then went to frolic in the water, which was warmer than that of the highland lakes of Gling. Brugmo shed her feather cape and waded in, and Meza had removed hers but had yet to reach the water when a tree by the lake was transformed into a fierce, pale-faced general.

'Ha!' he shouted. 'Our wise Dharma King said we should wait for you here.'

Meza threw on her feather cape, but hesitated when she saw the panic-stricken Brugmo in the water.

'We are fairies from Heaven, not ordinary women,' Meza shouted.

'You may be lovelier than fairies, but you are humans from Gling. My Dharma King says he will love you more than Gesar ever did if you will come with me and return the treasure you stole.'

Brugmo cried out piteously in the water, 'Help me, Meza.' She had taken off all but a silk shift, and as she made her way to the shore, trembling, the wet silk clung to her body. Her face was white with shame.

'Good sister, I will divert the young general's attention while you fly away with the treasure,' Meza said tearfully, as she removed her feathered attire and put it on Brugmo.

'Which one of you is Gesar's favourite consort, Brugmo?'

Glancing at Brugmo, Meza said with a sweet smile, 'I am the famed beauty, Brugmo. I will pay my respects to the King of Minyag. As for my sister, let her return home to tell all that I am safe.'

He sized them up with his eyes, but did not speak.

'Look at her,' Meza said. 'She has exposed her body to you. She panics at the first sign of trouble. Does she behave as a principal consort would?'

That convinced him. 'I will be lenient, as long as you do not resist.'

But when she heard Meza's words of criticism, Brugmo pushed away her fears and said, 'Taking one step forwards is worth a hundred fine steeds, and taking a step backwards is worth a hundred yaks. A hundred men stare and a hundred women sigh over their ill fortune when they see me. I am the favourite consort of Gesar, the Queen of Gling, whose beauty is known far and wide.' Her coquettish glance so flustered him that he opened a sack made of human skin, from which a whirlwind emerged and sucked both women inside. He slung the sack over his shoulder and set off for the capital city. The women, crowded against one another inside the dark sack, found it pointless to complain.

When at last they were let out of the sack, Meza saw that Brugmo had turned into a sparrow, while she, too, appeared to have become a bird. Human noise pounded their eardrums like thunder. Looking up, they saw the two kings of Minyag sitting high on their thrones, like towering mountains. The Dharma King said, with great satisfaction, 'It was a trick. How else could a sack of human skin accommodate two humans?'

Now Brugmo realised that she, like Meza, had been turned into a nondescript bird, and she chirped angrily. Fearing the loss of her beauty even more than that of her life, she flew up to peck at the king's eyes, but he shook the bronze bell in his hand and its golden light knocked her out of the air. 'Change,' the king said.

The women resumed their human forms.

'Which of you is Brugmo?'

'I am,' Brugmo replied quickly, afraid that Meza would try to impersonate her again.

'Bind her and nail her to a pillar.'

His brother was about to stop him but the Dharma King said, 'Trust me.' He continued, with a smile, 'So you are Meza.'

Meza silently looked away.

'We had the good fortune of meeting years ago. Do you not remember? Since I am generous, I have not told them to drive bronze nails into you. When you were still in the demon country, I went there to speak with the demon king. I tasted the wine you offered me, which is why I am being kind to you now.'

'If the king is truly kind, he should not forget his pact with Gling.'

Her words outraged the Dharma King. 'It was my brother's kindness years ago that stopped me attacking when Gling was weak. But now Gling treats Minyag as if it did not exist. No gratitude has been shown us, not even a simple greeting on the wind. Now that Gling has grown strong, it forgets its earlier connections and, worse yet, you have come to steal our treasure. You will be followed by an army led by Gesar. You repay kindness with ingratitude.'

'You cannot call yourself a fine horseman if you use your whip on a donkey. I will speak with you only if you do not mistreat the queen.'

He ordered Brugmo to be untied. Seeing how gentle the Worldly King was with Brugmo, Meza thought she might be able to help Gesar and save Brugmo if she could find a way to rid them of the vicious Dharma King and work on his younger brother. So to the Dharma King she said, 'The demon king treated me with loving kindness in his country – how could I forget him? Minister Sheng-ngon and I vowed to avenge him. Great King, Sheng-ngon is now the leader of what was left of the demon country. If he will join us, we can wage war with Gling. What concerns me is whether the great king can ensure success.'

'Very well. I will send my brother to the demon country to plot with Sheng-ngon.'

'I am afraid the Worldly King would find it difficult to . . .'

'You are right. My brother mistakes cowardice for kindness. Yes, Yu-ngog Tonpa, you stay with Meza and keep an eye on Brugmo. I will go to Sheng-ngon and return in a few days with good news.' He mounted a bird and flew to the north.

With Yutse Tonpa gone, Brugmo and Meza did their best to charm the younger king. Although enchanted by Brugmo's beauty, he soon tired of her talk, and chose instead to drink with Meza, whose sincerity endeared her to him. Meza's thoughts were on Gesar, who had been speaking again of returning to Heaven. 'Am I capable of becoming immortal?' she asked Yu-ngog Tonpa.

'Some say one must practise magical skills, like my brother, others that it depends on one's fortune. I do not know . . .'

Meza began to weep. 'My body will turn to smoke and ashes in this world.'

Yu-ngog Tonpa took her dainty hands in his. 'Gesar will eventually return to Heaven. But if you are willing to stay in Minyag, you and I could live together into old age.'

'Great King, Gesar would never let his consort become another man's wife.'

'Then I will wait until he returns to Heaven and come to you.'

Then Meza told the king the truth. 'It is not as the Dharma King thought. There is no plan to conquer Minyag. But if you will help me, perhaps Gesar would allow me to stay here as your companion.'

That night they performed the rite between husband and wife. Then Yu-ngog Tonpa opened the eighteen store houses under his control, and Meza searched through them until she found a piece of snakeheart sandalwood in a black metal case. With it, they would be able to travel safely through China's sweltering forests because it cured miasma sicknesses. Then, as Yu-ngog Tonpa slept, Meza slipped out of bed and found the room where Brugmo was imprisoned. She helped Brugmo into her feathered cape and told her to hurry back to Gling with the claw and the snakeheart sandalwood. Brugmo wasted no time and, rising into the evening sky, flew towards Gling in the moonlight.

Meanwhile, Yutse Tonpa flew to Sheng-ngon, who knew that the King of Minyag had arrived when he heard his laughter. He had been wondering why Meza and Brugmo had not returned from their trip to Minyag, and opened the gate to welcome his guest, eager to hear of the two consorts. The King of Minyag quickly told Sheng-ngon of Meza's plan and asked him to summon his army.

'I must see a written message from Meza.'

Stamping his foot, Yutse Tonpa said, 'There was no time for her to write one.'

'Does the king have a token from the consort?'

He did not.

Now everything became clear to Sheng-ngon: Meza and Brugmo were trapped in Minyag and he was to relay that information to Gesar.

'Neither Meza nor I have forgotten the old king,' he said, 'but without a letter or a token from her, I cannot follow your orders.'

Yutse Tonpa had no choice but return to Minyag, and Sheng-ngon sent a message to Gesar. When Yutse Tonpa returned with a token, Sheng-ngon readily gave his consent, agreeing that twenty-one days later the armies of the former demon country would join forces with Minyag to attack Gling.

Returning from the demon country in high spirits, Yutse Tonpa had a welcoming feast prepared and ordered Meza to be his companion. Raising her cup to congratulate him, she was uneasy and, fearing that he might ask after Brugmo, she kept his cup filled. Soon he fell into a deep slumber.

Sheng-ngon set off to see the king. After hearing his report, Gesar said, 'What do you plan to do?'

'I will take my troops to the place designated by the King of Minyag. When the time comes, the armies of the demon country, under a red banner, and the Minyag troops, under a black banner, will arrive at a place where Gling has prepared an ambush. We, on the inside, and you, on the outside, will join forces to destroy Minyag,' Sheng-ngon said.

Gesar turned to Gralha, who was at his side. 'Sheng-ngon is a brave and clever man. You may rely on him in the future.'

'To reach Minyag you must cross eighteen dangerous snow-covered passes,' Gralha reminded the king. 'Foot soldiers cannot possibly reach it on the agreed date.'

Telling his attendant to bring him several green horsetails, Gesar told Sheng-ngon that if they were tied around their waists, they could cross safely.

Sheng-ngon arrived in Minyag on the agreed day, and Yutse Tonpa had a banquet spread for him and his senior generals. Yu-ngog Tonpa, unsettled by his brother's determination to invade Gling, tried to dissuade him, saying that no one in the world could match Gesar's powers. 'Great King,' Sheng-ngon responded, 'calamities are not prevented because you have closed your eyes, just as thunder will rumble even though you have plugged your ears. Gesar will attack no matter what.'

Ten days later Sheng-ngon led the Minyag army into the Gling trap. At first the Minyag soldiers put up a fight, but then they saw that the men from the demon country had turned against them. By dusk, half of Minyag's soldiers had been felled. Then Gesar rode into the battlefield and captured the King of Minyag. With a groan, the king closed his eyes and bared his neck for the sword.

'Wait,' Gesar shouted. 'I hear remorse in this man's sigh. Yutse Tonpa, tell me what is on your mind.'

'King Gesar, all I ask is that you think of the pact between our countries and treat my people well. And my brother, Yu-ngog Tonpa, is a kind man and loyal to Gling. If it please you, spare his life.'

'I should despatch you to Hell, but your words have swayed me. Do not fear. I will lead your soul to a pure Buddhist land.' Then a bright light emerged from the palm of Gesar's hand, and Yutse Tonpa's body fell to the ground, yet his soul rose to a Pure Land where there was no fear or happiness, and no desire.

The Story
Khrothung's Death

When he saw that Gesar had sent away the King of Minyag's soul, Khrothung called on the King of Gling to raze Minyag to the ground. But Sheng-ngon counselled kindness.

Gesar smiled. 'Sheng-ngon is right. I will take only a few of my ministers with me to bring back Meza and the magic braid. That will be enough.' Then, mounting his horse, he set out for Minyag. As they galloped, the horse sang, in a human voice, 'I fly like a harrier hawk. My tail spreads like a waterfall a thousand *li* deep. I call to the gods in the sky, "Help us open the doors to Minyag's snowcapped mountains."' And the towering mountains that stood shoulder to shoulder on the border began to move, revealing a series of canyons. As the King of Gling and his entourage rode into the dark valleys, Minyag, which had been sealed off behind the mountains, was opened up to the world.

At the Minyag palace, Yu-ngog Tonpa and Meza walked down the steep steps to greet them. After presenting Gesar with a *hada*, Yu-ngog Tonpa said, 'Honourable King Gesar, Lion of Gling, thank you for not sending my brother to Hell. Now, if you will spare my people from the suffering of war, I am prepared to offer you everything in Minyag.'

'I did not bring a single soldier with me,' Gesar reassured him. 'Gling does not covet a drop of dew from Minyag, nor will we take even a hint of fragrance from your grassland flowers. You may continue as King of Minyag.'

Meza offered her exquisite hand to Gesar. 'Honourable King, I was born in Gling and was my parents' favourite daughter before I became your loving consort. But I served the king of the demon country when I was trapped there, and I caused you to lose Gling's great hero, your dear brother, Gyatsa Zhakar. Now I have once again become a consort of another king. Great King, I do not wish to travel further between men. I beg you allow me to stay in Minyag for the rest of my life.'

Gesar helped her to her feet. 'Meza, you are free of any guilt. The people of Gling know that, and so do the deities in Heaven. Hurry now, and prepare to return to Gling with me.'

With a wave of his hand, her feathered cloak wrapped itself around her; another wave sent her up into the air. She circled above the Minyag palace three times, calling in a crane's voice her joy and sorrow.

Yu-ngog Tonpa felt as if a knife had cut through his heart but, not daring to show his grief to Gesar, he welcomed the king and his ministers into the palace for a banquet, asking what other treasure he sought from Minyag. Gesar told him of the gemstone-studded braid of the *yaksa*.

Yu-ngog Tonpa knew of the *yaksa*'s existence because Asal Lokhra had been a close friend of his brother, but he did not know where the man practised his magic. He gave Gesar the same keys he had given to Meza, saying, 'I cannot help you with the braid, but you may take what you like of our treasure.'

Gesar and his men went to open the storehouse, and there they found a jar made of rock from a meteorite, filled with oil from a musk deer's heart. Yu-ngog Tonpa told them to smear it over their bodies, and it would protect them as they passed through the dense Chinese forests, which were infested with poisonous snakes and vermin.

Then Gesar returned to Gling with his ministers.

When news of the king's return reached Brugmo, she emerged from the palace to welcome him, dressed in her finest robes. Her oval face was like the early-evening moon, her arched brows like distant mountains where the snows had just melted. When she looked around, it was as though a breeze were caressing the surface of a lake. She glowed like a dream.

She handed the treasure she'd brought from Minyag to the king.

'We will all remember the contribution you and Meza have made,' Gesar said.

Brugmo was not entirely happy to hear that, but Gesar changed the subject, asking if anyone knew where Asal Lokhra could be found. His question was met with resounding silence. 'Can it be that there is no such *yaksa*?' he cried.

The ministers hung their heads, but Khrothung looked smug. It had been only a few days since his fate had hung in the balance in the dungeon, and his face still bore a sallow sheen, the colour of dust. But he sat up straight, his neatly trimmed beard glowing, and said loudly, 'The chief minister knows everything. At least, a chief minister *should* know everything.'

But the chief minister was silent.

Khrothung went on, 'If the king had taken my life, there would be no one to tell him where the *yaksa* is now. If the king does not know where he is, then the demon in China will not be overcome. If the demon returns to life, not only will China sink into darkness, even Gling. . . .' He glanced at Gesar's face and his tone changed. 'I was about to tell the king that Asal Lokhra lives on a copper-red mountain near the border between Gling and Minyag. Years ago, when Gling was at war with Hor, I met him when I followed a herd of wild horses over the border. We fought, from the mountaintop to the foothills, yet neither one gained advantage, which made us appreciate each other's skill. We burned incense and pledged to share hardships in this world. But the king, like everyone else, will not believe that I can obtain the gemstone braid from him.'

'Bring it back and then we will believe you,' the chief minister said.

Khrothung rolled his eyes. 'That means nothing if you do not believe me. Only the king . . .'

Gesar laughed. 'You still bear a grudge even though I have yet to determine your punishment for plotting to usurp my throne. And you should not forget that after I became king I did not punish you for banishing my mother and me, and that after the battle with Hor, I forgave you for plotting with the enemy. Why would I not believe you? Just tell us how we can obtain the gemstone braid from the *yaksa*.'

Khrothung's forehead beaded with sweat as he heard the king list his crimes. 'I thank the king for sparing my life. I will do my best, but the king must know that I can meet the *yaksa* only at a particular time. I have yet to recover from my imprisonment – I cannot yet undertake such a long journey.'

'When can you leave?'

'On the fifteenth of next month.'

'Then I will wait until the next full moon, on the fifteenth. But remember, leader of the Tagrong tribe, this is the last time I will entrust you with such an important task.'

Khrothung began to regret his importunate offer before he reached his fortress. Gesar had spared his life many times, but perhaps this time he was doomed. Khrothung *had* met the *yaksa* once, but they were not sworn friends, as he had boasted. They *had* fought on the copper mountain, but Khrothung had lost. Asal Lokhra had roared with laughter before spreading his cape and flying back to the peak. And, worst of all, the gemstone braid was an amulet that protected the *yaksa*'s life, so he would not give it up easily. Khrothung considered his predicament: punishment for his crime of plotting to usurp the throne had yet to be determined, and now he had added the crime of deceiving the king. He could not see how he would be allowed to remain alive in Gling. That thought cost him sleep and his appetite. Then one night he sat up and gave himself two savage slaps. *Who told you to be a hero?* he berated himself.

He recalled that when he was young, his family had not wanted him to grow up to be daring and rash, and had used magic to make him timid and suspicious, but ambitious. The thought brought tears to his eyes. *I do not weep for myself. I am old and not long for this world. I weep for my son Tonggod, who would have been alive if not for my ambition. I weep for the Tagrong tribe, which will earn the people's enmity.*

After Gesar had become king, the people of Gling had stopped worshipping their false gods and had turned to Buddhism. But Khrothung had a secret room in his living quarters where he kept an ancient idol. Now he crept to it and knelt before the idol. 'If it please you, give me the power to overcome this trouble.'

But the ferocious eyes of the idol were empty of light, and the lamp Khrothung held flickered and went out. In the darkness, Khrothung begged, 'If you cannot help me, cause me to fall ill until the fifteenth has passed.'

He left the secret room and lay on his bed. He felt frail. His god was making him ill, he thought. So he moaned when he awoke the next day, but the second moan had not left his mouth when he realised that he was well. His heart was beating normally, blood was surging in his veins, and his sex was as erect as a spear.

'I'm sick,' he said to his wife, when she came to offer her morning greeting.

Seeing his ruddy face and bright eyes, she smiled and gave him a bowl of fragrant tea to rinse his mouth.

Khrothung smashed the bowl against the wall and screamed, 'Why do you not believe me?'

He remained in bed until noon, when he summoned Dongtsan.

Real tears brimmed in his eyes when he saw his powerful son. 'I think of your brother whenever I see you.'

That saddened Dongtsan also.

'I'm dying,' Khrothung said mournfully.

'Father shows no sign of illness. Did you have a bad dream last night?'

'A disease in my heart is bringing me death,' he shouted, in a shrill, womanly voice. 'Gesar is leading me to my death.'

'Father, the king has just spared your life.' Dongtsan frowned.

'Leave me!'

'Father—'

'Go!'

The fifteenth of the month soon arrived.

Knowing that Khrothung would not come alone, Gesar sent attendants to fetch him, but a pile of rocks outside his fortress stopped them. It was customary in Gling to indicate that someone was seriously ill by piling rocks at their door. So the attendants returned to the king, who knew that Khrothung was playing tricks again. This time he sent Danma, and Michung, who was adept in medicine.

When he saw that the rocks had fooled Gesar's messengers, Khrothung had congratulated himself and hopped out of bed to enjoy a fine meal. But when his servants came to say that Danma and Michung were at the door, he got back into bed and told his wife to prepare tea.

His wife told the visitors that Khrothung did not want his illness to offend the honourable guests, which was why he had stayed away. She asked them to tell the king that, regrettably, Khrothung would be unable to accompany him on his expedition to China.

'The king had anticipated the illness of the leader of the Tagrong tribe,' Danma said, 'so he has sent Michung.'

Khrothung, of course, was even more adamant that he would not receive them.

'Then we will take his pulse with a hanging thread.'

A red thread was extended from the bedroom through a crack in the door, which would enable Michung to interpret the patient's symptoms from faint tremors on the thread. Khrothung tied the other end of the thread around the neck of a parrot, but Michung saw through the trick. Khrothung then put it on a cat, but again Michung was not deceived. Khrothung finally had no choice but to put it on his own body, and wrapped it around his little finger, making Michung laugh. 'The pulse is steady. Can it be that he is feigning illness?'

At this his wife was ashamed. She went into Khrothung's room and told him to get up. He refused. As a last resort, he told his wife to inform Danma and Michung that his upper body was burning like fire, while his lower body was as cold as ice. She tried to help him by laying him out in a spot where *yin* met *yang*, where his upper body was in the bright sun and his lower body in shade. Just then, Danma and Michung stalked into the inner room, and did not know whether to be angry or to laugh when they saw how Khrothung was tormenting himself. At the sight of them, Khrothung feigned death by holding his breath, closing his eyes and thrusting his legs out straight.

Danma thought that Khrothung was indeed dead, but Michung knew better. He winked at Danma, who picked up Khrothung, carried him out of the fortress and put him on his horse. They set off for the palace, and Khrothung realised that they would not carry him to the king if they believed he was truly dead. Then he knew that to deceive King Gesar he must truly die. So he closed all the orifices in his body and stilled his blood. He sent his soul out of his body, and bribed the soul-catchers with treasure to give him three days before they took him to the netherworld. He reasoned that Gesar would not want a cold dead body, so his tribe would take it back. He would revive himself once he had returned to his fortress.

On that day, everyone at the palace knew that Danma and Michung had brought back Khrothung's corpse and at least half had seen it lying on a square rock west of the palace. Gesar came to the rock, where he touched the body; the arms and legs were ice cold. Bending, he whispered into Khrothung's ear, 'Are you really dead?'

Khrothung did not respond.

'I think not.'

Khrothung's soul trembled as it drifted in the sky above him, but made no sound. Gesar felt the ruffling of a cold breeze, so he looked up into the sky again and said, in a loud voice, 'It seems that Uncle has truly left us.'

Thirty sutra masters arrived to sit around the rock and recite sutras for the departed spirit. Thirty python trumpets and thirty white conch trumpets sounded together. A giant pyre was set up, with Gesar's instruction that a cremation be held the next morning before sunrise if the dead man did not revive.

'Uncle Khrothung had powerful magic,' Gesar announced. 'He probably cast off the old body with its bad legs to retrieve the braid from Asal Lokhra. If that is so, then he should have returned by tomorrow morning.'

Hearing this, Khrothung regretted what he had done, but, with all the people around him, he could not possibly return his soul to the body and agree to take the king to *yaksa* Asal Lokhra. But his soul flew to the red copper mountain where he had encountered Asal. There he saw no living thing, only chill starlight cascading onto the mountaintop. At the break of day, his soul returned to the palace, and he saw that the people had already placed his body on a pyre. Women lamented as they threw fragrant petals onto his body.

King Gesar summoned a torch, one comprised of three true fires – air, stone and wood – which would sever all the human entanglements of a lifetime. 'Send someone born in the year of the tiger to light the pyre.'

Danma took the torch from the king, who instructed him to open the gate of fire from the east side. At this, Khrothung's soul flew down to put out the fire, and a swirl of cold air blew over everyone nearby. But the true fires continued to burn brightly, and Khrothung called his soul back into his body. Once there, it was bound so tightly by the rigid, cold flesh that when he tried to shout for Danma to stop, and to beg the king's forgiveness, he could not open his frozen mouth. He tried to open his eyes, but the heavy lids had stiffened. Then the fire gate opened and a jubilant flame rose up the soaring pyre. A column of thick smoke slanted up into the sky and, with a loud *crack*, the pyre collapsed. Those present thought they heard a startled scream, though they saw nothing but white-hot flames.

Gesar sat motionless, his eyes closed and his palms together as he recited a sutra for the body burning in the pyre. He heard Khrothung's soul circle him, chirping like a bird. He felt it land on his shoulder, and heard it speak in a human voice: 'Drogod Tenzin.'

'I know. My celestial mother told me last night in a dream, but I wanted Uncle to say it himself. Khrothung, your remorse at the moment of death has delivered your soul to the Pure Land in the west.'

Khrothung's soul circled above the ashes, watching people collect pieces of bone in a pottery urn. They gave blessings as the urn was sealed. Then Khrothung's son, Dongtsan, took the urn, with some of his people, to the mountain where Tagrong's soul bird resided.

The Storyteller
In Minyag

Jigmed came to a small school, which had only one teacher. The students were not at their teacher's side. Puddles surrounded by green algae dotted the tiny sports field. The teacher, a wide-brimmed hat on his head, sat on the steps reading a book. This was holiday time for mountain schools – they had been given two extra weeks to help at home. Farmers' children cleared weeds from the fields; shepherds' children helped to take the flocks to their summer pastures in the mountains.

When he heard Jigmed's footsteps, the teacher removed his hat, and offered him tea.

Jigmed asked what the teacher was reading. He replied that it was a book about the countries of the world, at least two hundred. 'Grungkan, the number of real countries is far greater than those in your stories.'

Jigmed's response touched the teacher's heart: 'Though you know a great deal about the world, who knows about you and this small place?'

The teacher put his hat back on, covering his eyes, and Jigmed changed the subject. 'I'm looking for a place called Minyag.'

'A place of legend.' The teacher took Jigmed into the classroom and, with the pointer he used to help students recognise written characters, showed Jigmed a map. 'These are real places, and Minyag is not among them.'

Jigmed left the school and walked to the village below, where a family was building a new house. The masons were making a stone wall, while the owner had set up a wok beneath a walnut tree. He asked Jigmed to stay for a while. 'Songs from a *grungkan* would be a great blessing for our new house.'

The masons stopped working to listen to Jigmed sing. When he had finished, the people blessed each other.

'I'm looking for Minyag,' he told them, and was greeted with laughter.

'Where you have just come from and the places you will pass through when you leave, all of this was ancient Minyag,' he was told.

'Really?'

They pressed their faces close to his. 'Can you see that we look different from you?'

Sure enough, they all had a pointed, slightly crooked nose, and brown eyes.

'And don't we sound different?'

So these were the remains of ancient Minyag, where broad valleys had been opened up and where wheat and barley grew on the land between the forest and the water. Symbols of luck were drawn in chalk on the gabled walls of stone buildings. Walnut and apple trees surrounded the villages, and clumps of burdock grew at the edge of the barley threshing ground. The wind blew long strands of cloud over the open valleys.

That evening he sang for the people at the threshing ground and spent the night with the masons in their tent. 'Minyag, Minyag,' he mumbled, as he fell asleep. The place seemed peaceful, devoid of any trace of magic. That night he had another dream.

The man came to his dream again. He sat down in Jigmed's head with his legs crossed but, unlike previous times, he was quiet.

'King?' Jigmed asked gently.

'Yes,' Gesar replied, in a low voice. 'Today I despatched Khrothung.'

Jigmed let out a soft, startled cry.

'I came to the human world to kill evil spirits and demons, but now I have killed a human being.'

Jigmed remained silent.

'I heard a cry. Why were you startled?' Gesar asked.

'You changed the story.'

'Should not Khrothung have died thus?'

Jigmed held his tongue.

'Or perhaps Heavenly secrets should not be revealed.' His sarcasm was unmistakable. 'But his body has turned to ashes and his soul has been directed to the Pure Land. Do you expect him to return to life?'

'He was feigning death.'

'I know that. But he refused to admit his mistake and ask for my forgiveness even when his body was placed on the pyre.'

'But he did! After Danma lit the pyre he crawled out to beg your forgiveness.'

'He was burned to ashes and his soul landed on my shoulder like a bird.'

'You have changed the story,' Jigmed muttered.

'Day will break soon, so I must leave you. I regret Khrothung's death. My mission was to kill demons, not to take human lives.'

'He was not a good person.' Jigmed felt he should console him.

'He forced me to kill him.'

Jigmed held his tongue.

'But I am a deity, and there was no need for me to kill a human.'

'You are also human, and that is why you are unhappy.'

'Why do humans make other humans unhappy? Sometimes Brugmo and Meza make me sad. So does the chief minister. Even my human mother.'

A cockerel crowed in the village, and Gesar said, 'Perhaps Khrothung is not dead. Perhaps it was a dream.'

'I don't know. But I beg you to stop coming into my dreams.' In the dream Jigmed knelt down.

Gesar stood and, shrouded in the dusty early-morning light, said firmly, 'No matter what you say, the story is different now.'

When he woke, Jigmed ran outside, only to see a mist rising slowly from the river valley to the hills. The king's words rang in Jigmed's ear. 'The story is different now.'

Khrothung had died, and his soul had been led to the Pure Land, but . . . Jigmed tried to remember Khrothung's original end. Standing in the damp fog, he panicked: he had lost the end of the story. But at last the end played out vividly before his eyes.

He pressed his head against a rock, and felt the coolness course through his body.

The Story
Treasure and Vows

'Now I am a cruel king,' Gesar said, to the chief minister, after delivering Khrothung's soul.

'You are a fair and just king,' the chief minister replied.

'Who was Drogod Tenzin?'

'An earth god from the land between Gling and Minyag.'

'Is there nothing you do not know?'

Detecting the sarcasm in the king's voice, the chief minister said, 'Is the king referring to the fact that I do not know where Asal Lokhra lives? I really do not know, for I had never heard his name before.'

'Like Gesar, King of Gling, who had never heard of a country called Minyag, which was right under his nose.'

'Honourable King, I know you are troubled by Khrothung's death. Relieve me of my post if you must punish someone.'

Without a word, Gesar went back to his palace, but he sent a message that the chief minister should guard the palace while he took a few men with him to seek out the earth god, Drogod Tenzin.

The chief minister laughed. 'I am relieved that he overcame his anger so quickly.'

When they reached the red hills on the border, Gesar stamped his feet to summon a local god. Danma asked why he did not kneel before the king, and the local god knitted his snow-white brows and said, 'I do not know which country I belong to.' He added, with some pride, 'A god has no country,' and told them that he had been on that land for more than a thousand years, long before the border between Gling and Minyag was created.

Growing impatient, Danma tried to force him to kneel before the king, but the old man's body sank into the ground only to pop up again elsewhere. 'The king is responsible for the people, the livestock and the crops. But I am responsible for the essence of the land, the veins of metal in the mines, and things invisible to the human eye.'

Gesar had been sunk in gloom since the death of Khrothung, and this god amused him. When Danma raised his bow, Gesar transformed himself into the twin of the greying old god, forcing Danma to lower his bow.

'So you are not human,' the god said.

'He is the king sent by Heaven to rule Gling.'

A rainbow appeared in the sky, and faint music could be heard.

'So, you came from the home of the gods?' the god asked.

Gesar smiled, unsheathed his sword and waved it. A thread of silver ran through the hill, a growing mineral vein the earth god had been nurturing.

Now, finally, he was willing to kneel before Gesar.

Gesar, still in the guise of the old earth god, said 'No. You are kneeling to yourself. Now, tell me where I may find Asal Lokhra, the *yaksa*.'

'I cannot . . .'

Gesar raised his hand, and a wind twirled the earth god like a spinning top. He was brought to the edge of the Earth, to the icy void, where there was no beginning and no end. He wept when he was jerked back to the hillside.

'Tell me.'

'Cross two red mountains and a black mountain ridge, and you will find Asal's land. But no one who has searched for him has ever returned. The grass and trees and the water that flows from the mountains are poisonous. On the black ridge stands a lone tree, under a rock that has existed since the day Heaven and Earth were separated. The rock is the centre from which Asal roams. But, please, do not harm him.'

As he spoke, a thunderclap sounded and the *yaksa* stood before them. His body stretched up into the sky; among his tangled locks was a braid studded with bright gemstones. He was weeping and his great teardrops fell onto the copper red earth, giving off the scent of rusted iron.

'I will not hurt you,' said the king.

The *yaksa* shook his head, and his teardrops flew to the lowlands between the mountains and made pools. 'King Gesar, you do not know. I have been able to cultivate my magic for hundreds of years without causing trouble in the human world because I rely upon those who know of my whereabouts to keep their vow of silence. Every knot on my gemstone braid is a symbol of a promise to keep my secret. For years, people have kept that secret, as have the birds in the sky, and the King of Minyag. But my braid will loosen now that Drogod Tenzin has opened his mouth.' The *yaksa* stumbled down the mountain. 'My body and strength are simply an accumulation of energy. I do not eat or drink, and I do not harm anyone. Indeed, my presence has prevented evil spirits and demons from causing trouble. Drogod Tenzin, is this not true?'

'They wish to borrow your treasure. They will take neither your life nor your land,' the god said.

'You broke your promise,' the *yaksa* roared. 'Once you told them my secret, my strength began to fail and my body will soon disappear.' His figure and face were blurring. 'Gesar, from now on no one will practise magic simply because they enjoy it, and no one will keep a promise.'

He cried when Danma took out the bamboo claw to remove the braid. 'Foolish man, that is useless now that the vow has been broken.' His voice and body faded, and the copper mountain became a little darker. The gemstones from his braid fell to the ground, and rolled to the feet of Gesar, who was staring blankly at the void Asal had left. They glittered as they cooled and re-formed. The king's attendants sprang into action, using grass, horsetails, silk thread, even hair pulled from their heads to string the stones together. Once the treasure was in his hand, the king prepared to leave. The earth god asked them to leave the stones with him so he could bury them in the ground where the mountain peak had first risen up. The stones would grow again to nurture the land, and the mountain would be covered with a dense forest and clear streams.

Danma, who thought that Gesar would regret having eradicated a harmless *yaksa*, for he had questioned all of his actions following the death of Khrothung, snapped at the old god. 'Why are you chattering like this? Do you expect a reward?'

'We should make recompense to Drogod Tenzin,' Gesar said.

'If the king plans to bestow a reward, please give it to the land, not to me.'

'If I do, will the land grow in the way you described?'

The god waved his hands earnestly. 'My land and I need no reward from you.'

Gesar laughed. 'My wish is for this land to have forests and clear waters.' And as he spoke, a flock of birds flew above them, bringing seeds they had collected from all corners of the world. Gesar said to the god, 'Now a single rainfall will bring trees and grass to your land.'

'But the flaming mountain has baked the clouds dry.'

'I will see that the ground receives the rain for which it thirsts.'

Seven days later they were back in the palace. The king ordered the chief minister and Prince Gralha to keep watch over the country, and told Gralha to behave as a king. The chief minister asked him to return quickly, for he feared he might not see the king again. Shanpa Merutse, looking older than ever, was also eager for the king's return.

Instead of wine, Brugmo and Meza gave the king two sharp arrows with the wish that their husband would return soon.

And so Gesar left Gling, accompanied by Danma, Sheng-ngon and Michung. As they passed the copper mountain, Gesar summoned the god of rain to send water to the barren land.

The Story
The Demon in China

Gesar and his contingent travelled through the dark country of China, where the days were pale and the nights dark grey. The light grew even fainter as they neared the centre of the country. On the last night, they camped in a dense grove of bamboo and the sky was darker and deeper than they had ever known it.

When they pitched their tents, the demon in the palace shuddered, and the bamboo around the campsite turned into poisonous snakes. Gesar melted the musk deer's heart fat, from the Minyag treasure, over a flame. Its strange scent repelled the snakes. When a miasma rose, he took out the piece of snakeheart sandalwood.

'Sleep. Tomorrow morning we will enter China's palace city,' Gesar said.

'How will we know when morning comes?' asked Danma.

'We will wake when birds begin to search for food and flowers bloom. That will be the morning.'

'How can flowers bloom where there is no light?' Sheng-ngon asked.

Gesar was silent.

On the move again, they saw flickers of light by the roadside. Looking closely, they saw that it came from inside the buds of flowers. In the dense darkness, they came to a bridge made of Chinese white jade. The princess appeared to greet them at the middle of the arch, a lantern in her hand, its light shrouded in dark cloth.

'I have been waiting here for three hundred days,' she said. 'I despaired of seeing you.'

'You know I have come to kill your mother,' Gesar said.

'I am the emperor's daughter.'

Their journey into the city was like a dream, the houses and wells, and the goods in marketplaces dimly outlined. The darker shadows that moved like emptiness were humans; thick black cloths covered their lanterns, too. In the circles of fainter shadow the people conducted their business, gossiped, kissed, read books, breastfed . . . It was almost as though the furtive dark brought them a special pleasure.

The princess took them to the city's finest inn. There, dark shadows flitted back and forth and hot tea and delicious food were placed before them. Then the princess went to tell the emperor that the King of Gling and his retinue had arrived in China.

'How dare he come without my permission?' the emperor snarled.

So Gesar sent Sheng-ngon into the palace as his emissary. Sheng-ngon could hear the emperor's voice but could see nothing except the golden dragon chair, whence a lethargic voice said, 'We will meet your king in the square before the palace.' And so the meeting was arranged for the fifteenth day of the fifth month, when two auspicious constellations, the Ghost Mansion and the Tree Star, would be aligned.

To mark the day, the emperor allowed a crack to open in the sky to let a little light in so that the people could witness the occasion, and he ordered nine more layers of heavy black curtains hung around the room where the demon's body lay.

And so Gesar met the Chinese emperor in the palace square.

When a ray of natural light shone through the clouds and lit the square, there were thunderous cheers from the crowds.

'My people have such love for me that I cannot often leave the palace. I do not want them to cheer,' the emperor said.

'Perhaps they applaud the change in the weather.'

'My people are happy to allow me to order the weather. It saves them the trouble of doing so.'

'It is too dark.'

'But we do not have hurricanes or floods, and the sun never bakes the land dry. The people can still see.'

'They secretly use lanterns.'

'Will you not eat the fruit and drink the tea before you?'

'Without the sun, the fruit and the tea have lost their fragrance.'

The emperor leaped to his feet. 'Have you come to insult me?'

'I have come to help your country see daylight again.'

The emperor's hand grasped the hilt of his sword; legions of bowmen appeared on the city wall, crossbows at the ready.

Gesar conjured up thousands of troops, and panic gripped the crowd. He raised his voice: 'Do not be afraid. The warriors of Gling and China are holding a tournament.'

The crowd calmed.

'I suppose we must have a tournament,' said the emperor.

Both sides agreed to begin with a horserace, starting in the square and ending at the sacred Mount Wutai. A Chinese general mounted his wind-chasing horse while a Gling general rode a green jade-bird steed. They shot out of the square like bolts of lightning. The emperor and the king spoke quietly and drank wine together. Soon they heard the sound of hoofs, and the Gling general rode up carrying a fern from Mount Wutai. The Chinese general was nowhere in sight. His wind-chasing horse had been in the lead but had fallen: its eyes, used to darkness, could not stand the strong light at Mount Wutai. Both horse and rider were injured, and shame had caused the general to slit his throat.

The enraged emperor flicked his loose sleeves, closing off the corner of the sky that had been opened, and the land was again submerged in darkness.

Then Danma, glowing in his golden armour, took up his bow, and all eyes were drawn to him. He loosed an arrow that sliced through the air and through the black magic, and the grey mist began to recede. The sky grew light, the sun touched the mountains and rivers. Fish at the surface of lakes dived to the depths, and birds folded their wings over their eyes. Like his people, the emperor covered his face when the sun fell once again on his land, where a dead silence still lay. But the light, travelling to every corner, buzzed like a bee.

Gesar transformed himself into a golden roc, and carried Sheng-ngon and Michung to the city, where he found the palace swathed in black curtains. Searching through dark, serpentine hallways, they found the demon empress's body.

'Put her in a steel coffin,' Gesar said.

They took Asal Lokhra's gemstone braid, wrapped it around her three times and slid her into the cold silence of the steel box. Then Gesar took them to the place where the sky met the land, at the end of the earth, and there he put down the coffin. With a blazing torch, he set fire to the body and watched it burn to ashes.

The emperor and his people heard a wind begin to stir the grass, the trees and the still surface of lakes. As they slowly opened their eyes, they saw birds in the sky and flowers turning to face the sun. A rich scent rose up from the damp earth. The people ran home to wash and dress themselves in bright clothing.

But the emperor thought he heard a shrill scream, and called, 'Empress!' But all he saw was a roc bring its wings together before him, then a smiling Gesar, who said, 'Your empress was a demon.'

The emperor of China fainted.

It was dusk when he awoke. He gave an order from his bed: 'Seize Gesar and tear his body into a thousand pieces.'

When he next opened his eyes he saw a smiling Gesar looking down at him. 'You may do as you will to me. I shall not resist. But you must come to your senses – and trust the gods.'

'Hang him!'

Gesar was hanged on the city's gate tower. Three days later, a minister came to report to the emperor that birds came daily to feed Gesar with nectar and fine juices. So the emperor ordered Gesar to be put into a dungeon filled with scorpions. Instead of stinging him, they bowed to him. The emperor then had him thrown from a high cliff, but birds rose up from the ocean to catch him and carry him back to the city. The emperor had him burned, but after seven days and seven nights, the pyre became a lake and in the middle of the lake was a sacred *ruyi* tree. Gesar sat on the cloud-like crown of the tall tree.

At this the emperor came with his senior ministers to beg his forgiveness.

'The demons have been dispelled from China,' said Gesar. 'I wish the emperor and his people eternal peace and happiness.'

The grateful emperor said, 'Your home is in a high, bitterly cold country, while mine is a country of abundance. I am old and and my daughter is too frail to rule. Stay here and share the throne with me.'

Gesar told him that the princess had a strong will, and was concerned for the people's well-being. Her sex did not preclude her from becoming a good emperor. Then the emperor bade Gesar farewell, and told the princess to accompany them to the border.

The Story
Shanpa Merutse's Death

In early spring, Gesar and his retinue reached the border with Gling. The first to welcome them was the earth god, who brought treasures from the mountains, followed by the generals and ministers who had made a special trip to wait at the border. 'Prince Gralha and Brugmo have been waiting eagerly,' they told the king.

'This is happy news.'

'The chief minister is still doing well.'

'That is good news too.'

'Prince Gralha deals with matters in a serious and thoughtful manner.'

'This sets my mind at ease. So what is the bad news?'

'With heaven's protection, Gling has not suffered from storms or plagues of insects.'

'What is the bad news?'

'The chief minister told us not to mention anything that may worry the king.'

'I am already concerned.'

The old general, Shanpa Merutse, was not well. Prince Gralha had brought him from Hor to the palace for treatment, but he had not improved. Gesar knew that Shanpa Merutse should have perished on the battlefield when they had fought Khridan Gyalpo, and that it was only through the protection of Gyatsa Zhakar's soul that he had survived for so long. But his later years had been worse than death, and it would be deliverance for him to end his life soon.

A red-crowned crane landed beside them. One of the ministers took the letter tied to its foot and presented it to the king. It was from Shanpa Merutse, who had learned of the king's return. Afraid that he might die before Gesar reached the palace, he asked for the king's permission to meet him halfway for a final farewell.

Prince Gralha rode alongside the dying Shanpa Merutse. Coughing blood, Shanpa Merutse said him, 'I am honoured to have served such a heroic king.' When they saw the king's banners, he ordered the blood to be wiped from his mouth, had a comb run through his silver beard, and mustered the strength to sit up. When the king jumped off his horse and strode over, Shanpa Merutse spoke: 'Honourable King, I am a sinner, yet the king has granted my last wish. But I no longer have the strength to show my respect.'

'Shanpa Merutse, you committed a crime against Gling but since then you have proved your loyalty to the country. The sun and moon bear witness to your deeds.'

Shanpa Merutse smiled, and kept his gaze fixed on the king as the light died slowly in his eyes. It was the king himself who closed them.

Gesar was lightheaded after too many toasts at the welcoming banquet, but the chief minister told him it was time to receive his subjects. Gling had become such a powerful country that it took nearly four hours for all to pay their respects and seek his blessings, ministers, generals, chiliarchs and centiarchs whose names he knew, and ranked palace attendants. Although this pleased Gesar, Brugmo noticed his knitted brows.

Tapping his head, made heavy by wine, Gesar said, 'I am trying to recall a familiar face I have yet to see. It is that of my valiant consort, Atag Lhamo. Brugmo, you are the principal consort but Atag Lhamo has fought for Gling and now guards the border alone. How could you have forgotten her?'

Brugmo lowered her head.

'Woman, I thought the flames of jealousy had finally died in your heart.'

'Atag Lhamo is very ill. That is why I did not tell her of the king's return.'

'Fetch someone who serves General Atag Lhamo,' the chief minister ordered.

'You did not call her a consort, but a general,' Gesar said.

'My king, that is a display of my respect for her. She has not only the beauty of a consort but also the courage of a general.'

A man with a fair complexion and intelligent eyes approached, and Gesar asked, 'What do you do for the consort?'

'I interpret and make maps. I have come with a letter from General Atag Lhamo.'

'Hand it to me.'

'The king is aware that the general cannot write. She dictated to me and I have committed it to memory.'

Atag Lhamo's message was filled with deep affection: she said she did not regret having betrayed her brother for the well-being of her people, and that although she and King Gesar had spent more time apart than together, the pleasures enjoyed by a man and woman were worth more than gold, and she would savour them all her life. She was happy that, even though she was a woman, she had fought for Gling in battle. But, despite it all, she had been born into a demon country: before pledging her allegiance to Gling, she had feasted on human flesh and slept on the skins of victims. Now, because of this, she was ill. Confined to bed, she missed the king, longing for his tender affection, but she knew that the king had crossed high mountains and forded great rivers to subdue a demon in a foreign country, and since her days in this world were numbered, let this letter be her farewell.

As they listened to the fair-skinned young official recite Atag Lhamo's words, the king and his minister wept. Brugmo lowered her head in shame, and her tears soaked into her skirt.

'Rkayngkar Perpo!' Gesar shouted.

The celestial horse came to his master and, with Gesar on his back, flew to the border pass that Atag Lhamo guarded. But he was too late. She had died a few days earlier, and her people now knelt at Gesar's feet, weeping.

'Why are you not conducting the deliverance rite for her?' Gesar wondered.

'The general asked not to have one.'

A lama who had come to recite a sutra for her was turned away. 'Reciting sutras is like summoning ghosts,' she had said. The lama had shaken his head and said that Gesar had not completely changed her nature: she was still a demon.

Before she had died she had told her servants, 'Do not let that Buddhist monk near my body. He speaks sutras but thinks of horses and silver. He says he can deliver souls, but that is empty talk. When the king comes, give him these few tokens from me.'

The Storyteller
Saving a Wife from Hell

The storyteller at last uncrossed his legs and stood up. Tossing the colourful ribbons on his hat, he began to sing:

'Gold and silver combs in her hair,
Like stars in the sky,
Offer them to the king.

Strings of coral and amber from her neck,
Like flowers on the grassland,
Offer them to the king.

A silk dress on her body,
Like a rainbow in the sky,
Offer it to the king.

The white helmet on her head,
Tempered by demon fire,
Offer it to the king.

Three golden arrows in a quiver at her waist,
Gifts from the king,
Offer them to him.

Atag Lhamo, born in the demon country,
Sent away at the king's order,
Wishes Gling ten thousand years of prosperity.'

Jigmed's song brought tears to the eyes of the audience, but a young lama jumped to his feet and interrupted, loudly accusing Jigmed of attacking his master and all Buddhist doctrine: 'How dare you reject the Buddhist teachings?'

Jigmed was no good at dealing with people outside the stories. 'I'm just telling a story. I'm a *grungkan*, a—'

The lama smacked his palms together. 'It makes you a demon.'

The people who, a moment before, had been moved by the story now shushed Jigmed. He stood up. 'You all know that I'm just—'

The lama clapped his hands again, and Jigmed packed his things, frightened by the vicious looks on so many people's faces. He could not stop shaking as he walked along the road, but reminded himself that the gods wanted him to tell the story, that he had nothing to fear. He thought of going back to finish it, but he lacked the courage. As he put the town behind him, he hated himself for his cowardice. At last he stopped under a giant pine tree, sat down and leaned against the thick trunk to catch his breath. He soon fell asleep.

It was so quiet when he woke that he could hear pine cones falling to the ground. As he lay listening, he composed himself. It was his destiny to tell the story, so why should he be afraid? He had heard of storytellers being chased out of other places. The reason was always the same: the words and deeds of the characters in the story went against Buddhist teachings. It had happened to an older generation of storytellers, when the story of Gesar had been banned in many temples.

He walked on and finished Atag Lhamo's story in the next village, where more than a dozen people listened to him.

After her death, Atag Lhamo's soul drifted for forty-nine days before it was escorted to the halls of Yama, the Lord of the Underworld.

Yama was startled. 'You are half woman, half man,' he said. 'Your mouth has the stench of death and the blood has not yet dried on your hands.'

Atag Lhamo, too, was surprised, for she had felt her own existence without sensing her body.

'Who are you?' Yama shouted.

'Atag Lhamo, consort of Gling and its border general.'

Yama burst out laughing. 'You performed too few good deeds in the human world, so now your demon nature is revealed.'

'Killing demons is not a good deed?'

'Building and repairing roads are better.'

'Guarding the border to protect the people?'

'You have done nothing but slaughter people.'

A thumb-sized white figure appeared on her right shoulder. 'Powerful Yama,' it said, 'Dharma judge of good and evil, as this woman's journey god, I know her story. She was a heroine of Gling, the incarnation of a hawk, and the consort of King Gesar. Please send her to Elysium, for she has performed many exceptional deeds.'

Then a small black figure materialised on her left shoulder. 'I am also her journey god. She is a descendant of the nine-headed demon. Since she was three she has slaughtered countless fowls and animals, powerful high officials, heroes, great horsemen and long-haired women. How can such a demon's soul be delivered? She must be sent to Hell.'

Yama told the devils to bring the scales. The devil working it whispered into Atag Lhamo's ear. She replied that she had nothing to give him, since she had lost her body. And so she was weighed eighteen times, and each time the little devil told Yama that the woman's evil deeds outweighed the good.

So Atag Lhamo's soul was sent to Hell.

The Story
Saving His Wife from Hell

After Atag Lhamo's body was burned, on a mountaintop near the northern border, Gesar shut himself away and recited sutras to deliver her soul to the Pure Land. He summoned a *yaksa*, who told him that Atag Lhamo's soul had lingered for a long time before being led away by Yama's little devils on the day before the king's arrival.

With a cry of dismay, Gesar mounted Rkayngkar Perpo and gave chase, but by the time he reached Yama's hall, Atag Lhamo was already suffering. He shouted for Yama.

'That man shouts and flowers rain from the sky,' Yama said to his servants. 'He must be a great saviour or a *sadhaka*. Ask him what he wants.'

King Gesar shouted again: 'Tell King Yama to come out.'

When Yama heard that, he knew Gesar had come for Atag Lhamo's soul, and he dawdled. In his impatience, Gesar overturned Yama's throne, then drew his crystal sword and swung it, almost breaching Hell's steel gate. That brought Yama out.

'You are not close to death. Return whence you came.'

Gesar had thought that Yama would bow down to him. But Yama disappointed him. 'Return to your life in the human world. I can tell that you have done good deeds, but you have also killed many people, so I could send you to eternal punishment.'

'I was sent to the human world by the Supreme Deity.'

Yama laughed. 'So you are the son of the deities, Thosba Gawa, King Gesar of Gling. Gesar, I know much about you, and you should know that in this place even heroes cannot conquer me. Look up – the blue sky is empty. No one will come to help you. No one will appear on the deserted road to guide you. I have ruled here since the day the Earth was separated from the sky.'

'You are unjust. Atag Lhamo should not be in Hell.'

'You are too late. She cannot be reborn until she has suffered for five hundred years.'

'I beg you, King Yama.'

'Return to me after five hundred years if you still care for her.'

Gesar drew his sword again, but with a simple flick of his sleeves, Yama returned the twisted steel gate to its original shape. 'All the souls brought here lack shape and substance, and all in this hall is an illusion. Go.'

'Must my Atag Lhamo spend five hundred years in Hell?'

Yama did not reply. He rested his hand on Gesar's shoulder and walked with him. They went a long way in the fog, and Gesar saw that Yama's land was composed of abysses, that the road was nothing but a series of bridges over them. They came to a place where they could see the sun; it hung in the distant sky, which shivered like a great curtain. 'This is where we part, Gesar. Perhaps we will meet again.'

'Is there another way I might rescue Atag Lhamo?'

Yama looked as though he wanted to say more, but then he dissolved into the mist, and so did the bridges and the abysses. Gesar and his horse were left standing in bright sunlight. After the deathly silence of the underworld, he felt as though he could hear the sunlight flowing. Gesar rode over the grassland, and after a while he spoke to his horse. 'The netherworld is different from the human world, where the countries have exact locations. The netherworld even exists within the human world.'

As he spoke, a clear voice came from the heavens: 'Thosba Gawa, son of the deities. You comprehend the meaning behind the *yin* and the *yang*, the real and the illusory. This wisdom will lead you to the truth.'

Gesar looked up and saw a bright cloud at the edge of the sky. The Guanyin Bodhisattva was sitting upon it, precious vase in hand. Gesar felt as if he had been glued to the saddle. 'Guanyin Bodhisattva.'

The Bodhisattva smiled. 'Why did you go to Yama?' she asked.

'To rescue my consort.'

'She was a demon.'

'But she pledged her allegiance . . .'

'I will not interfere with Yama's affairs. You must speak to Padmasambhava, Master Lotus. But for now, go home. You have offended Yama and you will fall ill. When you are well again, go to Master Lotus.'

As she spoke, the Bodhisattva's figure faded away.

Gesar did indeed fall ill upon his return to the palace. He prayed to Heaven: 'Supreme Deity, please do not let me die, but let me go to Heaven with dignity.'

He heard only thunder that sounded like a dragon singing.

Within a month he had recovered, and told Brugmo that he was going to see Padmasambhava.

In the past, whenever Gesar left, Brugmo had tried to stop him. Now she felt a sharp pain, like lightning, tear through her. She prostrated herself before him and said, 'If the king is leaving, he should take Brugmo with him or she will die from a broken heart.'

'Why must you try to stop me every time I embark on a journey?' Gesar asked unhappily.

'My husband, I was wrong in the past when I stood in your way – it was because of my selfish love for you. But now I am afraid that you are returning to Heaven, and that you will leave me alone in this world.'

'I do not know how long this trip will take, but I am not going to Heaven.'

Brugmo bowed her head.

Gesar then summoned his ministers. 'I am going to consult with Padmasambhava. While I am away, you must keep the peace. The hunters must put away their bows and arrows, and the fishermen leave their nets to dry in the sun. Remember this.'

He transformed himself into a twinkle of bright light and flew into the western sky.

Master Lotus lived in the Country of Yaksas, a land crossed by treacherous paths through valleys of thorn-covered trees and poison-oozing rocks. Gesar was astonished that the master ruled such a terrifying place. But the palace itself was different. Its walls shone like crystal in the sunlight. Something that might have been music and might have been fragrance swirled in the air. Gesar suddenly smelt his own scent – the odour of a corpse, of rivers of blood flowing on a battlefield. The white-clad attendant lifted an urn and poured the blessed water of compassion over his head to purify him, and then his skin carried only the strange scent of the sandalwood tree.

Master Lotus appeared. 'Other than this small palace, all else about this country is worse than the Gling of many years ago.' He laughed. 'If I had not been so tired, you would have had less to do.'

'The Guanyin Bodhisattva said you could offer guidance.'

'The Bodhisattva is never content to see me idle. But what can I do for you?'

'I am here to ask if you will tell me how to rescue my consort.'

'You are over-zealous in coming so far to save the former princess of a demon country,' the master said. 'Think hard. Is there anything else you wish to ask me?' His voice grew softer. He took the urn from his attendant and flicked some water into Gesar's face.

Gesar heard himself say, 'I wish to know how much longer I will stay in Gling, and how the black-haired people of Gling can continue to live in peace.'

The master sent spokes of light from his body and through Gesar. Rising from his throne he sang a Buddhist hymn.

> 'The fine steed must gallop often,
> The weapon of wisdom must be polished,
> Karma must protect the body like armour.
> Gling will live in peace.'

With these words the master vanished, along with the palace.

It took Gesar nearly three years to return home.

Gesar could not see the chief minister among those who came to welcome him home, and went to find him.

'May the king pardon your old minister for not going to welcome him,' Rongtsa Khragan said weakly.

'Has the physician examined you?'

'Great King, I am not ill. I am more than a hundred years old. I have seen how Gling was born and how it has prospered, and I do not want to leave, but soon I must.'

Gesar clasped Rongtsa Khragan's hands.

'Why did it take us so long to get back?' Gesar asked his horse, after leaving the chief minister.

'On the way home you went to a distant country,' the horse replied.

'Where did I go?'

'You were there in your dreams as you rode on my back. You went to the future.'

The Storyteller
The Future

Jigmed's constant wandering was getting harder. But he trudged on, for he was on his way to Khampa, where Gesar was revered.

One night he came to a post office in a small town. The clerk told him he could use the phone, and was shocked when Jigmed didn't know how. Jigmed took out an impossibly wrinkled business card and gave it to the clerk so that he could dial the number. When he was handed the receiver, he heard only the buzz of static. Then the old scholar's voice spoke: 'Hello?'

Jigmed found it hard to talk to someone he could not see.

'Hello?' the voice asked again.

'It's me.'

'It didn't take you long to look me up.' The old scholar was laughing.

'Walking is becoming harder for me. But I'm not weary. I just feel an ache in my back.'

'Then see a doctor.' Before hanging up, the old scholar told him to memorise the phone number. Then Jigmed went to the town's clinic, where a doctor made him stand before a machine to X-ray his back. He told him he had healthy bones.

'Is there anything in my back besides my bones?' Jigmed asked.

'What else do you think is there?'

'An arrow.'

On the road once again, he felt the arrow in him, from his neck to his crotch, making it hard to walk. He wondered why, after so many years, it had begun to hurt. Gazing into the sky, he was reminded of what King Yama had said to Gesar in the story: 'Looking up, the blue sky is empty.'

Deity, do you plan to retrieve your arrow? he asked silently. The thought brought gloom to his heart. *Deity, do you plan to take back your story with the arrow?*

After he had walked for some time, he reached an intersection where the air was full of dust from passing trucks. He asked a passer-by where the three roads led.

'Grungkan, this one is for you. It will take you to the Ashug grass-land,' the man said, pointing to the quietest road.

The Ashug grassland: the birthplace of King Gesar.

That night he spent the night on the grassland. The Yalong river roared in his ears and the stars sparkled above him. When he woke the next morning, he knew he had not dreamed. The invisible arrow, which he could neither touch nor see, was still there, making the trek painful and difficult.

At sunset he arrived at a temple, where the lamas were rehearsing a play about Gesar, under the direction of a Living Buddha. The young lamas, whose faces were painted and who wore gaudy costumes, came onstage amid rhythmic drumbeats. Lamas playing immortals began to dance gracefully around Gesar, who wore his golden helmet and golden armour.

'Which scene is this? The one in which the king returns to Heaven?' Jigmed asked.

'This is the hero's birthplace, so the people enjoy watching his birth,' the Living Buddha said. 'But I could make arrangements for you to sing about the king returning to Heaven.' The Living Buddha did not take off his dark glasses, but Jigmed could feel his sharp gaze on him. 'Grungkan, you carry a smell with you.'

'A smell?'

'A smell of the end.'

'Am I about to die?'

'I sense the end of the story. Will you sing the last part, the end of the hero's story, for us here?'

The play was still going on when the sun set and the first stars leaped onto the canopy of the heavens. That night, the Living Buddha brought Jigmed's meal and invited him to tea. Jigmed told him about the place where he had been chased away by lamas for performing Atag Lhamo's disrespectful words about monks. The Living Buddha smiled but did not comment. But he asked Jigmed, 'Are you sure you are ready to perform the ending?'

'I cannot walk any longer.'

Then they spoke of how many *grungkan*s were reluctant to sing the last scene of the hero's story, because they feared that once they did, the story would leave them. Jigmed told the Living Buddha that if he took his story to the city and recorded his songs the government would look after him for the rest of his life, and then he spoke of the female storyteller: how they had met at the radio station and their recent encounter. He even mentioned her gold tooth and how the old lady had kissed him before he had left. Jigmed laughed. 'The story she recorded isn't complete either. A cat ruined the tape, and she can't re-record what was lost.'

They sat quietly as they watched the moon break through the clouds in the eastern sky.

Once again, Jigmed did not dream.

The next day, as noon approached, he still did not know whether he would sing. The Living Buddha took him to see the temple's newly constructed Hall of Gesar. They started on the second floor, where many portraits of Gesar were displayed. Some were painted on canvas while others were carved from stone. He was portrayed galloping on horseback, stretching his bow to shoot an arrow, swinging his sword to kill a demon, frolicking with beauties. There were relics, too: saddles, a helmet, quivers, steel bows, bronze swords and magic implements, all collected by the Living Buddha, who claimed that they were the tools

Gesar had used in the human world. Jigmed asked if he could touch the objects, for with his bad eyesight he could not see them. They were cold and hard, and he could not sense whether they were true relics.

In the centre of the dimly lit hall, Jigmed stood before a golden statue of Gesar flanked by the generals who had helped him to build Gling. He called their names one by one: Rongtsa Khragan, Prince Gralha, General Danma, the old general Xinba Muiraze, Prince Yulha Thoggyur of Jang, Princess Atag Lhamo of the demon country and Gyatsa Zhakar, who had died too young. The hall seemed to tremble when he said the last name, so he repeated it, but this time nothing happened.

Then Jigmed turned to Gesar, to the glittering statue of the deity, the hero of his story and the decider of his destiny. 'Great King!'

Gesar, riding Rkayngkar Perpo back to the palace city, thought he heard the call. He straightened in his saddle, and this time heard it clearly: 'My destiny, my king.'

He knew it was the storyteller. As he listened, his body rose into the air, though his horse kept trotting. Gesar heard Jigmed ask, 'Haven't you always wanted to know the end of the story? The moment has come.'

Then Gesar found himself in the Ashug grassland thousands of years later, in his future. He did not know how he could have come there, but it was familiar, this place of his birth. He saw the lamas, dressed in red robes, playing brass horns as they enacted what he had done after coming to the human world. Then he saw his own statue, and the storyteller touching its feet with his forehead.

He heard Jigmed ask, 'Will I end the story? If so, take away the pain you have caused in me. I'm old – I can no longer bear it.'

'What pain?' Gesar asked.

'Did you forget the arrow you put in my body?'

'Arrow?'

'I can't hear what you're saying,' said the Living Buddha.

Jigmed turned and smiled at the Living Buddha. 'I'm begging the deity for mercy.'

Later the Living Buddha would tell of how he saw with his own eyes the statue raise its hand and gently brush Jigmed's back. And he told them of the clink of steel on the stone floor as the arrow fell from Jigmed's body – the arrow would become the most sacred relic of the temple. As it fell, Jigmed felt the story begin to leave him; like dust stirred by a strong wind, it flew into the sky. He knew he must sing. He picked up his lute, put on his storyteller's hat, and walked onto the stage where the monks were still busy rehearsing. Everyone held their breath.

Jigmed sang once more before the story left him. As the last words left his lips, his mind went blank. He did not even remember to look up to see if the human king still lingered. But the Living Buddha had caught the last of his song on a small tape recorder.

The half-blind *grungkan* stayed in the temple on the grassland, and every morning he groped his way to the hall to sweep around the statue of Gling's king and his ministers. He grew old there. When there were visitors, the temple played the final passage he had sung, and he would raise his face to listen intently. And sometimes, when the great hall was quiet, he would touch the arrow, and feel the chill and heft of steel.

The Story
The Lion Returns to Heaven

Gesar's birth mother had died during the three years he was away.

Brugmo fell on her knees before him when he returned, but Gesar sighed. 'I must know where her soul went.'

His magic had grown in the years since his visit to Master Lotus and the Bodhisattvas, and now he summoned the soul-snatcher from King Yama's realm, who told him that his birth mother had also been sent to Hell.

Gesar returned to Yama's hall.

'You, Yama, are unable to tell right from wrong. My mother lived a life of compassion, but you send her to Hell.'

King Yama rose from his throne. 'Lion-like King, whose fame and power reach far and wide in the human world, you had Heaven's blessing to kill demons in the human world, but you have killed humans. There was not one war that did not take human lives or cause the people to lose their homes.'

'But that was my crime, not my mother's.'

'The rule of karma dictates that your mother suffer for you.'

Gesar raised his sword but the blade passed harmlessly through Yama and his attendants. Then he recalled the incantation that Master Lotus had given him, and he sheathed his sword. As he spoke the secret words, Yama disappeared, and the cast-iron gate to Hell rumbled open. Inside he saw thousands of suffering souls, but not his mother or Atag Lhamo. So many souls had sunk into Hell that they were piled in heaps, filling the narrow passageways. Gesar raised his sword to clear a way through.

'Weapons from the human world are useless here.' One of the guardians of Hell had approached him.

'But I must find my mother.'

'To do that you must deliver all of the souls.'

Gesar saw that the torture the souls suffered far exceeded just punishment for the crimes they had committed, and he was filled with compassion. He prayed to Padmasambhava, Guanyin Bodhisattva and all the Buddhas in the Western Heaven for the souls to be released from their suffering and to enter the Pure Land in the west.

As he finished his prayer, the souls rose out of the abyss of darkness and up into the sky on their way to the Pure Land. Among them he saw his mother and Atag Lhamo, but they did not recognise him, and disappeared in a ray of celestial light.

King Yama reappeared. 'Thank you, King Gesar. So many years have passed but not a single person has ever accumulated as many good deeds as it takes to deliver all of the souls that crowded Hell. For at least the next thousand years I will not have to concern myself with making space for new ones.'

Gesar could not understand why he had been unable to rescue his consort when he had come the first time, yet now he had succeeded in saving all of the souls.

Waving his hands, Yama said, 'Ask Padmasambhava.'

Gesar rode back to Gling. He had only just dismounted when his horse, without waiting for its saddle to be removed, ran to the mountain to join the horses grazing there. A message from the chief minister was relayed to Gesar: 'I dreamed that on Gling's sacred mountain the feather of a hawk was ruffled by the wind. If that feather should fall, would the greenfinch show compassion and care?'

Then the king knew that Rongtsa Khragan's time in the human world was nearly done. He went to his bedside, where others had already gathered. A light glowed in Rongtsa Khragan's dim eyes when he saw the king. 'Gesar, allow me to address you not as my king but as my dear nephew.'

'Uncle, please tell me what is in your mind.'

'I have enjoyed more glory than anyone in all the generations of the three branches of Gling, and that is because I have followed you. Great King of Gling! My last wish is for the people of Gling to enjoy everlasting peace and prosperity.'

At these words his eyes closed. Gesar and the others stayed by his bedside as he spent his last hours in the human world. Just before daybreak he awoke, and gazed at the faces of the people with whom he had spent his life. As the sun lit the peak of the sacred snowcapped mountain, he smiled and breathed his last. In that moment, a white horse galloped out of the radiant light in the sky, then disappeared, like the faint glow of a rainbow. When the people turned back to look at the bed, Rongtsa Khragan had vanished, leaving only his clothes and the fading warmth of his body.

Counting on his fingers, Gesar realised he himself had been in the human world for eighty-one years. It was time to return to Heaven. He ordered that all the treasure be taken from the palace and distributed throughout the country. After three days of feasting and music at the palace, he summoned Prince Gralha, who came with an offering of a longevity *hada* and with a plea: 'The king is not bound by a life span, like the rest of the humans. Please, remain for ever with us.'

Everyone in Gling, the ministers and the citizens, begged the king to stay.

Gesar sang a song he had composed:

> 'The ageing roc must fly high,
> Because the wings of the young rocs have grown strong.
> The old lion must leave the mountain,
> Because the claws of the young lions have grown sharp.
> The moon will set in the west,
> Because the sun is ready to rise in the east.'

Then he proclaimed that Gyatsa Zhakar's son Prince Gralha would become King of Gling, and led Prince Gralha to the throne.

'My good nephew Gralha, I have done all I can for Gling. But you need not fear for Gling's future. The demons have been subdued and are now guardian deities of Gling.' Gesar called to Khrothung's son, Dongtsan, and spoke to the two young men together. 'I have delivered Uncle Khrothung's soul to the Pure Land, ending his tangled deeds in this world. And Tonggod of the Tagrong tribe sacrificed his life for Gling. So, Gralha, you must treat your brother Dongtsan well. And, Dongtsan, you must show your brother Gralha respect.'

The brothers embraced, and pledged to love and respect each other, in life and in death.

Then Rkayngkar Perpo, the celestial horse, whinnied three times, for he knew it was time for him and his master to return to Heaven. The steeds who had galloped to fight in all corners of the land gathered around him – the white-hoofed horse, the white-coated pearl horse, the flame-red horse, the thousand-*li* night-running horse, the red-maned hawk-eyed horse and the green-haired, snake-waisted horse.

'My friends,' Rkayngkar Perpo said, 'we have travelled countless roads together and have fought countless battles side by side. Now my master will return to Heaven and I will go with him. I bequeath my saddle to Prince Gralha's fine horse. May each of you leave behind a great reputation.' Then, with one last long whinny, he rose into the sky.

The thunderbolt arrow in Gesar's quiver bade farewell to the other arrows. 'I am returning to Heaven with the king. But I will come to you if the signal fires of war are lit again.' With the help of a bow, the arrow flew into the air.

Gesar's demon-slaying sword bade farewell to his other weapons. 'You must show the razor edges of your blades to Gling's enemies but the blunt edges to each other.' With a red light it flashed up into the sky.

When Gesar saw that his horse, arrow and sword were circling in the sky, waiting for him, he spoke his final farewell. For the last time he blessed the land of Gling and every living thing on it.

Spring thunder rumbled as the gates of Heaven opened to reveal Gesar's celestial parents and ten thousand deities gathered to welcome home their son, Thosba Gawa. Celestial music and the scent of strange flowers filled the land. A pure white *hada* hung down from Heaven. Gesar walked slowly towards the path that had opened to the heavens, Brugmo and Meza at his side. They turned back one last time to gaze at Gling's mountains and rivers, and its people. Then they rose up to the gates and entered as a gentle rain began to fall.

Gesar never again came down to the world of humans. But the story of his heroic deeds is still told.